RENOUNCED

BRIDGET E. BAKER

For Cassidy

Not everyone is born with all of their family. Sometimes our closest family is found along the way.

Thank you for always supporting me.

Dad is working.

He's always working.

My friends' dads only work during the week. They come home for dinner. Not my dad. He's always working. Nights. Weekends. All week long.

"But you promised," I whine.

Dad hates it when I whine, but I can't help it. I can *see* the beach and the waves and the people through the window. And he did promise we could go to the beach today. He *promised*.

Dad crouches down next to me and opens his arms.

I step into his hug without thinking. He works a lot, but I know he loves me.

"I did promise, little lamb, and I'm so sorry, but something came up. Something urgent—that means that it can't wait. Besides, the beach isn't safe today. There are far too many jellyfish out there."

I stiffen. It hurt so bad when that jellyfish stung me last time. I remember the purple flags that were up all over the beach that day. I'll never ignore that warning again.

Dad releases me and stands up, turning toward his lab,

like always. I drag myself toward the family room. Maybe I can watch a cartoon or something. Except when I pick up the remote for the television, it's sitting on the windowsill and I look outside.

There aren't any purple flags. The flags are green. Bright, dark green. I frown. "Dad?"

He pauses with his hand on the doorknob—about to disappear. "Yes?"

"Why do you have to work? What's wrong?" I don't ask why it's more important than I am, but I want to. My lower lip trembles.

Dad's sigh is heavy, which probably means he's mad. His work really is important. I know that, but I'm not sure why. He releases the door and walks toward me. He sits on the couch and pulls me up next to him. "You've been sick before. You know how lousy it feels."

I nod.

"Here in the United States, we have medicine when that happens. We have lots of different kinds of medicines, actually. Some help remove the sickness that makes you sick, and some make you feel better while your body eliminates the illness. But in some places, they can't afford either kind of medicine. In some places, when people get sick, they suffer a lot more than we do. And often, they die."

"Like mom died?"

He swallows. "Not very many people are in a position to help those sick kids or their sick mothers." He frowns. "People might contribute money to help pay for the medicine, or they could even go overseas to try and help treat a few of them." He shrugs. "But it doesn't really solve the problem."

"So are we going over to help?"

Dad squeezes my hand. "Not right now, no, but my training at school makes me uniquely capable of helping people. What I'm trying to do is make medicine that will be cheap, accessible, and that will save those kids' lives."

"Why does it have to be you?" I glance sideways at the green flags flapping happily in the wind. "Why can't someone else's dad do it instead? Maybe only this week?"

"Oh, little lamb." He scoops me up and puts me on his lap. His hand brushes my hair back behind my ear. "I know you want to see me more often. I know it's hard for you to understand why I'm always busy. I could spend less time working on this, this week, this month, this year. I won't lie about that, not to you. But sometimes in life, because of the gift of our intelligence, or because of our hard work, or because of a bizarre fluke of luck, we're the ones who are in the right place. We're the ones with the right skillset to do something hard. Sometimes we're the only ones who can accomplish what needs to be done."

"And you're the lucky one?" It doesn't feel very lucky.

He laughs. "Not lucky in the way that you're thinking. Not like I found a pot of gold."

"How then?"

"I'll give you an example. If a lady by the name of Marie Curie hadn't been born in Poland or had scientist parents, and if her mother hadn't died when she was ten, she might not have worked quite so hard, or learned quite so much. She was so cold one winter—without money for proper lodgings or heating—that she wore all of her clothing at the same time to keep warm. But thanks to her dedication and sacrifice, she was able to discover radioactivity. She was the first woman to receive a Nobel Prize."

Marie Curie. That sounds familiar. "Didn't she die from radiation?"

Dad looks like he accidentally smashed his finger. "Okay, well how about this one. If two parents by the name of Augusto and Michaela Odone hadn't had a son with adrenoleukodystrophy, they would never have studied as hard as they did. They never would have financed an international meeting of scientists and discovered a treatment for that rare illness."

"They saved a lot of kids? Like millions?"

Dad frowns. "It's not always about the total number of people you save. They could have simply enjoyed the time they had with their son. Or they could have had a son who wasn't sick at all, but neither of those things are what happened. Sometimes the world places us in a position to help others, and when it does, it's our job—" He shakes his head. "No, not our job. It's our *duty* to rise to that call. To do whatever it is that we're uniquely situated to do."

"You have to save the world, because you *can*?"

Dad nods slowly. "One day this will make more sense. And one day, you might be in a position to do the same." He kisses my forehead. "I promise that we'll go to the beach this week. I'm so close to the answers we need, little lamb. I promise."

"Okay." I turn on cartoons, but I don't find anything good. While a dumb cat chases a smart mouse all over the screen, I can't help but hope that I'm never like my dad. I don't want to be in the right place. I'd prefer not to be lucky.

Because it sure seems like saving everyone else is a crappy job.

❧ I ❧

RUBY

When you finally get home after a long day, you sink into a comfortable armchair and put your feet up. You sigh with relief, because the world outside falls away. That's what home means—the place you *belong*. The place you can rest.

I haven't been *home* since the day I thought Wesley Marked me.

My understanding of who I *am* has fundamentally changed in the past few weeks. I discovered things about my dad, my aunt and uncle, and even about myself that I wish I had never learned. But unlike the old Ruby, I don't shy away from that kind of thing. Not anymore.

It was the hardest few weeks of my life, and the cost was devastating, but we saved the Marked kids—mostly.

For the time being, anyway.

Now that the threat of Tercera, the virus that has held us all hostage for more than a decade, has been eliminated, I'm not sure who I am or where I belong. For almost my entire life I've been Ruby Behl, but now I know that I was born Ruby Ruth Thomas. And worse, more than half a million people insist on calling me Ruby Solomon.

And Her frigging Majesty.

For so long, I've been taking things one day at a time. One hour at a time. Heck, even sometimes one minute at a time.

I haven't had the time to even consider my plan for the future, but now the future is here, so I have to figure it out.

What comes next, what comes *after,* may be the scariest thing I've ever faced, because I can't blame anyone else. My next move is entirely up to me.

At least for now, I'm not alone making it. Every day, Aunt Anne and Job and I work to make sure the Marked kids have the medical support they need to survive their recovery and transition to adulthood. Now that they're off the suppressant, most of them are dealing with malnutrition, the surges of adolescence, and the ravages of damage from year two of Tercera.

Some of them are recovering well—some are pretty rough. But at least World Peace Now, often shortened by citizens of the Unmarked to WPN, has sent consistent supplies and we have a facility set up to help. Even so, every night, we're exhausted. We could reclaim an empty building somewhere in New Orleans, but the Marked have already claimed most of the ones in the best shape—and we can't really justify ousting them.

The weather has been nice enough that it's easier to camp out behind the clinic in tents also sent by WPN. We're all so tired by the time the sun sets that we usually make dinner over a campfire and relax. It will get old eventually, but for now it's been an adventure. It's nice not to be running from anything, or desperately working under some kind of time crunch. When he has time, Sam's brother Rafe comes and joins us. The conversations are never boring, not with Rhonda and Job and Rafe around to keep things interesting.

"So we all know that Ruby has kissed two guys," Rhonda says. "But what about you, Sam? Is Ruby the only person you've ever kissed?"

How did I never think to ask that question?

Sam tenses, like a bird about to take flight. "Does it matter?"

Oh, now I really want to know the answer. Is he nervous that I'm the only person he's kissed? Or is he embarrassed that he's kissed a lot?

"I think it does," Rhonda says. "The entire world knows about Ruby's infamous kiss with Wesley."

"Not the whole world," I say. "I mean—"

Rafe laughs. "Well, the Marked all know. It's all the guy talked about. And I bet the Unmarked have all heard, since Fairchild's son was Marked and left as a result of it."

I shake my head. "I had nothing to do with him being Marked."

"But you were miraculously spared," Rafe says. "Tell me that hasn't made the rounds."

"Okay, but what you asked about was me," Sam says. He might have avoided the question initially, but he'll step up to spare me harassment. Bless Sam.

"True," Rhonda says. "And you still haven't said."

"A few women have tried to catch my attention," he says.

That's an understatement. He was practically hunted back among the Unmarked. As a legend in the competitions there, and with his good looks, not to mention his dad's position as their leader, Sam was quite a catch.

"But I managed to avoid being kissed by any of them."

Probably by hiding and never speaking a word that wasn't strictly necessary.

"However, Ruby wasn't my first kiss."

I straighten in my chair. "I wasn't?"

He swallows, his eyes meeting mine and then flitting away.

"Who else?" Part of me wishes we weren't sitting around a fire with three other people. I wish I'd thought to ask this before now, when we were alone. "Do I know her?" Please don't let it be Rhonda. Surely she wouldn't have asked if it was her.

"I don't think so," Sam says, "though Rhonda has met her. She was in the clinical trial with me—her name's Lydia."

I blink. "She contracted Tercera." He said so. In the middle of the trial. He wasn't sure whether it had been *given* to her, or whether it was an accident. He never mentioned that he liked her. But I'm suddenly scrambling to do mental math. Is there any way she survived? Could Aunt Anne have given her the cure? Sam's cure? Any way I look at the timeline—I don't see how that could be possible. It's been just over three years, and it's a three-year course.

"I thought you liked Ruby from the time we were children," Job says.

Sam rolls his eyes. "I've always admired her, but I wasn't gross. It didn't turn into more until fairly recently."

Oh. So he *did* like this Lydia.

"You had a lot in common," Rhonda says. "You both received top marks in everything—that's why she was selected to join the trial."

"And she only accepted because I did." Sam's lips are tightly pressed—he feels guilty about it.

I don't mention that both Sam and I have only kissed one other person—and both those people are now dead. I'm sure he's thinking the same thing. I'll ask him more questions later, but for now, it's time to somehow change to a happier topic. "Yellow," I say.

Sam's head whips toward mine. The flames from the fire cast shadows across his perfect jaw. His eyes glow golden in this light.

"For our house, I mean." I smile. "You asked me yesterday what color we should paint our future home."

He blinks.

"Dude, your hotdog is on fire." Rafe sounds almost gleeful. He's got a weird sense of humor.

Sam snatches it back and blows out the flames licking its surface, swearing under his breath. "I was making that one for Ruby."

"I like mine lightly toasted," I say. "With the surface just barely wrinkled, not charbroiled."

My huge boyfriend stuffs the entire thing in his mouth at once, licking his fingers one at a time. "You distracted me."

Which was my intention. "Sorry about that," I say. "But I've been thinking about it, and I think that would be a fun color. If you hate it, I guess blue is fine."

His lips curl into a beautiful smile. "I'd like a sunny yellow."

"Oh please," Rafe says. "You wouldn't like it. If it were up to you, you'd live in a cave. And *if* any part of it was painted, you'd choose pitch black."

"Or camouflage," Rhonda says. "So no one would ever find it."

Job laughs.

"Not anymore," Sam says. "First, I'm not twelve, and second, thanks to our efforts of the last few weeks, we no longer have to live in fear."

"Right now Her Royal Majesty's house is white," Job says, "with huge columns and a massive wraparound porch."

My hand tightens on the stick I've been using to roast my dinner for the past few days. I know he's kidding with the 'Her Majesty' stuff, but it still annoys me. And that house is *not* my house. "What do you think these hotdogs that WPN sent are made of?"

Rhonda frowns. "What were they ever made from?" She shrugs. "Innards no one wants to eat? Bits of meat all mashed together with glue."

I hand my stick to Sam.

"You have to eat something," Sam says.

I grab a can of baked beans. The more I think about meat, the more disgusting it seems. "I'm fine."

He frowns, but doesn't argue.

"So tell me more about this house," Rafe says. "The one you two are going to live in together. Where exactly is it located?" His eyes twinkle, as if he's asking us about the magical island on which we ride friendly, fire-breathing dragons.

"It's got a porch," I say. "But it's much, much smaller than the terrible house Solomon built back on Galveston Island."

"I like that palace," Job says. "If Adam doesn't want it when he steps in for you, I'd be willing to take it off his hands."

"Her mom lives there, dummy. And stop distracting her," Rhonda says. "I want more details about this perfect dream life."

I roll my eyes, but I kind of like talking about it. "It's only one story, so I'm not always climbing up and down stairs. The kitchen is small, but has great storage so I can make whatever I want without walking all over the place."

"There's a smokehouse out back," Sam says. "For me to cure meat from the animals I hunt. We might even set up a little roadside stand somewhere if traffic between settlements picks up enough to justify it."

"And do the birds and rabbits come do the housecleaning?" Rafe snorts. "Because I feel like I've heard this fairy tale somewhere."

"Hilarious," I say. "I plan to do my own cleaning, but I do want a little mailbox near the road that has a built in birdhouse and feeder above it. Sam will *not* kill any little critters that come to live on our property."

"Unless they're ruining your greenhouse," Sam says. "Then all bets are off."

"And we live on the same street as Uncle Dan and Aunt Anne and Rose."

"What about us?" Job asks. "Rhonda and I are welcome, right?"

"Depends who you marry," I say. "But if they don't annoy me, then yes."

"What about me?" Rafe asks. "Are men-children welcome in this post-pandemic Disney World of yours?"

"Of course," I say. "In fact, you can stay with us until you find or build your own place."

"How magnanimous of you," Rafe says. "But none of this is ever going to happen."

"Why not?" Sam's scowl isn't playful.

"You're an attack dog," Rafe says. "No matter how long you pretend you aren't, you'll never fit on someone's lap. And you won't ever end up living in a little yellow house on the end of a street full of smokehouses and cupcake bakeries."

"I didn't say anything about a cupcake shop," I say. "I don't even like cupcakes."

"Everyone likes cupcakes," Rhonda says.

"The point is that this is never going to happen," Rafe says. "None of it. Tercera may be gone, but the world is in a shambles. Who do you think is going to be cleaning up the mess while you two are hiding away on your idyllic street?"

Sam shrugs. "Don't know, don't care."

I'm not sure whether he means that, but for the first

time, I wonder. Can I really hide while someone else fixes things? Is our job really done? Because as much as I want that little yellow house on the perfect street . . . I'm worried it's not realistic. I'm worried Rafe is right.

I deserve a home after the misery I've endured, but sometimes we don't get what we deserve.

Ruby's delicate, perfectly proportioned hands are scrubbing the spatula all wrong. Plus, she made dinner, so she shouldn't be washing dishes.

"Here." I bump her hip with my own and snatch the crusted spatula out of her hands. "Let me." The casual contact between us isn't a surprise anymore, but it still sends a thrill through me. *Mine.* Something primal inside of me smiles smugly.

I've finally gotten every single thing I ever wanted.

I still wake up at least once a night in a cold sweat, worried it's some kind of trick, but every time I do, things are fine. Ruby's close, just like she is right now, and all is right with my world.

Even if she's scowling at me.

"You're just as pretty when you frown, you know."

"Sam, you always do the dishes." Her voice is accusatory.

Because I do them the right way. "I don't mind."

"You will, eventually," she says.

"I won't." I'd never be annoyed by anything as inane as dishes. "Go sit down."

She rolls her eyes and huffs, and I want to toss the dishes back into the soapy water and pull her into my arms. But then, I always want to do that. It's where she belongs: with me, safe and treasured.

"I don't want to sit down. I want—"

"Ruby?" Mr. Fairchild, Port Gibson's mayor, walks toward our tiny campfire from the main hub behind us.

I'm sick of being stuck in a campsite that essentially doubles as Grand Central Station, but Anne took over the plasma center and is ruling it with an iron stethoscope. Ruby's older half brother Adam sent pretty nice tents and gear, so I can't complain too much, but people just come and go without much concern over a perimeter or security.

Not that we're really in much danger anymore.

But if you're always vigilant, you're less likely to get ambushed. And I had no idea Mr. Fairchild was even in Baton Rouge, much less on his way to see us. Frank is going to get an earful later. Maybe an extra five-mile run and a few hundred push-ups will help him remember to follow the protocols.

I dry my hands and force a smile. "Mr. Fairchild."

"Hey." The haunted look is back in Ruby's eyes—the hollow, pained look that always surfaces when she thinks about Wesley.

I hate it.

"Someone in a WPN uniform, named Frank, maybe? He said you'd be over here."

Yep, Frank is in very, very warm water.

Mr. Fairchild's hair sticks up on one side, and he looks thinner than he did the last time I saw him, which wasn't even that long ago. He's not handling Wesley's death any better than Ruby.

"Take a seat, please." Ruby waves at the stumps we've positioned around the fire. Somehow she always makes everything seem so natural, so *right*.

"I'm sure you're busy." Mr. Fairchild shoves his hands in his pockets, his breath coming out in puffs in the brisk evening air. "I don't mean to keep you. And actually, I came to see Sam, mostly." His face swivels toward me.

My eyebrows lift.

"You may not have heard, but Gavin Quinn is the interim chancellor, and—"

I grunt. "Kang said."

"Right." His feet shuffle in the dirt around our campfire. "The thing is, he's a bad person." He looks up at me quickly and then drops his eyes again. As if he's afraid of me.

Maybe he is. My dad was far worse than a 'bad person,' and I'm his blood, like it or not. "Okay." I wish I knew how to put people at ease like Ruby, but that's never been one of my strengths. He's either going to spit it out, or he isn't.

"Adrien Kang asked Sam to come," Ruby says. "He strongly suggested that he'd like to nominate Sam as the next chancellor."

Mr. Fairchild's eyes widen. "Are you interested in that?"

I shake my head. "No."

"Right. I didn't think so, but it's good to hear."

Ruby puts her hands on her hips. "Good to hear? Sam would make an excellent chancellor." Since I know she has no aspirations for me to rule at all, I'm not sure why she's so upset, but it's cute that she's defensive.

Mr. Fairchild frowns. "It's not that Sam wouldn't be great, but I was hoping he might support me."

"*You* want to be the next chancellor?" Ruby's hands fall from her hips and her shoulders droop. "Really?"

"It's not that I want to run things, exactly," Mr. Fairchild says. "It's more that I don't see anyone else who would do any better. The thing is, leaders usually come from one of two places. People who want the power, who want to control things. Those are people like Quinn or

Roth." He clears his throat and glances my way apologetically.

It's unnecessary. I know what he means.

"But the other camp—well, that's people like me. People who don't really want to run things, but they know that someone has to do it, and they want to help people." He looks down at his shoes and kicks at a hard patch of dirt. "Without Wesley, I don't have much reason to—I don't have . . . " He clears his throat again. "It might give me some purpose. And I think I can help." He glances out at the Marked—er, formerly Marked—kids walking down the street past our campsite.

They're no longer dying imminently of Tercera, but they were all on a hormone suppressant for close to a decade—that doesn't come without repercussions. There's no telling how they'll recover from whatever damage the virus did before it was halted. Some of them will deal with permanent organ damage. And, of course, they have no real support system. They've been living in a weird limbo, and now they have nowhere to go and no one to help them. Unless someone steps up. It seems like Mr. Fairchild may be offering to do just that.

"Your son was Marked."

"Only for a few hours," Mr. Fairchild says, "if what he said about how Ruby's blood saved him was true."

"It's enough," I say. "You thought he was infected for much longer."

"He lived among them and fought for them," Ruby says. She's so ridiculously smart—on the exact same page as I am already, without any discussion.

"Did that time help you feel some compassion for them?"

He nods slowly. "I think it's our duty to integrate them into our communities in whatever way they want to join us. We can provide jobs, food, training, and shelter."

"Medical attention?" Ruby asks. "Because that's going to be ongoing—some of them suffer from permanent conditions."

"And the babies," I say.

Ruby closes her eyes, and I know she's thinking about Libby and her baby, Rose. Libby died, but Rose survived. She's not the only baby who made it through . . . without a parent. Or with only one parent. "You'll help them?"

"What about WPN?" Mr. Fairchild asks. "I'm not trying to worm out of helping them, but surely WPN will do its part."

Ruby sighs. "I don't know how long I'll have any say in what they do."

"You're their queen," Mr. Fairchild says. "Aren't you?"

"For the time being," she says, "but I've spent less than a week in Galveston in the past decade."

"It does seem strange," Mr. Fairchild says, "that they'd choose you, but they're an odd people. They sent that air strike and that enormous force to Nashville to defend you. It seems they accept you as their leader."

No one can say they didn't come through for Ruby, that's for sure.

"You won't be alone in helping the Marked," Ruby says, "but if you can reassure us that, if you're voted in as chancellor, you'll do whatever needs to be done for those who can't take care of themselves in any form, you'll have our support." She walks toward me, and I lift my arm without thought.

She nestles her head against my chest and my world is right.

"Is that correct?" Mr. Fairchild pins me with an earnest look.

I nod.

"You'll come to Nashville and speak on my behalf?" he asks.

"It's in two weeks or something now?" Ruby asks.

"The actual vote is set to take place in twelve days, but the nomination requires twenty members of the Centi-Council to vouch for you. I think I'll get that many, but it might be close."

"Which means you may need us earlier?" Ruby asks. "Like in the next ten days."

"Eight would be better," Mr. Fairchild says.

Ruby nods. "Alright. We'll head that direction as soon as we can." Her lips twist a bit, and she says, "We just ate, but are you hungry? We can—"

"Thank you." Mr. Fairchild shakes his head. "I'm going to head straight back. I forgive you for Wesley." His face crumples and I realize he's fighting back tears. "But I can't—"

Ruby steps away from me and hugs him. "It's too hard," she whispers. "I understand."

I wish I could effortlessly comfort people. I wish I knew the right things to do or say. After a moment, she steps back and Mr. Fairchild turns to leave. He reaches the edge of the campfire's glow and spins on his heel. "Thank you, Ruby, for remembering him. And for everything you've done."

She nods and her lips flatten together. "Of course."

Very, very few people have thanked her for what she risked, what she sacrificed, and what she accomplished. She hates when it happens, but it hasn't occurred nearly enough in my opinion. It raises my impression of Mr. Fairchild a bit.

I finish up the dishes to give her a chance to recover.

But of course, she's not doing that. She's looking over some kind of spreadsheet under the light of a lantern and fretting instead—I can tell because she's biting her lip. "What's wrong now?"

She doesn't even hear me.

I sit next to her on a campstool and lean toward the spreadsheets.

"Oh." She blinks. "Sam. I forgot about the dishes and you did them all again, didn't you?"

I shrug.

"I'm sorry. It's just that Adam asked me to look over these trade agreements, and I swear, they make no sense. The projections Aunt Anne has been bringing for the recovery on the Marked and the supply lists or items and provisions we'll need, those I understand. But this?" She leans back and her campstool wobbles.

I wrap an arm around her. "Is this what we're going to be doing now?" I shift a little to catch her attention. "Trade agreements?"

She frowns. "Not, like, forever, no. But for right now—"

"A day turns into a week. A week turns into a month. That's how they get you."

"Who?" She smiles. "Who's going to get us, exactly?"

"We need to decide what *we* want, and then we need to make a plan for how to get it."

"What do you want?" Ruby's index finger traces down the side of my face.

I can't think when she touches me, especially not when she touches me like that. Innocent, light, but with purpose. My mouth goes dry. I inhale sharply.

Long, heavy strides come toward us from the main campfire and I stifle a groan. I can't get a single second alone with Ruby. Ever. "Hey, Rhonda." If my words are clipped and a little unfriendly, well. She should learn to read the room.

Or, you know. A small, outer campfire.

"Don't mind me, you two." She's like a toddler with a pocketful of gummy bears. "Carry on, carry on. I'm just tired and I have early shift tomorrow, so." She points at the tent she shares with Ruby.

"Have I mentioned how annoyed I am that your aunt won't let me sleep next to you?" I arch one eyebrow. "As if I'd do something *inappropriate*."

Ruby giggles. "I wish you would."

My heart hammers, but now is not the time. Not for fingers against my jaw. Not for lips pressed against her neck. Not for my hands around her waist. I inhale to clear my mind. "Look, as long as we whisper, Rhonda can't hear us. And we need to talk about this."

"You're not usually so serious." Ruby rubs her lips together, with her eyes on my mouth, which she always does when she wants to kiss me.

"I am serious." I take her hands in mine to give myself something else to look at. If she keeps staring at me like that, I'll kiss her again and we'll never discuss any of this at all.

And we need to make a plan. Without an objective, we'll drift along, buffeted by whatever winds and waves crash over us. "What do you want?"

"Well." Ruby stands up.

I straighten. Her head isn't far above mine, even with me sitting and her standing.

She braces her hands against my chest and then trails her fingers slowly across my collarbones to my shoulders. "I want to see you every day."

I want to stay on task, but my brain has gone on strike. Every muscle in my body has frozen in place. The place where her fingers rest against my shoulders tingles, and I want—*more*.

She squeezes my shoulders, and leans down until we're eye level. "I want to feel your lips against mine." She presses her mouth against me and I'm gone. Vapor. Defenseless, for once in my life. Her mouth only moves against mine for a moment before she straightens. "I want you with me all the time. And I don't want to get badgered, and bothered, and dinged, and pestered every second of every day, not anymore."

"So you don't want to rule WPN?" My eyes can't seem to leave her mouth.

She shakes her head. "Not at all, no."

"Do you want to live in a small town? Or a large one?"

She shrugs. "As long as we have our yellow house, together, I don't care."

"What do you want to do all day?"

She smirks. "I have a few ideas."

I groan. "I mean, what do you want to do with your life."

She beams. "I knew what you meant, but man this is fun. You fill me with light and joy, Samuel Roth. Some days, I still can't believe you like me."

It's my turn this time. I lean close, gather her against me, and whisper against her ear. "I don't *like* you, Ruby Behl. I love you."

She stiffens. I know why—I called her Behl. But honestly, I have no idea what to call her. Her name at birth, Thomas? What everyone from WPN calls her, Solomon? What Dan and Anne usually call her, Behl? Or Carillon, her adoptive father's real last name? It's a confusing mess.

"I don't care what your last name is," I whisper. "And one day soon, I hope it'll be Roth and we won't need to worry."

She relaxes against me then. "That's what I want in my future." She slides onto my lap, and the world is right again. "I want to be Ruby Roth." She freezes. "I never realized quite how corny that sounds until right now."

My arms tighten. "It's not corny. It's perfect."

She laughs. "Alliteration isn't perfect. It's corny, but I love *you* too much to care."

"Good."

"So here's our plan, Mr. Organized."

"Tell me."

"We head back to WPN tomorrow."

I lean back enough so that I can see her face. "Tomorrow?"

"We have to be in Nashville in eight days. We have reliable transportation and fuel now, and we don't need to worry about Marked attacks, but it'll still be a full day trip."

"Okay. And what do we do for the next week, then?"

"We figure out how to get Adam to agree to take over for me." Ruby shifts and lays her head against my chest. "Right?"

"And once we've foisted rule of WPN onto Adam permanently, and we've helped Mr. Fairchild become Chancellor Fairchild, what then?"

"What do *you* want?" Her voice is soft, and I realize she's tired. "Because I bet I'll like it, whatever it is."

"I'd like to live somewhere small," I say. "Somewhere simple—somewhere we can both have jobs that mean something. Maybe you do research or become a physician and help people who have the flu, or who broke an arm. And I can . . . I don't know what. Set up home alarms."

She laughs. "Yeah, right."

"I'll find something," I say. "Now that defense from a hostile enemy and infected rogue teens isn't an issue, I'm sure I'll find something else I'm suited for."

"I'm sure you will."

"But I want a family with you, someday, when you're ready, and I want it in a small town, without a lot of huge problems."

Ruby nods her head. "That sounds nice. I think we've dealt with our allotment of huge problems for both our lifetimes." She looks up at me. "Don't you?"

"Couldn't agree more." I wrap my arms around her tightly and she snuggles against my chest, her face pressed against my heart.

After she falls asleep, I carry her into her tent and tuck her in next to Rhonda. I can't keep myself from pressing a kiss to her forehead before I leave. After the last few weeks, sometimes the state of the world today doesn't seem real. I don't go very far to reach my own cot. Job and I are sharing a tent six feet away. He's brushing his teeth with water from a tin cup when I come out of Ruby's and Rhonda's tent.

"The girls are out?"

I nod.

"You make her happy," Job says. "I haven't really acknowledged that, but I probably should. I was worried at first, for both of you, but I'm glad I didn't stop you from dating her."

Job? Stop me? I don't laugh, but it's hard. "Uh, thanks."

"You going to sleep?"

I shake my head. "Ruby and I are heading to Galveston tomorrow. I ought to let Rafe know. Can you keep an eye on her for a few minutes?"

"She's not in danger, you know," Job says.

I don't bother arguing. If he's not going to be vigilant, I'll find someone who will be. Ruby hates when they hover, so I keep the WPN guards a few dozen yards out. I stop on my way to Rafe's and let them know to fall in closer. Frank annoys Ruby to death, but he's very dedicated. And he's not a bad shot, either.

Even knowing she's safe, I hate leaving Ruby alone. Too many rotten things keep happening around her. I jog to the hospital where Rafe is still presiding, and I don't slow down until I round the corner to his room.

"Sam?" Rafe's eyes widen when I push through his door. He's looking over papers at his desk, but he shoves his chair back and stands up.

"Hey."

"What's wrong?" He frowns.

"Nothing." I wish I knew how to talk to him. It's not like I was ever going to be a champion conversationalist, but the years when I had food and a roof and safety and he was on his own, clawing out some kind of survival . . . Well. Thinking about the disparity between our past doesn't help. He knows I'm glad he's alive. He knows I feel guilty. Rehashing it is pointless. "I'm leaving tomorrow."

"You're here to say goodbye." His tone is flat, borderline angry.

"Well, not goodbye. I'll be back in under two weeks, I imagine."

"You're going with Ruby?" Rafe's eyes flash. "To Galveston again?"

I nod.

"Of course you are." He sits back down and turns his attention back to whatever document he was reading.

"Are you angry about that?"

He snorts. "No."

"You sound angry."

He spins around and stands again. "And you're acting like your girlfriend, now. Poke, poke, poke."

"I wish I could talk to people like she can," I say. "Then maybe . . . "

"Maybe what?" Rafe squares his shoulders, his feet set shoulder width apart.

"Maybe I could talk to you."

Like a kite with its string cut, all the tension evaporates. "What?"

I think hard. What would Ruby say? "I'm sorry we abandoned you. I'm sorry you were alone." My voice drops. "I'm sorry I failed you."

Rafe's boots clomp across the tile floor. "You're an idiot. You should apologize for that, too." His lips twist up and his arms cross over his chest.

"I am sorry," I say. "For all of it."

"You're an idiot for thinking I blame you for any of that." Rafe sighs. "I've spent ten years being angry all the time, and sometimes I think it's the only thing I really know how to do anymore. Even when I'm not mad, I can't seem to help myself."

"I'm sorr—"

"Stop," Rafe says. "I was angry all the time . . . so I wouldn't feel scared and sad and alone."

Now I really have no idea what to say.

"So if you want to apologize for anything at all, you should apologize for leaving me tomorrow, for running after your girlfriend, wherever she goes, instead of staying with your family now that you have one."

She is my family, more even than Rafe, but pointing that out won't likely improve his mood. "I'll be back," I say instead. "I do love you."

Rafe nods. "I know you do." But he also knows I love her more, and that hurts him. I'm sorry about that too, but it doesn't change the reality. He turns back around and walks across the room to his desk robotically, then sits down and picks up his papers. "Be careful."

"I'm always careful."

"You're never careful." When he turns to face me this time, he's smiling.

"I need to be alive to keep her safe."

"Maybe one day I'll meet someone I care about like you love her."

"Doubtful," I say.

Rafe throws a stapler at me.

I snap one hand out and catch it. "Thanks. Ruby's been saying how she wanted—"

He whips a wadded up ball of paper at me next. "Has she been wanting garbage too?" He rolls his eyes. "Get out of here, big brother." His voice is barely a whisper when he says, "But come back soon. I'll miss you."

That's the hard thing about having people you love. It gives you more to worry about. We leave first thing the next morning. The fifty WPN guards Adam insisted on leaving are delighted to pull up stakes and return home. There's not a soul on the road between here and there— although crossing the Atchafalaya swamp is still harrowing, especially as we pass the sections where the road on the other side has crumbled away, the enormous, compromised concrete pylons jutting up from the swamp like jagged teeth badly in need of a dentist.

"We need to put maintenance on this road at the top of Adam's list," I say.

"Agreed." Ruby's hand finally releases mine as we exit the bridge.

It's nice to cross the bridge from Texas City to Galveston without worrying about armed guards or David Solomon, but I don't expect Adam to be waiting for us on the steps of Josephine's palace when we pull up.

Ruby wastes no time hopping out of the side door of the SUV. "What's wrong?" She slams the door.

I jump out of my side and circle around.

He has bags under his bloodshot eyes. "What took you so long?"

"I know I was supposed to be here a while ago," Ruby says, "but I sent you a message. I said I'd be delayed."

Adam frowns. "But I replied and said it *was* urgent and you needed to come immediately."

Ruby's eyes meet mine and she looks as confused as I feel. "Huh?"

Adam gestures. "Never mind. Let's just go. They're inside right now, waiting, and they're all angry."

"Whoa," Ruby says. "I didn't get another message from you. I told you we'd be delayed and that you'd have to deal with Sawyer yourself." She blinks.

"It's not only Sawyer. That's the reason I said I couldn't handle it alone."

Ruby grips my hand in hers. "We didn't get another letter from you. Who exactly is waiting?"

"All seven Port Heads," Adam says.

RUBY

Adam pivots on his heel and starts for the stairs.

"Wait." I throw up my hands. "Adam."

He spins around, his eyes wide.

"What's going on? Why are they all here?"

"Did you really not get any messages from me?" Adam blinks. "I've sent not one, but two separate messengers. The Port Heads have been insisting on a celebration and they . . . " He shakes his head. "I explained all of it, in great detail."

Sam shrugs.

Adam swallows slowly. "Two messengers have gone awry? The roads aren't bad between here and there and . . . that's bad." He walks toward me and drops his voice. "Look, the Port Heads *have* been getting my updates and they all know about your miraculous healing of the Marked kids."

"First of all, I didn't heal them—"

Adam shakes his head. "You stood up in front of twenty thousand WPN citizens and allowed yourself to be Marked. You pled for a cessation to your father's plans to wipe them out. You claimed we could heal the illness that decimated the world—and for the first time in more than ten years of desperate hope, you did what you promised, what no one else could do—not scientists, not men of God, *no one*."

"And now the Port Heads want to steal the credit." Sam slings an arm around my shoulders.

"That's about it," Adam says.

I think about two messengers going missing—possibly a runaway if only one disappeared, but two? I've grown to love my WPN guards, even the awkward ones like Frank, but that doesn't mean I can trust them all. "Let's go inside. We can talk it over."

Adam clears his throat. "They're meeting together right now—discussing the plans for a celebration tour."

The audacity. "Here? At my mom's house?"

Adam shifts awkwardly. "King Solomon's residence always served as a sort of—"

"Palace." It's only a vastly oversized colonial-style mansion, but I always kind of thought it kind of looked like one. I exhale. "Fine. So they're waiting to ambush me."

"Not exactly." Adam shoots a knowing look at Sam. "I think they're glad you're not back. Two days ago, Sawyer Blevins arrived from New Orleans. Rosa Alvarez arrived later the same day. Then yesterday Terry Williams from Tampa and Quentin Clarke from Savannah showed up. Dolores Peabody got in some time late last night, and Steve Young's and Jose Fuerte's boats docked early this morning."

"They coordinated it," Sam says. "There's no way they didn't."

"It seems likely," Adam says. "And they say that since you're still too busy, they should move ahead with the celebrations among WPN without you."

"I don't really mind," I say. "So what if the people credit them?"

"They argued against the whole thing," Sam says. "They

tried to *kill you* instead of letting you rule, and then when you outsmarted them, they came while you were in quarantine and told you that sparing the Marked was a huge mistake. If you hadn't defeated them, they'd have *killed* them all, and they certainly wouldn't have made any effort to heal them."

"The one who ought to take the credit for all this is Adam," I say. "He sent the air strike that freed Aunt Anne, and then he sent the supplies to the Marked—when we needed to distribute the cure, and again over and over since. Plus, if he takes the credit, the people will be happy when he takes over."

My half brother scrunches his nose. "About that."

"About what?" The last time this came up, he didn't seem to hate the idea of ruling in my place. Wesley was concerned he'd usurp my crown—not that I'd mind as long as he was a good ruler.

"I hate all of this," Adam says. "Not to mention, the people don't like me."

"You'll only need to handle things for a while," I say reasonably. "Until you can transition the government to some form of democracy."

Adam laughs. "Okay."

"I mean it," I say.

"The citizens of WPN practically worshipped David Solomon," Adam says softly. "He saved them from Tercera, you know. These communities are composed of people who listened to his warnings and joined his followers. Then they all watched as the rest of the world, people who called him a lunatic, died *en masse*."

I haven't spent much time thinking about what the early days would have been like here in Galveston. My family and I mostly hid in a tiny cabin on the edge of civilization, and even there, Uncle Dan said it was scary. Really scary. But these ports are major hubs. David Solomon secured them, wiped out the government, and took whatever they needed to keep his people safe. He was a sociopath, and a narcissist too, but he was also an effective leader for an apocalypse, I guess.

"He was like George Washington," Sam says. "They say that the early Americans would have made Washington king if he'd been willing to accept it."

"Solomon was no George Washington," I say. "He didn't stand for freedom or—"

"The point," Adam says, "is that as much as they loved your father, and they did love him . . . they love you even more."

I blink.

"He kept them safe, but you eliminated the threat that put them at risk, not just here, but for the entire world."

"Did they get the memo where my dad, like the man who raised me, is the one who *created* Tercera in the first place?"

Adam's smile's sad. "The truth doesn't matter nearly as much as the perception. You went to the Marked camp and came back unmarked. You opted for a Trial by Fire, which you escaped unharmed. You went back to New Orleans with the specific purpose of helping those kids . . . and you asked for our help in bringing the Unmarked, the only other real political force in America, to heel. They obeyed your orders each time, and you succeeded in negotiating your aunt's release and healing the Marked kids—an uncontested miracle. Even your boyfriend was miraculously healed after being shot. That story kind of primed the pump, you know."

Sam whistles. "Yeah. If they revered Solomon, they're going to adore you."

"They do." Adam shrugs. "Your approval ratings, if something like that existed here, would be through the roof."

"I don't see why that would bring the Port Heads down on us." I can't put off facing them for much longer. They'll have noticed the cars and the guards and realize I'm here. I still can't think of the two missing messengers without becoming quite uneasy. "What do they really want? They can't be this upset and bothered by the lack of a party."

"The Port Heads have been King Solomon's delegates in each major WPN hub, and by extension, they enjoy his popularity." Adam glances over his shoulder.

The front door's opening, Dolores' severe grey bun clear even in silhouette. Ugh.

"The people didn't like how they tried to take you down," Adam whispers. "Word got out after their test questions that they tried to harm you."

"So they're here to what? Convince me to like them?"

"Or at least get the people to think you do," Adam says.

"I don't like them much," I say. "Except for maybe Quentin, Jose, and Terry."

"You should replace them," Sam says, "if you don't think you can trust them."

"We may have to do that." My head begins to ache, and I haven't even walked into Mom's house yet. I've never been more sure that I need to pass this mess off to Adam. "But for now, let's hear them out."

"Ruby? Is that you?" Dolores' voice causes my eye to twitch.

I force a smile and march toward the front of the house, hiking up the stairs purposefully, Adam on one side, Sam on the other, my guards falling in ahead of and behind me.

"You have quite the honor guard." Sawyer Blevins' voice is droll. Almost bored. "Which I hear are no longer necessary, now that the Marked pose no threat."

I'm pretty sure I'm staring at my major threat right now. "Hopefully I won't need guards at all very soon." I glance sideways at Sam—our little yellow house is coming up quickly. Please, oh please.

Sam shrugs. "It wasn't Tercera that made the world a dangerous place."

I barely keep from rolling my eyes. I reach the top step and look past Dolores and Sawyer to the other five Port Heads, crowded into the entryway, peering around to see me. "To what do I owe the pleasure of *all* of you, here in Galveston? Another test, perhaps? Or are you here to whip the citizens of WPN into a frenzy in the hopes they'll oust me themselves?"

Adam's jaw drops.

I might be a little more annoyed than I realized. "I won't beat around the bush. You weren't invited. You aren't welcome, and I'm irritated that you're all here."

Jose Fuerte laughs from the very back: deep, hearty, and full.

A few of my guards snicker, but at a baleful glare from Adam they fall silent.

"Since no one seems to have any explanations handy, why don't we head for the Garden room, where we can discuss it privately." I shove past Dolores and Sawyer, and the others shift out of the way. Sam and Adam shoulder their way past as well.

"That was awesome," Frank whispers.

I nearly trip over him, but I don't slow down until I've swung past my superfluous butler, inherited from my ridiculous bio father, and into the idiotic 'garden' room where he always held large meetings. The conference table is polished to the same high sheen it always has been—from the day good old Solomon demanded my blood to heal himself from the Tercera I infected him with, to the day I met my charming Port Heads for the very first time. I march to the front of the table and take a seat.

My heart twinges as Adam and Sam take up seats on either side of me.

I miss Wesley.

Sometimes it crashes over me like a wave. Like a tidal wave. I draw in a ragged breath.

The Port Heads filter through the door slowly, shooting forward in abrupt fits and starts. I only sat in a bumper car once Before—before the world collapsed, before life as everyone knew it died—but this reminds me of that. As if they're all moving toward me against their will, jolted forward by the person to their left, to their right, and directly behind them.

Eventually, Jose takes the seat closest to Sam, and Steve takes the seat next to Adam. The others pull out chairs up and down each side, the wooden legs scraping against the hard floors.

"I suppose this is where a good leader would set you at ease," I say. "I should apologize for snapping at you and tell you that, of course I'm always happy to see you." I cross my arms and lean back in my seat. "But no one has ever called me a good leader, and I won't lie and tell you that I have no idea why you're here. You're in disfavor with the people for your pernicious attempt to end my life and grab more power for yourselves. You came to counsel me *not* to try and save the hundred thousand Marked children who were eking out an existence to the north of your cities and settlements, no thanks to any of you *Godly* people, and I ignored your hideous advice. At great risk to myself—" I nearly stumble, thinking of Wesley's death. "And at great cost, we found a cure to the virus that has stalked us all for more than ten years. You'd like to claim credit." I stand up and brace my hands against the tabletop. "But I won't allow that travesty."

Seven sets of eyes widen in alarm. Seven heads start to turn toward one another for support, but think better of it.

They stare at me in horror instead, as if their own worst nightmares are being shoved in their faces.

We've lived through an apocalypse, and they're afraid of little old me. I won't lie and say I don't enjoy it a little.

I sit back down. "Why don't you each tell me why I shouldn't *eliminate* you right here and right now, and replace you with people who respect me. People who care about others. People I can *trust*."

No one says a word.

I lift my eyebrows.

Seven people begin to talk at once.

"Let's start with you, Jose, the person I dislike the least." I lean forward and rest my forearms on the table. "Why should you keep your job?"

"Your Majesty—"

"Also, no one should call me that. Plain old 'Ruby' is fine. The 'Majesty' and 'Highness' and all the other queen words and what-have-you are all nonsense."

Jose clears his throat. "Ruby, I've never done anything but support you. I never tried to overthrow you. I believe if you check the record, you'll see that you answered each of my questions during the trial correctly. As I believe your father intended, I asked questions to test your intentions and your ability—not your functional knowledge of Biblical trivia."

"You aren't on trial here," I say. "And I asked you to go first precisely because I recall that exact thing. But Jose, I want you to tell me what you do to serve, and how you act as the best leader for your port and your people. Why are you the best person to rule them?"

Jose swallows. "I'd love to bring you out to Carmen to see." He spreads his hands out. "I can say many wonderful things, but if you come to see our port, our people, and our commerce, I think you'll understand. And you can ask my people yourself. If they didn't want me to lead them, I would gladly step down."

An idea strikes me then. A beautiful, perfect idea. I'm embarrassed I didn't think of it sooner. "Jose, you're brilliant."

I pause for a moment. With their notoriety, they'll undeniably have a leg up in any kind of election we hold . . . but that doesn't mean they can't lose. And it doesn't mean we shouldn't let the people decide whom they want. Plus, it'll be the big first step toward freeing all of WPN from the ridiculous monarchy Solomon created. "I've decided that we will have a celebration after all—in each and every port. I'll come out to visit, and I'll let you show me the job you've done." Another idea strikes me then—a way to use my popularity to ease this transition . . . and oust the lousy Port Heads too. I can't quite suppress my smile. "And once I've had my tour, and a celebration in each location, we'll hold an election."

"An election?" Sawyer coughs. "An election for what?"

"Why, for the position of Port Head," I say, "of course."

"We're going to have to win an election?" Rosa's eyes dart right, then left, then back to mine. "In our own ports?"

"Does that really alarm you?" I feign complete innocence. "I'll give each of you the chance to show me exactly what you do, how you run the area, and what your goals are. Once that's done, if I don't deem you utterly unfit, then you'll be one of the names on a ballot and we'll let the people decide."

"That's a horrible idea," Dolores says. "It undermines your authority."

I very much hope it does, but I don't say that. "How so?" I shrug. "Do you think I wouldn't win an election? Do the people not have confidence in my leadership?"

No one else says a word. Adam's beaming when I leave —dismissing the Port Heads to their residences on the island. Except one of them doesn't leave. He remains seated. Adam and Sam stand up, and so do I, but he stays in his seat even then.

My cousin, Sawyer Blevins, clears his throat. "I was hoping to have a word with Ruby."

Sam opens his mouth, but I shake my head. "It's fine."

He and Adam walk toward the door. "We'll be right out here, in case you need us." Sam holds my gaze for a few beats, letting me know he'll be listening. I nod, and he steps out.

"Thank you," Sawyer says.

"Did the others ask you to stay behind and plead their case?" I arch one eyebrow.

Sawyer frowns and pats the seat next to him. "Nothing like that. In fact, I'm not on especially close terms with the others."

"No?" I find that hard to believe. "You're the Port Head closest to me. You were Solomon's blood relative. You're saying the others don't sort of look to you as their *de facto* leader?"

He shrugs. "If they do, they've never been good at showing it."

I finally sit. "What do you want, then?"

"I'm worried about you," he says softly. "I know you don't want this—"

"Oh." I snort. "This is where you offer to step in and help me. To guide me. To be a good cousin."

He shakes his head. "Young people always know everything." He sighs. "No. I don't even want that. I'm too old and too tired to want to deal with all the nonsense. Part of me doesn't even want to rule New Orleans anymore."

There's an exhaustion underlying his words that actually convinces me more effectively than an hour of talking could. In spite of myself, I actually believe him. "Okay. Then what?"

"Did your father ever tell you about our history? Our time together?"

I shake my head. I don't really want to hear about Solomon, thank you very much. I almost open my mouth to tell him that, but I can't quite bring myself to do it. As much as I hate my biological father, I suppose part of me wants to hear something positive.

"Your grandfather, my uncle, was a moving man of God. People came from hundreds of miles away to hear him preach." Sawyer's eyes glaze over and he gazes out the window. "He *moved* people. He *changed* them. Not, like, they felt something and moved on. No, people gave up things after meeting him, after hearing him speak. He was that powerful."

"My grandfather?"

"My mother's brother," Sawyer says. "That's how I'm related to your father, and to you. He was my first cousin. His father and my mother were siblings—very close, in fact. Best friends."

It's hard for me to think about that—about having a whole family I never knew.

"Elias Thomas—Solomon's father—did a lot of good. Government officials came to him for help. Political leaders were always asking for endorsements. But in the process, he also amassed quite a fortune."

Of course he did. This is more what I was expecting.

"Except, after he died unexpectedly in a car accident," Sawyer says slowly, "and they read his will, he left every cent to the church. He left David nothing."

Huh. I didn't expect that twist. "I bet he was angry."

"Furious," Sawyer says. "Livid, even. He came to me, asking me for evidence that his father was out of his right mind. I helped him look, but it was hopeless. His father was quite purposeful and had spoken to nearly everyone about his intentions—everyone other than his son."

"But then how—"

"David met your mother not long after this all went down," Sawyer said. "He had inherited his father's flock, and they were generous and grateful for Solomon's guidance in their time of need. That's when he changed his name, you know. He told them it helped him move on—that he had been transformed. He realized that although he hadn't gotten his father's wealth, he had something almost as good—the root of his father's wealth."

I should have known.

"He needed to look the part, however," Sawyer says. "He was quite a womanizer, but he needed someone who looked like a preacher's wife. Someone smart, beautiful, and well spoken."

"She was married." I frown.

He shrugs. "Her family had an impressive name and she was *unhappily* married. Easy enough to fix."

Yuck. "But how did—"

"I'm getting there," Sawyer says. "Your father was very upset when Carillon stole you, but he wasn't willing to sacrifice his money tree—not right when it was finally blossoming. He kept pursuing you, secretly, and finally he came into some information." He pauses, probably wondering how much I know. "He found out about Tercera, but wasn't in a position to stop it."

"That part I know."

"He and I discussed how he might use that information to keep himself and his family safe."

Use it to keep his family safe? And become a dictator. Gross. So Sawyer was as bad as Solomon.

"He discovered the accelerant in your father's lab." His hands open and close rhythmically. "I begged him not to do anything with it, but he felt he had no choice. It was the only way to ensure he could protect his people." Sawyer shakes his head. "No matter what I said, I couldn't convince him."

"And my father ushered in the end of the world," I say. "With a lie the likes of which hasn't been told before or since."

Sawyer's face is pale, his hands no longer opening and closing, but trembling as if he can't quite stop them. "I'm sorry, Ruby. I'm sorry that I couldn't convince him that it was wrong. I want you to know that, although David Solomon made some significant mistakes, not everyone in your family supported those decisions. Plenty of the Thomas family, and the Blevins branch, actually worshipped God. I'd be happy to help guide you, if you ever want it, but not so that I can control what you do. I can't express how pleased I am that you're like your grandfather—that your main goal is to serve and protect."

For the life of me, I don't want to believe it, but he actually seems genuine.

Or maybe I *do* want to believe him. I certainly don't love the idea that I'm descended from a monster. It would be nice if I could trust Sawyer and believe that my biological father was merely twisted up and confused by perceived injustice—that I'm not prone to the same megalomania and greed.

"I appreciate the offer," I say. "And I'll certainly let you know when or if I want to know more."

Sawyer stands up then. "I'd also like to be the first to offer my resignation."

My jaw nearly drops. "Excuse me?"

"I'm old," he says. "As you've pointed out, I've made some critical errors. When you were speaking earlier, I realized that you're correct. Surely there are people much better qualified than I am to serve the people of New Orleans."

Somehow, his determination to quit annoys me. If I

can't quit, he can't either. "Well, for now, let's not do anything hasty. Why don't you stay Port Head until I'm able to come and see New Orleans and we can ascertain whether there are other acceptable candidates. The last thing we want to do is throw things into turmoil unnecessarily."

He half bows. "As you command."

Ugh. I don't want to command anything. I wish he didn't annoy me so badly—it would be way easier for me to figure out what to do with him. I force a smile as he leaves.

"That was amazing," Adam says the second he's gone. "Sam and I were just talking about how far you've come since that first meeting with those bullies. They had no idea what hit them this time."

"But what did Sawyer want?" Sam asks.

He's asking as a courtesy. There's no way he didn't overhear, not with his listening skills. I roll my eyes. "You've told Adam already, I presume."

Adam's sheepish look confirms it.

"You should have let him quit," Sam says. "It would have made your job easier."

I shake my head. "Not really. We need a smooth transition—not chaos and drama."

Sam's voice is soft, and there's no censure in it when he asks, "But how are we supposed to meet with each port, celebrate, get a tour, and hold an election, before the Unmarked vote on their new chancellor?"

"I forgot about that entirely." I swear under my breath. "Well, we'll have to set up as many as we can, then head out to Nashville, then come back." I shake my head. "There's no helping it."

"You plan to go to Nashville and lend Fairchild your aid, then?" Sam asks.

"Of course." It's the least of what I owe Wesley's dad.

"But he *asked* for you. I suppose if I have to, I could just send you."

"I won't go without you," Sam says.

"What about the Galveston celebration?" Adam asks. "If we pick a date tonight, you can announce it in tomorrow's Sunday sermon."

How could I have forgotten that today's Saturday? I swear again.

"I hope you're getting all that out of your system before tomorrow." Adam smirks.

"Shut up," I say.

"Ruby!" Josephine practically shouts from the end of the hall. "You're home."

Like Galveston could ever be my home. I almost laugh. "I'm here," I admit. At least that much is true.

"I'm so pleased." My mother jogs down the hall and opens her arms for a hug.

I step toward her, half reluctant, half eager. As her arms wrap around me, conflicting emotions continue to tumble around. She abandoned me. She married a madman—an abusive, narcissistic villain. And she stayed with him after discovering her pregnancy, putting me at risk from the day of my birth. But she also killed him in the end, preventing him from harming me permanently. She has stood up tall and managed everything she could while I pursued what I felt was more important, over her suggestions.

And whatever her faults, she clearly loves me to the extent of her capacity. When she finally releases me, she forces a smile.

I hope my forced smiles don't look quite that pained.

"I have some news," she says.

Oh, no. Not more *news*. "Great." I groan. "May as well lay it on me."

"I've been investigating—discreetly, don't worry."

"Investigating what?"

"Your father's . . . activities."

Huh? "His trade agreements? His plans for expansion?" I snort. "I'm not sure I care much about any of that."

She clears her throat and looks down at her feet. "I've been able to locate four children whom I believe might be . . . related to you."

Oh, great. I can see why she might fixate on that, and I suppose it's better to know. "Wonderful. Well, it looks like I'll be here a few days, so that will give me plenty of time to meet them." I glance at Adam. "Also, how quickly can we throw together some kind of celebration for the people of Galveston?" I'd far prefer that we send the provisions we'd use for a party to the recovering Marked kids. But I do understand the reason for and importance of allowing people to find joy where they are. As they are.

"One week," Josephine says, "should be—"

"A week?" Sam grunts. "Surely you can do something sooner than that."

"Three days?" Adam shrugs. "It won't be spectacular. It won't be fitting with the inspiration for the celebration, but we can throw together something in three days."

Josephine frowns, but she doesn't argue.

With the way today is going, that's a major win. "Great. Party here in three days, then on to New Orleans to remove Sawyer Blevins from office."

Mom's jaw drops open.

I use one finger to close it. "Better get used to shock. Now that I'm back, a lot of things are going to be changing."

❧ 4 ☙

SAM

Ruby looks at the Bible as though it might bite her.

"You can touch it, you know."

She jumps and turns toward me slowly. "Half of this book is full of nonsense—lists and bizarre things that make no sense. You know that, right?"

I shrug.

"Wait, are you religious?" Her face brightens, the corners of her mouth turning upward. "How did I not know this?"

The hopeful gleam in her eye makes me nervous. "Don't even think about it."

"If you've read the Bible . . . " She stands up, stalking toward me slowly as if she doesn't want to startle me. "*You* could give the sermon."

I'm full on smiling now. "Have you heard me say more than twenty words to anyone but you? Hard pass."

"I can't believe my boyfriend reads the Bible."

"I think there's more to the world than we understand, and I've read every great text at least once. I find a lot of comfort in many of the stories, especially the New Testament ones."

"You could knock me over with a feather," she says. "At least suggest an inspirational topic I can share today. They may like me well enough, but if I get up and bumble around in front of everyone, they might change their mind. Then it'll be an uphill battle to convert this idiotic monarchy to some form of democracy and get out of Dodge."

"You still want to leave?" I channel every bit of nonchalant I can, but I'm nervous about her answer.

She crosses the room and bumps on my leg until I swing sideways in the chair. She sits on my lap and leans up close. "Of course I do," she whispers. "The very second I can oust the leeches my dad appointed and make sure WPN is in good hands, we're gone. You and me, small town, meaningful jobs, but nothing major. We'll be together, and we'll have simple, low-stress lives."

The anxiety I didn't realize I had melts out of my shoulders.

My lips are just brushing against hers when someone knocks on the door to the office.

"Who is it?" Ruby's voice is delightfully annoyed.

"I have the children gathered as you requested." Josephine.

Ruby stiffens against me and stands up. She brushes off her pants, as if that might prepare her in some way to meet half siblings she didn't know she had, who only exist because her biological father betrayed her mother. "Right." Her lips twitch, and I wish I could pull her back down.

I wish the whole world could disappear sometimes. We've done our part. Why does this kind of thing keep cropping up? "You want me to come?"

Ruby's eyes widen. "Always."

I stand up too, and she grabs my hand, our fingers interlacing. It's still shocking to me that with as small as her hands are and as large as mine are, they fit together so easily.

"I'd love to put this off, but they didn't do anything to me. I keep reminding myself that they didn't wrong me, and if we're leaving as soon as we can, I can't delay anything. Right?" She looks up at me, her fringy blonde lashes almost disappearing over wide, uncertain blue eyes.

"Right." I squeeze her hand and we walk toward the Garden room where Josephine's cook, Laura, has left a plate of cookies and fruit with a pitcher of lemonade. As if food will make this easier, somehow. Although, if they're young enough, maybe it will.

Adam's waiting outside the Garden room, his arms crossed over his chest, his eyes unsettled. He's not as large as I am, but he's close. Military energy, wide build, tanned skin, and a competent bearing. I could take him out easily, but he's more than an adequate lead guard for WPN. Ruby pauses in front of her half brother and they exchange some kind of glance before she moves past him and into the room. I'm not sure what Ruby's expecting when we walk inside—mini-Adams?—but I wasn't expecting the diverse mix sitting awkwardly in chairs, picking at tiny cookies.

"Hello," Ruby says brightly. "Thank you all for coming." She looks around with a bewildered look on her face. "Where are your mothers?"

"Queen Josephine said they should stay outside," a tall boy says, his voice cracking. He's gangly and blond, and he looks about twelve or thirteen. He's the only one of the four who looks anything like Ruby or Adam. Not that they look very similar, but their coloring and their noses are close at least.

"I miss my mom," a small girl with floofy hair and dark brown skin says. Then she gulps loudly and looks pointedly at her hands.

"I can ask them to come back in," Ruby says.

"No, don't." A boy who looks even younger than the girl shakes his head vehemently. "My mom's always shushing me, and if you're my sister, I want to talk to you."

Ruby's mouth turns up. "I want to talk to you, too. And I think I should make something clear. We believe I am your half sister, but that also means you're one another's half siblings. Take a look around. Whether you have other family at home perhaps, I don't know, but you have us now, and I'm happy to know about each of you." Ruby pulls out a seat and sits, pouring herself a glass of lemonade and absently wiping a few drops that spilled while she looks at the children gathered.

As shocked and stressed as she must be, she's kind, she's considerate, and she's composed, welcoming them in a way their father never did. My love for this woman overwhelms me sometimes, and I wonder how something so good could have come from someone as depraved as Solomon. Maybe, as Sawyer said, Solomon was merely a corrupted soul. Perhaps that's true of all people who have gone bad—it happened thanks to a twist of fate, combined with their own poor choices.

"How about we introduce ourselves?" Ruby smiles. "My name is Ruby. I was raised as Ruby Behl. It's a very long story I won't bore you all with, but I found out recently that David Solomon was my real biological father. I know he wasn't an especially nice man, and I won't be upset if you don't have good things to say about him. Or if they *are* good, that's alright, too. I want to be clear that whatever your feelings are, they're okay here, with me. Always."

The dark-skinned girl glances at the redheaded boy as if checking to see whether the other child believes her.

"I'll go first," the awkward boy says. "My name is Alex. I'm thirteen years old. My mom was a widow, and Solomon came to our house to . . . I don't know. To tell her it would be okay, maybe." He frowns. "He did a little more consoling

—" He clears his throat and looks pointedly at the two younger children. "Anyhow, here I am. I didn't see him very often before he died, and that was okay with me."

"And what do you enjoy doing?" Ruby asks.

"I'm a farmer," he says. "Mom and I live pretty far down the island, and we grow crops—tomatoes, sweet corn, onions, and peas."

A farmer? No wonder we didn't see many vegetable gardens. Solomon has commercial farmers. It's smart—but I hadn't given it much thought. He and his mother would have been easy to hide, that far out. It makes me wonder how Josephine found them in the first place—maybe combed through his routine for the past fifteen years and retraced the contacts he had in which she wasn't present. That's what I'd have done, anyway.

"That's wonderful," Ruby says. "In fact, maybe you can help me understand how the crops work around here, and how you're paid for your work."

He smiles shyly at her.

I wonder about any economy that relies on thirteen-year-olds and their widowed mothers for its crop production, but that's a question for another day.

"I'm Paul," the tall, thin Asian kid next to Alex says. "I'm fifteen, and I'm in the musical performance track. My mother plays organ for the Sunday sermons." The pride in his voice is clear, and I can guess how Solomon met his mother.

"That's wonderful," Ruby says. "I have no musical talent at all, but I appreciate listening to those who do."

He beams.

"Who's that guy?" the redhead asks, tossing his head my direction.

Ruby snickers. "*That guy* is Samuel Roth, my boyfriend." She glances back at me. "He seems a little scary possibly, or intimidating, if you don't know him, but he's so *good* that he'd never do anything to harm anyone. In fact, sitting in here with him is probably the safest you could ever be."

The redhead's eyes widen. "You're the one who shot everyone."

"What's your name?" Ruby asks, pointedly not answering that question in the affirmative. "And how old are you?"

"I'm Roger," the chatty boy says. "And I'm six going on sixteen, my mom says. I'm not sure what that means, but she always says it with a big sigh, like it's not very good."

"What things do you enjoy doing?" Ruby asks.

"Playing with trains, mostly," he says. "And I love drawing. I could draw you some really pretty pictures to put up on your walls. I noticed they're really boring and just plain white when I was coming in here."

Ruby laughs. "I'd love that. You're right. They are boring."

"My mom says my drawings are all really good. She saves them all in a box forever and ever."

I'll just bet she does.

"And what about you?" Ruby asks the little girl softly. "What's your name, sweetheart, and how old are you?"

The little girl doesn't look up.

"I'm always nervous meeting new people too," Ruby says. "If you'd rather not talk today, that's fine. But I'm happy to meet with you another time. I'd like us to be friends. It looks like we're the only two girls—that makes us sisters."

A moment passes in silence, and then another. Finally, the little girl looks up, her brilliant golden eyes flashing. "I'm Amber."

Clearly named for the striking, bright, golden color of her eyes.

"It's wonderful to meet you, Amber." Ruby smiles.

"I'm seven."

"That's a wonderful age. So much to learn and so many things you're old enough to do." Ruby points at the untouched cookie on her plate. "You don't like sweets?"

She shrugs, her tiny shoulders barely moving. "I don't like most things."

"Well, I hope I'll be an exception. I hope we'll be friends."

Amber's eyes meet Ruby's and the side of her mouth turns up in a very small smile. "Me too."

Ruby chats with them for a few more moments, and then she stands up. "I'm not sure whether you've heard, but I have a Sunday sermon to give in an hour or so. I'll be announcing what I hope is a fun surprise today, and I thought I'd tell my *family* first—we'll be having a big celebration right here on the island."

"What are we celebrating?" Alex asks.

"The cure to Tercera has been found," Ruby says. "And administered, for the most part. I think that's cause for celebration, don't you?"

"So it's true?" Paul asks. "Tercera is gone?"

"Well, the virus still exists," Ruby says. "But it's not hanging over our heads anymore. We have a cure for it."

"If we're righteous then we're safe," Roger says. "God only punishes the wicked."

Ruby's lips twist. "Well, in my experience, no one is really one or the other. We all have a little good and a little bad mixed up together, and we get to choose which one to grow by our actions. Regardless of your feelings on that issue, everyone is safe now, wicked or not." She gestures to the table. "You are welcome to stay as long as you'd like, and when you're ready to leave, if you want to attend the sermon—" She stumbles a bit on that word. "You and your mothers will have seats near the front."

"What about my father?" Paul asks. "And my sister and brothers?"

Ruby blinks. I'm sure that she, like me, didn't give much thought to them having families of their own, but of course it's not like Solomon would prey only on widows. "Of course they're welcome too."

After the meeting, Ruby closes herself in the office, staring at the Bible with the same intensity she brings to bear on all her problems. Adam's standing outside the door, so I take up a position on his other side.

"Do you think she'll tell everyone about him?" Adam asks.

I shrug.

"Her mother is dead set against it. She says that Ruby can't incriminate Solomon without losing the people's support." Adam sighs. "She might be right."

"She might be wrong."

He shrugs. "I wish I knew what to recommend."

"Ruby wasn't raised for running a government like this," I say. "She hates it. We just want to leave, but she won't do that until she's confident that the people of WPN will be alright."

"You mean she wants to make sure another Solomon doesn't rise up to replace him."

That's what I mean.

Five minutes until her sermon is supposed to start and she still hasn't left the office. I tap on the door and enter. She's poring over a dark brown book that looks an awful lot like a journal.

It's definitely not the Bible.

"Are you ready?"

"Do you know what this is?" She snaps the book closed and waves it at me. "This little brown book?"

I shake my head.

"It's my dad's book of dirty secrets. He's got evidence of all kinds of distasteful, nasty things in here. Prominent members of the community here in Galveston, and of each

WPN settlement. Even Unmarked officials, like your father, are listed. In fact, if we'd taken the time to look into it, we might have figured out that your dad was my dad's partner. He knew that, too. Obviously. He knew when you sat here across from him, but he didn't tell you." She shakes her head in disgust. "Is that what it takes to rule? Lies? Deceit? Blackmail?"

"When you're a dictator—a tyrant—who rules by fear, yes."

She stands up. "I can't do that. Not ever, even if it's only for a short time."

"So you're going to tell the people about Solomon?"

She looks at the ceiling. "I don't know. I want this to be a smooth transition. I don't want a revolution on my hands, and Josephine says that the only way to ensure it goes well is to let their positive memories of him transfer to me."

"But that feels gross."

She nods. "It's time to go, though. I know it is." Ruby straightens her shoulders and marches to the door. "Let's go."

The trip to the conference center is uneventful, even with masses of people waiting in long lines outside. They stand a little straighter as we drive past, many of them pressing hands to their mouths or their hearts. Josephine and Adam aren't wrong. They look at Ruby with adoration, devotion, and awe. It's a look I recognize.

Because it's the same way I've always looked at her.

Her hand trembles as I help her out of the car. "Maybe I shouldn't have worn a pantsuit," she murmurs. "Maybe I should have let Josephine dress me in that stupid ball gown."

"You need to be yourself," I say. "That's enough—it's always been enough."

Her eyes meet mine and hold my gaze. Something inside her stills then, and she nods. "Thank you." She pivots on her heel and marches down the hallway that leads to the back stage entrance. I'm glad to have Adam handling most of the details so I can simply stay close to her this time.

Finally, she reaches the steps up to the stage, and I stop at the edge of the curtains, while she continues out to the podium.

Applause begins as soon as they see her. Calls of "Queen Ruby!" and "Her Majesty!" flood the air.

She steps up and drags the microphone down slowly until it's at the right level for someone of her diminutive size. "Thank you for that wonderful welcome."

More applause.

"I won't lie and say that it comes easily to me—talking to you like this. In fact, I don't really think I'm qualified to teach you much of anything. As you all saw the last time I was up here, I know very little about the Bible, or about God's will."

She looks down at her feet for a moment, as if considering something. When she looks back up, her face is resolved. Confident. Almost eager.

"The fact is, I shouldn't be up here at all. I'm not a queen." She removes the circlet Josephine insisted she put on in the car and sets it on the top of the podium. "You only call me your queen because my biological father, David Solomon, declared himself your king."

Murmurs. Jostling. Awkward silence.

"I didn't even know we were related until a few weeks ago, and today, for the very first time in my life, I sat down to study the Bible with the hope I might learn something I could share with all of you. I've been reading it off and on for a few weeks now, and I'd like to know more about it than I do, but I'm still a far cry from an expert of any kind."

A few odd hoots and hollers.

"I've been focusing on the New Testament. I feel a

kinship with Jesus in those accounts—he's a God I can get behind. He didn't ever shy away from people because of their circumstances or their illnesses. No, as far as I can tell, his entire goal was to heal, and heal, and heal some more. He healed everyone who was broken, everyone who was scared, and everyone who was alone. He didn't discern whether they deserved his healing—he welcomed all of them the same way." Her shoulders square. "My father might have acted pious, but even in the short time that I knew him, it was clear to me that he was not. He was a terrible person who beat my mother, who beat me, who turned his back on the wounded, the ill, the needy. He took and he took and he took, and he rarely gave anything at all —and only when he thought it would get him something greater in return."

Gasps. More murmurs. Scared and confused and angry faces.

"I know. It's appalling that I should say something like that about your leader. I know you loved him. When I go over the facts in my mind, there's no way I can take over leadership of his people without making it known how he came into power in the first place. My biological father, David Solomon, started a relationship with a married woman—my mother Josephine. Her first husband knew he was a bad person, and after I was born, Donald Carillon stole me from David Solomon."

The audience is absolutely shocked.

"And I'm eternally grateful that he stole me."

They don't know what to think about all this.

"Donald Carillon loved me. He wanted to make the world a better place. He spent years studying viruses and vaccines—and in the process he created a virus known as Triptych. He created it in order to create a vaccination that would be able to keep everyone safe from as many horrible viruses as possible, for as cheaply as possible. It was a noble goal, but evil men, like John Roth, the former leader of the Unmarked, and David Solomon, your king, conspired against him. John Roth stole the virus that should only ever have existed in a lab . . . and released it. David Solomon knew all about it. He also stole the accelerant and used it to wipe out the government. It kept all of you safe, but it killed millions and millions. Who knows how much earlier the cure my adoptive father developed might have been released if not for those two men and their selfish actions."

Angry confusion spreads. People don't believe her—they don't want to, anyway.

"Hear me out," she calls, "please. Just listen until I'm done explaining, and then you can decide what you think."

They settle down, but they don't look any happier or any more satisfied.

"Your lives were kept safe by David Solomon, and I appreciate why you'd be grateful for that protection in a terrifying time, but he used religion to shackle you, to blind you from the truth, and you can see it if you'll open your hearts to what I'm saying. God is real—I truly believe that. I've seen too many miracles, too many unexplainable events, to argue otherwise. But we have to be careful that we're doing what he would want. Many people encouraged me to keep all of this from you." She shakes her head. "I considered it, to my everlasting shame."

She swallows.

"My dad did a lot of bad things, but he thought that keeping you safe—a very noble goal—would justify his reprehensible actions. I couldn't in good conscience do bad things for noble reasons, not unless I wanted to become like him. I don't want to do that, not ever. That's why I have to confess that when I requested the Trial by Fire, I knew that I couldn't be infected by Tercera. My adoptive father, Donald Carillon, had given me antibodies as a child, which I didn't discover until recently—just before David

Solomon died. They prevented me from ever contracting Tercera, and I knowingly deceived all of you. I'm very sorry for that."

Now they're definitely angry. Tight words. Angry gestures.

"But."

They fall silent immediately, almost as if she cast a spell on them.

"That's not the whole story, either. I did that so that I could prevent the Cleansing—the elimination of every person infected with Tercera—that David Solomon and the other Port Heads planned. I did it for the right reason—but it was still wrong. I see that now, and I vow that I'll never lie to you again. Never. I'll only do good things for good reasons."

"You may be asking yourself how I can believe in God—I'm a little heathen who learned about her parents and the Bible and all of this recently." She walks away from the podium and toward the audience. She drops down on her knees so she's not above them all. "It's because I see God in each one of you. Each of us is good. Bad and good, mixed up together. We all make good decisions, and sometimes we make bad ones, but we have to try and make more good than bad. We have to strive to grow all that is good within us. When we make mistakes, we must apologize and try to improve."

She shakes her head.

"It's that simple. Today I met the brothers and sister that my biological father left behind—a testament to his ongoing duplicity to my mother. But in them, I didn't see his sins. I didn't see his wickedness. No, my siblings are beautiful humans. They, just like every single one of us, have the chance to make choices every single day. In my Bible study after meeting with them, I read about Jesus with his disciples. They were fishermen, like many of you are. Jesus filled their nets to overflowing in one story. I'm sure that would have made them all rich, but it seems like that wasn't his goal, not really."

She pauses. "I'm not an expert at any of this. I'm sure most of you could quote some of the things I'm reading for the first time. But to me, it sure looks like, although God could give us anything or everything, that's not what he does—for a reason. After he showed the men that he could fill their nets, that the fish obeyed his call, he asked those men instead to leave all of that behind and follow him—to become *fishers of men*."

Ruby's face slowly pans from one side of the room to the other. "Today I'm asking you to do the same thing. While most of the world suffered, you have prospered here. You have fished, grown crops, traded, and manufactured amazing items. God has blessed you with fish, so many fish. But we all need to remember that having an abundance of fish has never been the end goal. On Jesus' behalf, I'm asking you to become people who take care of others, and I want you to make that decision yourselves, not because a government is telling you to do it. I want all of us to make more good decisions today than we did yesterday. I don't want power, and I don't want to be queen. It's not an insult to you fine, hardworking, Christlike people, truly. Jesus didn't want the power and honor of a title or a crown. He wanted to change people, to encourage them to be better than they were. He wanted improvement for the people, and consequently the world, around him."

She straightens purposefully. Her eyes flash.

"We've healed the Marked children from Tercera, and we've eliminated its stranglehold on the world, and it took us a decade and innumerable lost lives to do it. Now we need to leave our fishing nets behind. We need to walk away from our desire for power. Instead we need to seize upon what Jesus asked us to do—we need to be fishers of men. It's time for us to welcome those Marked kids who want to join us into our communities. We need to send aid and education and supplies for those who wish to create and improve their own space. We should be taking care of them no matter how or where they choose to live, and if they want to come here, we should welcome them into our homes. It's our obligation as followers of Christ to teach them, feed them, and clothe them. It's our obligation to be better today than we were yesterday. I'm certainly going to try my very hardest, and I really hope you'll all join me."

Silence.

I'm genuinely worried that she gambled and lost. No one looks pleased. No one looks happy.

Until I realize what I'm seeing: they're wrecked, many of them sobbing. They're ready to follow her and do just as she says. Finally, someone at the front of the audience begins to clap, and then everyone else picks up the gesture until their support is nearly deafening. I scan the audience as I always do, seeking for anyone who means her harm. Most of the faces are puffy and red. Most of the eyes shine, with hope.

And for the first time, I fear that it might be a ridiculous dream that we might ever leave here and live somewhere small. Somewhere comfortable. Somewhere like we discussed.

Because Ruby is magnificent, and they'll never let her go.

RUBY

I cannot get away from here fast enough.

Of course, what I want doesn't matter. I've got four more sermons to give on the day that never ends. My distaste for addressing crowds notwithstanding, these people didn't do anything wrong. If they want to connect with me after the major changes I'm requesting they make, I can't deny them.

As they rush the stage, my security team panics—most notably Sam. He looks ready to tuck me under his arm and rush us back to Mom's house.

I shake my head at him and wave the others back. These people don't mean me any harm. I can tell that much from their broken expressions. What makes me happy is the hope underneath the nervous sadness.

It'll kill Sam, but I can't help myself. I hop down from the stage and walk down the center aisle. People rush from either side, reaching for me, calling to me. It's so bizarre that these people, who have studied God and the Bible for decades, are listening to my guidance, but for some bizarre reason, they are. Even now that I've confessed my deception. Even now that I've told them the kind of person my biological father was. Even after I begged them to throw their aid behind a group of people they've been taught to fear and hate.

Which means these Christians are better people than I had any reason to expect, given their leader. They really do believe in what the Bible teaches, and that lifts my spirits unimaginably.

So I show them.

"Of course I'd be happy to meet your daughter," I tell one woman.

She thrusts her young child outward, pushing her past the other women and men blocking her path.

"I'm Hildie," the girl says. "I pray for you every night." Tears stream down her face as she reaches for me.

I let her take my hand and I crouch down until we're at eye level. "Thank you," I say. "I need every prayer I can get."

She beams.

"We pray for you too," a young man who can't be much older than I am says, his arm around a girl my age. "Every morning and every night."

"And us," a woman with white hair says, her hand shaking as she presses it to her tear-stained face. "Thank you for telling us the truth, and for putting us back on God's path."

"You all must choose your own path," I say, "but you can't do it without knowing the truth."

Heads nod.

"Queen Ruby," a woman calls. "My name is Gretchen, and I've got a tree full of oranges back at home. I'd be happy to bring them to you so you can take them to those children."

"And I have a big, empty house," a man says. "My wife passed and I don't need the space. I'd be happy to give it up, or to welcome children into our home."

And they go on and on and on. Offers of aid. Blessings on me. Gratitude for what they've received and for my sermon.

In spite of Sam's pained expression and nervous eyes, I move forward.

Until Josephine steps up to the podium. "As I'm sure you can see, Her Majesty Queen Ruby loves each and every one of you a great deal. It's for that very reason that we must ask you to leave." She inhales slowly. "She has several thousand people waiting outside for their chance to hear her speak and meet her if she has the energy for it."

I expect them to ignore her, to linger, and to keep asking and shouting and pressing against me.

But they leave, filing out quickly and efficiently.

My second sermon, and my third, fourth, and fifth are much easier. The terror of my chosen direction is gone, leaving only my growing faith that this was the right thing. An infection can't heal until the pus is drained. These people are good underneath. They want to be righteous and kind and generous. They've been living out here, huddled away in fear for a decade, but now that we've eliminated Tercera, they seem increasingly ready to throw those nets away and pursue their new vocation: providing aid to those in need.

I'm proud of them, really proud.

Even someone as dark as David Solomon couldn't infect them. He ruled by fooling them, but once their eyes are opened, they fling their arms wide. By the time we return to Josephine's home, we can't even drive up to the front of the house. Boxes, crates, baskets, and bins clutter the driveway, the front yard, and the surrounding areas. I can't help but look inside the boxes nearest me as we walk toward the front doors of the stately white house.

Oranges. Lemons. Bread. Wheat. Beans. Clothing.

Blankets. Flashlights and lanterns. It's all here—delivered by zealous, excited citizens, eager to serve.

"Your Majesty." Josephine's housekeeper, Mrs. Johnson, waves.

What now?

We climb the rest of the way up to the main house to where she's standing on the porch. "Yes?" I ask.

"I've been compiling a list—people have been coming by all day. They're offering their homes, spare bedrooms, and sheds that could be modified to be a safe and comfortable living space. They're all ready and willing to welcome the formerly Marked into Galveston. I'm not sure precisely, but it looks like we have room for more than ten thousand."

Not all the Marked will want to leave, or will have any interest in joining WPN for that matter, but some of them will. Some will want a chance to become a part of a society with jobs, opportunities, and infrastructure. Surely some of them will want to have a childhood and an education. Thinking about the generosity of the people who formerly considered these kids to be a threat, of their willingness to open their homes to them, this time I'm the one who's crying. "I can't believe it."

Sam wraps an arm around me. "You did this."

I shake my head. "I haven't done a thing. These are the people of WPN. I haven't been fair to them. I've judged them and their hearts because of their leader. But how often do leaders fool us? I had no idea how much good they would do without compulsion, if only they knew of the need."

"You inspire them," Adam says. "In a way I never could."

I roll my eyes. "Please. You sent loads of aid to us already."

"From our government stockpiles. This was offered

freely from the citizens. It's not the same." Adam surveys the boxes and bins through the front window of the house. "A lot of that will spoil soon. We'll need to sort and prioritize, sending the perishables to Baton Rouge right away."

"We need someone to organize immediately and to coordinate our ongoing efforts—to direct what goes where." I didn't realize people would jump to bring things and make room quite this fast, but I'm pleased they listened. "Who do you think might be able to handle this?"

"Your mother has a wonderful head for this sort of thing," Adam says. "It'll be sort of like running the household and your father's appointments, only a little more complicated and rushed."

I should give her more credit than I do, maybe. She has been pretty competent at managing the details of things, and that's no small feat with a group this large. "But she's already managing the details of the celebration," I say. "I can't really ask her to do both—at least, not for the next few days."

I wish Wesley were here. At times like this, the reminder of his loss aches deep in my soul. He was brilliant at this type of administration. "If Wesley's dad wasn't otherwise occupied," I say, "he'd be amazing at this."

"You need to start meeting people here," Sam says. "You can't rely on your Unmarked family and friends to run WPN."

He's right, of course. "Alright, then let's set up some meetings with the people Solomon used for this sort of task." I'm reluctant to trust anyone he chose, but some of them might be alright. And undeniably, they know how things work here much better than I do.

"There is the matter of the two messengers who went missing," Adam says quietly.

Sam's shoulders straighten. "You and I will deal with

that while she meets with your cadre of helpers to work on the administrative tasks."

Adam clears his throat. "That's just it. The messengers were my guards, but the only people who knew what message I was sending were—" he lowers his voice "—administrative people."

"So we meet with them with her, and deal with this after she's gone to bed." Sam crosses his arms over his chest.

"That's a better plan," Adam says. "And I'll have their personnel files brought."

I'd like to disagree with them, but it's obvious that someone either didn't want me to return, or that one of the Port Heads wanted me to look derelict in my duties. Either way, I've got enemies who aren't afraid to kidnap . . . or possibly worse.

"I do have men sweeping the area, attempting to discover how far the messengers made it, and where they went awry." Adam steps out the front door and begins talking to one of the guards, ostensibly to line up a group of people who can help us.

Josephine walks down the hall. "We have a lot to do," she says. "I've asked Mr. Peterman, your father's former Storehouse Coordinator, to manage in the short run—a lot of those donations will spoil if they aren't delivered immediately." She sighs. "And Mrs. Johnson and I have drawn up a short list of items we'll need for the party in three days."

I don't often want to hug my mother, but right now, I don't resist the urge. "Thank you."

"Did you think you were alone here?" Her voice is soft. "You did something amazing today. You inspired your people, and now they love you more today than they did yesterday. I didn't think that was possible." She steps back, her head bowed. "I advised you poorly. I told you not to confess any of those things about David, and I thought I had your best interest at heart, but I fear I was being self-ish. I might have been hoping that no one would find out anything you shared for myself instead of what would be best for you or for them."

My mom's actually human—and I find that I like her much more for it. "It was a gamble," I say. "I really did think, and not only with that first sermon, that you might have been right. They seemed pretty hostile when I told them that they'd been led by a man who cared more for himself than the will of God."

"They believe all of this led them to you," Mrs. Johnson says. "And I agree with them. A ruler who does God's will— who heals, who cares, who saves."

Oh, good grief. "Well, I'm just happy that you're taking care of a lot of these things." I sigh. "I was beginning to feel like Atlas, trying to hold up the world."

"Did you think you had to do everything yourself?" Mrs. Johnson laughs. "We're all here for you."

And it turns out, she's right. The next few days fly by, between coordinating the ongoing donations, my upcoming trips, and the details of the party. The weather appears to be cooperating, at least, for us to hold the celebration outside, on the beach. WPN has maintained the seawall, creating a beautiful, sandy beach down the main strip. An area I recall as child is still there as well, called the Pleasure Pier. We'll have carnival rides for the kids, and food stands, and at Adam's suggestion, donation bins scattered around for nonperishables.

The night before, we have almost everything ready to go.

"Ruby?" Sam's voice is tense. That's never good.

I look up from the checklists I've been reviewing. My eyes were nearly crossed from the paperwork, but it all looks in order. "Yeah?" Adam's standing just behind Sam. Now I know it's nothing good. "What's wrong?"

"We found the messengers." Sam's face is grim.

"They're dead." I close my eyes and hope they'll correct me.

They don't.

"Who would *kill* them?" I ask. "Just to delay me?"

"It had to be the Port Heads," Adam says. "They were planning to take over in your absence."

"We both fear that they'll decide to move to Plan B," Sam says.

"Which is?"

"It appears that one of them intended to release the information that you had antibodies to Tercera." Sam glances at Adam. "We found a box of fliers in a shed, smearing you, essentially."

Adam sighs. "If you'd listened to Josephine or me and not told the people everything." He shakes his head. "They planned to delay your return, and then undermine your rule. But now, if they can't do that . . . " Adam clenches his fists.

"You think they might try to kill me next?" My eyebrows rise.

"It's pretty easy to assassinate someone," Sam says. "We'll work as many angles as we can, but unless we keep you away from anything public—"

"Which we can't do right now." I shake my head. "There's no way to transition a government from a monarchy to a democracy without ever talking to anyone or explaining the purpose."

"Our only solution is to be a little more aggressive in flushing out the people working against you," Sam says.

More aggressive, coming from Sam, doesn't sound good. "Don't kill them."

"If you eliminate the source of the danger, the threat disappears," Adam says. "I know it sounds extreme, but how many lives hang in the balance?"

It certainly seems like something David Solomon would do, which is how I know it's wrong. "But if you're willing to sacrifice innocent lives hunting down the wrongdoers, where do you draw the line?" I shake my head and stand up. "No. You'll have to cover as many angles as you can for now, and we'll come up with a plan to trick them."

"But, you can't—" Sam starts.

"We can only—" Adam says.

I throw my hands up. "This is a security issue at this point. If you have ideas for how we can trick whoever opposes me into betraying themselves, great. You can obviously do some searching as we travel port to port. But I won't skip out on talking to the people, and I won't kill the Port Heads, and I won't delay our plans. All of those options would be a win for them."

Sam and Adam institute a litany of protocols—from even *more* of the irritating guards, to advance prep on each location for the celebration, to snipers waiting in adjacent buildings to secure any threats. It reminds me to an uncomfortable degree of the measures employed by my bio father, but no one will be harmed unless they're a threat, so I don't argue.

Mom and Mrs. Johnson bombard me with tiny details, but it's not so bad. In my seventeen years of life, I've never planned a single party. It's actually kind of fun. "Yes, two colors of cotton candy is fine," I decide. "Pink and blue."

I've never had cotton candy.

"Sure, the band should play lots of old songs—things that were popular Before." I smile. "It might have bummed people out years ago, but now we can welcome back the life we once had. We don't need to fear dancing or interaction or anything that has been too big a risk."

I'm surprised when Sawyer comes by to wish me well— and make sure that Sam and Adam have taken reasonable measures. "I'm worried," he practically whispers once we're in the Garden room.

Sam's sideways glance tells me that Sawyer's concern doesn't reduce his suspicion of my cousin's possible involvement.

"Why did you show up?" I ask. "The day I arrived, every single Port Head had only recently come."

"I received a message," Sawyer says. "It was printed on a white card." He pulls a paper from his pocket. "It strongly encouraged me to come." He hands the paper to me.

Sawyer:

We have spent too long worrying only about our own ports. It's time we come together, for the good of World Peace Now. A more virulent virus than Tercera threatens to end all we have created: misperception. Anyone who refuses to fight it will be destroyed by it.

It's not signed. "Why didn't you show me this before?" I arch one eyebrow.

He shrugs. "I thought it might have come from you, honestly."

"Everyone would have gotten one," Adam says. "We could demand to see each Port Head's notes and the one who doesn't have one is the sender."

Sawyer's eyes brighten. "That's a good idea."

"But it would tip our hand," Sam says. "And a cunning manipulator would have sent one to him or herself as well."

My cousin's shoulders slump. "What do we do? I'm worried about you coming to the celebration."

"Perhaps you could make the presentation there instead," Adam says.

Sawyer shakes his head. "The people don't want to hear from me—but you could do a virtual speech, from the safety of your home. A broadcast would keep you safe, but give the people what they want."

Sam taps his lip with his forefinger.

"No," I say. "I won't hide. We proceed as planned."

Sawyer stands. "The Port Heads have a lot of secrets. Your father knew most of them, but I know quite a few as well. I'm happy to—"

"Thank you. I may take you up on that later, but for now." I stand too. "I'm trying to avoid judging anyone by their past."

By the time he's gone, Sam is pacing. "I think we should have asked what he knew. We could investigate—corroborate his stories and then—"

"We can revisit that in New Orleans," I say. "But we don't have the time right now to sniff out what's real and what's not."

"We've been trained to do just that," Adam says.

"He's been trained longer," Sam says. "He might be trying to manipulate us."

I don't think so—he seemed genuine. But it's so hard to tell.

Less than an hour later, Dolores Peabody shows up at my front door. I groan. "What now?"

"She's no worse than Sawyer," Adam says. "He makes my skin crawl."

I shake my head. "Alright, let's talk to her."

"I'm starting to hate the Garden room," Adam says.

"I think I should talk to her alone." I glance at Sam.

He nods infinitesimally. He'll stand outside the door so he can hear and provide feedback, but Dolores will think we're alone and speak more freely.

For the first time ever, Dolores' hair isn't in a bun. She's gotten it cut in a very cute bob, and it's not grey, either. "You dyed your hair?" My eyebrows rise.

"The last ten years haven't been big on celebrations and parties," she says. "But now that the threat of Tercera is gone, and we're going to be interacting more, I felt like it was time for a . . . refresh."

And now that her job is on the line—unless the people like her. I'm not sure whether this is sad or inspiring. "Did you need something?"

She drops her voice. "I was inspired, Ruby." She swallows. "I won't lie and say that I was excited to discover you existed, or that your father had left control of World Peace Now to an untested, immature child. I worried you'd ruin us—everything we built. And I lost track of the real purpose in our community. You have proven that I was dead wrong—and that God works in mysterious ways. I wanted to apologize, and to warn you."

A chill runs up my spine. Warn me?

"You may have already considered this, but it wasn't happenstance that brought all of the Port Heads to Galveston at the same time. I received a very curious note." She hands me a white card that looks identical to Sawyer's, but for the name at the top. "Someone is working against you, I fear."

"Do you have any idea who it might be?"

She inhales slowly. "I've known Sawyer Blevins for a very long time, and in case you didn't know this . . . " She leans toward me. "He actually sort of helped David—your father, I mean—get his start. I've always wondered whether he was jealous of David's power and success."

"You think my cousin is plotting against me?" I try to sound shocked.

She shrugs. "I don't say that lightly, truly. But you should also know that Rosa had an . . . inappropriate relationship with David." Her lips twist.

That's not the biggest shock of the week, but it turns my stomach anyway. Will I never stop finding out gross things about my biological father?

"And you should also know that Jose and Steve both killed someone—"

Killed someone? I mentally shake myself—somehow

we've descended into the exact type of thing I didn't want Sawyer to share—prejudicial history about each one of her rivals without any context. "Dolores."

Her eyes widen.

"As it happens, my cousin told me exactly the type of relationship he had with my father, and his reservations about David Solomon's behavior, Before and recently. I'm more interested in whether you know of any particular plans anyone had to harm me."

She bobs her head a few too many times. "Of course you are. I'm sorry to have come and said—"

I place my hand on top of hers—in part to calm her down, but also to see how much of this is feigned. Her hands are trembling. I wonder what it cost her to come here and tell me these secrets, even if I don't particularly want to hear them, and if I don't trust the source. I snatch my hand back. "Look, each of us has a past, and when viewed without context, it can be pretty prejudicial." My dad *stole* me from my father—if I didn't know the reasons why . . . I'd hate him. But I don't. "What I'm really interested in hearing—"

"I was in love," Dolores says. "Deeply in love, when I was your age." She freezes, and then her hand slowly rises to trace the edge of her pearl necklace.

I blink. This is a significant change of pace.

"I tell you this only because it appears that you are also . . . devoted."

I nod.

"I thought there was no better man than the one I loved and admired. He told me he loved me too. We spent all our time together, and I trusted him, implicitly."

"I think—"

"He married my sister, Ruby." She's not making this up. The raw pain on her face can't be faked. "Their engagement." She looks up at the ceiling and then wipes a tear away. "I walked inside one day, and the perfect, kind, honorable man I loved . . . was kissing her, not me. And then he confessed that it had been slow in coming, and it began with admiration, but . . . " She shakes her head. "Sometimes the truth is right under our noses and we miss it."

"I'm sorry," I say.

"I refused to go to their wedding. I refused to talk to my sister at all," Dolores says. "And when Tercera spread, I called and warned my entire family—but not her. She caught it . . . and died."

This is *so* not how I expected this conversation to go. Not who I thought this woman was. "People are complicated," I say. "But you can't blame yourself—"

"Oh, I do," she says. "Every single day. But my point in this is that sometimes the people you trust the most aren't who you think they are." She glances at the door. "Don't close your eyes to the things that are right in front of you. Especially not right now."

I'm not sure what else to say. I'm sorry about what happened to her, but I'm not worried about Sam. Plus, I don't have a sister. Ha.

She stands up abruptly. "I'm sorry if this visit seemed . . . alarmist. I was trying to help."

I actually believe her. My two least favorite Port Heads have possibly become my favorite, in a bizarre twist. "If you hear of anything," I say. "Any plans or plots, maybe you can come tell me about them *before* you travel to Galveston to meet in secret next time."

The color drains from her face and she nods. Then she scurries out.

"What do you make of that?" Sam asks.

I shrug.

"I'm moving Sawyer and Dolores down on the list of suspects, and Rosa up." He glances at Adam. "I know you're not desperate to take over for Ruby, but another child of Solomon might be—we should find out whether Rosa has children. And I'm not saying that Sawyer and Dolores couldn't have come to her to throw off suspicion, but we've been watching them all, and I haven't seen any of them meeting or communicating amongst themselves. It would be odd that both of them would have coordinated something like this—that they both approach you and confess even though they sent the messages."

I hate all this—distrust, trailing people, lies. It makes me sick. "I agree. I think it's likely that they actually feel guilty." But now I really can't get out of here and start looking for a little yellow house soon enough.

When the day of the celebration dawns, I don't even argue with Josephine when she brings my outfit, a pair of slacks and a cute floral print blouse. "At least it's not a ball gown."

"Don't be silly. You can't ride the carousel in a ball gown."

The carousel? Is she serious? "What about the Ferris wheel? Will it be operational?"

Josephine frowns. "I'm not sure whether—"

"It's fine. You don't have to tell me no. I'm sure Sam and Adam would never approve it." Too easy for me to get shot, I'm sure. Josephine leaves so I can get ready, and I take a moment to breathe in and out. I'm almost never alone. Lately, it's been never.

But I can't sit around enjoying the solitude forever. I fumble my way into the fancy dress slacks and navy and red rose shirt—the flattering cut almost making it look like I've got curves. I'm barely dressed when someone raps on my door. "Yeah?"

Sam cracks the door open. His eyes are more green than golden, and his smile is wide. "You ready for your party, *Your Majesty*?"

I hate when people call me that. Hate, hate, hate. Except for Sam. A shiver runs down my spine at the words. "I am."

Instead of gesturing for me to leave, he steps through and closes the door behind him. "Me too." He's wearing dark jeans and a navy polo shirt, his hair pulled back to showcase his ridiculously beautiful jawline.

"Aren't you worried we'll be late?" I glance at the clock. The party starts in less than fifteen minutes.

He shrugs. "It's not a test or a sermon. It's a party. They can survive without you for a few moments." He crosses the space between us in a heartbeat and opens his arms to me.

I couldn't stay away if I tried. My arms circle his waist, and his head comes down to mine. I've kissed Sam so many times now that I long ago lost track, but my heart still races as his lips meet mine. My hands still tighten on the muscles of his lower back. The butterflies in my stomach still swoop and dive riotously.

He murmurs my name, and I forget to breathe.

Sam's hands, his strong, fierce, competent, positively deadly hands, cup my jaw, his thumb stroking my cheek gently, and I melt against him.

"They might not even notice if we don't go," I whisper.

"I'll be so relieved when all this is over and we aren't stealing snatches of time—five minutes here and ten there." His breath warms my face when he sighs resignedly. "But you do have to go. You haven't announced your intention of voting on a Port Head for Galveston—and that's step one to convincing them that you can step down and let Adam take over for you."

I close my eyes and lean my head against his chest, listening to his steady heartbeat. His arms wrap around me and squeeze me against him. "Fine."

"We'd better go."

"Promise me you'll ride the carousel with me." I look up at him.

His eyes widen. "Excuse me?"

"Josephine says there will be a carousel, and I've never been on one. I want to ride a horse next to you."

He chuckles. "If you insist, but it had better not be pink."

"I think you look good in pink." I look up at him. "If anyone can pull it off, it's you."

He rolls his eyes. "Let's go."

From the moment we leave my room, I'm under careful watch. Guards aplenty, an armored car, radios from advance teams. It's absurd. "You'd think I was a fascist leader or something." I shake my head. "The people like me—surely this is overkill."

Adam doesn't respond, looking straight ahead at the route down Seawall.

Sam takes my hand in his, but he doesn't say anything either.

"They're just taking care of you," Josephine says from the back row of the SUV. "You should be pleased they care."

"To recap the plan," Adam says through his radio, "we're stopping just in front of the entrance. Ruby will address the people briefly, and then we'll open the pier. Priority is given to any citizens with children between the ages of two and sixteen."

He keeps going, outlining the details, but I already know them. Citizens will be celebrating up and down the beach on either side, and my words will be broadcast to them all at once. Food stands are set up on either side of the pier, and of course up and down the pier itself.

And then we're there and it's time. The large two-story building at the front of the pier looks freshly painted, though I don't recall discussing that, and there's a beautiful facade on the scaffold Josephine approved to be erected in front of it. The car stops, and I climb out slowly, blinking at the sunshine that wasn't nearly this bright through tinted glass.

Thousands upon thousands of people are gathered in every direction. They wave, they cheer, and they beam at me. They must not realize how truly average I am in every way. At least I won't have to worry they'll figure it out for much longer. Today will be another huge step toward a successful transition—and our freedom.

I walk across the wooden planks of the pier and climb the steps slowly, Adam in front of me, Sam behind. And finally, I reach the top. The microphone is already live—I can tell from the tiny hum and the almost silent whine that emanates. I worried I'd be more nervous today, but with so many people so far away, I can't make out many individual faces, so it's easier somehow.

I step toward the microphone. "Good afternoon," I say. "And welcome to Galveston's celebration of life and health!"

I wait for a moment until the cheering quiets.

"I'm delighted to be here for this purpose and excited for what the future holds for all of us." More cheering, of course. I've come to expect it at this point. "I've also been very personally touched at the generosity you've all shown. In response to my pleas on Sunday, you have far exceeded any hope I had for donations. So many of you are willing to open your homes and your storages to make room for the Marked. It's been miraculous to witness."

More applause.

"Today I have a bit of very exciting news. I've decided that the people of WPN are clearly guided by God, and that you're readily able to follow a good and noble path. In light of that, I think you should have a much more active role in government."

Murmurs. They don't understand what that means. No problem, I'll explain.

"In the past, David Solomon appointed men and women to run the day-to-day affairs of each major port city and the surrounding areas. I agree that they need governance, of course they do, but I don't believe I should be appointing those rulers for you. I want you to choose your rulers yourselves. I'm going to travel from port to port, make these announcements, ask them for their help, and then stay long enough to witness an election of the first freely chosen representative of the people."

Intermittent cheers. For a fresh new idea, that's enough, I think.

"And that holds true for Galveston, too. There's no reason you shouldn't be governed by someone you choose. So once I'm done traveling to each of the seven ports, I'll return here and you'll elect your first representative."

"We want you, Ruby!" a woman in front of me shouts.

"Ruby!" A man next to her yells.

Within seconds, the entire group is chanting my name. Good grief. Wrap it up, Ruby. This is not going well. Regroup later. "I'm delighted to hear your enthusiasm and support for my plan." Yes. Pretend that's what this is. "I'll be sure to print up more details and have them distributed before too long. But for today, let's celebrate the future together!"

Adam's lips are twisted with suppressed mirth.

Sam's mouth is a flat line.

He should be delighted—no one shot at me, not even once.

But a few moments later, after greeting dozens and dozens of people, we reach the carousel. "There aren't any horses," I say.

"It's more a spinning swing," Josephine says. "But I couldn't bring myself to tell you that earlier."

"At least I won't be on a pink pony," Sam says.

"But you can't sit next to me, or hold my hand." I frown.

"Just get on," Sam says, gesturing.

I grumble, but I do it, stuffing my legs under the bars and sitting in the metal seat. Sam does the same behind me. I twist around so I can watch him struggling to fit his legs into the tiny metal bucket seat.

A few moments later, the ride is full, and everyone steps back. Then with a grinding, halting whir, it starts. The swings turn round and round the base, and as they do, they lift up in the air, our feet dangling farther and farther from the ground as the swings shove outward. The speed increases more and more until I can't take a bit extra, and then finally, after a moment of whizzing round and round, it slows and our feet slowly float back down to the ground.

"That might have been more fun than a plastic horse," I admit.

Sam's eyes are squinted. "Don't make me do that again."

I laugh. "I won't. Not today, anyway."

But I insist we try all the rides other than the Ferris wheel and the freefall, which Sam and Adam both agree are too hard to secure. Then, in possibly the riskiest move of all, I try a hot dog from one of the street carts. "What kind of meat did you say this is?" I ask.

Sam shakes his head. "Better not to ask."

It's surprisingly delicious—I try not to think about how it was made. And I chat with hundreds and hundreds of smiling people. We discuss the Marked. We discuss the future. We discuss the Bible. And they all thank me—even though I haven't really done a thing for the people of World Peace Now—not really.

Finally, though, the sun sets. The chill in the air deepens, and even with the lights on all the rides lighting up the sky, it's time for us to head back home. "Keep celebrating,"

I say to the citizens who protest my departure. "It's just that we have to be up early. I'm leaving for New Orleans tomorrow." Our spirits are high when we reach the large white colonial mansion.

Until we open the car door.

The smell hits me like a kick to the knee. Sharp, pungent, and stomach twisting. "What is that?"

"Fish," Adam says. "Rotting fish."

I jog toward the front door, eager to see what in the world is wrong. My guards scramble to get out in front of me, and Sam sprints around me, halting my progress.

"Let us check it first." He's terse, but I don't blame him. Something is clearly wrong.

A large basket of fish is on the front porch—and someone scrawled something on the floorboards in front of it. *You aren't queen. Leave or else.*

Nothing like a basket full of rotting fish guts to drive their point home. Clearly not everyone loves me and my sweeping changes.

I kick the basket out of the way, moist goo spilling over my boots. Blech. "Looks like we've still got some work to do," I say.

Then I walk past it—putting it behind me figuratively and literally. Because it'll take a lot more than stinky fish and anonymous messages to change my course. Clearly these people don't know anything about me.

But they will soon enough.

❧ 6 ❧

SAM

"God won't actually protect you," I say. "You know that, right?"

Ruby scowls. "You're being ridiculous. I'm not made of tissue paper."

Says the woman who weighs 90 pounds—when her hair is wet.

"First you said no to the boat travel."

I grunt. "It would have taken a full day. In case you forgot, we're due back in Nashville in a few days to help Wesley's dad."

Her face falls. "That was a low blow."

I shouldn't have said Wesley's name—she's right. "Boat travel takes two full days, not five hours."

She shrugs. "Days with you. Days off, kind of."

I hadn't thought of it like that. "Adam says they only traveled via boat so often because they couldn't risk driving through Baton Rouge, whereas we have friends there. It made sense for us to stop and drop off supplies."

"Like you said, Baton Rouge is full of friends. So what's the big deal?" She stares out the window.

"You can't just hop out of the car—it's reckless enough

in Baton Rouge, but with someone trying to kill you, you really can't do it in New Orleans."

"I wanted to tell Rafe about the aid from WPN myself," Ruby says. "So sue me."

The pavement beneath us zooms past at fifty miles per hour, which is probably a little too fast with the state of roads these days, even on a highway, but my reflexes aren't strained. I place my hand on her knee and squeeze. "I'm sorry. I'm not trying to upset you, but it's my job to keep you alive. Please help me do that by waiting for me to give you the all clear. Okay?"

"I guess the dead messengers and the baskets of rotting fish don't exactly fill you with peace and calm."

"Nor does the fact that New Orleans' Port Head is Solomon's first cousin."

"I thought he was off the short list," she says.

"He's off the top of the list," I say. "But the list of Port Heads is already short."

"Rosa is extremely obnoxious," Ruby says. "Is it wrong that I'd almost prefer it's her, and not my one blood relation?"

"You have Adam," I say. "And the other kids Josephine discovered."

She sighs. "But they know as little about our past as me."

It's hardly surprising that she enjoyed hearing about her grandfather. It's hard to live with the knowledge that your parent is a complete waste of space. I'm the expert on that.

"I'll wait when we arrive." She shifts toward me and places her hand over mine. "I shouldn't have ignored you, but I'm sick of people acting like I'm special."

"You're in serious denial," I say. "You've always been someone special to me, but no matter what anyone says, you matter to those people in Galveston. You're more venerated than even the royal David Solomon was. You healed their world and then told them the truth about it. You didn't decide that the Bible was stupid—even if your dad taught you that. You look at everything with an open mind and hope for the best. And best of all, you inspire the best in people for whom it doesn't even come naturally."

"Well, that's a little generous," she says. "But I hope even part of that is true, because I'm not looking forward to doing the whole song and dance all over again in New Orleans."

"I'd far prefer to do it on the second day," I say, "so that I have at least twenty-four hours to secure the venue."

"You sent your team ahead," she says. "Trust them."

I swallow. "They never do as good of a job as I would, and I don't know the guards that well yet. For all we know, one of them killed the messengers on a Port Head's orders." I shake my head. "No, I would far prefer that you not address the citizens of New Orleans until tomorrow night."

"They need a day to nominate other representatives who can take Sawyer's place," she says. "And then a day to get out information on the vote. And then a full day to vote."

"I know why you planned it the way you did, but I don't have to like it."

"They may not react the same way as the people of Galveston. They don't know me at all."

I squeeze her leg again. "I know you—and trust me. They'll love you, too."

True to her word, Ruby listens to me respectfully and patiently when we arrive. The line all the way down the street of citizens waiting to enter the super dome surprises me. "Didn't Sawyer say this place holds eighty thousand?"

Ruby gulps.

"Why are there people waiting outside?"

I really hope it's because they haven't opened it up yet.

But the gargantuan auditorium is already full to bursting. Plus those long lines.

"Welcome, welcome." Sawyer is beaming as we drive up, his arms spread wide. "I can't tell you what a delight it is to have you here in New Orleans at last."

"Adam," Ruby whispers, "how many WPN citizens did you say there are?"

He shrugs. "We haven't done a real census in a while. We estimate between five hundred and eight hundred thousand for the entirety of WPN."

"Wait, we don't have a system in place that creates identification for each person?" Ruby asks.

"Identification?" Sawyer asks.

"Ruby was wondering how many citizens live here, in New Orleans specifically." Adam looks pointedly at the line of people extending down the street.

"If you include the surrounding areas, we boast close to a hundred thousand adult citizens. We aren't quite as sure about children. We do have birth certificates for each one that was born in a New Orleans hospital, but as you know, many of them have chosen home births in the last decade." Sawyer points at a set of doors that lead into the back of the super dome. "We are ready and waiting for Your Majesty. We can't wait to give you a big New Orleans welcome."

Something about him reminds me of David Solomon— even if he's not as obviously disgusting. "I'll go in first, scope things out, and then I'll come back for Ruby."

Sawyer frowns, but doesn't argue. "Of course." His smile snaps into place almost immediately, and he leads me through the doors, down a hallway, and up a sequence of stairways. "You'll find that we followed your instructions to a tee, and we also added quite a few security checks you didn't require for the citizens. My sweet cousin Ruby has quite a few novel ideas. I hope the citizens here embrace them as warmly as in Galveston." He winces. "But just in case they don't, we're ready."

For the first time, I actually like him. He truly seems to care about Ruby's well-being and success.

Fifteen minutes later, I've reconfigured some things and assigned new guards, but he really did follow my instructions, and he added some sensible precautions based on the location. I switch the position on the snipers I brought with me after seeing the stadium myself, and then we're finally ready. "I'm coming down," I tell Adam via the radio.

"Ah. You have little communication earbuds," Sawyer says. "Very good."

I walk through the doors and out into the open. "Ruby."

She turns toward me and smiles. Something in my chest eases at the sight. I shouldn't fret over leaving her briefly, not with Adam around, but I do. No one else, no matter how good, is quite the same as me. "Ready to go?"

I nod.

"Great."

Her hand's trembling when she takes mine in the hallway, but by the time we've climbed all the stairs, she's calmer. "It'll be like the celebration," I whisper.

"How so?" She shakes her head. "They don't know me at all. They might despise me."

"With so many people, you won't be able to see their faces, so it won't be nearly as scary."

Her face turns slowly upward. "You knew that's why I was less nervous?"

"I mean, *I* can still see their faces, but a normal person can't. So I figured that would help."

She laughs. "You're ridiculous."

"You're amazing, and inspirational, and they'll adore you. I know it." I press a kiss against her lips and then plunge us forward, into the blindingly bright lights of the stage.

In spite of my motivational speech, I'm not quite sure how they'll react to her. She's a usurper here, and a relatively ignorant and faithless one. But I shouldn't have worried. She gets better every time. Sawyer walks to the podium first and smiles and waves. "I have the rare privilege of introducing my beloved cousin to you. I loved her father, in spite of his limitations, and I find that every day I know Ruby, I am more impressed than the last. Please provide a big welcome to Ruby Solomon."

They cheer the second she approaches the podium. She beams too, as if she's delighted, not scared and frustrated to be doing yet another speaking engagement. She turns slowly from the right to the left so they can all see her clearly. A month ago, she'd have hated wearing the sheath dress Josephine chose for her. A month ago, she'd have been miserable in her skin with this many people staring.

Not anymore.

Today, she practically radiates authority and competence. I'm unbelievably proud.

"Thank you so much for your kind and enthusiastic welcome. I'm shocked, frankly, that so many of you turned out to hear me speak."

More cheering.

"I'm sure you'll have heard rumors by now from Galveston."

The crowd falls silent. Much more quiet than I'd have expected with a group this large.

"You'll have heard that I've basically denounced the actions of my biological father, David Solomon. He shot Donald Carillon, my mother's first husband—a man who raised me kindly and with great care. As a result of his actions, the virus you all know as Tercera was unleashed on the world. And instead of throwing all his efforts into locating the cure Donald Carillon had developed, David

Solomon used the excuse provided by the ravages of Tercera to create an empire for himself."

Not a single sound. If I dropped a pen on the floor, I wouldn't be the only one who could hear it—everyone would. It's that quiet.

"He succeeded in amassing all the power he ever wanted, and I want to be clear that I don't blame any of you. What you saw when you listened to him speak was a man professing to follow God. All the evidence you had supported that conclusion. If you are anything at all like the good people I have come to know and love in Galveston, you are people of faith, people of kindness, and people of trust. I appreciate all those qualities a great deal. Unlike my biological father, I will never abuse your trust. My promise to you is this—you deserve better than my father gave you, and I intend to rectify his unconscionable failures."

She lays out her plan for a representative of the WPN citizens to be selected in each major port city. "Sawyer Blevins served my father for many years. He was David Solomon's first cousin, as you all know."

I glance back at Sawyer, resplendent in a three-piece pinstripe suit. Dressed well, standing solemnly, he paints a picture of total regret for the sins of his cousin, and support for Ruby. I wonder whether it's real. Ruby insists he wants to step down—I'm not sure whether to credit that claim either.

"I have every faith that my cousin has served you to the utmost of his abilities, doing what he felt was right, but the fact remains that you never chose him. I'd very much like for all of you to have a voice—a vote—an opportunity to express who you'd like to lead you and what your vision for our future includes. This person should be someone you believe will do his or her utmost to educate, organize, and protect all of you."

She launches into her other goals—serving the needy,

specifically the now healed Marked population. "Like you, they have no culpability for what happened to them. They have suffered alone for too long."

The applause is deafening. Truly.

Ruby may have worried, but she has the people of New Orleans just as wrapped around her finger as the people of Galveston. Perhaps more.

"I'm sorry to express that my cousin Sawyer has informed me that he does not wish to continue to serve as the Port Head here. I certainly understand his desire to step down, and indeed, I can relate to his desire to live a quieter, calmer life. He'll be taking me on a tour of New Orleans tomorrow, but I want you all to do me a favor—reach deep and ponder tonight. If you could submit nominations of people who might do a good job serving as your representative tomorrow, with signatures ratifying those nominations, we'll put together a ballot for Sawyer Blevins' replacement. Sawyer and I will interview them tomorrow night and those we approve will speak to you the very next day, just as I have here. Directly following those speeches, every adult seventeen years of age and older will be allowed one vote."

She beams at them. "I hope that our community will welcome these new changes and grow right along with them." She tells the same story she shared in Galveston—how Jesus asked the disciples to leave their nets full of fish and serve as fishers of men. They go just as wild as the people in Galveston did.

Sawyer gets up when she's done. "Thank you for warmly welcoming my cousin. I hope my news doesn't alarm any of you. I'm not planning on leaving New Orleans, but I feel that it's time for someone new to lead us toward the sweeping changes that are coming. I'm excited for our future and I have a lot of faith in our community, our new queen, and the God who brought her to us."

Sawyer certainly seems to be well loved, at least here. And he's not waffling on his promise to Ruby that he's not interested in ruling any longer. That reaffirms my hope that he's not the one behind the missing messengers and the fish —which means Ruby's safe. Even so, when he provides us with a nice dinner, in between the first and second speech, I insist on tasting the food for Ruby before she eats. Better safe than sorry is a cliché for a reason. The second round crowd is a much smaller group—maybe only ten or fifteen thousand people who couldn't fit in the first time, but they're already primed. When she reaches the point where she mentions that they'll be taking nominations, someone shouts, "Queen Ruby! You can represent us!"

Hundreds of others cheer at the same time. "Ruby! Queen Ruby!"

She turns toward me and widens her eyes. It's no use, though—when the people love you, they're going to request that you stay, every time. She inhales deeply and smiles at them. "Unfortunately, I won't be able to rule all of WPN *and* New Orleans as well. But I promise this won't be my only visit. You won't be strangers to me."

Thunderous applause.

I'm beginning to worry that this transition is going to take a while. I don't see Ruby fobbing things off on Adam any time soon. Ugh.

"Will you be staying with me at the Capitol Building?" Sawyer asks.

I grunt.

"We decided it might be easier for Ruby to rest in the smaller house you said David Solomon usually used," Adam says.

Sawyer's eyes widen. "He only stayed there when Queen Josephine wasn't with him." He clears his throat. "If you gather my meaning."

Judging by the way Ruby's face falls, she does understand him. For the first time since we arrived, my hands ball up into fists and I have to suppress the urge to punch him. What was the point in telling her that?

She frowns. "Then perhaps the Capitol—"

Oh, no. Now I really want to pound him into the ground. I take Ruby's hand quickly. "We've already sent scouts to secure the smaller house. I'm sure it'll be just fine." We are not going to move to the Capitol Building and compromise Ruby's safety because he's made her feel gross about her stupid bio dad's love shack.

"Plus you hate being stared at and admired," Adam says. "Small will be much more comfortable and easy to manage than large."

Adam walks toward the waiting cars, and Ruby and I follow him. If she looks back over her shoulder and waves bye to her cousin, well, I ignore that. He may be better than we thought, but I'm not rolling out a red carpet for the guy.

"I'll be prepared to receive you in the morning for the tour of New Orleans," Sawyer says.

"I can't wait." Ruby actually seems to mean it. I hope, for her sake, her cousin is the relatively decent guy he seems to be.

The drive to the small house we prepared isn't long— and the house looks just as it did in the photos Sawyer sent over. Small, no more than three or four bedrooms, clean, white-washed, with pansies in window boxes out front, and best of all, it's located on the outskirts of the main part of New Orleans. No other houses nearby appear to be occupied, which makes our job both easier and harder. After I run through the details of last-minute checks with Adam, we head inside.

Josephine saw to the more mundane details, like sending a cook and cleaning crew ahead to ensure the place was in order. When we walk through the door, the rich smell of garlic bread and spaghetti sauce fills the entryway.

"I'm starving," Ruby says.

I don't smile—she wouldn't appreciate the humor in the difference between her version of starving, which consists of a small plate of pasta, and mine, which would be a full pot—but my heart smiles inside. "Me, too." Now I do smile—I can't help it—at the thought of her eyes when she sees me pile up my plate. She sees me eat daily, and she looks shocked every time.

We practically jog into the kitchen, Adam at our heels.

"The men and I are taking our food to go," he says.

Ruby's head whips around. "What? Why?"

He swallows and glances my direction. "You've been pretty busy lately, and well, we noticed you haven't really had any time alone."

I've liked Adam ever since I found out he was Ruby's brother. Unlike Wesley, I never suspected he wanted to usurp Ruby's power. But now? Now he's a competitive candidate for my second favorite person in the world.

"Oh, that's thoughtful," Ruby says. "As long as you don't feel put out by that—"

Adam shakes his head. "We needed to have some people in the neighboring houses either way, since they're vacant. They pose too great a threat for anyone who means you harm. It was that or burn them down."

Ruby blinks. "Uh, okay."

And then they all file out, including the housekeeper and cook. Ruby grabs a plate and begins to shovel pasta on to it. As I suspected, it's a moderate amount. I wait until she's done and dump the rest of the contents of the pot onto my plate.

"Parmesan?" she asks, a long cheese grater and a hunk of cheese in her hand.

"Can you even believe they have that?" I shake my head.

"It's bizarre, living like this. Fresh dairy products that we didn't make ourselves. A cook. A housekeeper." I sit down at the wooden farm table. "I hate it."

At the same time, she says, "I love it."

Our eyes meet.

"You do?" she asks. "You hate parmesan?"

"You were only talking about liking cheese?" My eyebrows rise.

"Not exactly." She gulps and sets the cheese down on the table. "I mean, I hate ruling. I hate talking to people and announcing things. I hate being in charge. But I like that there's actual commerce, and that they have the capability to make work easier and more efficient. It's almost like Before with World Peace Now, and without the threat of Tercera looming, things will only improve."

"You remember the good things from Before." I pick up the cheese and grate it for myself. Then I hold it over her plate.

She nods, and I grate some for her, too. "What do you mean, the good things?"

"You remember movies and parks and a variety of delicious food."

"That implies those were less important than the bad things." She presses her lips together. "Which are?"

"Politics and warfare and greed. The more people have, the more they want."

"I'm not sure that's always true," she says. "But I know it's a problem."

"It's *the* problem. Power corrupts, but absolute power corrupts absolutely."

"Who said that?" Ruby picks up her fork, but she doesn't take a bite.

I eat one, hoping to encourage her. "I don't exactly remember. Some baron or other. Maybe Baron Acton? I think that was it. He also said that great men are almost always bad men."

"That's a depressing thought," Ruby says.

"Are you going to eat?" I twist my second bite on my fork.

Ruby nods. Then she bows her head and closes her eyes. Is she *praying*? She opens her eyes and takes a bite.

"What was that?"

She shrugs. "Look, maybe there's a God and maybe there's not, but I've never been the kind of person who thinks it's right to only talk to someone when I want to ask for something. I figure on the off chance he's really up there, I should make an effort to, I don't know, say thanks, and, like, check in sometimes."

Unbearably adorable, always, and definitely not a bad person. Such a good person.

"I hate how long this is taking," she says. "And I know we need to get back in two days so we can head north to Nashville. I know you wanted to be done with everything by then."

I swallow my half-chewed spaghetti. "It wasn't a very realistic timeline," I admit. "Not for transitioning the government of an entire group of people."

She sighs. "So you're not mad?"

When I straighten in the wooden chair, it creaks in protest. "Of course I'm not mad. You're . . . I don't know how to describe it."

"What?" She drops her fork. "You don't know how to describe me?" She wipes her mouth. "Am I messy? Do I look ridiculous?"

"I mean, when you're talking to your people—when you're explaining your plans—the word I'm searching for is *magnificen*t. You're breathtaking up there."

She laughs. "Don't be goofy. It's not as awful as I thought it would be, but I'll be relieved when it's all over."

Will she? "You're a natural at public speaking," I say. "And the people adore you. Josephine and Adam were right about that. I'm not sure they'll accept any kind of resignation you try to give."

"Just like with Sawyer, they won't have a choice." She takes another bite and sets her fork down. Her small hand reaches across the table and rests on top of mine. "I promise, Sam. We're transitioning this, and then we're leaving."

I hope they let her.

The next day, Sawyer insists on showing us oil rigs, both onshore and off. Then we taste beignets and gumbo, both better than I expected, and we visit fields of strawberries, corn, and even orchards full of blooms that he assures us will become peaches before too much longer. We finish the day with a tour of the perfectly maintained Capitol Building.

When we finish, there are boxes and baskets and bins of donations lining the steps of the building, much like those in Galveston.

Sawyer blinks. "What are—"

"Oh, we're used to this," Adam says. "These are donations from your local population—for the Marked kids, I imagine. The people listen to Ruby's concerns and immediately step in to help."

Many of the crates hold things we saw today—berries, fruits, pecans, even fish. Luckily these aren't spoiled. Adam steps to the side to task some people with the transportation and organization of the newly donated supplies.

"I really had no idea so many things grew in Louisiana," Ruby says. "It's remarkable."

"You haven't even been down to see the fishing operation yet," Sawyer says, "or our burgeoning textile manufacturing production. We've begun to branch out, and we now make more than just cotton print fabric. We have a whole line of synthetics."

Ruby's right—it really is almost like Before within the WPN settlements.

"Unfortunately, we don't have any more time on this trip," Ruby says, "but I look forward to seeing more the next time I'm able to come out."

"Ah, yes," Sawyer says, "it's time for you to review the nominations for my replacement and meet with them."

"Again, I do appreciate your help today," Ruby says. "But I'd better see to those nominees."

Adam clears his throat to make it plain that he's back and ready, and Sawyer and his men disappear back into the Capitol Building. "Where are the nominees?" Ruby asks. "I can't wait to meet with them."

"You're not going to like this," Adam says, "but . . . there aren't any."

7

RUBY

"There aren't any?" My voice is far too shrill. I clamp my lips together and think. Could this be Sawyer's doing? Could he be pretending not to want to remain as Port Head, while secretly preventing anyone else from becoming his competition? But my people were outside on the steps of the Capitol Building all day, collecting nominations.

Is it possible no one here *wants* to manage things? Or maybe it's just that no one else feels qualified. That possibility didn't even occur to me until now. People always want the chance to do better than someone else, but in a world where this wasn't an option until yesterday . . .

"Not a single person brought a nomination?" I glance around furtively. "Maybe they need a bit more time. The sun hasn't set."

"There are a few people who had eighty or ninety signatures, but no one showed up with a hundred." The line of Adam's mouth is tight—resigned.

"Well, Sawyer says he's done, and I'm not coming out here to run things," I say. "Where are the people with the signed nomination forms?"

It takes us a few moments to track them down, but once we do, Sam and Adam and I march up and down the streets of New Orleans, getting enough signatures to qualify two nominees: Hector Garcia and Isabelle Chanticleer. I breathe a sigh of relief once it's done. "Now we need to find these two and make sure they're not total loons. It wouldn't do to replace Sawyer with someone even worse."

"Now, now," Sam says. "We don't know Sawyer well."

My shoulders droop. "You're right. I'm sorry, it's just that—"

The corner of Sam's mouth twitches. "There may not be anyone worse."

I roll my eyes. "Stop."

I'm pleasantly surprised that Hector seems bright, motivated, and intelligent. He's also very interested in improving the plight of the average citizen of New Orleans and lays out a plan with a list of changes he intends to make if elected.

"You're saying that people aren't allowed to change careers?" I ask.

It sounds uncomfortably similar to the Unmarked rules —you select a path and you stay on it. I'm ashamed to say I never realized it was such a restriction on people's freedom until Hector points it out.

"Let's just say that it's strongly discouraged," Hector says. "The reasoning is that job changes lead to inefficiency."

"It's not only in New Orleans," Adam says. "That's World Peace Now policy everywhere. I have often wondered how someone can know whether they want to do something or whether they're good at it if they haven't tried it yet."

Hector shrugs. "It also keeps anyone from advancing in their career, unless the administration selects the individual for a promotion specifically."

"Which means they're indebted to the Port Head for the position, further securing his or her power," Sam says.

Isabelle is, if possible, even more impressive. "I spent all day today making a list of improvements we could institute, and a proposed timeframe for their implementation. I also chose the priority level of each item, in my mind, based on the number of citizens impacted, and the harm that results from any delay."

I review the lists she hands me, which includes a number of initiatives to further the freedom and rights of women, and my hope for the future grows. Surely the people of New Orleans will see that either one of these nominees will do an excellent job representing their interests—and that choosing someone who is passionate about improving their lives is a large improvement over an appointment of someone the monarch likes. I really hope this is a big coup—for democratic ideals.

The rest of the night flies past. "I'm so glad we brought as many people from Galveston as we did," I say.

"I'm glad we did too," Adam says, "but with most of our security team handling election-related protocols, there aren't many people available to ensure your safety."

"I don't like that at all," Sam says. "Unfortunately, even with Sawyer bowing out, I feel like the ballots need to be collected and counted by people who don't have a vested interest in the outcome. That means you, me, and the six guards we didn't assign will have to handle security."

"At least the citizens appear to love Ruby as much here as they do in Galveston," Adam says. "Which means—"

"It's only sideways attacks by jealous Port Heads we'll have to keep an eye out for." Sam still seems to wish I'd let him just *eliminate* the threat. At least he hasn't made that request outright.

The next morning, when we're preparing to introduce the two candidates for New Orleans' first election, Sam is just as abrupt and rude to the new candidates as he ever was to Sawyer. My cousin is accustomed to it, but Hector and Isabelle appear quite alarmed at his tone.

"You will not approach Ruby, or turn toward her rapidly. You will not threaten her in any way."

Isabelle and Hector nod a little too much.

"My staff will check you for weapons now, and again right before the speeches."

"Sam," I say. "Surely—"

"We talked about this," he says.

He's right. We did.

"She's not Fidel Castro," Sawyer Blevins says. "We all love her, and none of us mean her any harm, I assure you."

Sam scowls mightily. "Nevertheless, you will all follow the rules I've outlined."

"Of course," Sawyer says. "Whatever you say."

And then it's time to talk to the people of New Orleans again. This time, everyone who travels out fits in the stadium—barely. Which means we're looking at only eighty thousand or so citizens who have turned out to see the speeches and vote. It's still a fabulous showing, given that Sawyer estimates they have just over a hundred and ten thousand adult citizens in the surrounding area.

They're just as enthusiastic when I welcome them as they were the first day. They don't seem quite as excited about Hector, Isabelle, or even Sawyer as they did two days ago. In fact, a lot of citizens call out things as the new candidates present their plans. "We want Ruby!" and "Queen Ruby!" and even "Move to New Orleans!" are not only shouted, but picked up as chants over and over.

I ignore it—best not to encourage them, I think. Once Isabelle and Hector have both finished, to very limited applause, I stand back up. "Well. I think you're a lucky group of people with two wonderful options to represent you for the next two years."

They cheer, but it feels half-hearted for some reason. Adam comes up to the front then, to help me outline the details of how the vote will work, and how ballots will be structured.

"What about write-ins?" someone yells loudly. "Can we write in another representative?"

I freeze. They only had a day to nominate. What if there's someone else, someone they'd prefer, who didn't get their nomination in? "Well, I suppose if you manage to find someone you can write in that all of you can agree upon, that's alright as well. But they'd still have to win a majority of votes."

Cheering. And more chants of 'Queen Ruby.' Ugh.

Alright. Well, I'm just excited that they're excited.

"For the next term, we'll be better organized. We'll have a longer nomination period and more time to get the news out—time to campaign even. But for now, we're choosing a sort of interim representative, and I appreciate your patience and understanding. I'm sure whoever you choose will do their very best to represent the interests of all the New Orleans citizens—and of course, Sawyer will be around to help transition them to the role. Right?"

The people start to chant my cousin's name. I glance back at him, wondering if he has any suggestions. He shrugs and points at the podium.

I nod. If he'd like to talk to them, it's fine with me.

He walks slowly to the microphone. When he smiles, the crowd goes wild. I suppose they're used to hearing from him weekly. It makes sense they love him. "Citizens of New Orleans, we are staring out at a bright new world."

Cheering.

"We have a fearless, brilliant, and inspired leader."

More applause—almost frenzied.

"And as is appropriate, we're now selecting someone to represent each of you and your needs, your interests, your goals. You should think long and hard about which of those candidates will be able to manage the minutiae of the day to day, as well as balance each of your needs as the world shifts and changes around us."

This time they're more thoughtful. It's what I've been hoping would happen. They really do listen to my cousin.

"I loved the passion Hector expressed. He's clearly going to be a powerful ally for each of you tradesmen in negotiating wonderful deals with other ports. He also has plans to allow you all more freedom in picking where and how you want to work and excel. All of those are great things. Wonderful ideas." He turns his head to the right, glancing at Isabelle. "And who wouldn't support more opportunity for our wives, our daughters, our sisters, our friends. I'm embarrassed that these reforms are necessary, and I apologize for the ways I've failed each of you. Isabelle is also, from what I can tell, quite organized. I'm sure with her at the helm, the flagship New Orleans will charge dead ahead—on time, and on track."

He steeples his hands on the top of the podium. "I'm grateful to my young cousin for giving me this chance to thank all of you. It has been the singular pleasure of my life to guide you, to teach you, and to work alongside you for the past decade. It has been a very trying time, a terrifying time in so many ways, but I've always been able to rely on the goodness of my citizens—and watching you pull together and support one another, well. It came as no surprise to me to see the generous donations you poured out at the Capitol Building. Of course you're ready to transition, as Queen Ruby asked, into fishing for mankind—you've always been the most kind, the most generous, and the most charitable of people. Thank you for your patience with my shortcomings, and I wish you all the very best in the years that lie ahead of us."

The crowd goes wild, shouting "Sawyer" and "Ruby." As far as send-offs go, it wasn't a bad one at all.

And then we wait while the people vote.

With so many individuals gathered, it's relatively easy to set up two dozen voting booths in the surrounding area, but it still takes a very long time to work our way through all the citizens seventeen years of age and older. And then we have to start counting the ballots cast, which is a whole other ordeal. Sawyer has taken the initiative to provide simple sandwiches and water for the gathered crowd while they wait for the results, which was brilliant. Maybe he really does care about the people.

"Your Majesty?" Frank's voice still bothers me, but I've gotten more used to it. Even if he won't stop referring to me as 'Majesty.'

"Yes?" When I look up from the small wooden chair in the tiny side room of the super dome to meet his eyes, I realize that he's not the only guard tasked with counting ballots who has shown up to talk to me. There's a whole flock of them.

"You told us to let you know if we noticed an anomaly?" He clears his throat and blinks. Then he blinks again.

"What's wrong?" I look from Frank to the other guards. "Has someone threatened you?" Sam's been worried about me, but what about my guards? If something goes wrong, they're the ones who are really at risk. "Or other voters?"

They all shake their heads.

"What's wrong then?" I lift my eyebrows.

"You did say that write-ins were allowed." Frank shuffles his boots across the ground.

"Who are they writing in?" Ugh. What if there are hundreds of write-ins? Tallying all that will take forever.

Frank looks at the other guards and then turns back to me. "You, Your Majesty. They've written in your name."

Oh, good grief. "How many of them have written in my name?"

"More than half off the ballots I've counted," Frank says.

Adam's laughing loudly behind me.

"Obviously I'm not going to be their representative." I sigh. I don't even want to stay in WPN territory. So far I'm doing a miserable job of governing anyone, and I'm definitely failing spectacularly at transitioning them to a republican form of government. They're voting for their sitting monarch as their representative? Ugh. "Alright, well, for now, tally those, but obviously I'm not an option. So we'll select the person with the most votes that *aren't* for me."

Frank's still frowning.

"What's wrong with that?" I want to get in a car and drive home. Not back to Galveston, but back to Port Gibson, to a time when the most complicated question anyone asked of me was what I planned to make for dinner.

"Well, if we exclude the ballots that write in your name, the person in the lead is another write-in candidate."

I stand up and begin pacing. The guards shift and jostle, trying to make room for me to do it in this tiny space. "Who?"

"Well." Frank grimaces. "I know you said he's not running, but other than yourself, Sawyer Blevins is winning by a wide margin."

I swear under my breath. I can't ask him to keep ruling —not after he's been clear about how much he wants to be done. Why do the people only want representatives who don't *want* to lead?

"You can't let them choose," Sam says, "and then not honor their decision."

"But I can't make my cousin do this when he wants to step down either." I lean back in my chair until my head rests on the top of the wooden chair back. I close my eyes. "I hate this."

"You can at least ask him whether he'd be willing," Sam says. "If he's been doing it this long, he could handle it for two more years, I'd think."

I want to scream. So we'll just have the same Port Head we've always had? The one appointed by my father? Someone who doesn't even *want* to do it anymore? How can I have made no progress, in spite of my best efforts?

"Why?" I shake my head. "Why wouldn't they vote for Hector or Isabelle?"

Adam's eyes are sad. "Hector's Hispanic, which is certainly a minority group here, and Isabelle is a woman."

"*I'm a woman*," I say. "And they're apparently scribbling my name down all over the place. Plus two other Port Heads are women."

My brother shrugs. "They've known Sawyer for a long time—he's a known quantity. And as to voting for you, they all see you as God's miracle. Your charity, your concern for others, those things just confirm it in their minds. For all their organization, neither Hector nor Isabelle spoke their language up there. They didn't mention God, or a plan, or a calling." Adam shrugs. "I can't even blame them for wanting you to relocate here. They're a larger port than Galveston, and they produce a lot more, and they know you didn't grow up in Galveston and don't have loving memories of your father. If I were here, I might beg for the same thing."

By the time the last votes are counted, nothing has shifted. Almost seventy-five percent of the people wrote in my name. Of the rest, less than five percent voted for either Isabelle or Hector.

Which means nearly fifteen percent of the people wrote in a vote for Sawyer. So, if you exclude my name, he won by a landslide.

"I need to talk to Sawyer," I say. "Can someone bring him in?"

"Sorry." Adam bobs his head. "I'll get him."

Sam laughs. "You gave them the chance to pick someone new, but this is a pretty bold step for them. Even selecting the man they're accustomed to is still progress. In two years, they'll get the chance to do better. Hopefully they'll have learned something between then and now and either Hector or Isabelle or someone new will take over."

I guess so.

Sawyer shows up a moment later. "Ruby?" He glances around the room. "Is everything alright?"

I nod.

"Do you need to leave? I can make the announcement if you'd like."

My shoulders droop. "That's the thing."

"They wrote in your name, didn't they?" Sawyer smiles and shakes his head. "You can't blame them. We are the biggest single settlement, and we are close to Galveston. We've outpaced Galveston for years in terms of production of, well, of everything. And they adore you."

I sit down at the desk and brace my hands against the wood. "They did write in my name."

"But surely you can simply choose the second person they voted for—Hector and Isabelle can't have received the exact same number of votes."

"Surely," I say. "In fact, Hector won by about three dozen votes."

"That settles it, then," Sawyer says. "I'm sure that—"

"But Sawyer," I say. "The people wrote in another name in large numbers."

He freezes, his brows pulling together. "They did?"

"Yours."

His mouth dangles open. "Mine?"

"You didn't expect that?" I ask.

He shakes his head. "I thought they'd be happy to be rid of me, honestly."

So did I, frankly. I don't think that's written on my face, or at least, I hope it's not. "Well, they wrote in your name more than three times as many times as they voted for Hector. So I can definitely go out there and announce Hector," I say. "But I did say that write-ins were allowed if the winner *wanted* the job." I look at him pointedly. Asking without asking.

He clears his throat, but doesn't say another word.

"I hate to ask this, because I know the job is tedious and exhausting and you've done it for a long time, but . . . "

"Will I serve for another two years?" He frowns.

I nod.

"I guess so," he says. "But maybe we can have Isabelle and Hector both work with me—in positions where people will get to know them. I do think both of them would be good candidates to take over."

A brilliant idea, honestly. "They could do Sunday sermons sometimes too, if they have any interest. It might help them connect and share their vision."

"And give me a break," Sawyer says. "It feels like double duty, trying to lead them spiritually *and* politically."

When we announce the results, together, the people cheer loud and long. Sawyer asks Isabelle and Hector up and discusses the ideas he has to bring them and their ideas into government roles, and the people seem to love that idea, too. By the time we finish and reach David Solomon's old house, I feel better about the progress we've made, even if it's not what I hoped to accomplish.

"Thank goodness that's all over. Tomorrow, once we're back in Galveston, we can go over final details of the trips I'll be taking to the other ports, and then drive straight to Nashville."

"I like that plan," Sam says.

"We do have a lot of final details to review," Adam says. "The upcoming visits, the trade agreements we still haven't finalized, and the ongoing plans for support with the Marked—including integration for those who would like to join us."

I force a smile, knowing it's probably pained. "Maybe you can figure some of that out."

My half brother grimaces. "How did I know you were going to say that? But Sam and I have been talking about my coming with you. As captain of your guard, I really ought to go on the trip to Nashville, for instance."

"So that's a no to handling some of the administrative stuff?" I sigh melodramatically. "Did I mention that I'm so ready to take a break from this?"

"It's cute that you think a trip to Nashville to manipulate council members will be a break." Sam's so beautiful that even when he's mocking me, I want to kiss him.

I laugh. "But it's not *me* on the hook this time. We're going there for *you*," I tell Sam. "They want to hear from John Roth's son, the famed athlete and soldier."

"Fairchild implied he wanted me there," he says, "but I very much doubt I'm the draw. I imagine the support of the queen of their biggest rival government will carry a lot more weight than the opinion of their disgraced former leader's son."

I really don't think anyone with the Unmarked cares who I am or what I do, which after the past few days will be a huge relief. The last time I went, they didn't give me the time of day—until a small army showed up to force them to release Aunt Anne. But even if Sam's right, at least I won't be in charge of a single thing—I'll just be sharing my two cents on who would make a good replacement. "I'll be sure to pack a ball gown this time." I smirk. "Because for once, I get to be eye candy, right?"

Sam stands up. "We better get to bed. It's going to be another long day tomorrow."

"That's my cue to head out," Adam says.

I stand up too, slowly. "You're going to insist I sleep in another room again?" I lift my eyebrows.

My boyfriend's strong hands circle my waist and pull me close. His breath on my face soothes me, wiping out the misery of the election failure and my stress about the next few weeks. "I've never been the boss of you, not when we come right down to it. You ignore me, or cajole me, or badger me until I give in." His mouth comes down over mine slowly. Too slowly.

I go up on my tiptoes, pressing my mouth against his. His hands tighten on my waist. My heart lurches dangerously in my chest. I twine my hands around his neck and his lips turn upward in a smile.

I love *feeling* him smile against my mouth.

"No matter where we go, you're home for me," he whispers.

"Same."

"You and I both know that we're being smart—not getting carried away." His voice is a low murmur. "But no one else will know what we're doing in the same room together, and your people don't need any reasons not to listen to you. Not right now."

I groan. "I know that."

"So we'll keep being smart."

"It's hard," I complain.

He chuckles. "You have no idea how hard." He brushes another kiss across my mouth. "But I love you enough to do hard things—most any hard thing."

My heart skips a beat. But he's right that I can't really risk anyone assuming anything untoward, not right now. I need the WPN citizens to love me . . . at least until I can transition them into a form of government where the people have the power, and not one monarch.

I'm not sure how long I stand in the kitchen with Sam's arms wrapped around me, but it's not long enough.

It's never long enough.

Eventually, he insists on walking me to my room and closing the door. I brush my teeth and change into pajamas, and then I fall asleep to the sound of Sam talking to one of the guards in the family room. Even though he's not sleeping next to me, he's close, and that's enough. I know I'm safe.

The next morning, the drive back to Galveston is uneventful. I didn't expect this, but when Sam pulls up in front of the huge white columns of Josephine's mansion, I'm actually happy. It's not *home,* but it feels more like home than any place I've been recently.

Adam and Sam are directing the re-deployment of the two hundred and some guards we took with us to New Orleans when Josephine rushes down the front porch steps, her long jacket open and fluttering behind her. She's not smiling, which is odd. She's usually happy to see me.

"I'm so sorry." Her breath is labored, her cheeks flushed.

"Why?" I slam the car door, remembering that the last time I got back to Galveston, the Port Heads were here to ambush me. I know we left Sawyer with his hands full back in New Orleans, so it can't be the same problem as last time.

"I assumed they were from the Unmarked, or I'd never have welcomed them onto the island. But once they were here, I figured I should let them stay until you returned."

I scratch my left eyebrow and glance at Sam and Adam, who have both frozen and are turning slowly toward my mother.

"Who is here?" Sam's already terse demeanor is even tighter, sharper somehow. "Who did you *welcome* inside?"

Josephine's eyes widen and she gulps. "They say they're an envoy from another government." She bites her lip.

"What government?" Don't panic, Ruby. Don't panic. "Not the Marked, and not the Unmarked?" Who else is there?

My eyes meet Sam's. Surely if anyone else in North America had survived in significant numbers, we'd know about them, right?

"Where are 'they'?" Adam asks. "And exactly how many foreign individuals did you welcome to Galveston?"

Sam circles the car and takes up a defensive position next to me—as if there are snipers lining me up in their crosshairs this very second.

Josephine says, "Only a few—"

"Thank goodness," Adam says.

"—hundred." Josephine smiles. "Which isn't that many, when you consider they've left their entire people and come out to introduce themselves. I put them on the other end of the island, just in case they turn out to be worse than they seem."

Sam and Adam both swear, loudly.

A few hundred?

"Oh, calm down." Josephine steps toward me, rolling her eyes as she does so. "You two are so reactionary. The young man in charge is the son of their president, and he's delightful, especially when he smiles." She drops her voice. "He gets these two dimples." She shivers. Shivers! Like she *likes* him.

Sam's and Adam's eyes both go huge and round and their nostrils flare. It's as though Adam's slowly turning into Sam, the more time they spend together.

"He's *delightful?*" Sam asks softly.

"He really is," Josephine says. "He's funny, and charming, and he came with a lot of gifts. And, I know you and my daughter are . . . " Josephine clears her throat. "Dating, or whatever it is you're doing. But he came with a proposal, which I insist you at least listen to."

"What kind of proposal?" Adam's voice is tight.

I notice for the first time that Sam has unholstered not one but *two* handguns, and he's gripping them a little too tightly for my comfort. "Don't shoot anyone, Sam."

"I'm not promising anything," he practically growls.

"The boy's name is Kimball, and he's twenty-two years old, and he's the son of the president of CINOW, a conglomeration of the survivors that occupy the land formerly known as California, Idaho, Nevada, Oregon, and Washington."

"What exactly does he want to talk to me about?" I ask. "If it *is* me he'd like to meet."

"Oh, it's you," Josephine says. "We talked about you quite a bit after he arrived last night."

The muscle in Sam's jaw that I usually love is working overtime.

"What does he want?" I grind out.

"He'd like the cure to Tercera, of course," she says. "They've done a much better job of caring for their Marked children than we did, I'm happy to say. You'll love that." She beams. "And his father was hoping the two of you might hit it off and want to get married." She avoids Sam's face. "It would be a wonderful way to join the two governments peacefully, don't you think?"

8

SAM

Do not shoot Ruby's mother. Do not shoot Ruby's mother. Do not shoot Ruby's idiotic mother. Because.

It would be a waste of a bullet I might need when I meet this Kimball and he smiles with both of his dimples.

"Where did you say you put these soldiers?" I force a smile.

Judging by Ruby's expression, my smile isn't very reassuring. I drop it.

"They're on the far end of the island. The Palisade Palms, if you recall, was a building we kept in good repair so that we could access Ruby's father's lab should the need arise. But it hasn't been kept at full occupancy, and David was renovating the Galvestonian next door when he passed away." She gulps again, as if only just recalling she's the one who killed him.

"You put them there?" Adam frowns. "There's no security set up to patrol that area."

"There are the perimeter guards," Josephine says. "And trust me—the delegates from CINOW don't mean us any harm. I'm sure of it."

"Oh, you're sure?" I force myself to holster my guns. "Well, no need to worry about *hundreds* of completely unknown hostiles from another government if you're *sure*."

Ruby places a hand on my forearm. "It's alright." Her voice is soft, soothing even.

"Alright?" I want to kill them all to secure the island again. I want to take Ruby and run somewhere they can't see her. Or talk to her. Or harm her.

But am I this upset because of the threat another government poses? Or because the *charming* delegate, whose father is president of some big government, wants to *marry* Ruby sight unseen? When I think about that, I'd like to rip his dimpled head right off his body.

But I'm not a Neanderthal.

And Ruby loves me.

So like always, I shove that jealousy, that irrational idiocy, deep deep deep down inside and slam the door on it. I breathe in and out. And then in and out again. "Today is the eighth day from the day Fairchild asked us for help," I say.

Ruby nods. "I know."

Of course she does.

"We need to leave for Nashville today—tomorrow at the latest." Her shoulders droop. "Which means I guess I'll have to go meet him right now."

Adam explodes in a very satisfying way, as do a handful of his most outspoken guards.

Ruby frowns. "I'm sorry. Did I step into some kind of alternate world where my guards are actually in charge of me?" Her eyes flash. "Your job is to keep me safe. My job is to decide where I go and to whom I speak." She shakes like a dog coming out of a lake. "Now back off. If you can't be reasonable, Josephine and I will drive down to the Palms alone."

We've pushed her too far, which means there's no

chance she'll relent. That's on us. "It's fine," I say. "I'll come with you, and Adam will select two dozen guards—"

Ruby opens her mouth to argue.

"They have hundreds of soldiers," I say. "I won't agree to less than two dozen."

"We don't know that they're all soldiers," Ruby says.

But Josephine doesn't contradict me, which tells me they are.

Ruby must understand that too, because she rolls her eyes. "Fine," she says. "Two dozen."

We pile back into the SUV for a drive down Seawall Boulevard. I toss my head so Adam knows to take another car and coordinate the other hundred or so men that will be arranging themselves unseen up and down the way, from Islander East to Beachtown. I'm fairly confident I can keep Ruby safe, if they mean her harm, but it's always nice to have the upper hand when things go sideways.

The streets of WPN look exactly as they always do. People going out to grab things, people chatting, people turning to wave when they realize Ruby's in the vehicle. She hates it, but I love how much they appreciate her. It *almost* makes me not mind being here. Not quite, but almost. Then I think about how much of her time they take up and I'm glad we're getting away as soon as possible. To live our own lives instead of facilitating theirs.

How did Josephine get all these troops installed in the Palms without worrying the citizens of Galveston? "No one appears nervous. What did you tell the people about the soldiers?"

Josephine frowns. "Why would they be concerned? They arrived on foot, but I moved them from the bridge to the lodgings in standard issue large black SUVs, and I had them drive down the beach after sundown. No one thought anything of a sanctioned group of people driving down the road."

I suppose in a place with a constant influx from other ports, all of them in well-maintained vehicles, even dozens of cars, when driven past after dark, don't raise alarm bells. Sometimes the differences between WPN and the Unmarked still surprise me.

I'm prepared for a barricade. For snipers. For any kind of hostile interchange.

But as we approach the Palms, I scan the horizon, uniquely equipped to anticipate with my exceptional vision.

Of all the scenarios I prepared for, none of them included an even mix of men and women, all tan, all toned, all young, milling around the pool and walking down to the beach.

"*Those* are the soldiers?" I lift my eyebrows.

Josephine and Ruby squint.

"Where?" Ruby asks.

I wait for them to be close enough to see.

"They look like surfers." Ruby swivels around to look at her mother. "Did you say they were soldiers?"

Josephine sighs. "I told you they weren't threatening. They approached with a white flag, and trucks loaded with kiwifruit, medical supplies, and walnuts. I'm telling you, I wasn't being naive. It's a friendly group."

My shoulders relax, but I feel the beginnings of a headache forming at the base of my skull. What exactly are we in for? What kind of leader sends his son to flirt with the queen of a rival government? Adam's SUV pulls into the parking lot first, followed by mine. I stop next to his, and the other four take up places on either side of us. "I'm ready," Adam says into my earpiece.

"Me too." I turn toward Ruby and nod. "We can get out. But keep close to me until we're positive you're not in danger. Sometimes things that don't look threatening still are."

"Like a slow loris," she says.

"Huh?"

"It's a little monkey-looking critter," she says. "It lives in Asia and India. They're adorable, but they have venom sacks in their armpit, and if they lick it, their bite can kill you."

I swear, I never know what her enormous brain is going to come up with next. "Yes." I imagine a monkey that licks its armpits and try not to laugh. "Exactly like that."

She smiles. "I'll follow your directions, I promise. I just want to figure out what the heck is going on so we can get to Nashville already."

Thanks to that odd conversation, by the time we climb out of the car, the guards have already spread out.

"You must be Ruby." A tall, dark-haired man in swim trunks walks toward us from the back of the East Palms building.

And this must be the son of the president of CINOW. He would have to be tall with a rippling stomach and broad chest. Why couldn't he be short? Or bald? It wouldn't bother me if he had a paunch, or maybe a really big nose. Sadly, his nose looks fine—like it's never been broken in a fistfight—but fine. He looks like he spent an hour and a half styling his short hair.

Maybe I should consider getting a haircut regularly instead of yanking mine back in a ponytail every day.

But Ruby loves me. I know she does.

I won't let this guy make me act like Wesley did. We've been through too much for that.

"I'm Ruby," she says. "And you are?"

He smiles, and just like Josephine says, he has a dimple on both sides of his mouth. His teeth are perfectly aligned, but huge. Like horse teeth. "I'm Kimball Ryson." He keeps walking toward us alone, as though he hasn't noticed the twenty-six armed soldiers in position to blow his head off. He holds out his hand. "Nice to meet you."

Ruby's eyebrows rise. "Over on the West coast you still shake hands?"

He laughs. "Not at all, but that's why we're here." His voice drops to a much more intimate volume. "We heard from some people heading our direction that a Queen Ruby found the cure for Tercera."

She smiles. "Well, it wasn't me so much as a group of us, but yes. We did." She glances back at me. "My chief of security, Samuel Roth, actually had the cure all along."

Kimball's smile broadens. "It sounds like we have a lot to talk about." He gestures behind him. "It's a beautiful day —not quite California weather, but not far from it. Any chance you'd like to talk down by the water?"

"Of course we're happy to share the cure," Ruby says. "But unfortunately I'm in a bit of a rush right now. I hadn't planned to stay in Galveston for more than a few hours before departing again. Your arrival took us by surprise."

"Shocked might be a better word," I say.

"Samuel?" Kimball turns to face me. "That's your name, right?"

I nod.

"Thank you. You have no idea how transformational this will be for us. We have an infected population of nearly three hundred thousand. Ruby's mother told us that you had nearly a hundred thousand taking a hormonal suppressant as well. We only wish we'd realized that worked as a stopgap sooner and could have saved more. But I won't lie. It hasn't been easy to take care of them without risking ourselves."

"You've cared for the Marked kids?" Ruby asks. "You provide them food and shelter and clothing?"

The smile slides from Kimball's face. "Of course we do."

"How many citizens do you govern on the West Coast?" Ruby asks.

"Just over a million," Kimball says. "Not counting those infected and living on a suppressant."

Ruby's lips compress. "No one did much for the Marked kids here. They were left to fend for themselves."

His mouth drops open. "That's terrible."

"I couldn't agree more." Ruby shakes her head. "I'd love to go chat with you by the sand—did you know that I haven't spent a day at the beach since I was five years old?"

"That's a travesty." Kimball tilts his head. "Of epic proportions. We need to do something about it immediately."

"That might be overstated, but either way, I don't have time right now. If you can tear yourself away from the surf to travel down the island, I can meet with you for an hour or so before we leave."

"An hour?" Kimball's frown looks almost too perfect. "I'm afraid that's not enough time to discuss the things I've been tasked by my government to cover. Would it be impertinent of me to ask what's so pressing?"

Impertinent? Did he grow up in a historical novel? What a pretentious idiot.

Ruby doesn't seem to mind, sadly. Or maybe she's just polite. "It sounds like you're the only government on the West—we had no idea you were even there—but on the east side of the country, there are three main groups. The Marked, whom we recently began treating, and World Peace Now, sometimes referred to as WPN, where you are currently. The third is the Unmarked, and Samuel's father led them until very recently."

"He didn't happen to be brought down by something to do with not alerting anyone to the existence of the cure, did he?" His smirk irritates me badly.

"My father didn't realize it *was* a cure," I say. "He thought it was more of a preventative." Why am I defending him? I haven't spent a single day mourning him.

He was a terrible father, and morally bankrupt in every way.

"In any case, there's a sort of leadership vacuum there right now," Ruby says. "And they've asked Sam to come up and help them select a new leader."

"Sam?" Kimball looks from Ruby to me and back to Ruby again. "Who is also your boyfriend, I assume, which is why you need to go along."

Ruby blushes. "He is, but that's not why I need to go. He's perfectly capable of going without me."

Oh, no, I'm not about to leave him here with her. "Ruby's opinion and support means as much to Wesley's father as anything I might say."

"Who's Wesley?" Kimball's eyes widen. "I really am the odd man out, here."

"None of this concerns you," Adam snaps. "We need to get back—Her Majesty has a lot to deal with before she leaves."

"Her Majesty?" Kimball's mouth twitches with suppressed laughter.

"I can't seem to get them to stop saying that," Ruby says. "I know it's ridiculous. My deceased biological father was a bit of a narcissist."

"I'm sure you'll eventually prevail," Kimball says. "You don't seem like someone who gives up easily."

"Not usually," Ruby says. "And I am sorry not to have more time, but you can see that this can't really wait."

"Where are you headed?" Kimball asks. "Because I'd be happy to accompany you."

Before I can object, Ruby says, "I'm sure you understand that you can't just drive a few hundred men to Nashville, not while the Unmarked leadership is in turmoil."

His smile spreads across his whole face, his dark blue eyes intent on her. "Oh, I don't need to bring anyone along, and I can't imagine the Unmarked would feel threatened by little old me."

This time it's Ruby's mouth twitching with suppressed laughter. "You'd have to put on a shirt, you know. I doubt they'd appreciate you parading around in swim trunks."

"I think I can manage that." He glances over his shoulder. "How much time do I have to tell my people where I'm going and throw some things into a smaller bag?"

"We leave in three hours," Ruby says.

"Let me know where, and I'll meet you in two." This time, when Kimball reaches out his hand, Ruby shakes it.

"Well, it's nice to meet you, then, Kimball Ryson. I hope I won't regret allowing you to accompany us." Ruby shakes his hand a moment longer than she should.

"Oh, I'm positive you won't."

But I sure will, because I'm pretty sure killing the son of the president of CINOW would be a mistake. Even so, I'm not ruling it out just yet.

9

RUBY

"I can't stand that guy," Adam says the second we close the door.

"Why are you riding with us now?" I put one finger on the middle of Adam's forehead, which is right between the driver's and passenger's seats, and shove him backward. "Buckle up."

"I only rode in the other car so I could give orders to the hundred and fifty soldiers you'd never have approved," he says.

"Please tell me he's kidding." I glare at Sam.

"Okay. He's kidding." Sam keeps his eyes on the road, the coward.

"So you two just ignore me now?" I shake my head. "I liked it better when you didn't get along."

"Honestly, you'd think she'd listen to us," Adam says.

Kimball was perfectly polite, just as Josephine said he'd be. "I think it was a nice change of pace to find out about another government because they want to extend an olive branch. It certainly beats having guns pointed at our heads, like WPN did the first time we met them."

"Better to face a gun in the face," Sam says. "At least that's honest."

"Kimball has been nothing but friendly to us." I wish Josephine hadn't taken Adam's place in the other car. I'm sure she'd back me up. Or if they weren't back with their parents among the Marked, I'm sure Rhonda and Job would back me up. "I need more family here—someone else to support me when you two gang up."

"Adam *is* your family. He only agrees with me because I'm the one talking sense. You can't trust that guy," Sam says. "That's all we're saying."

I look from my brother to my boyfriend. "Honestly, you two. Is it because he was wearing nothing but swim trunks?" Both of them look just as good with their shirts off—they shouldn't be annoyed that someone else makes time to work out.

"He was wearing swim trunks?" Sam asks.

"Was he?" Adam shrugs.

I roll my eyes. "Alright, be ridiculous. I don't care. We have a long list of things to do, and another set of bags to pack, and then we're all off, bound for Nashville and a totally different problem. So don't fault me for being glad this new development is low drama."

"So far," Sam says.

"I'm surprised you didn't refuse to let him come—all alone though he'll be."

"I considered it," Sam says. "But . . . "

"You knew I'd make sure his rooms were bugged," Adam says. "So if he plans to send any of his soldiers to attack, we'll know well in advance."

"Tell me you didn't." I look from Sam to Adam and back, but I can't tell whether they're kidding. "You bugged his rooms? Are you serious?"

"I told your boyfriend I was a quick learner," Adam says.

"You didn't lie." The corner of Sam's mouth turns upward.

"You hated Adam when you first met," I say.

"You did?" Adam asks.

"To be fair, I hate everyone when we first meet," Sam says. "But it didn't take me long to decide you were alright."

"Oh my gosh." But we're finally back to the house. I hop out the second the SUV stops and trot up the stairs. Even so, Sam's by my side as I reach the front door.

"Don't be mad," he says.

"That you're domineering and possessive?" I straighten my shoulders and put my hands on my hips. "That you're trying to tell me what to do?"

"I'm just doing my job." He sticks out his bottom lip. "I'm so sorry, Your Majesty," he says. "I'll never step out of line again."

I punch his arm as hard as I can. "Owww," I say.

"That happens every single time." His smile is smug. "I only want to keep you safe."

"Said like every overbearing parent, boyfriend, and misogynist throughout time."

He ducks his head a little. "Are you really mad? I don't stop you from doing anything—I just try to work around your decisions to keep you safe."

It's true. And I do have a target on my back—the Port Heads don't love me. "I know."

"If you're really upset, you need to tell me. I'll always listen."

I step toward him and he wraps his arms around me. "I know. I'm not really upset, and I don't care whether you like this guy or not. I know we can't trust him. But we have more than enough problems—we don't need to make any more by imagining issues where they don't exist. Let's take him for face value unless we have reason not to, okay?"

"I'll try," Sam says. "It's just that in my experience, there are far more lousy humans walking around making decisions than good ones."

"My big, hot pessimist."

Sam's head lowers until his lips are hovering over mine. "Say it again."

"You're big."

"Not that." He smiles, which only makes him even hotter.

"You're mine?"

"Better," he whispers. "But no."

"You're hot."

"Bingo." He kisses me then.

"Am I the puppy in this scenario?" I pull back so I can see his eyes clearly.

"Excuse me?" Sam blinks.

"You lead me along so I'll say the right thing, and then you reward me when I do."

"You're saying a kiss from me is a reward?"

I love when he's smug. "I guess I am."

"Then I guess you are like a puppy, but a very cute one."

"You two are adorable," a man says from the bottom step.

I'm accustomed to the sounds of other people around—I'm incessantly surrounded by guards. But I know that voice, and Sam stiffens when he hears Kimball.

"She said two hours," Sam says quietly. A little too quietly. He's less deadly when he's barking about things. It's when he's quiet that I get nervous.

"He said we're cute," I whisper. "Hardly an attack."

Sam grits his teeth. "We have a lot to do yet."

"I won't get in your way." Kimball drops a bag on the bottom step and sits down. He pulls out a book.

"Is that *Harrison's Principles of Internal Medicine?*" I ask.

Kimball's head whips around. "What?"

I walk down a few steps and peer at the cover of his

book. It is. "Why are you reading *Harrison's Principles of Internal Medicine?*"

"I'm in medical school back in Sacramento," he says. "I'm studying to be a doctor."

"How old are you?" Sam asks.

"Twenty-two," Kimball says. "How about you?"

"Sam turns twenty-two in a few weeks," I say. "You're really in medical school?"

He shrugs. "Sort of—I mean, it's not like it was before the world died, right? But CINOW has two medical schools. One in Seattle, one in Sacramento. We start college at seventeen, usually. I finished a year early and started at sixteen. So I'm about to start my third year of medical school, which means I'll be doing a lot of hands-on clinical stuff."

I'm jealous. I wish we had something like that. "The Unmarked mostly do internships, like where you shadow another doctor."

"That doesn't sound very comprehensive," he says with a frown.

"It's not," I say. "We need to improve that, for sure. I'd be interested to hear how you put your program together."

Adam clears his throat and taps his watch.

"On the road," Kimball says. "We'll have plenty of time to talk on the way, I'm sure."

"Oh, you won't be traveling with us," Sam says.

I turn around to glare at him. "Rude, geez."

Sam forces a smile. "Or perhaps you will." He turns to Adam. "You'll need to make sure he's been thoroughly searched."

I huff. "Is that really—"

"It's fine." Kimball stands up. "I have nothing to hide. Search away."

The next few hours fly by—but luckily Josephine packs

my bag for me. This time she doesn't pack a ball gown. "What? Nothing frilly or fluffy?"

She lifts one eyebrow. "You're going to address heads of state." She pats a bag on the bed. "A business suit is a much better call for that. They need to see you as older and more professional, not regal or stunningly beautiful."

Just when I'm ready to write her off, she surprises me with insight. "Alright, well, thanks."

"Do me one favor?" She crosses the room until she's standing right next to me.

"What?" I'm immediately suspicious. She never asks me for anything anymore, but she used to, and it was always something I couldn't give her. Like forgiving her husband David Solomon, or even harder, trusting him. Hard pass. I wonder what she'll request this time.

"You love Samuel Roth."

"Is that a favor?" I ask. "Because if so, I'll grant it."

She smiles. "I know you don't want to hear this, but you're very young. Seventeen is . . . " She looks upward as if asking God for his help in getting through to me. Like I'm a rebellious teen who's sneaking out and smoking pot or stealing cars. "It's just awfully young to make any permanent decisions."

"Mom, I'm not like seventeen-year-olds were Before. My entire life is different. I'm like . . . like a thirty-year-old."

"I was thirty when I left Donald Carillon," she breathes out. "And that was a mistake."

She's never admitted anything like that, never. I'm not sure what to say, but I'm suddenly full of questions. "Why?" It seems the safest thing. Maybe it'll encourage her to say more.

"Donald was brilliant," she says. "I don't suppose he ever told you where we met?"

I shake my head.

"He was my professor." Her cheeks flush bright red.

"He wasn't."

She nods shyly. "I was in the very first class he taught, although he was only a graduate student then, so we weren't breaking any rules. He was the smartest man I'd ever met."

My mom was a scientist? Josephine? I'd been wondering how I could have an aptitude for science, since my father, Donald Carillon, isn't really my father. I'd thought maybe Aunt Anne inspired me. It never occurred to me that my love for STEM might come from my mother. "You went to—"

"Berkeley," she says. "It's where Donald went after MIT."

I've never even considered how many things I can learn, just by asking her. She lived through almost everything that's a big grey blank spot in my past. "Was he a bad person?" I know my biological father David Solomon was, but I've never had the courage to ask about the man I loved, the man who raised me—because he was also the man who made Tercera, effectively destroying most of the world. The second thing kind of seemed to eclipse the first. I haven't really allowed myself much time to think well of him.

"He wasn't a bad person," she says. "He was a good man. Not very balanced, sometimes, but I thought he would make me happy. But Ruby, he didn't. He cared so much more about his work than about me, and when we couldn't have children . . . " She shakes her head. "I think it broke something between us. We couldn't recover."

"You tried?"

"For five years," she says. "I miscarried four times."

"Do you think he went crazy when he heard you were pregnant with me?" Maybe that's why he stole me.

She shakes her head. "It was possible you were his—we both knew it. In his heart, David knew it too. But at the time we discussed it, and we didn't care, David and I. We were in love, and I was desperately hoping that Donald was the problem and I'd finally have a healthy pregnancy."

I don't want to know any more about that. Truly. "But Donald stole me."

"He knew that David hit me," she admits, her eyes downcast and her voice small. "He saw him, once."

"Really?"

"Not in person, but on a surveillance tape." She shakes her head. "The whole thing was very messy. I made a lot of mistakes, Ruby. I'm not perfect. That's why I can tell you this. I believe you love Sam, and I can tell he loves you, but no one would blame you for evaluating your options— you're only seventeen. Don't make any permanent decisions unless you're one hundred and ten percent sure."

"Mathematical impossibility," I say.

"You're so much like him," she says. "Like Donald, I mean. And I'm glad of that."

So am I. And I kind of don't hate that she's trying to be a mom, even if she's clearly trying to get me to date Kimball. As if I ever would. Even so, it's nice that she's trying to give me motherly advice. "Thanks, Mom. I'll give it some thought."

When we finally emerge with my two suitcases, Adam frowns. "That's going to be a tight fit."

"So tack another SUV onto the motorcade," I joke. I can't imagine he's planning less than a hundred guards, seeing as we're venturing into Unmarked territory. Ridiculous. As if they'd hurt me. As if they even could with Sam around.

"Ruby, do you remember how long the drive to Nashville is?" Adam asks.

I shrug. "Not really. I don't think we've ever gone directly from here to there."

"Two days, if we take a car. At least fifteen hours. It's

almost three in the afternoon. Sam said you were supposed to be there today."

Well, crap. "Maybe we could—"

"I assumed you knew we were going to fly." Adam tosses his head at one of the men behind him and he grabs my suitcases.

My mouth goes dry. "Are you serious?"

"Deadly serious." His head tilts. "You know we have fighter jets—did you really think we'd go by boat to Mexico?"

I hadn't given it much thought.

"We maintain dozens of fighter jets, and at least a dozen commercial planes." Adam shrugs. "We don't often take them to places outside of World Peace Now for obvious reasons."

"Like what?" I can't think what obvious reasons we'd have for *not* flying instead of driving.

"Transportation when we arrive, for one," he says. "And then there's the issue of finding a clear runway."

Ah. Duh. "So, where will we land in Nashville?"

"When I sent men before, we scoped out the area and found a mostly clear spot not too far from town—it's a private hanger that I'd guess Roth kept clear."

"Roth?" Sam turns the corner, a duffel bag in one hand. "My dad?"

"Didn't he have a plane?" Adam asks.

Sam nods. "He did. One or two, both small. He hardly ever used them, but I saw him leave in one a time or two."

"See?" Adam smiles. "And now you get to fly as well."

"I figured," Sam says.

"But you let me talk about the drive?" I shake my head. "Thanks a lot."

"I thought you meant a figurative drive," Sam says.

I roll my eyes. "Let's go."

Kimball doesn't look surprised when our SUV lets us all

out on a small runway a few miles down from the white columned mansion.

"You assumed we were going by plane?" My voice is a little irritated, but I can't seem to help it.

"We came by plane from California to just outside of Houston." He shrugs. "Otherwise it would have taken us *forever* on uncertain roads."

Great. I'm the only idiot.

"I expected a larger plane," Kimball says. "What's this? An Embraer 175?"

"You just know something about everything," Sam says. "What a gift to have you along."

Oh my goodness, Sam is adorable when he's jealous. I smile at him. "I love you."

The frown melts off his face. "We'd better go." He takes my hand in his and we climb onto the jet. It's a surreal moment—walking up the steps into a plane as though the world didn't actually crash and burn.

After takeoff, Sam and Adam get into some kind of heated debate about guns.

"The Glock is like the Toyota of the gun world," Sam says.

"Right," Adam says. "It runs well, consistently, and never lets me down. It also has two more rounds than your Beretta."

"And my Beretta is heavier," Sam says, as if he's heard this a million times from idiots. "Which might matter to people for whom a few ounces makes a difference." Which his expression makes clear is definitely not him. "I'll take a fine-tuned precision instrument any day over one you're billing as 'reliable.'"

"What about the extra two rounds?"

"I don't need them," Sam says, as if that's his bull's-eye.

If I have to listen to any more, I'll scream.

Kimball's reading again, so I lean toward him. "You're

clearly serious about studying, but haven't you read that already?"

He nods. "Of course, but my first rotation when I get back is internal medicine. Most of the material made sense, but not all of it, and if someone's sick, it's not like I can say, 'Hey, can you hang on a sec while I look up what to do for someone who's coding? Thanks.'" He laughs. "Better to know it cold."

"I guess."

"What's wrong with you?" He closes his book.

I slump in my seat. "Nothing."

"You don't want to be queen."

"No," I say. "I don't. At all. I should never have been ruling anyone. It was only a bizarre fluke that led to me being here at all."

"Which probably means you're the leader they don't deserve," he says.

I shake my head. "I've made mistake after mistake." I tell him about the debacle with Sawyer.

He laughs. "Rookie mistake, believe me. I've been watching my dad for a while now. People almost always vote for the devil they know."

My eyes widen. "What makes you think he's a devil?"

He shrugs. "Maybe he's not. But you said they wrote in your name, too, right? How many?"

The half wail kind of sneaks out. "Writing in my name is the opposite of encouraging. They like me because they think I cured Tercera."

"I know you said it was in your boyfriend's blood, but didn't you figure that out?"

As quickly as I can, I explain what happened. How my dad kidnapped me from my birth parents—and then how he created Tercera. We're both silent for a moment then, and I realize that Sam and Adam aren't fighting anymore.

They're listening to me, sharing our whole story with a stranger.

Oh, well. I have no idea what versions he's already heard from whatever people fled across the country. He may as well hear the truth. I forge along and tell him the rest.

"You lost your best friend?" He shakes his head. "And your dad." He sighs. "I'm sorry. That all really sucks, but it helps me see how lucky the people of World Peace Now are to have you, someone who only wants what's best for them. Someone who wants to free them—from the threat of a virus, from their own ignorance, and from their own idiocy."

Heat rises in my cheeks. "That's really nice, but I think you weren't listening. The cure was actually—"

"Oh, I was listening before, and I'm listening now. We've only just met, but I can already tell that you do this a lot, where you act like you didn't do something amazing, even though you did."

I swallow. "Either way, the point is that now, since John Roth is gone, the Unmarked have to choose a new leader. So we're going to help them make the right call."

"You're sure this Quinn is a bad guy?"

I can't help my scowl. "He didn't send aid to the Marked, even after he knew we'd developed a cure. In fact, he did nothing at all until he saw WPN doing it, and even then he waited a few days."

"Not altruistic," Kimball says, "but still maybe not villainous. It bodes well that he didn't like John Roth, based on what you told me about Sam's dad."

I glance over at Sam, who's scowling. I hope he's not mad I was discussing his dad. "The point is, I know that Mr. Fairchild is a good person. He was fair in Port Gibson, and Wesley was the best person ever."

"You said he didn't pursue locating Wesley's little sister."

I swallow. I did say that.

"And that when your aunt showed up, Marked, but with a message, he turned her away."

Actually it was worse than that. I cringe a little when I say, "Technically . . . he imprisoned her."

"Instead of listening to her?"

What if he's right? Does Fairchild deserve our support? The plane is landing now, so luckily I can just drop the whole thing. But his questions stick with me. Are we right to help Mayor Fairchild? Will he do a good job? How can you ever trust that anyone else's intentions will remain noble? Isn't Sam always talking about power corrupting, and absolute power corrupting absolutely? Ugh.

What if Sam throws his support behind the wrong person? I used to blame my parents for making such poor decisions, but the more decisions I'm stuck making the more I wonder . . .

Will I do any better? Or am I taking the first steps toward dooming the world . . . again?

With no one to blame but myself.

10

RUBY

Nashville was definitely better the last time we came—the time they had Aunt Anne locked up and were planning to kill her.

Although, maybe it's my own idiosyncrasies that makes me feel this way.

"They're trying to be nice," Sam says. "They thought this would make you happy."

They put us in a ridiculously large mansion, and everyone keeps calling me Her Majesty. When they discovered I came with Sam, Adam, Kimball and a few dozen guards, they assigned me a cook and housekeeping staff, whom I'm pretty sure are here to spy on me.

My head might explode.

"I hate being pandered to," I say. "And I figured at least here I wouldn't need to argue with people about being treated like royalty."

Sam's eyes sparkle, but he doesn't actually laugh, or even smile. He knows I'm that close to exploding. "At least the porch is nice. And you said you liked the pancakes."

I roll my eyes. "What was I going to say?" I glance behind me to make sure no one has snuck out of the house to listen in. "She was staring right at me, asking whether I liked breakfast."

"So you didn't like them?" Sam tilts his head.

"They were fine! I don't like people hovering and cleaning around me and acting like I'm a celebrity."

"You're the queen of WPN," he says. "I know you don't want to stay in that position, but to the rest of the world, you're a big deal. No matter whom they elect as chancellor for the Unmarked, every council member knows that you—with one little crook of your finger—could crush them." He shrugs, the muscles of his chest rippling a bit. "You can't fault them for trying to make sure you're happy."

Honestly? I thought they'd see me as a joke. "The last time I was here, no one took me seriously."

"Until a thousand troops and a fighter jet threatened to level them."

"Fifteen hundred troops and two fighter jets," I say. Not that it matters.

This time Sam does smile. "It's nice to be holding all the cards for once," he says. "You can admit that, at least."

The door bangs open and both of us turn to see who it is now.

"Morning," I say.

Kimball sets a glass of orange juice on the table in front of me. "This is from Madeline, who was going to bring it herself, along with a basket of biscuits."

"Did you tell her that I don't need a second breakfast?" I widen my eyes.

"She seemed to believe you needed more nutrition than you're currently getting." His eyes scan my bony frame. He doesn't seem to disagree with her assessment. I'm not in the habit of slapping people, but if I were, I might slap them both.

Sam never, ever makes me feel like a truant child. He jokes sometimes about how I need to eat more, but for some reason it doesn't bother me when he does it—and he doesn't shove biscuits and pancakes in my face and make big eyes about how I'm not eating them.

I need to calm down.

But I've never been asked to recommend someone to a council of any kind, let alone the governing body of most of my growing up years. Six months ago, I'd have trembled at the thought of answering to Mayor Fairchild. Now Sam and I are supposed to go speak on his behalf to all his former colleagues and bosses. It's disconcerting to say the least.

Sam sits up straight and his eyes go glassy—which means he's listening to something on his earpiece. "Someone approaching." He scans the tree-lined drive, his shoulders relaxing. "It's just Mayor Fairchild."

"Which means it's time."

The door bangs again and my brother shoots out—probably because Adam's listening to the same feed in his earpiece. "You look very professional," he says. "I like the suit. Josephine pick that out?"

I nod. It's scratchy, but the black pinstripe with a shell pink undersweater makes me look five years older, and I need every extra day I can muster.

Adam scans past me and his eyes stop on Sam and then widen. "Don't you look impressive?"

Sam scowls.

"He's right—I like the suit." I smile. "We're like the grown up versions of Ruby and Sam." I stand up.

"What about me?" Adam asks.

"You're always wearing a suit," I say.

"I'd still like for someone to notice it every once in a while."

"I would have made a real *splash* by wearing my swimsuit," Kimball says. "Except you all seemed to think that would be inappropriate."

Until he mentions the swim trunks, I don't really study

him. But now that he's brought it up, I can't help but notice that his suit looks like the kind that fancy lawyers in Aunt Anne's favorite legal shows used to wear. It's not showy or ostentatious, but it's clear Kimball's family has real wealth. Which I guess is the point. "You cleaned up alright," I say. "Who would have thought that the California surfer tagalong wouldn't embarrass us?"

"Ha."

Mayor Fairchild reaches the front step, and I sling my shoulder bag over my arm. "Are they ready for us?"

"I came to see whether you were ready for them," he says. "They'll be accommodating of whatever schedule you need to keep." He drops his voice. "I heard you came by plane."

I suppose I should have looked into the extent of my power and privileges the very second they crowned me— for the first time, I'm realizing that I have a lot more options at my fingertips than I've really processed.

The thought embarrasses me.

Why should I have a plane when most people are lucky to have a bike?

Why should someone make me pancakes when the Marked have been struggling for years not to *starve*?

I think about the little girl who set this all in motion.

She was starving, and Wesley, Mayor Fairchild's son, gave her a basket of food. Some bread, some apples, some cheese.

That one thing was a tremendous violation of protocol.

And she died as a result of it.

The world isn't right, and we've barely begun to set it back on track. I should be taking stock of what resources are at my disposal and using them all to fix the wrongs that surround us. I square my shoulders and swallow. "Meeting with the council is the only reason we've come to Nashville at all." And as soon as we're done, I'm going to double down on evaluating our resources, reallocating them where they're needed most.

Sometimes I have these moments, brief, poignant, where it feels like I'm a stranger in someone else's body—where I almost step outside of myself and think, *who is that?*

I have one of those moments as we walk down the tree-lined path. Sam and Adam fall in easily on either side of me. Kimball and Mayor Fairchild walk in front of us, chatting. And dozens of guards move down sidewalks on either side of us, taking up positions out front of and behind where I am, communicating with Sam and Adam via earbud.

All these people are moving around frantically to keep me safe.

Me.

I'm still the same, tiny, young, inept bumbler who couldn't pick a career path. I'm the little girl who hid in a closet while my dad bled out. And for some reason, all these people care about what I say and do.

It's a strange, incomprehensible fluke, of course.

If I hadn't been related to the infamously awful David Solomon.

If he hadn't destroyed the government and used the proliferation of a deadly virus to seize control, protecting enough people that he had someone to rule over . . .

Then I wouldn't be Queen Ruby. I'd be 'trash collector Ruby.' Or 'stick-your-eye-over-a-microscope Ruby.' Or maybe even 'piano-playing Ruby.'

There's only one surprise that has happened in my life that felt magical, that felt meant to be, that felt like it was a connection *I* made, myself, because of who I am. I reach for Sam's hand and he takes mine immediately. Our fingers twist together and something inside of me feels *right*. I'm not a stranger in someone else's life. This is my life—things are just weird right now. If we push through, we'll get to that small town. We'll find meaningful jobs that matter where no one is looking to us, expecting huge things of us. We'll be together, working toward something that matters, but not something *epic* or *life-changing*.

That's what I want—not all this absurd hoopla.

Stay the course until you can change direction. That's all we need to do. Take the next small step, and the next small step, and the next small step until we've walked through the hard part.

As we climb the steps to the administrative offices of the Unmarked, set up in the former Tennessee State Office building, I focus on this small cobblestone in our current path. The next little thing I need to do in order to get where we're going. It's hard not to think about the last time I climbed these steps—I was holding Sam's hand then too. Which reminds me of one of the first times I held Sam's hand—as we crossed from the mainland onto Galveston Island. We took the old service road, and we had to cross the metal beams that connect that road on the cutout they made for ships to pass. And the dozens of times I held it between those events.

This little walk in to chat with some people about their new leader is nothing to any of those times—to the times where we faced terrible danger and the horrifying unknown of a pandemic-threatened world.

This little step is a figurative piece of cake by comparison.

So why do I feel a vague sense of unease I can't quite pinpoint? I should feel confident and calm. I shake off my ennui purposefully and force a smile when Sam's brows draw together. I know what that look means.

He's worried about me. He wants to keep me safe.

I wish it were that simple. We walk through the grand front doors of the enormous limestone building, and it's time. All eyes turn toward us. Most faces smile—but not in a very convincingly genuine way.

What are they thinking? That I'm lucky? That it's unfair? That they wish they could trade places with me? Or do they hate me?

I wish I knew.

Or maybe I'm glad that I don't.

I focus on the little piece of space right in front of me. And it's nice that we aren't tackled this time or threatened. We don't need to hold a gun to anyone's head either, so that's a major improvement. A tall, flinty-eyed man in a brown uniform stands directly in front of us.

I remember him, Commander Drake. He doesn't appear to have suffered any permanent damage from the rock-in-a-sock he took to the head. I can't decide whether I'm pleased or disappointed. He wasn't very nice, and Sam did what he had to do.

But this time, Commander Drake is beaming. "Your Majesty." He gestures toward an open set of double doors.

The council chamber.

Last time I forced my way inside, clutching my dad's old briefcase to my chest because it was our only evidence that John Roth had been sitting on a cure, without being quite sure how effective it might be.

This time, we're invited, but then and now, a hundred sets of eyes swivel in our direction. I swallow and try to remain calm. My heart doesn't get the memo and practically gallops out of my chest. Hopefully none of them can hear it.

"Samuel Roth." Interim Chancellor Quinn doesn't smile.

"I'm guessing he didn't send the chef," Kimball whispers. "In fact, he doesn't look too pleased you guys are here at all."

I snort. "He's not a fan, no. He was Sam's father's rival."

"Not much of a rival," Sam says. "More of an irritant."

"More than an irritant now," I say. "And just as bad as your dad ever was."

"True."

"When you're done whispering, I hear you'd like to make a statement." Chancellor Quinn's lips press together so hard that the lines around his mouth deepen.

"To be clear," Sam says. "I was asked to come and make a statement. I don't really want to be here at all."

"Duly noted," Chancellor Quinn says. "But if you're ready to approach?" He steps away from the podium on the raised dais and waves at the microphone.

Sam squeezes my hand one last time before letting it go. I watch, my eyes transfixed on his broad shoulders as he walks toward the front of the room. He never wanted anything to do with any of this—he is as far from his father as anyone could be—but he's here because he wants to do the right thing. I'm proud of him, always.

He doesn't waste any time. The second he's in front of the microphone, he starts speaking. "My name is Samuel Roth. Most of you likely don't like me very well because of my association with my father." He pauses and scans the room, analyzing their expressions, probably. "I don't even blame you for that. He was a terrible man. Believe me, I've known that for longer than anyone. He was charming, brilliant, effective, brutal, and utterly selfish. It's a terrifying and devastating combination."

Sam looks at me and I throw him a thumbs up. I don't care if it's cheesy. It's not like anyone is paying attention to what I'm doing back here anyway.

And it makes him smile.

"I doubt my father held me in much esteem. It didn't seem to matter much what I accomplished or what I was able to do. He certainly never showed me affection or praised my efforts. He might have cared for me, but only inasmuch as I represented a legacy he planned to leave. The Unmarked are well rid of him. That's my point."

Murmurs begin in the gathered crowd. He better get to the point quickly. I've learned a few things about managing crowds, although not groups this intense, certainly.

"I'm telling you these things because I hope, perhaps out of naive optimism, that the governing body of the Unmarked can choose a better chancellor this time."

"Whom do you support?" a woman near me shouts.

"That's a good question. As I understand it, Interim Chancellor Quinn is running unopposed. To run against him, someone needs the nominating vote of twenty members of this council."

Heads bob.

"I think a vote for Interim Chancellor Quinn would be as close as any of you could come to voting for my father."

He pauses then. Sam's gorgeous face rotates slowly from one end of the room to the other. He doesn't flinch. He doesn't look away. He challenges each and every one of them and every single person drops their gaze from his before he moves to the next person. Finally, he speaks again. "I would support *anyone* against him. He's as selfish, as greedy, and as morally bankrupt as my father—and my father spoke of him as though he were nearly an equal. He could do more to ruin the future of this government than almost anyone I've met."

Chancellor Quinn's face is bright red, and if he had a gun, I imagine he'd be trying to use it.

"Luckily, it won't be quite so dire as that," Sam says. "You have another option. I've known Mayor Fairchild for quite some time, and I'm sure many of you have known him longer than I have. We haven't always gotten along, and we haven't always agreed on everything, but he's always been mostly reasonable and typically fair. Justice is a moving target in real life, but from my experience he tries to hit it whenever possible."

Mayor Fairchild's face isn't glowing, but he looks satisfied. That's about as unqualified a recommendation as Sam's likely to give anyone. He should be delighted.

"I hope you don't mind if we ask you a few questions," the woman near me shouts again.

Sam shrugs. "I'm no expert, but sure."

"Do you consider yourself an Unmarked citizen?" the woman asks.

Sam blinks. "Of course I do."

"But you've accepted a rather critical position among the leadership of World Peace Now, have you not?" Her eyebrow rises sharply, and I realize she's been gunning for him.

"I am Chief of Military and Strategic Defense for Ruby Thomas Carillon Behl Solomon, yes."

I've never heard anyone give every single one of my names like that. It's bizarre. Part of me likes it—it kind of sums up everyone I am. The name I'd have been born with had things not been upside down: Thomas. The name of my kidnapping dad: Carillon. The name he took to keep us safe and hidden: Behl. The name my biological father took in order to invoke a Biblical leader as he usurped the government and ran his cult: Solomon.

I bet it confuses the crap out of everyone in this room, however.

"How can you possibly fulfill the duties of that position with World Peace Now without violating your duties as a citizen of the Unmarked?" She stands up. "In fact, how have you been fulfilling your duties as the second-in-command of security for Port Gibson? What about the Unmarked citizens there? Are you keeping them safe?"

Sam rolls his eyes, and the audience doesn't like it, muttering and grumbling and shaking their heads. "The greatest threat to the Unmarked, as evidenced by their name, was the threat of contracting Tercera." He folds his arms. "By abandoning my post, and by extension, them, I was able to accompany Ruby on her travels. Together we uncovered the truth, that I was carrying the cure in my blood. Placed there secretly by my father—the one I recently decried, and who I helped kill."

"But once you'd found that information, did you rush back to inoculate the Unmarked citizens?" she asks. "Your own people?"

"I gave my blood to two other Unmarked citizens to administer to the people who were actively *dying*," he says. "They've got plenty of subjects now who are able to replicate the same virus that is saving them from Tercera." He shakes his head. "And I'm happy to make another blood donation today before we leave."

A man near the front of the room with a shock of white hair that almost reminds me of Sawyer's stands up. "So you're leaving?" He looks around the room. "Where are you going? Back to Port Gibson?"

Sam sighs. "I'm returning with Ruby to Galveston. I'm keeping her safe there for the time being."

"So you're still shirking your Unmarked duties?" This time the person asking is in the back left corner. It's a very short man with a long mustache. "It sounds like you're more dedicated to WPN than to us."

"They welcome you?" A redheaded lady next to the mustached man asks. "I heard you killed over a hundred of them when you and Ruby sneaked onto the island looking for the cure."

"I didn't kill anyone," Sam says. "I shot threats as they appeared, but no one died."

"How many people did you shoot?" Chancellor Quinn asks.

He's planted all these people, of course, but they're still

effective. They're making Sam look bad—very bad. And he's getting flustered. "I always shoot exactly as many people as need to be shot," Sam says. "And not a single person more."

"Your father was a renowned sharp shooter too," Chancellor Quinn says softly. "It seems like you have more in common with him than I do. Split loyalties. Confusing motives. Deadly skill with weapons. And possibly a thirst for power?"

I'm about done. "You will shut your mouth, sir."

Every head spins toward me.

"Your Majesty," Chancellor Quinn says. "Are you weighing in on our proceedings, or are you issuing a command to your Chief of Defense?"

"You think you're so smart." I stalk toward the front, and when I reach him, I spin around and face the pit of vipers striking at my boyfriend. "All of you are nearly as morally bankrupt as Chancellor Quinn." I put my hands on my hips. "Sam and I are experts on lousy fathers. Believe me when I tell you that it's made us very good at spotting liars and narcissists." I turn sideways because I want to see Chancellor Quinn's face. "My peach of a father kept a little leather-bound journal, you know. It's chock-full of disgusting secrets. Things people wouldn't want *a soul* to discover, let alone an ocean of their peers. I think you might be interested to know that your name was written in that book, *Gavin Quinn*."

The entire audience has fallen deadly silent. I don't recall seeing his name in my father's book, of course. I slammed it shut almost as quickly as I opened it—vile notes and secrets are the crutch of a dictator. But I'm betting Chancellor Quinn has done plenty of things he'd prefer not be revealed. I'm glad I recalled Quinn's first name, though. It makes it a little more convincing as a bluff.

"I'm not my father." I look at the audience. "I don't believe in winning by destroying the people around me." I turn back toward the snake. "So I'm going to give you the chance to step down, *Gavin*. I'd advise that you call off your idiotic pack of dogs and apologize to my boyfriend Sam. And then you'll walk right out that door, forfeiting your position. The council will nominate a few other options—the best that they can manage—and they'll have a chance of escaping the disaster they've been barreling toward for a decade."

Now, if I'm right, if Quinn is as disgusting as I think, he'll take the out. He'll spare himself the indignity and leave.

He steps toward me, one hand balled into a fist.

"Don't make me tell everyone," I whisper. "Because I'm afraid I'd enjoy it a little too much, and I'd hate to owe anything to my father's memory."

"You're a real piece of work," he says, spittle flying from his mouth and hitting my cheek.

I don't even bother to wipe it off. I just smile.

Because he bolts past me and down the aisle.

The rush of adrenaline is one of the best feelings the human body creates, but I can't simply enjoy it. I've still got ninety-nine people looking at us as though it's up to us to tell them what to do next.

"Pardon me," Kimball says. "I'm not a citizen of World Peace Now, or the Unmarked, so I'm ignorant. But, isn't Ruby an Unmarked citizen as well as Queen of WPN?"

Heads swivel, and whispers grow. "Who's that?" "They brought him." "He looks familiar."

Oh, Kimball, you idiot.

I wave for him to come to the front. "We did come to present you with Sam's and my support for Mayor Fairchild," I say. "But we have more news than that. I'm sure you're wondering who this is."

Every eye widens. Every man and woman sits forward in his or her chair, peering at Kimball.

"I'd like to introduce you to Kimball Ryson, the son of the President of an organization that calls itself CINOW. I haven't yet been there myself to verify this, but he says they boast more than a million citizens, and another three hundred thousand or so who are still infected with Tercera. They came to us in peace, asking that we share our cure."

The explosion of talking and shouting takes me by surprise. I knew they'd have questions, but I didn't expect such a clamor. "—a threat." "—must respond immediately." "Can't possibly—"

I hold up my hand. "Please be calm. There's no need to overreact. We don't pose a threat to them, and they certainly aren't threatening us. When I first met Kimball, he was wearing a very different suit than this one." I smile. "He was wearing a *swim*suit—he had come to talk, but he wanted to do it in a nonthreatening way. He succeeded."

A few laughs. It's very hard to be angry and alarmed when you're laughing.

"Look. I know it's big news. I know it's alarming, but we don't need to overreact either. Did you know that the fever we feel when we're sick is actually our body's overreaction to an illness? People often believe it's something our body does to protect us, but it doesn't kill the virus or bacteria, almost ever. No, it only makes us miserable, and sometimes that fever even kills us. Humans act just the same in a macro view. We freak out, and often our overreaction is what does the most damage. So sit down and listen for a moment."

"I think I've heard enough." A man with a long beard by the window in the back stands up. He throws his hands up and looks around the room. "Ruby is Unmarked. She's calm. She's well spoken. She already runs WPN—and the Marked listen to her too, probably because she cured them. And her aunt and uncle have worked tirelessly to serve and protect."

I blink. What's he talking about? I expected an argument, but it almost sounds like he's *praising* me.

"I nominate Ruby Behl to fill the open council position, and to serve as our next chancellor."

"I second that," the tall woman from the back says.

Dozens of other voices shout as well, but shockingly, most of them are agreeing with them.

"Wait," Mayor Fairchild says. "Stop." He waves his arms and shouts and the people finally settle down. "I asked Sam and Ruby to come out and talk to you because I thought it would help me beat Quinn." He shakes his head. "I never wanted to be chancellor, but no one else was stepping up to fight."

Oh, good. "Yes, I agree. I think Mayor Fairchild would make a much better option. I formally endorse him, to the extent that any of you care about my opinion."

"You've misunderstood me," Mayor Fairchild says. "My son Wesley always thought the world of Ruby. He saw her work hard, learn skillfully, and serve willingly. He never had anything but glowing things to say." He inhales deeply. "I resented her when he gave his life to save her. I'm ashamed to say it now, because for the first time, I see what he saw. Ruby Behl is exactly what we need to lead our country. She's smart, capable, noble, and well spoken. And she's young enough to understand and adapt in this changing world."

Oh, no. No, no, no. I shake my head. "I can't possibly—"

"Why wait until tomorrow?" Kimball asks with a smile. "I think you're ready to vote today. Right now. Ruby Behl!" He pumps his hand in the air.

And the morons all cheer.

When this is all over, I'm going to punch Kimball in his

fat face. "I don't want to be chancellor," I shriek. "I didn't come here to—"

"That's why you're perfect for it," Mayor Fairchild shouts. "I agree. Let's vote now."

And then the worst thing to happen since Josephine told me I'd be David Solomon's replacement occurs, right in front of my eyes. The idiots who rule the Unmarked vote for me to take over as chancellor.

Unanimously.

And I run out the back door and puke into a wire mesh trashcan, trying to ignore the chattering of my concerned guards.

I'm wiping my mouth when Sam joins us in the hall. "Are you alright?"

"No, I'm not," I say. "I can't imagine how things could possibly get any worse." I cover my face with my hands. "Were you in the same room as me just then?"

"Sam?" an unsteady voice asks. Tentative. Unsure. And very, very female.

I open my eyes.

Sam turns slowly to face the most stunningly beautiful Valkyrie warrior I've ever seen. She's nearly as tall as he is. Her hair is long, almost black, and so shiny it practically blinds me. Her full lips part softly as she inhales. "It *is* you."

"Lydia?" Sam's still staring at her.

The name finally registers. *Lydia?* The one other girl he liked? The girl he kissed? I'm staring at Sam's Wesley, and she's *so* much worse than I imagined she could be.

I should have known better than to complain out loud. If I've learned anything in the last seventeen years, it's that things can always get worse.

11

SAM

I had one friend in the clinical trial Dad signed me up for.

One.

She held my hand when I got my injections.

I held her hair when she puked.

We'd help each other over the worst parts of the obstacle courses.

She'd call my name as she writhed in agony.

The single greatest blow I withstood in that horrible, three-month ordeal was when Anne Orien tearfully told me that somehow, inexplicably, Lydia had contracted Tercera. She said the rigors of the trial had left her particularly susceptible . . . and she began to immediately exhibit final year symptoms.

Lydia *died* of Tercera. That was a given.

Except that was clearly all a lie . . . because Lydia is right in front of me.

"No one has called me that for quite some time," she says. "Years, in fact."

I swallow. I have to say something. Anything. "You're alive?" Brilliant, Sam. Yes, point out that she's not dead.

She laughs. "What did they tell you?"

I'm not sure where to start. "How? How did you recover from Tercera? Did the trial work?"

Lydia's enormous, deep brown eyes widen. "Tercera?"

"Didn't you contract it?" Was everything a lie? But why?

"I didn't respond as well as you to the serum or the light treatment. The study was a failure, but your dad wouldn't pull the plug. He refused to give up on it, even with his own son at risk."

Everyone died but me.

And apparently Lydia.

"Did anyone actually die?" I'm not sure what to believe any more.

"I'm the only person Gavin Quinn was able to save," she says. "And I'm lucky he was willing to put forth the effort."

If Lydia escaped . . . my dad had to simply come up with an explanation, and what better way than something that left no body and no incriminating evidence behind. Tercera infection . . . earlier than normal progression. No one will search for her, no one will expect a body. She'd have fled to the Marked to spend her final months without risk of infecting anyone else.

"You've been . . . where have you been all this time?" I ask.

Lydia's cheeks flush. "No one could see me, obviously, or know that I was alive, at least not until your father died. And then, I couldn't leave for . . . well, for other reasons. But then Quinn came rushing home and threw his things into a bag. He said everyone was leaving—and he mentioned your name. That you were here. While they were rushing around, shouting, crying, I slipped out the back door and I came here without thinking about it."

"Leaving where?" What's she talking about? I open my mouth, but I'm not sure what to say.

Lydia narrows her eyes. "He said that she knew—that

the girl you were with threatened to expose him. That's why they were leaving."

"Expose what?" Ruby asks.

I almost forgot she was there. I spin around. "What was in your dad's journal?"

She shrugs. "No idea. I made all that up."

Lydia's jaw drops.

"Made up what?" I feel like they're in on a secret I don't share.

Ruby looks from Lydia to me, slowly. "David Solomon had a journal." She nods. "That wasn't a lie. But if Gavin Quinn's in it, I didn't see what it said about him."

Lydia starts laughing. It's big and loud and beautiful, as it always has been. "You're a smart one. Wow. I wouldn't have thought anyone could fool him, but you sure did. He came flying through that door, terrified. He told everyone to pack and that we were leaving in under ten minutes."

"Who is everyone?" I ask.

"His wives?" Ruby asks.

"He only has one wife, of course," Lydia says. "But he has a half dozen . . . partners? Maybe that's a better word. He calls them all concubines, including the two men, as if he's some kind of ancient eastern prince."

I'm gripped with a desire to hunt that man down and end him. Poor Lydia. He deserves to die slowly, with his intestines being tugged through—

Lydia's eyes widen. "Why do you look so angry?"

"I'm going to end him." My fists clench to keep from unholstering my Beretta. "How far has he gone?"

She laughs again, but I'm not sure why.

"What's funny about this?"

Ruby puts a hand on my arm. "Maybe get all the facts before you jump to any conclusions."

"Huh?"

"Based on the way Lydia talked about Quinn earlier, I

doubt he was forcing anyone." Ruby's whispering, but Lydia can hear her clearly, I'm sure.

"Not at all," Lydia says. "And he and I weren't romantically involved. I took care of things for them—cleaning and cooking and running errands as long as they weren't to places I might be seen by anyone who might have known me in Port Gibson. Quinn's definitely not conventional. No one would have accepted his bizarre family, but he didn't mistreat me or any of them."

I drag a deep breath into my lungs. "You're free now. Anyone can see you—and no one will harm you. I promise."

Her grin is so wide I can practically see her molars.

"Ruby?" Kimball's head pokes through the doorway. "Ah, there you are." He looks from Ruby, to me, and then to Lydia. "I don't mean to interrupt anything, but they're asking for you inside."

"I'd better go back," Ruby says.

"Oh." For the first time since the day she brandished that honey pot at me, I'm not sure whether I ought to follow Ruby inside.

Lydia might need me more.

Ruby doesn't seem to need anything from anyone these days, if I'm being honest. Not anymore.

"You can stay and catch up with Lydia," Ruby says. "Heaven knows you've got enough things to catch up on." I listen for hurt or anger or irritation and don't hear any. Her tone and breathing and facial expressions are all calm and even.

"Alright, if you don't mind."

"Don't worry." Kimball holds out his arm. "I'll take good care of her."

Instead of batting his arm away, or telling him to shut up, Ruby slides her arm though his and marches through the door. Before I have time to think about what that means, Lydia's talking.

"I'm so glad you don't have to leave right away." She wraps her arms around me and pulls me close for a hug.

It makes me shaky, and not in a good way. I try not to stiffen. She doesn't deserve to feel . . . rejected as a friend, but having her touch me, even innocently, feels *wrong*. Wrenchingly wrong. Thankfully she releases me quickly.

"So you work for the new chancellor?" Lydia tosses her head at the door. "She's a lot smaller and . . . I don't know . . . younger than I expected."

"She's magnificent," I say. "Truly, I've never known anyone like her."

"That's great." She swallows. "So do you have to go back in there soon? Or do you have time to, I don't know, go for a walk?"

Every single person in that room just voted Ruby in as chancellor, and they were ready to tear me apart for my split loyalties and relation to my dad. I'm not sure my presence will help her much right now. It's not like there are plotting Port Heads here who might try to take her out. "Let me check in with Adam first, but if he's okay with it, sure. I could take a walk, probably."

Her smile is as beautiful as it ever was, and I'm just so relieved that she's alive. The past few years haven't been full of rainbows and moonbeams. It's nice to find out that there were a few good secrets kept too. Even if she has had to hide all this time because of my dad. Will I never be finished with the fallout from the awful mistakes he made? Will people never stop blaming me?

I slide through the doorway and scan the room. It takes a good twenty seconds for me to spot him—talking to two of the guards in the corner. I could activate my earpiece, but then everyone else wearing one would also hear. I'm not sure Lydia needs that much attention aimed at her. I catch Adam's eye and he breaks off his conversation and jogs across the room. "What's up, boss?"

"Do you have things under control?" I ask.

Adam's lips purse with bemusement. "You think they're going to let Ruby out of their grips right now? Every single one of them is giving her their best advice, not only for running the Unmarked, but for integration of WPN and the Marked. I'm not sure that even *you* could pry her free."

"Oh, no, I mean, I was thinking of going for a walk, if you can handle things here without me."

Adam chokes.

I pat his back. "You okay?"

"Just surprised." He spits a wad of gum into his hand. "Sorry. That went down wrong."

"Good thing it came out," I say. "I've heard that when I give the Heimlich, I press a little too hard."

Adam grimaces. "Please don't break my ribs unless I'm actually dying."

"Noted," I say. "So are you alright here?"

"Uh, sure," Adam says. "I'm just not sure why—"

Lydia, tired of waiting, apparently, pushes around the corner. "Sam?"

Adam freezes. "Who's that?"

Why don't I want to explain? Maybe I'm embarrassed by the clinical trial. Or that I didn't even realize she hadn't died. Or that she's been suffering, hiding alone all this time because of my dad.

"I'm Sam's friend, Lydia."

"And you two are going for a walk together." Adam frowns. "Sure, yeah." He glances over at where Ruby's talking to a half dozen members of the Deca-Council with Kimball at her elbow. "Looks like *Kimball* and I have it covered."

"Good." And as an added bonus, I don't have to sit and watch Kimball fawn all over her while I try not to put my fist through his teeth.

"I thought you were smarter than this," Adam mutters.

"Excuse me?" My voice is low, thrumming with hostility actually, and I'm not totally sure why.

"That guy likes her," he says, his voice just as low. "I shouldn't care, I guess. I mean, they both love medical, scientific crap, and they both rule nations, and they're both absurdly beautiful. Actually, you're right. Take your walk. They make the perfect couple. Why fight it?"

A growl rumbles in my chest. "Shut up, Adam."

"You won't be able to hear a thing I say on your walk," he says. "Or see a thing they do, so you'd better get going."

I trust Ruby. Of course I do. And I haven't seen Lydia in *years*. I'm not doing anything wrong, whatever he may be implying. "I'll be back in an hour. Reach out on the headset if there's any trouble."

"Oh, I think you can already see the only trouble we'll be dealing with."

He means the councilors, surely. Ruby laughs and Kimball touches her arm. She leans toward him, not away from him. But I trust her—I know she loves me. And I'm not doing anything wrong, catching up with Lydia.

Adam's the one who's wrong.

So I pivot on my heel and walk out.

Lydia has to trot to catch up with me. "Is everything alright?" she asks.

If her hearing is even close to mine, she just witnessed every word of that interchange. "You heard everything, I assume." As I walk, she matches me, step for step. We're both quick, so we make good time. We exit the building and jog down the steps.

She doesn't say anything; she just keeps pace alongside me. Down one street, around a corner, and down another. It's peaceful, actually, jogging at my natural pace and not slowing down. Ruby's not really one for physical exercise, and her legs are *so* short. If I were dressed for it right now, I'd go for a good long run. As it is, I settle for a brisk jog instead. I'm not sure Ruby would even be capable of being next to me this long without talking, but Lydia's like me. She appreciates the silence. We've gone a few miles before I slow down, my shoulders finally relaxing, my irritation with Adam dissipating.

She swallows. "Ruby's your girlfriend, isn't she?"

Why hadn't I already told her that? "She is."

Her exhale is gusty and exaggerated. "I should've known you couldn't be single. You're *you*." She looks up at the enormous oak trees lining the street.

I stop in the shade, my head turning toward her slowly. "What does that mean?"

"Look in a mirror and you'll understand." Her smile is shy.

"Come on, you're just as good looking as I am." Something doesn't feel quite right in my belly. I shouldn't have said that. It's like I've lost my mind.

"I am?" This time, her smile is broader, more confident. As it should be.

"Of course you are." A memory of her mouth pressed to mine, my heart thumping in my chest, her hand brushing against my thigh, surfaces unbidden. I shake my head.

"Are you alright?"

I clear my throat. "I'm fine. Things are pretty crazy right now, but it's always nice to get good news."

"Is that all I am?" Her voice is breathy, sort of. Not quite normal. "Good news?"

I shrug. "Great news?"

She laughs. "Moving in the right direction, anyway." She steps toward me.

And I back up reflexively. "You're moving too."

"I always move toward you." She inhales sharply. "Even when I technically shouldn't, because you have a new girlfriend."

"We weren't ever—"

Her eyes meet mine, wide, intense. "Weren't we?"

I—I don't know. I'm not sure what to say. "We never—"

She steps toward me again. "You are the only man I've ever kissed. The only man I ever wanted—"

"Whoa." I put my hands up and back up again. "I do have a girlfriend, Lydia. Ruby."

I hate the hurt look in her eyes. "And clearly you haven't dreamt of me for the past few years the same way I have of you."

Oh, man. This is awkward. Adam was right. I should not have gone for a walk with her. I should have stayed in that building.

When she steps closer a third time, I don't have the heart to move away, nor can I. I've been backed into the trunk of a tree. I think about it from her perspective. To Lydia, we never really broke up. She and I were . . . not quite together, but we were something in that clinical trial. Something that mattered. Something that makes me feel guilty about my feelings for Ruby now. I should step away. I should tell her that I love Ruby, because it's true.

"I have, you know, dreamt about you, every day." Her eyes meet mine, and she doesn't even have to look up much. She's only an inch or two shorter than I am—several inches taller than even Rhonda. Her voice is low when she says, "and every night." Her hand brushes against my thigh again, just like our first kiss. "No one I've met has ever even come close to you, Sam. No one."

"I thought you were dead," I say.

"I'm not, though." She licks her lips. "I'm right here. Alive, and very, very well." She steps closer still, almost her entire body pressing against mine.

And I sidestep so quickly that she loses her balance and nearly falls headfirst into the tree that was behind me. Which makes me feel even more guilty, because a tiny part of me wanted to kiss her. Badly. I haven't dreamt of her for years, but only because she wasn't alive.

Or, at least, until right now, I thought she wasn't.

The Lydia I knew was strong. Almost unbreakable, like me. She was fierce, and funny, and kind. She made me laugh. She made the horrendous clinical trial almost bearable. And now she's here, and she wants me, just as I am. Ever since we found the cure, I've felt like I'm badgering Ruby to death trying to keep her safe—while she does all the important things and I buzz around her, adding very little.

I shake my head. What am I thinking?

I'm an idiot.

None of that matters. Ruby is *home*.

"I have to get back," I say.

"You love her, then."

"I do," I say. "A lot, and for a long time."

She doesn't ask anything else, just walks alongside me in silence. But when the council building draws into view ahead of us, she slows down and clears her throat. "I guess I should feel bad for telling you how I felt, but I don't. My claim precedes hers, technically."

"Your claim?" I shake my head. "You did nothing wrong," I say. Technically, I didn't either. It's not like we kissed. But we shouldn't have even come close. I'll have to evaluate why I waited so long to tell her what Ruby means to me.

"Well, I'm not hiding anymore," Lydia says. "And I find myself suddenly unemployed. So if you valued our friendship at all, could you maybe talk to that Adam for me? See if he can get me a job or something? I've still got the same accuracy and skill I always had—I've kept up my marksmanship and agility skills, even working for Quinn. I swear that even though you don't like me in the same way that I like you, I won't embarrass you if you're willing to vouch for me." She steps closer. "And maybe one other thing. Can you keep that embarrassing stuff I said between us? I'm not sure I could ever look at Ruby again if she knew that I—"

I nod. "Sure." I owe her that much for never questioning whether she really died.

When she beams at me, for a moment I wonder whether I'm making a mistake, finding her a position in security. She says she wants to forget what she said earlier, but . . . her eyes don't look regretful. I could find her a place somewhere else, probably. Somewhere far away.

Ultimately, though, she and I are the same, only her life was taken from her whereas I went to Port Gibson and reunited with Ruby. Getting her a job and helping her find a position near the only friend she has is the least I can do.

"I don't have to talk to Adam," I say. "I'm his boss." I start toward the council building again, walking as quickly as before.

"With the way he was talking to you," she says, "I figured—"

"He was sharp with me because he felt that you and I shouldn't be going out for a walk together." I glare pointedly. "Turns out, he had a little more insight than I did."

Her answering grin is dutifully sheepish. "Well, thanks. I really appreciate it. Even if you're already taken, at least we can still work together, right?"

"I guess." I jog up the steps.

"It means a lot to me to know I have at least one friend left," she says. "Thanks."

Her parents are both dead, just like mine. But that reminds me. I pause just outside the door. "I met Raphael," I say. "My little brother. Or, I guess technically Ruby found him for me, but the point is, he's alive."

Lydia drags a breath through her nose. "You think . . . maybe?"

Her sister was Marked right before she joined the trial

—both her parents had died. It's why she signed up. She had nothing left to lose.

"She was too old for the suppressant," she says.

"I may be a jock," I say. "But I can do basic math. She'd have been halfway through her final year when we discovered the cure."

Her eyes fill with hope. "So, maybe."

"Maybe. And Rafe kind of runs things, so the next time we're down, I'll have him search." I push through the doors and jog down the hall.

"Thank you," she says.

"Of course," I say. "I don't want to create false hope, but a few amazing things have happened."

"And I'm sure the future will do nothing but improve." She's half smiling when I push through the back door into the council chamber.

To my surprise, the council members are all gone. Adam's playing cards with Frank in the corner. And Ruby's asleep . . . on Kimball's chest . . . on the sofa in the corner.

"There you are," Adam says. "We wanted to just leave you, but Ruby insisted we wait until you were done with your . . . *reunion* with your friend." Adam scowls at Lydia.

Kimball's arm is wrapped around Ruby's small frame. They look . . . cozy.

It pisses me off.

"Well, I'm ready to go now."

"I'm Lydia." She holds her hand out toward Adam. "I hear that now the cure has been discovered, we can do this again."

He doesn't take her hand.

"Or maybe that wasn't right?" She glances at me.

"You haven't been inoculated yet." Adam's lip curls. "I'd hate to expose you unnecessarily."

"If she got sick, I could fix her immediately," I say. "No reason for you to be rude."

"Wait, *you* could?" Lydia's eyebrows rise. "I heard Ruby found the cure." Her voice is hesitant, unsure. It breaks my heart a little bit to hear it.

"Ruby figured it out," I say. "And she has antibodies in her blood, but the virus that gobbles up Tercera was hiding inside of me."

"That's amazing," Lydia gushes.

"What is?" Ruby stretches and rubs her eyes.

"Sam saved the world," Lydia says.

Ruby beams at me. "He really did."

And suddenly, I regret being annoyed that she was asleep on Kimball. I mean, it's not like I was here. All she was doing was sleeping. I know better than anyone how run ragged she's been. Everyone wants something from her, and it takes a toll.

"Well, whether you want to shake my hand or not, Sam has offered me a job, so we'll all be working together a lot in the future, and I'm delighted."

Ruby straightens. "Wait, what?"

Her reaction makes me think that maybe I should have run that decision past her.

But it's Kimball's smirk that really gets me. I really do hate almost everyone when we first meet, but I swear I dislike that guy more with every passing minute.

12

RUBY

I smile at Madeline, who has placed another platter of pancakes on the table. She curtsies, which is bizarre, and then ducks back into the kitchen.

"These pancakes are actually pretty good." I stab one more and drag it onto my plate.

Sam takes the rest of the stack and douses them in syrup. "I know you hate being in charge and yesterday didn't go the way you wanted, but the food is a dramatic improvement over our first trip together." He smiles. "Remember that rabbit you caught?"

I laugh. "That I made you kill and skin?"

"That stew." He cringes. "I don't miss setting snares for our meals and cooking them over a fire."

"Me either."

"Things have changed," Sam says. "But I hope you know that—"

"I'm going to kill her." Adam stomps through the door. "I'm going to wrap my hands around her throat and squeeze until she stops talking."

"Who?" I ask.

But Sam's face is unsurprised. He knows. "Lydia hasn't

worked in security for a few years, but she'll adjust to working with a team quickly, I swear."

"Oh, that's not the issue." Adam spins on his heel and glares at Sam. "She's telling all of us that we're cleaning our guns wrong. And then she told me that I cock my hip. She says if I stop, my aim will be nearly perfect." Adam's face turns bright red. "My aim is *already* perfect."

"Not beyond thirty—"

"No." Adam shakes his head. "Not from you, too. You go deal with her, and make her understand that her job is to be a cog in a wheel that I turn, or I will either kill her or quit."

"You can't quit," I say softly.

"And I doubt you could kill her," Sam says. "At least, not if you don't stop cocking your hip."

Adam lunges for him, and Sam's up like a flash and darting out the door. So much for a nice breakfast and a discussion about us post-Lydia.

"All the pancakes are gone?" Kimball sounds so mournful when he walks into the room and stares at the empty platter.

I laugh. "I'm sure Madeline will be out with more any moment." I stand up. "She seems to believe that I'm on the brink of starvation."

"Where are you headed?" He grabs a piece of bacon off the plate in the center of the table and stuffs it into his mouth.

Men are all the same. "I've got a huge stack of resolutions to review. Apparently interim chancellors can only do a very short list of things, and approving resolutions isn't among them. Which means they've backed up for weeks." I groan. "Not that I know what any of them mean. My head already hurts and I haven't even started yet."

"I'm sure you have plenty of people offering to help

you," Kimball says. "But my dad does a lot of this kind of stuff too, and I've been helping him since I turned twelve."

"Grooming you much?" I laugh.

"Oh, he has high hopes, my dad."

He looks nothing like Wesley, other than his coloring, but sometimes he reminds me of him anyway. His laugh, the mischievous glint in his eye. Something. It makes me happy . . . and sad.

"Hey, are you okay?"

He's observant and empathetic like Wesley, too. Maybe that's it. "I'm fine," I say. "You just remind me of my best friend Wesley sometimes."

"The one who died?" He cringes. "I'm sorry. Is that good, or just painful?"

"Both?" I shrug. "But probably mostly good. I think the saddest thing about losing someone is that you start to forget them."

"You lost your dad, too, longer ago than you lost your friend." He shakes his head. "My mom died almost ten years ago now, and I miss her every day."

"Ten years ago?" I close my eyes.

"She was a senator."

Oh, no. My horrible father accelerated her. "I'm so sorry."

"I don't blame you, you know." Kimball exhales. "Your dad was a lunatic. You couldn't control that."

I shudder. "Please don't call David Solomon my dad."

"Sam did, back at the Capitol—"

"I know," I say. "And that bugged me too. He's never done it before, but I think he was distracted."

"I'm sure. I can't believe he thought she was dead, and they had that horrible experience together, and now she's alive. That would throw anyone."

"Probably," I say.

"You're remarkably okay with it," he says. "If my

boyfriend had a super hot woman from his past show up . . .
it would tick me off, probably."

I laugh. "It would have made me insanely jealous a few
months ago." I snort. "Maybe even a few weeks ago."

"But not now?"

I shake my head. "Sam's the reason I'm so calm. He
taught me something, you know. He told me that love is a
choice, every day, every moment. We choose to be with
that person, and we choose to turn toward them, and that
choice is how we love them."

"But doesn't that mean that we can choose to *not* love
someone every day, too?" Kimball frowns. "I'm not sure
that reassures me."

He *is* a lot like Wesley. He would totally have said the
same thing. "People are always changing. Not in every way,
but in a lot of things. Josephine told me a little bit a few
days ago, about how she loved my dad—"

"I thought you didn't call David Solomon—"

I shake my head. "No, I'm talking about Donald Carillon, who I knew as Donovan Behl." I pause. "It is confusing. I'm sorry. I found out about each odd thing in
sequence, but it's a lot to keep track of when it's dumped
on you like it was."

"I think I've got it now," he says. "Your mom loved your
dad—and then she met your bio father."

"That's it," I say. "And I think the issue is that she
changed and he didn't see it. He didn't change alongside
her. But love is the choice that even when the person we
love shifts, when they grow or change or make mistakes,
we'll be there with them. We'll change and grow with
them."

"I like that," Kimball says. "But do you wonder whether
Sam's really up to it?"

"Up to what?" I arch one eyebrow. "To choosing me?
I'm not tall and gorgeous, but he doesn't care."

"Oh, believe me, you don't have to tell me why he'd choose you. No, that's not what I meant."

I blush. I really wasn't fishing for a compliment, but it's nice to get one anyway. "What did you mean?"

"A few things he's said just make me wonder. You're obviously a phenomenal leader. You inspire people. You want what's right. People see that, and they respond to it, but Sam seems to hate it. Will he be okay, changing like you said, while you grow into the leader these people clearly need?"

"But I don't want to keep leading them," I explain.

"You don't." His voice is flat, like he's not even questioning me. And that's why I know it *is* a question.

"Of course not. I hate all this. My plan is to integrate the Marked and the Unmarked and the people of WPN and then once they're all equal, slowly move the whole group of them toward being free—a real republic. Then they'll vote for someone new, and *I'll* be free."

"That's an ambitious and admirable goal," Kimball says. "Truly."

"Why do I sense a but?"

"Because that's going to take a really, really long time."

"Why do you think that?"

"Uh, because it's true. What you just laid out is ten years, minimum. And I know you're young, but that's still a long time."

Ten years? He can't be serious. "I think I can get it all done in six months."

He laughs. "Oh, Ruby."

"Look, just because your dad's president of CINOW, it doesn't—"

He grabs my upper arms. "I wasn't attacking you. I'm trying to be realistic, but that's fine. Maybe I'm wrong."

A tiny thrill shoots up my body when he touches me. I shake his hands away. "Look, I appreciate your input on these resolutions, but only because I want to get through them *faster.* You'll see. As soon as I'm done with them, I'll start making my plans for the transition, and then we'll present that to the council. While they're mulling it over, I'll head back to WPN to start my tour through the rest of the ports. On the way, we can stop in Baton Rouge and get you the paperwork from my aunt on the cure. You can take that, and several blood samples from Sam, of course, and head back home."

"Okay," Kimball says. "Whatever you say."

His poking and prodding notwithstanding, he's unbelievably helpful with the resolutions. He thinks of a dozen things I don't, and he does it effortlessly. "You're making me wish my dad had been a president instead of a mad scientist."

"You're just now thinking that?" Kimball winks. "Because that would have been my hope, like, the second I found out he created Tercera."

I slug his shoulder.

"That was pathetic," he says. "Like a kitten batting at me."

"You sound like Sam."

"Has anyone ever shown you how to throw a punch?" Kimball isn't laughing now. He looks deadly serious.

"Of course not," I say. "I'm so small that—"

But he's shaking his head. "You have Adam and a host of guards, I know. But even though you're small, there are quite a few holds you could learn, and some great blocks. You should learn them immediately, at least some basics."

Sam never mentioned that, but probably because it's not like anyone would ever get through him. But what if he's not around? He could be on a walk. He's been taking a lot of those lately.

Or what if we do change too much, and not together? I don't doubt that Sam loves me, and I surely love him. But there are no guarantees. He has to choose me every day, and if he doesn't . . . Maybe Kimball's right. It wouldn't hurt me to learn a few things about self-defense.

Plus . . . "He would be so *shocked* if I knew some moves," I say. "Alright. We finished this stuff way earlier than I thought I could." I wave my hand at the piles of paper.

He stands up. "Great. Let's go. We can practice in the courtyard—no one will even notice we've left."

"Wait." I fold my arms. "Why are you the one to teach me? What about my brother, Adam?"

Kimball shrugs. "The thing is, I've watched them. Sam's good, and so is Adam."

"But?"

"But I've been trained in karate since I was small, and a bunch of wrestling moves, too. Before I went through a growth spurt, I was worried I'd be short, so I learned some holds that are great for people who are smaller. If you want to surprise that boyfriend of yours, I'm your best bet. I can teach you something he won't expect."

The thought of shocking Sam . . . I love the idea. "We'd better hurry."

Kimball's a better teacher than I expected him to be. He's not quite as tall as Sam, or as broad, but he's awfully close, which means he's a good test subject to see whether the holds he's teaching me will work.

"This is a rear naked choke hold." He shows me how to lock my elbow with my other arm.

"But your neck is so big," I say.

"The advantage you have with Sam," he says, "is that he won't know it's coming. You can pretend you're going to kiss him, like this." He flips me on my back and holds himself above me, his head lowering slowly.

I'm already breathing heavily from the exertion of learning the wrestling moves, but when my heart races, it's not because of that. At least, not entirely because of that. "Okay."

"You can make him think you're going to kiss him, right up until the very last minute." His breath washes over me, warming my entire face. That's why I'm blushing, I'm sure. Then he stops. "But then, right here, when he's ready for that kiss." He wraps his arm around my neck and flips me over, locking his arm into place.

Ugh.

He releases me. "Your turn."

My back aches, and my hair is full of grass, but it's still a good feeling. I'm not very natural with this stuff, but I'm learning just the same. "Alright," I say. "So I lean over him like this." I can't quite brace myself over Kimball, he's too big and I'm too tired. But I lean against him like I would against Sam. "And then I lower myself down until—"

"Uh." A grunt. "What's going on?"

Sam.

I leap to my feet and run my hands through my hair.

Kimball's still lying on his back on the grass, a lazy look in his eye. I kick him. Hard. He's smiling as he sits up.

"It's not what you think." I gulp.

"I don't know what to think." Sam looks honestly baffled.

I can't think of a single thing to say I was doing, so I just confess. "Kimball was showing me some wrestling holds and a few karate moves."

Sam laughs.

An honest-to-goodness belly laugh bubbles out of his mouth.

He doesn't think the idea of women in security is dumb. Rhonda and Lydia have both worked with him, so that's not it.

It's the idea of *me* doing something to defend myself

that he finds utterly absurd. I'm not sure whether I'm more hurt or angry.

Probably equal amounts of both.

I stomp inside.

Sam grabs my arm, but I twist away. "No."

"What?" His eyes are wide. "Why are you mad? What did I do?"

"Nothing," I say. "*Nothing at all.*" He hasn't even been here all day. He's been with *her.* And that's when I realize that as zen as I've been trying to be, every minute that ticked by made me more and more nervous. And that makes me angry.

Sam scowls. At me. He never scowls at me. "Can we talk?"

If he were entreating me, maybe. But while he's angry? Even though he spent all day gone? I shake my head. "Sorry, but actually, you're right. The idea of me learning anything physical is stupid. Because I don't have time for that. Kimball and I were just about to go meet with some members of the Deca-Council."

Kimball, the darling, stands up immediately. "Right. I almost forgot."

"Should we change, do you think?" I look at the grass stains on my shirt.

"Probably." Kimball shrugs. "At least, I intend to."

"Then we'd better hurry."

I race inside and change into a pair of clean slacks and a red blouse. To his credit, Kimball's waiting on me when I get out.

So is Sam.

"I'm sure your friend is probably really lonely," I snap. "You ought to have dinner with her, surely. Don't bother coming with me. Adam and Lucas will be more than enough to keep me safe from the perils of the council building."

And then I duck out the door.

We're halfway down the sidewalk before Lucas and Adam catch up. "What's going on?" Adam asks, glancing back over his shoulder every few seconds. "Why are we running away?"

"We aren't," I say. "We're just in a hurry because we're late."

And in a bizarre stroke of luck, two members of the Deca-Council are actually at the chamber, eager to discuss the framework of my plans for integration. When there's a lull, Kimball leans over. "Still think he's going to effortlessly change alongside you?"

"Shut up," I say.

But secretly, I'm worried. What if he's right?

Ⅹ 13 Ⅹ

RUBY

It's easy to throw myself into the work. There's more than enough of it for a dozen people, let alone one. Even after the council leaves, their demands run through my brain on repeat. I've made so many lists that I need a list of all my lists. I've been lucky to have Kimball around. He's a third party who's not interested in the outcome, which makes him perfect to give honest feedback.

"You're like George Washington," Kimball says, once we're alone.

I pat my hair. "You like my big powdered wig?" I force a pained smile. "And my wooden teeth?"

He rolls his eyes. "You know what I mean. He shaped the nation—he set things in motion. And now, you get to do the same. The people love you—here, down in Galveston—they credit you with ending the pandemic. They credit you with fixing the world."

"People are dumb," I say. "I didn't do any of that."

"They believe it, and that's what matters. And I've heard the story. I'm kind of on their side. You did do it, and even without Sam's blood, you were well on the way to finding a preventative measure all on your own."

I shake my head. "My dad did that, not me. Adam's been telling you the wrong things."

"Look, Washington didn't singlehandedly rout the redcoats, but he got credit and people listened to him because of that. I'm not sure anyone else could have united the fragmented people in early America."

"Yeah, yeah, I see the parallel. WPN. Marked. Unmarked. And then me."

"You've got a leg in each camp. The Marked revere you—"

"You're getting that from when they locked me up? Or when they threatened to drain my blood until I was dry and dead?"

"The jokes are entertaining, but look at the facts. Of course the Unmarked are excited about the prospect of joining forces with WPN," Kimball says.

I straighten and stretch. I've been looking at requests, and inventory lists, and territory lines, and census data for too long. My back is killing me. "What are you talking about?"

"WPN has better tech, better infrastructure, and all the military power. The Unmarked are asking WPN to share everything they have . . . and offering virtually nothing."

"Allies are always a good thing." My stomach rumbles. Did we work through lunch again?

"Um, not necessarily. This is more like telling a needy neighbor that you're happy to share your barbecue. Then they show up with a box to steal your cable, a hose to take your water, and an extension cord to jack your electricity, too."

"Don't be so dramatic. The Unmarked have professionals and infrastructure."

"They have river ports that are barely scraping by and a

handful of people who understood things Before but haven't adjusted well to life in the brutal and unwashed present." Kimball frowns.

"You think WPN's going to be angry?"

He shrugs. "I'm not very religious. Maybe they'll be surprisingly charitable and generous. But if I were the neighbor about to have someone else sponging off my water and my power bill, then yeah. I'd be kind of ticked with the lady who rubber stamped it and handed them a hose."

Good grief. "Okay, well then we need to limit the how and the why. Maybe we focus on WPN sharing training and IP and less actual resources."

"That's a smart move. Mitigate the transfer to make it look like you're sharing knowledge more than anything else. Plus the citizens of WPN will be seen working to incorporate the new stuff, so that will alleviate any possible irritation." Kimball pauses. "Look, my point was this." He taps on the table. "Pay attention, Ruby."

I look over at him. "Yeah. I'm listening."

"You want to fob this whole thing off onto someone else—anyone else. I get that. It's not like you grew up hoping to become a greedy despot. However, if George Washington had walked away . . . America might not exist. If you want these people to pull together, which is better for the Marked and the Unmarked, you're the only one who can convince them all to do it."

That's unfair.

But possibly true.

Just or not, everyone seems to be giving me credit for the discovery of the cure. Sam's dad was too close to all of it for them to laud him. And even though my dad created the problem, he didn't mean to release it, and my actual father was a dictator, but his people loved him. So on all counts, everyone is poised to credit me, not discredit me.

The world is a strange and bizarre place.

And I know what my dad would say if he were here. He'd tell me the beach will have to wait when people's lives are on the line. There's no way for me to go back and get that time with him again, but it's hard not to remember that if he'd taken me that day, it would have been a memory I could have kept forever.

Similarly, if I do this, if I commit to trying to make this integration and union of the three groups here work, it won't be done in a day. Or a month. Or six months. It'll take time. It'll be obnoxious and exhausting. And it'll be time I can never get back. I'll become a different person than if I had just bailed and hoped someone else took over.

Staying might save the world.

But it might cost me Sam.

"We leave tomorrow morning," I say. "And you can get home soon after that. I'm sure your people are eager for your return."

The door to the small side office we've been working in opens. Sam steps inside. "I don't want to interrupt, but it's almost three o'clock. Did either of you plan to eat anything?"

"I've been in such a rush to finish all this so we can leave," I say, "but you're right. We should take a break."

"Will you finish it all today?" Sam takes in the stacks of paper scattered all over the table dubiously.

"I'm determined," I say. "And we'll stop in Baton Rouge to get Kimball what he needs to take back to CINOW."

"Is there somewhere to land in Baton Rouge?" Sam asks. "Or do you mean we'll go by car?"

I frown. "Going by car will take quite a bit longer. I'll ask Adam about the possibility of a flight to Baton Rouge. If that won't work we might be better off flying straight to Galveston and then driving to Baton Rouge. It has been a while since we were there. We should check in with Aunt Anne and Uncle Dan and Rafe. Don't you think?"

"My people's Marked population is stable," Kimball says. "So there's no rush on my end. I'm happy to stay and help as long as you need me."

I expect Sam to say something snarky, but he doesn't even frown.

"Have you eaten?" I ask.

Sam glances at me, unsure who I'm asking. "Me?"

I nod.

"I did, but I'm always hungry."

"Want to have lunch with me?" I smile.

"As your Security Chief?"

I shake my head. "As my Sam."

His smile is like the sunshine after a long day indoors. "Of course."

As simple as that, the tightness around my heart eases. We may not be changing in the same ways naturally, but if he's listening to me and I'm listening to him, we can work the rest out. I'm sure of it. I stand up.

"If you'll have Madeline send me some sandwiches, I'll put together a proposed list of tech that the Unmarked need most and the personnel they'd need to get them functional." Kimball smiles. "You deserve a break."

"You don't have to keep working," I say.

He shrugs. "I don't mind."

"I'll be back." I walk through the doorway and down the hall and Sam matches my pace like he always does when we're going somewhere together. As we walk out the exit and down the street, my hand swings at my side, only a few inches away from Sam's. I want to reach out and slide my palm against his. I would, normally, but everything feels strange. Almost like I don't know him or what he's thinking. We're almost to the house, where we'll have to interact with Adam and Madeline, and I still don't know what to say. At this point, anything will do. "What have you—"

"So I was—"

Sam turns to face me.

I look up at him slowly, unsure what he's feeling. Angry? Sad? Scared? Not scared, surely. It is Sam, after all.

His face gives nothing away—the Sam mask is firmly in place. Intense is the only thing I can read for sure.

I sniff. "You can go first."

"I wasn't sure what to say," he says. "I'm not sure whether I'm in trouble."

The corner of my mouth turns up just a hair. "In trouble?" I can't quite help my smile. "I'm not your mother."

"You're far scarier than she ever was," he says. "And I love you more."

At the word *love*, the air whooshes out of my body and I have to fight back tears.

Of relief.

"Hey, are you alright?" Sam's arms wrap around me to steady me. "When you weigh eighty-five pounds, you can't skip meals."

I laugh. "I'm fine."

He drops me like I'm a hot potato.

I catch his hands and tug them back around my waist. "But that doesn't mean I don't need you close."

Sam's body freezes, the muscles in his arms taut. "You're not mad at me?"

"Should I be?" This time when I look up at him, his eyes are sad and concerned and nervous. "What did you do?"

And it hits me like a load of bricks. He's been spending all his time with Lydia. I was worried he might like her, but I didn't think . . . What if he *did* something with her? Something he hasn't wanted to pressure me about . . . She's older and she's gorgeous and rage and despair both pulse through me in quick succession. I shove his arms away. "Did you do something?"

He should be denying anything. Everything. But instead

he blinks at me, like I've startled him. Like he doesn't know what to say.

"Did you kiss her?"

Sam swallows and shakes his head slowly.

"But you almost did." I'm the last person on Earth who should be judging him. I kissed Wesley. Twice. And he's denying it, if not very energetically. But his slow, guilty face means he wanted to, and somehow that still guts me.

"Lydia told me she had feelings for me." He runs his hand through his hair, dislodging the rubber band, and it tumbles around his face. "I care about her, too."

"What kind of feelings?" I try to keep my voice as even as I can.

He shrugs. "I'm happy she's alive."

I should have known he didn't kiss her—Sam would never do anything like that. He's not like me. He never messes up. But he *wants* to kiss her, maybe for the same reason I kissed Wesley. I wasn't *sure* about Sam and it scared me. He gave me space and time with no strings, no anger, and no hostility. Or, at least, not much hostility. He is a human being, after all.

And this is the girl he chose before me—my Sam doesn't choose people lightly. That means she meant something to him. The only reason they aren't still together is that he thought she *died*. And she's way more suited to him than I am. She's tall, tough, strong, fast, gorgeous, and a defense prodigy. Ugh. I hate this.

But I owe him the same patience and courtesy he gave me.

"When I kissed Wesley—"

Sam grabs my hand. "I didn't kiss her, I swear."

I squeeze his hand lightly. "I know that. I believe you."

He nods.

"But when *I* did, you dumped me."

His eyes look impossibly green in this moment, the

shade of the new oak leaves. "I only did that because you hid it from me."

"You didn't exactly come running over to tell me that Lydia came on to you several *days* ago."

"So are you dumping me?" Sam's voice catches. "If you are, just do it."

I didn't want him to break up with me, but I needed it. I had to figure out what I wanted. "Should I?" He seemed so sure then. I wish I knew what to do.

He shakes his head. "No, you shouldn't. I love you. That hasn't changed."

"But something major has." I think about what he's told me about the clinical trials—which is not much. He hates talking about them, but she shares that with him. And they're very similar. It's painful to consider, but they probably have more real similarities than we do. We share a history, but so do they—and they're both permanently different as a result of their past. Plus. "You're not too keen on me running the Unmarked and WPN," I say. "And it bothers you that I am." I don't want to say this next part. "I thought I could fob the whole thing off and be done with it, but I wasn't raised to do that. My dad taught me to do things *right*, even when they're hard. Even when I'd rather be at the beach." I inhale. "This transition from the current situation to a better one is likely to take a while. Not a few days or weeks or even months. I'll be at this for at least a year. Maybe more."

"I know."

"And you hate it."

"I do hate it," he says. "I hate the politicians. I hate the threat this all poses to you. But most of all, I hate that we can't *be* together except in little snatches of time."

He's right that I don't see him very much anymore.

"And I'm a bother to you, not a support." He throws his hands up in the air. "I don't belong here."

"You handled security in Port Gibson."

"Not for a president. Not for a queen."

I blink. "You don't think you're qualified?"

"I have a very particular set of skills," he says. "It lends itself to covert ops. Or breaking down walls. Or even taking out an army, but I'm not exactly a General."

"We're not at war," I say. "That's kind of my whole point. And the more I move forward, the less clear the path out becomes."

Power corrupts. He doesn't say it. He doesn't have to say it. I know he's thinking it.

"I choose you every day, still," I say.

"How can you choose me, if you're choosing the opposite of what we said we wanted?"

And that's the gist of it. We did agree to something, something I wanted too, but sometimes dreams and reality don't mesh. "I can't be who I am and walk away, Sam. I know you want me to do just that, but if you really love me, if you really know me, then you aren't surprised by what has happened. If there's a chance I can unite these three groups, if I can bring the best of all three together and make us all stronger, I have to try."

"We all become our choices over time," he says. "That's what makes us—not some innate qualities. You can still choose to walk away. Someone else will step in—they always do."

But Kimball's right about this. Sam either doesn't see it or he's intentionally looking away. I have a bizarre, unearned chance to do something *right,* and there's no way of knowing who else would step in if I bow out. It would be wrong for me to walk away.

It might break me.

But losing him could do the very same.

"What are you thinking?" I ask. "You never volunteer

anything. I have to drag it out of you, and lately, I just don't have the time or energy."

"You don't have time for anything anymore," he says. He doesn't sound bitter, but he does sound . . . resigned, and somehow that's almost worse.

"I don't know the right answer here. If I dump you, and I'm tempted to do it, it's not because I don't love you. It's because I do."

He shakes his head.

"Look, I know you love me, but I am who I am."

"This transition matters more to you than *we* matter?"

"You're saying our success is predicated on me adhering to a vision of the future we outlined over a campfire?" I want to curl up and cry. "Are you saying we won't make it if I don't walk away?"

"No, I'm not."

But to him, my acceptance of this task shows my lack of commitment, and I feel like he only likes the me *he wants me* to be.

"This might make you angry, but I have to ask." He inhales and then exhales. "Are you saying all of this, in any part, no matter how small, because of Kimball?" His voice is small, quiet, and utterly unlike him. "Because even I can see that he's like a grown-up version of Wesley."

"Don't be ridiculous."

"Am I?" He looks down at his feet. "Because I've thought a few times that if he hadn't died, Wesley would have been far better suited to helping you with all of this stuff you're doing than I am."

I reach for Sam's face and turn it back toward me. Then I kiss him, slowly, firmly, purposely. "I love you, Sam. I like you, too. When I want to kiss someone, it's always you. The person I want by my side in a boardroom and on a war field is the same person—you. The person I want to see in swim trunks . .

. is you." I brush my fingers across his lips. "There hasn't been much time for us lately, and we've had a lot of bizarre things tugging us apart. But there *will* be time for you and me during all this. It won't be in a small town like we planned, not yet anyway, but we'll have dinners. Meetings. Breakfasts."

"Okay," he says. "Alright."

"Alright, what?"

"If you aren't having second thoughts, then neither am I."

I kiss him again—and I don't have any thoughts at all, only feelings. All of them good ones. By the time we reach the house, Madeline's almost done with dinner. After we've eaten, I feel much better.

Kimball shows up a few moments after we finish, in time to clean up the leftovers. "I did the integration chart, and I've drawn up some preliminary state options. I'm thinking the Unmarked, with their almost four hundred thousand citizens, should get four or five states. I'll show you what I had in mind. And then the Marked would have two—or they can integrate into the others. You'll have to talk to them and figure out what they want. And then you make the ports in WPN into states—and you can set up some kind of local voting based on that. It would mirror the old United States plan, of course, and—"

Sam stands up.

"Hey." I grab his hand. "You can stay. I'd love to hear what you think."

He glances at Kimball. "It looks like you two already have it covered."

When he walks out the front door, my heart cracks just a little bit. Because if he's not even going to try and be a part of what I'm doing . . . I'm not sure how long we'll be alright.

❧ 14 ❧

SAM

The flight to Baton Rouge is uneventful, right up until the plane starts to descend.

Shouting from the cockpit has me sprinting to the front of the plane. "What's going on?"

"It's a—" The pilot squints. "It looks like a giraffe."

"You'll have to circle around." I can see them quite clearly. "It's actually a family of giraffes. A local zookeeper released the animals when the government was destroyed by the accelerant and city services shut down."

"What's going on?" My body blocks Adam from entering the cockpit.

"I'll go explain the ascent and circle," I say.

The pilot and copilot are both swearing quite a lot.

"I'm sure the plane is at least as terrifying to the giraffes as they are to you." I smirk. "Once you circle, I bet they'll have moved away."

They do, of course, and we're able to land safely. The hike from our landing strip to the edge of the Marked settlement is barely more than four miles, but Ruby's legs are so short that it's a real pain for her. She's always cranky when she has to hike. It's kind of cute, actually. I've learned not to talk to her, no matter how leisurely the pace.

"It's starting to get hot." Ruby tugs at the bottom of her blouse. "I think we need to make plans for transportation a little better in the future."

"Absolutely," Adam agrees.

"You need to make communication lines your number one priority," Kimball says. "We've got reliable phones lines and even cellular towers in each of our main cities. We got them up within four years of the collapse."

Bully for them.

"I'll have to see who we have with the knowledge—"

"I'm happy to send a team for you," Kimball says. "You probably already have all the equipment and structure in place. You'll just need to make repairs and updates, as well as—"

"We'll let you know if we need that," I say. "My father had a phone he used periodically, so there's some kind of network in place already. We'll definitely look into it."

"I'm sure the team Ruby selected as her executive committee will have the details on that," Kimball says. "They're heading straight for Galveston as a control center for now."

"I've been wondering about that," Ruby says. "Because the technology *is* already developed, and Solomon had plenty of other, more advanced things. So why didn't he have better long distance communications in place?"

"What are you really wondering?" Adam asks.

"I think he intentionally only allowed local telephones in each port, and no outside communications except with himself."

She's right, of course. It was entirely within his reach to make communications more accessible, so why would he limit them? Unless he had an ulterior motive.

"I think he wanted to keep the people isolated and in

the dark to control their ability to reach out to others. He could essentially tell the citizens of World Peace Now whatever story he wanted, and he'd only have word of mouth to combat his side of things—assuming the Port Heads maintained the party line."

"How 1984 of him," Kimball says.

"I'm pretty sure those principles go further back than that," Ruby says. "Dictators and monarchs have been around since long before America existed."

Kimball laughs. "I'm referring to a book by a guy named George Orwell. He wrote about a society where the government monitored everything and controlled everyone. Now that I think about it, that book is kind of like Solomon's guidebook, only in that story, they did away with religion, whereas Solomon harnessed it."

I hate how well read and knowledgeable this guy is, and that I can't even contradict him since I haven't ever heard of that book. Or any of the other stuff he offers, like advice on ruling and setting up republics and voting and redistricting. Or lively opinions on various medical findings. It almost feels like he and Ruby are speaking another language when he starts spouting off words like hematoma and aortic or cysto-something or other. Having him here makes me feel worse and worse about myself and what I bring to the table. Ruby picked me over Wesley, but she didn't want to rule then—and Kimball's an awful lot like Wesley, who she followed around for years.

There's a bit of a misunderstanding when one of Rafe's perimeter guards spots us and fires a warning shot, but it's quickly sorted out. "I'll just radio Rafe to confirm," a short black kid says.

I nod. "Tell him his brother didn't shoot you yet, but he's losing his patience."

He gulps. Luckily Rafe picks up right away. "You said they're on foot?"

"Rafe, it's me," I shout. "We came by plane, but had to land a ways off and hike."

Even through the crackle and pop from the old walkie, Rafe's signature laugh is loud and crystal clear. "I should have expected something like that. Yeah, let them through."

The kid's look is sheepish when he waves us past.

"They have preteens securing their perimeter?" Lydia has sidled up on my right side. "Really?"

"That kid's probably our age," I say.

"No way," she says.

"It's the suppressant." I shake my head. Anyone who hasn't seen the Marked *knows* they're on a hormone suppressant, but they don't *get* it until they witness it themselves. "They don't grow right, like they're suspended in time. It keeps them alive, but their bodies don't reflect the amount of time they've spent here on earth. You'll get used to it with time."

She shudders. "I hope not. Please tell me you aren't leaving me here."

"My brother's here," I say. "You'd be lucky to stay."

Her eyes widen. "I'm sorry. I didn't mean to insult them. I'm just surprised, that's all."

I don't meet her eyes. "Whatever you say."

Rafe's not alone when we reach him, but he waves us into the cafeteria of the hospital where they've set up their main administrative operation. I don't recognize many people. Sean, with his distinctive scar, Anne and Dan Orien, and their kids, Rhonda and Job. There are about two dozen kids I've never seen before, all of them gathered around a long table. They all stand when we enter.

"Who are all these people?" I ask. "Did we arrive at a bad time?"

As Rafe's scans our group, the WPN guards, including Adam, secure the perimeter. They may not be my friends, most of them, but they take to their training well, following the protocol I outlined perfectly every time. "You have a few new people now that you're back."

I clear my throat. "I'm not 'back,' at least, not in the way you're thinking."

My little brother frowns. "Then what—"

"Rafe, we can give you some time if you're in the middle of something," Ruby says. "But we have some pretty big news to share when you're ready."

"We all want to hear it," a girl with short, spiky hair and hard eyes says. "You've pretended to be some kind of dictator long enough, Rafe."

Ruby's head swivels around until their eyes meet. "Who are you?"

The spiky haired girl puts her hands on her hips. "I don't have to ask you that. You're Ruby Behl Solomon, erstwhile Savior, and Queen of WPN. The one who has been sending us truck after truck of badly needed and quite late supplies."

Ruby blinks. "I'm Ruby, yes."

"I'm Yvonne. And I'm the Marked representative from Lafayette."

"From Lafayette?" Ruby glances at Rafe.

"You didn't think Rafe ran every settlement?" Yvonne's eyebrows climb. "I swear, Rafe, you are unbelievably—"

"I did what had to be done," Rafe says. "And thanks to me, you're all cured. You're welcome."

"It was high-handed," a boy with hair black as pitch says. "But he's right that he did what no one else could. He summoned everyone who could travel without consulting with us, and that landed us all in a lot of trouble when that accelerant hit, but he provided food and shelter and nailed down the cure in time."

"For most of us." Yvonne looks terribly short on gratitude.

"So you're all . . . representatives of different Marked settlements?" Ruby asks.

"You Unmarked know nothing of our lives," the black-haired boy says. "Because you didn't care about us at all."

"We provided the suppressant for years," my aunt says.

"Your medals will be ready any day," Yvonne snaps.

"Stop," Ruby says. "There's no reason to fight right now. If you're the leaders among the Marked, then I need to speak to you all." She walks to the front of the room. Her eyes meet mine and she tosses her head slightly, asking me to accompany her. I jog to the front of the room, and she smiles at me. "This is going to be a lot of information. You might want to sit down."

They do, although you can tell by their faces that following an order from anyone, even her, chafes. I've been insisting they're much older than they look, but for the first time, I wonder whether that's true. What makes someone grow up? Circumstance? Experience? Or is it education and training? Because if so, they're the very age they appear. No guidance, no support, and no teaching from anyone more educated or clever in a decade. Hormones now raging for the first time in their lives.

It's very possible that we're dealing with a bunch of irrational children—who won't even allow anyone to call them children. I don't envy Ruby. In fact, for the first time, she may be facing an audience she can't cajole, charm, or convince.

"Before I begin, I'd like to know who I'm dealing with. I'll introduce myself, and I hope you will, too." She looks up and down the table, making eye contact with every person in turn. "As you may have heard, when I was a baby, a man named Donovan Behl stole me from the hospital." She doesn't flinch, or apologize, or look embarrassed. She's come to terms with her past. "His real name was Donald Carillon. His sister and her husband have been working here tirelessly for the past few weeks distributing the cure and directing the provision of any extra medical care you all need."

A few people murmur, but it seems she's right. They'd heard that part.

"That man created Tercera—not to infect people and destroy the world—but to create a vaccination he hoped would *spare* people. Ironic, but true. And through a terrible twist of fate, and a few evil men, his virus was released, but the two different defensive strategies he was creating both disappeared. One into my blood—a triple shot of anti-bodies—and one into the blood of my boyfriend, Sam. Again, ironic."

"You could say that again." Rafe smirks.

"Sam's little brother, Raphael, became one of your representative leaders in another bizarre turn." Ruby's eyes travel up and down the table again. "My actual biological father was even worse than the tragic Donald Carillon. His name was David Solomon, and he was the leader of WPN. He had just enough information about the release of Tercera that he was able to hide away and gather followers. My mother shot him not long ago, with some serious encouragement from me, and in another bizarre twist, the people of WPN made me their next ruler, a job I have never wanted. Now that you're up to speed on that, I'd like to hear from each of you as to who you are and where you call home."

"I'm Yvonne," the spiky girl says. "And I'm the chosen representative for the Marked in Lafayette. We were about twenty thousand people strong before the suppressant started failing."

"I'm Nathan," the boy with black hair and dark, almost midnight eyes says. "I'm the representative from Alexan-dria. We only had twelve thousand or so."

Beaumont. Lake Charles. Natchitoches, Shreveport,

Lufkin. All of them small. All of them proud. All of them independent.

"Some of us were pretty hard hit," Nathan says. "I think I only have about eight thousand alive in Alexandria now."

Ruby closes her eyes. "I'm so sorry."

"You are the one person who doesn't have to apologize," Yvonne says. "Well, maybe you and Sam." She purses her lips. "But you said you had news."

"I do." Every single eye in the room is on her. She's calmed them down quite a bit, listening to who they are and where they're from. But mostly, showing them she's a real person, and that she knows they're real people, too. Showing them she can listen. Every single day, I realize she can do something I didn't know she could do—connect with people in a way I never could. "I actually have quite a lot of news to share. I'd ask that you hear me out until the end before you react, if that's at all possible."

Heads nod all around.

"I have no interest in ruling WPN, as you all know. The only reason I took the position at all was so that I could halt their plans for a Cleansing of the Marked population—they meant to wipe you out entirely."

Grunts and scowls and huffs. They knew.

Ruby doesn't mention Rhonda or the ordeal she endured to secure control. If they've heard about it, which I imagine they have, not bringing it up will make them respect her more. She and Rafe had a real split over all of that. "I went back recently with the hope that I'd either pass control off to my half brother Adam, or that I'd be able to transition it quickly to a republic or democracy of some kind."

That grabs their attention.

"But will they continue to send us aid?" Yvonne's shoulders straighten and her hands brace on the table.

"What about the people who are saying some of us can

live there?" Nathan asks. "Who will make sure anyone who goes is treated well? Who will hold them accountable?"

They don't *want* her to step down. That takes me by surprise.

Ruby holds up her hands. "Hear me out. I hoped my brother Adam would take over, but he has no interest, and the people didn't really seem amenable to another turnover of leadership either. I realized quickly that it wouldn't be a speedy proposition, transitioning to another form of government entirely, especially with all the changes lately, like finding a cure for all of you."

"Something else you did," a boy in the back with nearly white blond hair mutters.

"The fact is, I'm going to have to make these changes one tiny step at a time," she says. "And that became quite clear when I tried to encourage the citizens of New Orleans to elect a representative themselves, instead of simply following someone who was appointed to rule over them. After finding two great candidates, both of whom had to be nominated, and then supporting them by having them speak to the assembled crowd, the citizens of New Orleans voted in the same person my biological father had appointed to represent him for the past decade." Her lip curls in disgust. "They didn't change a thing, even when I begged them to, and that tells me this isn't going to be a simple shift."

"So you're not quitting," Yvonne asks, "and leaving us to manage alone?"

Ruby shakes her head. "I'm not." She sighs. "But it gets more complicated, still. See, when I went up to Nashville to try and help the Unmarked make their decision on a new chancellor to replace Sam's dad—"

"They picked Sam, didn't they?" Rafe's arms are crossed over his chest, his eyes practically sparking.

I shake my head. "They hated me, actually." I snort. "I don't really blame them."

Rafe frowns. "Then who—"

"In a very bizarre turn, they elected *me* to take over—"

"You?" Rafe stands up. "How could they possibly want you? You're only seventeen."

Every eye widens.

"Yes, how could they?" My brother means well, but I still think he may need a good thrashing. He needs to learn when not to run his mouth. "Let's review. She, as a seventeen-year-old girl, traveled through Marked territory, which most of them wouldn't risk. She infiltrated WPN and found her dad's journals, discovering the truth that the leaders of WPN and the Unmarked had been concealing for ten years. She risked death and endured beatings from her abominable bio dad. She united the people of WPN. She fought her way up north and discovered the truth, and then she survived what almost no one else on earth did— the wrath of our dad. She defeated him with the help of her friend Wesley. Then she came back down here and convinced the Unmarked to free Anne Orien. They rushed down and saved all of you—and then she went back to WPN and subdued them. How could the Unmarked want someone that young, naive, and stupid to rule for them?"

"They get WPN's tech and trade partnerships," Rafe says. "I guess that part makes sense."

I am going to thrash him—that idiot.

"Yes, that's why they decided," Kimball says. "So that they could get WPN's tech."

"Who is this?" Rafe asks. "And who's that?" He glares at Lydia.

"Lydia is an old friend of Sam's," Ruby says. "She's not of strategic importance, so I'll let him introduce you later. But this is Kimball Ryson. He's the son of the president of another government, one that's one and a half million citizens strong. They call themselves CINOW, and they're located in the Pacific Northwest. They're comprised of the former states of California, Idaho, Nevada, Oregon, and Washington."

Every single eye is on Kimball.

"Hey," he says. "Nice to meet you."

"He came to ask for the cure," Ruby says. "He heard it existed from a few people who decided to escape the madness of WPN in light of Solomon's death, but you don't need to look so alarmed. They're friendly and have no intention of harming anyone."

"That makes an alliance with WPN a little more desirable for the Unmarked, knowing there's an outside threat." Rafe grunts.

"I'm not a threat, I assure you." Kimball's smile is a little more predatory than I realized before.

And I wonder whether he's being entirely honest. Are they a threat? Land is essentially unlimited at this point, but do they lack tech? For the first time, I begin to really think about what ulterior motives Mr. Surfboard might have. I'm ashamed I wasn't considering these angles before. It's kind of my job, after all.

"My point," Ruby says, "is that I'm now going to be combining WPN and the Unmarked into one government and one people. There's nothing to keep us apart, not anymore. And that logic also applies to all of you."

Every single one of the Marked representatives jumps to their feet, their eyes flashing, their hands going to their weapons.

I draw mine and hold it against Rafe's head. Adam's gun is trained on Yvonne. Every single one of my guards could put a bullet between the eyes of these kids before they could harm us. But they're all aiming at Ruby.

They may be young, but they know what matters.

"Whoa," Ruby says. "Everyone needs to calm down."

She turns toward me, and I know what's coming. No, no, no, don't ask it of me. "Sam, tell everyone to drop their weapons, please, and drop yours."

I hold her gaze.

"Sam." She's not upset. She's not terse. She's not even afraid, as far as I can tell. A million yammering heartbeats in this room, but hers is steady. "Please."

I grit my teeth, but I nod and lead the way by lowering my gun. It's one of the hardest things I've ever done.

"We mean none of you any harm, nor will I *ever* require any person or group to join with us who doesn't desire it." She sighs. "I'm sorry I didn't make that clear before. No part of our visit is a threat—not to you, or your people. I'll never threaten you."

Rafe drops his gun back into his holster.

Yvonne follows him.

And the others do the same, slowly, incrementally, until finally, no one is pointing guns at anyone else.

"The beginning is always the hardest part," Ruby says. "But I don't want this to be scary. I have prepared some paperwork that outlines what I'm offering. The Marked will all have several options. They can join the Unmarked. They can join WPN. You should know that both sides are going to be joining in the future, but obviously the cultures are not very similar. Or, if both of those options sound bad, the Marked may remain separate. You don't all have to do the same thing, either, if you are all amenable to this option. I'm fine with each citizen among you making his or her *own* decision—to join one of the other groups, or to remain in a Marked settlement. But before that vote can take place, you all have a decision to make. Because the other option you can choose is to be completely disassociated from both groups. To remain your own, sovereign people."

"I don't understand," Yvonne says.

"As the leaders of the Marked, I'm allowing you to opt in or out," Ruby says simply. "If you opt in, you'll become part of the integration. If you opt out, other than sending aid in the short run and sharing tech with you, we'll honor your geographical boundaries and leave you alone."

"You'll cut us off?" Rafe's nostrils flare.

Ruby shakes her head. "I hope very much that it won't be like that at all. If you choose to remain a separate entity, I hope we'll be friendly. I certainly mean to offer as much help as you'd like. But I won't force it on you, any of you."

"But if we vote to join you?" Yvonne asks.

"Then each citizen will be free to move—to WPN or to the Unmarked settlements. Or you can stay here. Depending on how those numbers work out, we'll assign your regions voting power and a representative."

"You're saying we can join this union, whatever it is," Nathan says. "Or we can stay solo."

I nod. "That's exactly what I'm saying. We haven't come up with a name yet, but when we do, it'll represent everyone who's a part of what I hope will be a free and prosperous new country. You are welcome to join, but there will be no hard feelings if you don't trust me. I completely understand the difficulty there."

As much as I hate the idea of Ruby ruling for a long time, even I can't deny that she's impressively good at it. By the time we leave the room, every single one of those representatives votes to join Ruby's new, as yet unnamed nation.

And I think if it came down to it, they'd die for her, too.

15

RUBY

"Of course I'll come with you," Rhonda says. "I'm so bored here that I almost painted my toenails."

I laugh.

"But seriously. You said you need me to help with inoculating the WPN citizens." She cocks one eyebrow. "Are you sure that's the reason?"

"What else would I need you for?" I glance from Adam to Sam. "I'm swimming in guards, in case you hadn't already noticed."

Rhonda glares at Lydia. "Oh, I noticed the extras."

"Do you know her?"

Rhonda's full lips flatten until they're practically white. She nods.

"You don't like her?"

"She's manipulative."

That's all I get? I'll have to press her later. I'm sure if he were paying attention to us, Sam could hear us right now, which means Lydia could too. They're chatting and laughing, so I'm sure they aren't listening, but if I were Rhonda I'd want to make sure übergirl couldn't hear me talking smack. "Well, I'm happy you're coming back . . . for more reasons than just your help with the inoculation," I confess.

"You're lonely," she says.

"Is it that obvious?"

"You look tired." She wraps an arm around my shoulders. "I'll have words to say to Sam, if this is how he takes care of you."

"She won't eat when she's working, and she's stubborn as a mule." I didn't realize Kimball had reached this corner of the room. "Don't be too hard on Sam. He tries his hardest. It's Ruby who won't listen."

"Looks like you're trying too." Rhonda glances at me meaningfully.

"I do every single thing I can think of to help Ruby."

Kimball's a little too flirty for my comfort, but what can I do about it? Kick him out and start a war? "Kimball has been a tremendous help, seeing as he's been raised to rule and I want nothing to do with it."

"I bet," Rhonda says. "Plus he's not bad to look at." She releases me and leans against the wall casually.

"That's on my résumé," Kimball says.

"Oh yeah?" Rhonda asks.

Kimball nods slowly. "It says 'killer smile' right under 'ab model.'"

"Sounds like California hasn't changed much," Rhonda says. "Even after a devastating pandemic."

"The truth is hard." He smiles.

And he didn't lie. He does have a killer smile. It doesn't make my stomach flip and flop, but it's beautiful.

Actually. I wonder whether Rhonda might like him. He's tall and ripped like Sam. He's got a great smile. He's smart and funny. And he's pretty impressive in his own right at hand-to-hand combat. He may not have the love affair with guns that Sam has, but he seems to know his way around a trigger, if his boasting can be believed. They might be perfect for each other. "I imagine you'll be spending quite a bit of time together."

"Kimball's leaving soon, isn't he?" Sam's voice is deceptively soft.

I jump. He snuck up on me too. I need to pay better attention to my surroundings when I'm chatting. "Actually, I'm not sure."

"I told Ruby I'd stick around as long as she'd have me," Kimball says. "Once I'm not helpful anymore, I'll head home."

"As soon as we get what we need here, including Job and Rhonda, I hope," I say, "we'll be headed for Galveston briefly . . . to explain what happened in Nashville, and then we'll go to Mobile. I can spread the news as I do my tour through the ports."

"Smart," Kimball says. "The people will take the news much better from you directly. You can assuage any concerns they have about the power shift."

"Ruby's a lot better at this than I realized," Sam says. "It seems intuitive, actually."

"She is a natural," Kimball says.

"Which means she likely won't need much help," Sam says. "So you can go home right away after all. It would be terrible if the infected citizens of CINOW were forced to wait on the cure so that you could flirt."

Rhonda laughs. "Oh, sorry." She covers her mouth with her hand.

Is she kidding? "I hardly think—"

Sam takes my hand. "It's just a joke, of course."

"Kimball's guidance has been indispensable," I say. "I don't think that was very funny."

Other than ducking his head a bit, Sam doesn't reply at all. But he stays by my side. If things are still a little bumpy, well, that's to be expected. With Rafe, Yvonne, Kimball, Nathan and the other representatives' help, we're able to assemble most of the Marked kids. None of the stadiums in Baton Rouge have been well-enough maintained to be safe, so we opt for the streets, but Adam and Sam work with Rafe to create a large tower and an amplification system.

I announce the recent events and our plans.

And the next day, they vote.

"It's kind of sad that all the Marked kids combined total less than a hundred thousand," Aunt Anne says. "Didn't you say there were that many people in New Orleans alone?"

I sigh. "Not quite, but close. Almost ninety thousand Marked kids are here, now that they've nearly all gathered for treatment. And Rafe says there were more than eighty thousand people in Baton Rouge, last they counted—before the accelerant and all of that."

It is sad.

"How long will it take to tally their votes?" Aunt Anne asks.

"Uncle Dan and Adam and Sam are running that part," I say. "And I can't say how happy I am not to be involved with one small aspect."

But in the end, nearly every one of the Marked kids votes to join under a combined government, but not to assimilate into either the WPN or the Unmarked settlements. Surprisingly to me, they all vote to submit to my rule.

Ninety thousand kids who can't trust anyone—why would they trust me?

"It's not really much of a shock," Rafe says. "You brought them the cure. You've sent them aid for weeks. And now you're offering to provide tech, jobs, training, and infrastructure. All the things they never had—and you're letting them *choose* whether to take it or not." Rafe steps closer. "They do trust you when they trust no one else. Don't let them down."

"I'll do my best," I say.

"I believe you," Rafe says. His voice drops and so do his eyes. "I'm sorry about what I put you through before."

"I told you she always does the right thing," Sam says quietly from where he's standing in the corner.

But Rafe barely knew his brother then, and now I'm taking him away again. "You could stay here for a while, Sam," I say. "If you wanted to spend some time with Rafe. I could let Adam take over—"

Rafe laughs. "I should have trusted Sam's word—and I should have accepted that he won't be parted from you. Ever."

If I hadn't been looking in her direction, I never would have noticed Lydia's scowl at Rafe's words. I might not have noticed when she ducked out the door and disappeared, either.

"We have a lot of details to address before you leave," Yvonne says. The others all chime in as well.

I'm still watching the door when Sam quietly follows Lydia out.

He may not be willing to stay in Baton Rouge without me, but he's not entirely focused on me anymore either. As I'm pelted with questions, I realize that maybe it's fair. It's not like I'm doing nothing but moon over him. If that's what he's hoping for, well, he won't get it from me. Probably ever.

My heart still squeezes painfully in my chest.

"It's not all going to be decided in a day," Kimball says. "In fact, your best bet might be for all of you to put your suggestions in writing and then submit a form. I know you're not accustomed to doing things this way, but now that you're going to be combining under one government with WPN and the Unmarked, I'm sure the tech can be provided for you to come up to speed on things like computers and printers." He glances my way. "Right?"

"Absolutely. In fact, the first thing we likely need is an accurate census that we can draw from the ballots recently cast. We can elaborate on those with the information on each citizen who wasn't old enough to vote—but right after that we'll need a list of what supplies you need in each area. Food, agriculture, tech, all of it."

The rest of the day disappears like butter on a hot pan, and the one after that does too. But then, finally, after some of the mundane details have been worked out, we're ready to head for Galveston. It feels like all I do lately is convince people around me that I'm the best person to run things— and I don't even want to do any of it. The irony is dreadful, honestly.

I hug Aunt Anne and Uncle Dan goodbye. "I hope you'll finish up here soon," I say. "And then you guys and Rose can come out to see Galveston."

Aunt Anne rubs the side of her nose. "We were actually thinking of staying here."

I blink. "But Uncle Dan has always run Port Gibson."

"We did that for the three of you," Uncle Dan says. "We never dreamed of hiding there forever." He shrugs. "They need us here. Ongoing medical care, setting up their infrastructure. It's shocking how much needs to be done, and they have no experts in, well, really, in anything at all."

"I get it," I say. "But don't forget that your kids might still need some of your expertise now and then."

"I hear you're going to be working on some kind of communication system," Aunt Anne says. "Then we'll only be a phone call away."

"I do hope the world is about to shrink down again," I say. "Now that people don't need to huddle and hide and isolate."

"Maybe we'll all have a trip to California in our future." Aunt Anne glances at Kimball purposefully.

"You'd be welcome," he says. "Maybe one of the only things that Tercera didn't change is the weather and the waves."

"I imagine real estate's more reasonable than it was," Uncle Dan says.

"Most of us have settled up north so far." Kimball beams. "So, not to sway you, but there are actually ocean front places available for free. We're planning to push for the resettlement of Los Angeles in the next year or two, with San Diego coming a year or so beyond that."

"Sign me up," I say. "I like Galveston well enough but—"

"It's not bad," Kimball says. "But nothing compares to San Diego."

"So I've heard."

"You should come with me and see it." Kimball's eyes stare into mine, bright blue and devastating.

When I drag my face away, Aunt Anne's mouth is hanging open and she glances from me to Kimball and then smiles. "Well. I look forward to an update just as soon as you can get those phone lines working again."

Rhonda stomps into the room, a huge duffel slung over her shoulder. It looks like she's been doing some scavenging.

"Wait until you get to Galveston," I say. "They have actual seamstresses and clothing companies making new stuff there."

Her eyes widen. "It won't smell strange? Or have moth holes I need to whip closed?"

I laugh. "None at all."

She drops the bag. "Then I'm going to be traveling a little lighter than I intended."

I roll my eyes. "Let's go."

Job's reaction when we reach the jet is the best, though.

"You are kidding me right now." His eyes are wide, his entire body frozen in shock, his jaw dropped so far it nearly touches his chest. "We're going to *fly* there?"

"We have to get the jet home somehow," I say. "But I'm glad you're impressed. This bodes well for the next few weeks."

He snaps to attention then. "You did say I'd have a research lab. That's true, right?"

"Oh, you will." I can't cram my agenda down people's throats with the Unmarked or the Marked yet, but no one within WPN dares contradict the *queen*. As much as it annoys me, their unquestioned devotion has some perks too.

As soon as the plane takes off, I close my eyes. Someone drops into the empty seat next to me. I open them reluctantly to see who it is.

Sam.

"You're not supposed to move around during takeoff, you know."

A smile plays around the corners of his mouth. "I'd heard that, yes."

"Where were you?"

"I wanted to talk to the pilot and copilot and learn what I could about the process."

"Always monitoring every angle. That's one of the things I love about you."

"Electronic things, mechanical things, they make sense to me intuitively, but I need to learn more about air strike capability. It hasn't been much of a concern until now."

I drop my hand over his huge warm one. "I've missed you."

He sighs. "Me too."

"I think I should start blocking off time for us. Breakfast, or lunch, or dinner. Or maybe all three."

"I do things other than eat," he says, his voice bemused.

"Then you pick something."

"I feel bad for mocking your attempts to learn self-
defense. I'm a little embarrassed I haven't taught you
myself yet, but maybe it's because you're so good at everything that I wanted something that was *mine*, my
contribution."

Does he think that if I can defend myself, I won't need
him? I squeeze his hand. "Sam, no matter what you teach
me, I won't be able to defeat someone your size."

"But maybe all you'll need to do is to shock them
enough to escape."

And if I need that, it means he's failed me. I can see
why he hasn't focused on this line of logic before now. "I'd
like that."

When he smiles, his chiseled jawbone, his high cheekbones, his full lips, and his sparkling golden eyes all sharpen
somehow.

It releases all the butterflies in my belly. "I love you."

"I love you, too. A lot. In pretty much every way."

I want to ask him about Lydia—all the jealous girlfriend
things. I want him to tell me she's nothing to him, and that
I'm still everything. But even asking makes me the needy
weirdo I never want to be, so I bite my lip instead. And
then I take a nap on his shoulder. Before I know it, we're
landing. Which makes sense. The flight isn't even an hour,
start to finish.

I'm sick of meeting with people.

I'm sick of talking to people—more like preaching to
them, here. But at least the Bible has some handy verses on
loving others and welcoming people into the fold.

I'm sick of people telling me I'm wonderful and cheering. It doesn't feel real, if I'm honest. Real people complain

and argue and throw you in holding cells. I keep waiting for the moment I find out that all the WPN citizens are pod people and I'm really going to be tossed in jail or fed to lions.

But that moment never comes.

Instead, the citizens of Galveston are wildly excited that I've managed to bring all these people into the same governing body. They're happy to help, happy to have the chance to win over the heathens, as far as I can tell. And far be it from me to deny them the chance to share something that matters to them. They all leap to help me line up the things we'll need to bring the Marked and Unmarked up to WPN standards.

I spend two full days signing requisition requests for the new telecommunication lines and reviewing the numbers of personnel, the lists of tech, and the quantity of each commodity we need to prepare for shipments up to Nashville, to Memphis, to Baton Rouge, to Alexandria, and to the other Unmarked and Marked cities.

Even so, before I know it, I'm packing. Time to go to Mobile and try to convince another round of people to oust the lousy representative that David Solomon chose in favor of one who actually wants to do good. Time to listen to more pandering and praise. And then I have to do it . . . five more times, once at each port. Ugh.

"Ruby, do you have a second?" Kimball's voice is nervous, probably because since we got back, he's been way down the beach. I don't know how he even made it all the way down here or who let him into my room.

I drop the pair of underwear I was packing and hope I'm not blushing too obviously. "Sure."

He glances at my suitcase.

Drat. He noticed.

He clears his throat. "Sorry to interrupt. I know you're leaving tomorrow."

"Right, for Mobile."

"That's kind of why I'm here." He shoves his hands into his pockets. He's wearing khaki pants, which is odd for him. He's usually either wearing a business suit or beachwear. I didn't realize he had other clothing.

"You're here because I'm leaving?" My eyebrows rise.

"Well, you know I offered to come, but one of Adam's guys stopped by to tell me that it's essential personnel only."

I frown. "Really?" One of Adam's men? So, one of Sam's men, is what he means, since Adam reports to Sam. I suppose I shouldn't be so surprised.

"As long as you need me, I'm here for you. My dad's not in a huge rush. Knowing the cure is coming is enough. But if you don't want me here, I can leave now." His brow's furrowed, his eyes conflicted.

I step toward him. "Kimball, you know that wasn't a message from me. Of course if you want to come, you're welcome. You've been tremendously helpful. So much of this is new to me, and you've been a wonderful guide, telling me what potholes to avoid and what things to do when I don't even know what to ask."

He exhales gustily. "Thank goodness. I was wondering whether I'd upset you somehow."

I shake my head. "Not at all. Truly, you've saved me over and over now. But I bet your family misses you. I do feel bad that I've kept you this long. I really ought to finalize some kind of official agreement of peace between CINOW and . . . well, we haven't chosen a name yet, so I guess I could sign for the Marked, the Unmarked, and WPN individually."

Kimball laughs. "Oh, we aren't worried about any of that. I've sent Dad a few letters, and like you suggested, I sent a few guys home with the doses of the cure like you said. He's already got our scientists working on replicating it. He sends his substantial gratitude." He braces himself against the large wooden post at the foot of my four-poster bed. "Actually, he said you should have insisted on something in exchange for that. You're new, so he's not going to hold you to your offer of the cure for free. If there's something we can do for you—"

"Stop," I say. "That's the old way. We can do better. If there's something like that I can share, I will. If there's something like that you can share, I hope you'll do the same. We won't repeat the sins of our past, and I hope you won't either."

Kimball releases the bedpost and steps closer, his body only a few inches from mine. "You're spectacular."

My heart races and my hands tremble. I can't quite breathe. What's going on?

"I've wanted to tell you that every single day since we met, practically. If your boyfriend is finally forcing me out, if it's time for me to go, then I can't leave without telling you. I know you don't know me very well, Ruby, but—"

"Stop," I say. "Don't."

"Don't tell you that I love you?" Kimball whispers. "Don't tell you that we're perfect for each other?"

I shake my head. "No. Don't say that, because it's not true. The person who's perfect for me is Sam. If you had any idea how much—"

"Oh, I know the history you share. I heard it in every single line of the story you told me. But shared history isn't enough, Ruby. It's not what keeps people together, and it's not what makes you a good match. It's shared vision, shared goals, and compatibility that matter if you're spending a lifetime with someone. I'm not ever going to pressure you in any way, but you should know that my dad would be *delighted* if we became engaged—and that has absolutely nothing to do with what I'm about to say. Nothing at all."

"Kimball, you know that I've needed your help. You

know that I'm eager to foster friendly communications between CINOW and—"

"Stop," he whispers. "That's not any part of *this*."

I look up into his eyes, and it's a mistake. A girl could get lost in those eyes, with that dark, almost black hair falling across his brow. But not me, because . . . "I love Sam. I'll always love Sam."

"If that's true, then I never had a chance," he says. "But when I watch you two, I see someone who dislikes everything you're becoming. He's pressuring you to leave, to run away from *who you are*, from what makes you different than everyone else out there. It's not that you're charismatic, which you are. It's not that you're absurdly likable, which you clearly are. It's not even that you're stunningly beautiful, which everyone probably appreciates. No, it's that you're so *good* that you're willing to walk a path you despise because you see that it's for the greater good. You'd rather tuck your nose into a book and research. You'd rather hide behind your brilliance, but you're not doing what you want like every other person in the whole entire world. You're stepping out of your comfort zone to be the champion of the disenfranchised. You locate and administer first aid to the lost. You encourage and cajole and bludgeon the selfish into being more than they are—and people adore you for it. You make the entire country the best version of itself, and you walk away without a single thing for yourself in the process."

I shake my head. "I'm so lost I have no idea what I'm doing most of the time—"

Kimball presses a finger to my lips.

And a single flutter forces itself free in my belly, and I *yearn* for a moment for a world that's different than this one. I wish I didn't love Sam so fiercely so that I could see what this is that I feel for Kimball.

But he's wrong that Sam and I only share a past. Sam *is*

my future. He's all I see. And if Kimball's trying to splinter that, the happily ever after that I deserve, then he doesn't really know me at all. And that's why he's not an option. Wesley could see me well enough to know that Sam was all I needed.

"Sam has never pressured me. He'd never do that. He's struggling now with figuring out what he wants in the future, but I don't fault him for that because I've changed *everything* on him. At the end of the day, if he doesn't pick the same future as me, I'll deal with it. I might even walk away from the world and watch it burn. The point is that my feelings for him don't leave any room for me to even flirt with someone else. I'm sure you understand that."

"I do," he says. "Believe me, I really do. It's one of the reasons I admire you so much."

"Good." My hands finally stop shaking. "And look, if you don't want to return home yet—"

Sam flies through the door like a heat-seeking missile and leaps for Kimball, hitting him in the jaw with a terrible crunching sound.

Inexplicably, Kimball takes the blow and comes back up swinging. The two of them roll around on the floor of my bedroom, smacks and whams and grunts filling the entire space.

My brain revolts at the thought. I am *not* one of those moronic girls who swoons when two guys fight about her. Is Sam really punching Kimball for telling me he likes me? This must be some bizarre, waking nightmare. Only, it's not. It's really happening.

Kimball ducks and backs up, and for the first time, there's a tiny opening between Sam and Kimball. Without thinking, I spring forward into that space. Sam's hand halts about half an inch from my abdomen, his nostrils flaring. But Kimball isn't as quick as Sam, and his fist connects with the side of my cheekbone, glancing off.

But even the glancing blow is *hard*.

I'm ashamed to say that I drop to the floor like a sack of potatoes.

And I wail. A little bit more than I probably should, but holy cow, it hurts. My entire face throbs. It's so much worse, even, than when David Solomon slapped me.

"You hurt her!" If Sam were a Doberman, he'd be frothing at the mouth and snapping his teeth.

I reach for him. "Enough. I was trying to stop the fight, and I wasn't thinking. I never should have flung myself between you two. It was an accident."

Sam collapses next to me like a puppet with its strings cut. "I'm so sorry."

Kimball's devastated, his gaze flicking from me in horror to Sam in rage.

"Just go, please," I tell him.

He leaves, thankfully.

"You didn't need to hit him," I say. "And we both know you were playing with him—letting him get a few hits in so you could whale on him longer. That wasn't kind."

He doesn't bother denying that. "But that guy's not who you think he is. Did he tell you that he knocked two guards out to get in here?"

"Because you wouldn't let him in?" The corner of my mouth twitches.

"Maybe," Sam says. "But he should have—"

I lean against Sam's chest. "Let's agree to disagree. I know you don't like him, and I get it. He basically came in here to propose, since you'd disinvited him on our trip."

Sam swears. "I'm going to—"

"I told him no," I whisper. "Of course."

"Duh," Sam says. "But the fact that he'd even ask you to marry him is ridiculous."

Only, I'm not sure Sam notices all the cracks in our relationship that an outsider might see. I wish he were right. I

wish the very thought of me with anyone else was absurd—
it certainly felt that way a few weeks ago. But part of me is
actually sad to see Kimball leave.

And I'm not sure what that means about me and Sam.
Nothing good, I'm afraid.

16

SAM

Ruby kicks a trashcan over, and bits and pieces of junk—including chicken bones from lunch, blech—fly across the floor. She freezes, unaccustomed to watching the results of a temper tantrum. It's not like she throws them very often.

"I swear, most days I have no idea what you see in her," Lydia whispers.

No one else could possibly hear her—she and I have hearing unlike the rest of the world. I sigh. "She's frustrated, and I don't blame her. Every single existing Port Head has been elected by the people to continue to serve. The very same people her biological father appointed before she took over are still in office, in spite of the choice she gave the people."

"How is kicking over trashcans and making a mess for the servants to clean up going to help?" Lydia's perfect brow is arched in disapproval. But then, she disapproves of virtually everything Ruby says or does. It grates on me.

"You've never done something stupid because you were angry?" I purse my lips, because Lydia does just that on a regular basis.

She crosses her arms under her chest. "All I'm saying is, she's in a position to do something about it, and all she's doing is complaining. If she doesn't like them, she should appoint someone else." She's not whispering this time, and it draws attention.

Adam's head whips around, his eyes flashing. "She doesn't want to appoint someone else. That's precisely the issue. She wants the *people* to choose someone better, someone she will be pleased is representing them. And now that she's gone to all this effort to give them this choice, they're choosing exactly what they already had."

"*Queen Ruby* could use a dose of that herself." Lydia's lips are twisted.

"What does that mean?" Adam asks.

"She doesn't appreciate what she's got," Lydia says. "That's all I'm saying." She turns on her heel and ducks out the front door.

"If you're not careful, your girlfriend is going to slit her throat," Adam says.

I roll my eyes. "Ruby won't slit anyone—"

"I'm not talking about Ruby." Adam scowls at me and stomps across the room toward Ruby. "Hey, maybe we go to the terribly unused gym that Quentin showed us and you can punch a bag instead of making a mess in here."

"I'm sorry," Ruby mutters, leaning over to clean up the mess she just made, and probably staining the knees of her fancy pants in the process. "I just don't understand it. How can I help the people if they're too stubborn and ignorant to be helped?"

It has been the same issue over and over. I get why she's frustrated, and I understand why Lydia's sick of hearing about it. Obviously what Ruby's doing isn't helping. She probably should either appoint new people, or blatantly tell the people she doesn't like the men and women who Solomon appointed. Short of that, they're going to keep voting for the people they think were chosen by God's anointed.

Rhonda pushes through the door, her eyes scanning the room. "I just heard. I bet Ruby's angry."

I shrug. "She didn't hate Quentin, at least. He's one of the better ones."

"Still." Rhonda shakes her head. "I thought she made it pretty clear that she loved the short lady. What was her name? Tina? She was fiery. I liked her, too."

"Yeah, well, maybe next election." Although, if we're still here, traveling from port to port in two years, I might take a page out of Ruby's book and start kicking trashcans myself. Or, you know, start shooting people. Something along those lines.

"Your girlfriend is outside, destroying the men in hand-to-hand. Something pissed her off pretty badly." Rhonda glances over her shoulder, like I'd better jog off to clean up my mess. I suppose technically it is my fault, since I brought her along.

"She isn't my girlfriend," I hiss.

"Tell her that." Rhonda scowls at me.

I walk toward the door.

"Don't you think it's a little unfair?" Rhonda whispers the question as I pass.

I pause. "Huh?"

"You sent Ruby's boy toy home with a sprained elbow and a limp, but you brought your little blast from the past along on the trip."

I don't pretend I don't understand her. "She's not a toy."

"And Kimball wasn't yours to break."

I pivot on my heel and glare at her.

"Has it occurred to you that if you're forced to beat your rivals into submission . . . maybe you're not as perfect for her as you think?" Rhonda steps toward me, her lips compressed.

"He wasn't a rival. He proposed to her, yes, as some kind of political alliance, but she turned him down flat."

"He didn't propose as an alliance, you dumb brute. You've changed so much lately that I can't even believe I used to like you," Rhonda says.

"Excuse me?"

"Are you pretending not to know I had a crush on you?" Rhonda's eyebrows rise. "Or are you pretending that you're not leading Lydia and Ruby both along, unsure which one you want?"

I swallow. "I want Ruby. Everyone knows that."

"Do they?" Rhonda tilts her head. "I wish I did. You're moody as hell. You stomp all over. Ruby and Lydia are both upset right now, but you're racing off after Lydia while Adam and I stay here with Ruby."

"Lydia has no one else," I say. "Ruby has three nations' worth of people who want to help her."

Rhonda pauses, and I wonder whether I've finally gotten through to her. "And why do you think Lydia's upset? Is it something that someone did or said to defend Ruby? Because if so, she has no reason at all to be angry, whereas Ruby actually suffered a big setback today."

I'm inches from the door, about to go check on Lydia. I can tell myself it's because Lydia's all alone, or that she's a threat to the others, but if I really think she's a threat, I should fire her. So why am I taking better care of Lydia than Ruby?

Maybe it's because Lydia's problems are something I can fix. And they feed my ego. What Lydia wants is my attention. If I go out there, the problem's solved. Ironically, Lydia's the one throwing a tantrum, even if she accused Ruby of it.

But I can't help Ruby—and she's surrounded by dozens of other people who can.

I reach for the door, but not for the same reason I was before. "Thanks, Rhonda," I say. "I needed that."

"I hope it actually helps," Rhonda says. "Because Adam and I were just talking about how we miss Kimball."

The door doesn't slam when I walk through it, and that takes a supreme act of will on my part. Rhonda and Adam are both my friends. If they're saying they miss Kimball, if Rhonda is warning me . . . things are worse than I thought.

The second she sees me, Lydia knees the guy she's fighting in the stomach and tosses him to the side. Rhonda was right—this was a tantrum to get my attention. "Let's go for a jog," I say.

Lydia smiles. I hate that she's so beautiful. It's distracting.

"Through the cemetery?" I toss my head. "The azaleas are still blooming."

"And I love all the Spanish moss," she says. "It's so . . . romantic."

Quentin may be a bit on the lazy side, but he keeps the city in wonderful shape. It almost looks the same way I imagine it did Before. It's warmer every day, and Savannah is humid, but there's a nice breeze, so it's bearable. At first, we just jog. It gives me some time to think. And unlike Ruby, Lydia's perfectly happy to enjoy a long silence. But eventually, I have to deal with this. "Lydia," I say. "The thing is—"

"You're mad about me beating up the men," she says. "It's bad for morale."

I swallow. "It's not that, precisely. It's *why* you were doing it. You and I talked about this before. You got upset in there that Adam called you out, but he did it because you were criticizing Ruby, my girlfriend, who also happens to be your *queen* and ultimate boss, and I can't have that on any level. You're acting out any time my attention isn't on you."

"I think not." She huffs. "I'm training the men, just as you tasked me to do."

She's going to make this hard. We're nearly a mile away. Plenty of distance to have a real conversation without worrying someone will overhear. I stop jogging and she stumbles a bit and then stops too. She turns around to see what's wrong. "We need to talk."

Her eyes widen. "About?"

"You and me."

Her heart races, as I worried it might.

"Actually, there is no you and me," I say. "But I think you're still hoping there might be, if you play your cards right. If you help me to see what a mess Ruby is—how she's not right for me."

Her face falls. "I'm not an idiot."

"No one has ever accused you of that."

"It's clear that you love her," she says. "But you're all wrong for each other. You see it too, but you're in denial."

"I'm not." If I grit my teeth, well, she's being annoyingly obstinate. "Why do you think I'm here? I'm telling you that this is *never* going to happen, what you want. I don't care about you like that."

Except, now she's smiling. "I've loved you for a long time, Sam."

"That sucks for you." I don't mean to hurt her feelings, but she's not listening. "I love Ruby, and I have for a very long time."

"Okay." She shrugs. "I'm patient."

"If you can't accept what I'm telling you and stop throwing fits, I'm going to send you away."

"But you haven't yet," she says. "And you're here, on a run with me. Not in there with Ruby."

My hands clench at my sides. "You don't know what you're talking about."

"Don't I?" Her eyes sparkle. "Alright, maybe I'm wrong, but it's a risk I'm willing to keep taking."

"Let me be as clear as I can. The next time you flirt with me. The next time you throw a fit like this that demands my time. The next time you annoy me in the slightest, you can't work near me anymore. I'll transfer you to one of the ports. Permanently."

"Okay," she says.

She doesn't flirt with me on the jog home. She doesn't smile at me. She doesn't stand too close. She doesn't do a thing wrong, but I feel like this entire attempt was a complete waste of time. When the house we're staying in comes back into view, I draw up sharply. "Did you understand what I was saying, Lydia?"

This time she's beaming ear to ear. "Oh, you were crystal clear. You love your girlfriend, and you're not at *all* threatened by your feelings for me. That's why you had to go for a five-mile run with me to tell me that, so far away no one else could overhear."

I'm going to put my fist through something any second. I know it. "That's not—"

"It's fine, Sam, I swear. You'll either realize I'm right and she's wrong for you, or you'll finally man up and propose to her. Either way, I won't have to wait very long for my answer. And you were right that the tantrums I was throwing aren't helping my case. They're too much like something she'd do. I promise those will stop."

"She doesn't throw fits," I say automatically. But also because it's true. Ruby gets angry sometimes, but she never engages in petty attention games. Never. It's one of the things I adore most about her.

But I do think about what she said the entire flight to Mexico. I'll either man up and propose . . . or I'll realize Ruby's wrong for me. She's right that eventually we'll either get married, or we'll break up. That's what happens. You either make a permanent commitment, or things don't work out. Ruby turned me down once before, but I was only proposing so I could help her take care of Rose. I was doing it for the wrong reasons.

We spend the next day touring all over the picturesque La Ciudad de Carmen. I never really relax, but I come as close as I possibly can to it.

"Mexico was wiped out," Jose says. "In fact, not a single soul was left alive when we decided to repopulate this area six years ago."

"That's so sad." Ruby's eyes are wide, her lip trembling.

"It was devastating," Jose's wife Lilian says. "But it has been nice to see life returning to the area, albeit slowly."

"None of the children?" Adam asks. "There weren't Marked here?"

Lilian shakes her head. "Unfortunately, no. I think that there were some pretty ugly wars that raged in this area in the time after the United States' government officials were wiped out. At least, David Solomon took credit for keeping the United States safe from that by using the military force he took over."

I try not to think about what things must have been like down here.

"And why did you decide to repopulate this area?" Rhonda asks. "It's pretty far removed from the other WPN ports."

"Ah," Jose says. "Well, the answer to that is right here. This area has always been the number one supplier of this in the Americas." He gestures to the grove of small trees behind him. The leaves are wide but also long, and they're a rich, deep green. "A single tree might have thousands of blooms, but usually only manages to develop about twenty or so pods a year."

"Chocolate." Rhonda sighs. "You resettled here for chocolate."

"In a world consumed with misery and ugliness," Lilian says, "we bring joy. Our port is able to bring simple pleasure to so many."

It's clear that it brings her a sense of contentment and peace to cultivate the cocoa trees here. Jose cuts one of the pods open and shows us the seeds from which chocolate is made, and lets us taste the pulp, too. "We make this into a sweet and unique liquor," he says. "And from the fruit you can create something like caffeine."

Ruby tilts her head. "All from the same plant?" She crouches down and touches one of the yellowish pods. "It's so strange that the pods poke off the side of the trunk like this, and down low, too."

"Actually, it makes sense." Jose shrugs. "It's how the seeds are best spread. Boars and other animals find it easier to reach the fruit at this height. Then they either eat the fruit and discard the seeds or . . . " He points at the ground.

"They poop them out," Ruby says, "fertilizing them in the process."

"Exactly," Lilian says. "It's because of that excellent process that when we returned, there were trees for us to harvest our first rounds of chocolate from."

"I won't complain," Rhonda says. "I'm delighted that you're here."

"Me too," Ruby says.

The rest of the day passes quickly—there are many other products grown and manufactured here, but they're all secondary to that one. I'm not sure whether it's the distance from the other ports, the beautiful weather, or the agricultural nature of Carmen, but I relax, just a bit.

"I'd like to level with you about something." Ruby's fork pauses over her chocolate cake. "I haven't been this blunt elsewhere, but something about the time spent in your company makes me feel different about you."

Apparently I'm not the only one who let my guard down. I scan the people at the table. Everyone seated came here with us, except for Jose Fuerte, his wife Lilian, and their four daughters, all of whom are older than both Ruby and I.

"You know that tomorrow I'll be looking for nominations from your people for other representatives."

Jose smiles. "I heard, yes."

"You're not worried, because in every single port, the current Port Head has always won that election by a fairly wide margin, even in New Orleans, where Sawyer's name wasn't even on the ballot."

He shakes his head. "No."

"No?" Ruby drops her fork. "Why not? The other Port Heads have all been nervous."

"I don't want to run things here anymore," Jose says. "I'd been asking your father to replace me for years."

Ruby blinks. "You're kidding."

He shakes his head. "I don't like telling people what to do. We're all happy here, as you can see, and I'm sure there are plenty of people who will do a much better job than I ever did. I only kept this position because your father didn't trust anyone else."

"Oh." Ruby looks around the table. "Do you have any suggestions, then?"

The second daughter, Mabel, clears her throat.

"Did you have ideas?" Ruby asks softly. "Mabel?"

"My mother would be a wonderful representative." Mabel's beautiful dark eyes fill her entire face. "And for the last year or so, she's been running things anyway."

"Is that so?" Ruby's face turns toward Lilian.

Jose's quiet wife blushes and wipes her mouth with a white napkin. "This area is very conservative. I'm not sure they'd vote for a woman."

"I suppose we'll find out tomorrow," Ruby says.

"Because I'd be happy to have you take the place on the ballot that would have been occupied by your husband."

And two days later, for the first time since Ruby began all of this, someone who wasn't appointed by David Solomon wins—by a wide margin. Jose's wife is as gracious and kind as ever when she murmurs her gratitude and promises to do her very best.

Ruby's smiles are genuine when we return to the house we're staying in that night. "Finally." She sighs. "Finally the people elected someone else, even if it's the wife of someone who stupid David Solomon picked."

"You like Jose," I say. "You can admit that much."

She nods. "I do."

The sun is setting behind her, casting her features in soft light. "Would you like to go for a walk along the beach?"

"Yes," she says. "Yes, I really would." She practically skips down the steps, leaving her shoes in a pile on the last step. "What a great idea."

For a moment, the same girl who told me she'd like to live in a small town looks up at me, her eyes light, her smile warm. I take her hand in mine, and the world is absolutely perfect. She doesn't talk as we walk, and our hands swing in perfect balance, my huge fingers not overpowering hers at all. For the first time since we traveled to Galveston and Ruby did her first Sunday sermon, everything feels perfect.

I swing Ruby into my arms and spin her in a circle, our faces only a few inches away. "I love you."

"I love you too," Ruby says, her eyes never leaving mine.

"Then marry me."

Her eyebrows draw together. "Why are you saying that?"

"Because you're perfect for me, and this moment is perfect, and the rest of the world and our lives might not be, but we need to appreciate the perfect moments when they come."

She stares at me for a long time. She reaches for my face and trails one finger down from my temple to my jaw, and then to my mouth. I can't keep from leaning into her hand. She's still everything I want, even now. Even though things have changed. I've never been more sure in my life.

"I do love you, Sam," she says. "But no. I won't marry you."

17

RUBY

Sam almost drops me. "*No?*"

I pat his arm until he releases me. I need to stand on my own two feet for this conversation. Like a chasm has opened underneath me, my heart shrivels inside my chest and my breath hitches. I've put this off for too long. I can't avoid it any more. "And it's more than that." I swallow and steel my resolve. "I'm dumping you, Sam."

His gorgeous, angelic face blanks. "Why?"

How can I even answer that? Sam has always had all the answers. He's been the one who was one hundred percent sure every step of the way. About me. About us. About the world. I'm the mess who doesn't know up from down. I'm the one who can't even figure out my own name, much less the name of a new nation I'm supposed to be *leading*.

"You're asking me for the wrong reasons."

"Because we're perfect for each other?" His eyebrows climb his forehead. "Isn't that the very best reason? Because I can't imagine my life without you? Because I love you?"

But the truth hits me between the eyes and suddenly

everything is crystal clear. "You're proposing right now because you're scared."

"Scared of what?" Sam looks around as if a bear might barrel out of the cocoa tree orchard next us and roar in his face. That wouldn't make him nervous, because big old Sam would just shoot it in the head and we'd continue on our walk.

Bizarrely, that kind of threat doesn't faze him at all.

No, he's afraid of something else entirely. "You're afraid that you and I *aren't* right for each other. We've been slowly drifting apart for weeks now, and you can deny it, but I've seen the desperate glances Lydia lobs your way. I'm not angry about it—I get it. You two are alike. You're two bullets in the same chamber, as it were."

He winces.

"Or you know, a gun analogy that makes sense. Look, my point—"

"You're dumping me because of Lydia?" His voice sounds broken.

"No."

His shoulders slump. "I don't understand."

"I'm well aware," I say. "And I think I'm only just beginning to comprehend myself. But look, Sam. You aren't proposing because you want to race off into the sunset with me. You don't want to marry me because you can't imagine a moment of your life where I'm not the center of your universe. A month ago, yes, that would have been why. But now, you're not even sure you want to be where I'm going."

He looks so heartbroken, so *wrecked*. Probably a lot like I looked when he dumped me. After I kissed Wesley. It's monstrously unfair of me. It's not like he's done anything wrong—I'd put money on it.

But maybe that's why I have to do this. Because he never would do anything wrong. So I'll never be sure that he won't always wish he had . . . unless he's free to do whatever he'd like. "Sam, I love your fierce heart. I love your brilliant mind. I love your quick wit. I love your resilience. I love your goodness. I love most everything about you."

"You just love Kimball more."

I laugh then, the sound more like the bark of a seal. "Uh, no. I see parts of Wesley in Kimball, probably more than really even exist. You were right when you said I barely know him. I hope Kimball is as good as Wesley was. I hope that his country stands for the things he insists it does. But I'm certainly not going to run away from you to chase after some mirage."

"Why are you running from me, then?"

"I'm not," I say. "I'm running toward something that matters to me, deeply." I try to figure out what I can say to explain the sense of purpose I've found. "My dad wanted to fix the world, and instead he decimated it. He failed utterly and completely, thanks in large part to his hubris, his pride, and his messy, messy personal life."

No one can argue with that.

"But he taught me that we *should* want to improve the world, and through an odd twist of fate, I'm in a unique and bizarre position to do it. How could I ever look at myself in the mirror without disgust if I walked away from this opportunity to fix what he broke? I can take something shattered by Solomon and my dad and my aunt and uncle a little bit too, and I can glue it together, and sand it. I can smooth it over and I can repaint it in shining white. *I* can do that. Little, unimpressive Ruby. What kind of message will that send to the women of the world? That they can literally do *anything.* And I know it's not what you want—"

"You're wrong," Sam says. "I've been watching you and I get it—"

"But you're not with me," I say. "You still long to be free, to get away from the crowds and the brokered deals, and the miserable mess of it all. You're like a leashed dog, pacing, drooling, longing to be off the leash and running on the beach. I won't be the one holding that restraint, Sam. I won't."

"I want to be here, pacing and drooling," he says. "I do."

If only he'd said that analogy was all wrong. If he'd said there's no leash, and he's no dog, but he didn't. I'm not wrong. He's pacing, and he's drooling and I can't be his master. I can't be his boss. We have to be partners, or this will never work.

My heart cracks clear down the middle when I tell him the absolute truth. "I won't do it. I wasn't saying this for dramatic effect. I'm finally able to do what I should have done the moment I decided to start down this long path. I'm ending things with us, Sam. For good."

Tears stream freely down my face, but when I turn around and walk back alone to the house we're staying in, he doesn't stop me. And that's how I know it was the right call. Even if it feels like my heart just went through a food processor. The rest of the trip passes in a blur, the joy I found on the beaches and the calm breezes gone. The peace of the smell of roasting cocoa, evaporated.

Smell and color and joy disappear from my life, and I am merely going through the motions. Eat. Sleep. Smile. Talk. Try not to break down bawling. On the plane, Sam sits down at the front, so I march on past to the very back, noting with a flare of anger that Lydia takes the seat right next to him, smiling and laughing the entire time.

At least Sam looks as miserable as I am.

Not that I'm staring.

"What are you doing?" Adam asks.

"Huh?"

He sits next to me. "You dumped Sam? Are you trying to shove him right into her arms?"

I press my lips together. I don't have to explain my decisions to anyone else.

"I know I didn't grow up with you, which means I never cut the hair off your dolls, or poked you in the side until you cried. I never told anyone about the boys you had a crush on, or told you that your left eye looked bigger than your right."

"Wait." I widen both eyes. "Does my left—"

"Focus, Ruby."

"On what? Get to the point."

"Sam is a moron, as I have been telling him daily, but he's *your* moron, and nothing in this wonky world makes sense unless you two are together."

"I don't have the energy to fight with you, Adam."

"Great. Then don't. Stand up, march up there, I'll come with you if you want, and tell Sam you were wrong. Smooch and make doe eyes and then the world can be right again."

"No."

"No?" Adam fumes. "What is wrong with you two? You're as idiotic as he is."

"He's miserable with me right now," I say, "and until—" I choke. "*Unless* he comes around to the idea of needing me no matter what, unless he gets on board with being my partner in this plan, our relationship will never work. Right now, I'm tugging him along next to me like a guard dog. I can't do that. I won't marry a canine."

"Then don't marry him. Keep dating him for now." Adam scratches his head. "I'm confused about this analogy. What would turn him into a man again?"

"He proposed to me, Adam," I whisper. "And he did it because he's scared of how he feels about Lydia. Or he's scared about how unsure he is about me. Either way, the biggest issue is that until now, *he* was the one who *got* this stuff. He knew what I needed and what I felt and he was so *sure* and now he's all wibbly wobbly. I can't have him being like that. I need solid, strong, positive Sam back."

Adam wraps an arm around my shoulders. "Oh, Ruby. In

life, no one is *never* wibbly wobbly."

"What I mean—"

"I know what you mean. Up until now, Sam has been superhuman. I've seen that too. But he's unsure and he's scared, and that's *life*, chica. It just is."

"You've spent too long in Mexico."

He laughs. "Maybe so, but I'm still right. You're punishing him for being unsure? We're all unsure. Your job, as his partner, is to be sure when he's not, and he'll do the same for you. You put him up on this pedestal and now you're close enough to see that he's human too. I just hope that by the time you come to grips with that, he's still absolutely gaga for you."

Adam's an idiot. Sam was scared, and I did the right thing turning him down.

I'm almost positive that I'm right.

Also, I'm only seventeen. I won't even be eighteen for months and months. Marrying anyone is stupid. I wrap myself in every argument I can think of for the next few hours, until our plane lands outside of Galveston. And then I brush past Sam and Lydia and down the gangway. I'm certainly not going to wait around and hope that Sam comes and tries to talk me out of anything.

Like I did when he dumped me.

The only thing more pathetic than regretting my bold position would be skulking around and making that regret obvious. Or watching him flirt with Lydia. Doing much more of that might kill me.

But the second my feet hit the ground, I know something is wrong.

Josephine's wringing her hands, her eyes teary.

"What happened?"

"CINOW attacked us a few hours ago. They dropped bombs on Beaumont and Lake Charles."

Lake Charles is a Marked settlement, but Beaumont's a

WPN one. "How many died?"

She shakes her head. "We're not sure. I sent teams to assess the damage and evacuate anyone in danger. I wasn't sure what else to do. No one has attacked, well, *anyone* since Before."

"How do you know it was CINOW?"

"Who else would it be?" Josephine practically wails. "They had fighter jets. And from the early reports, very, very few people survived in those cities. They made more than one sweep."

"But why?" It makes no sense. "Why would they attack us?"

"They want what we have." Adam got off after me and is standing right behind me. "They sent Kimball to find out all that he could. No wonder he was so willing to travel with you anywhere. He saw all the maps—he knows everything."

"If he knew everything, he'd have attacked Galveston," I say. "He'd have aimed for me."

"Maybe he was," Josephine says. "Maybe . . . maybe I was wrong to encourage you to spend time with him. I'm so sorry."

"Why would he think hitting those places would harm me?" I ask. "It makes no sense." But nothing about the thought of Kimball attacking makes sense.

"I disseminated a false schedule of where you'd be and when," Sam says, his face grim. "I had you arriving today in Lake Charles to begin the integration of the Marked settlements."

I thought the world felt upside down before. Now my ex-boyfriend is glaring at me and talking about how the other guy who proposed to me not long ago might have just tried to kill me.

Fabulous. Maybe if I'm lucky, by dinnertime, a zombie version of Wesley will show up and try to eat my brains.

18

SAM

"No, we cannot bomb CINOW." Ruby's eyes get that look in them, the one that means she's set and she isn't backing down. "First of all, we have no real proof that the attack was actually carried out by them."

"Oh, well, then maybe it was the Marked who leveled their own city," Rhonda says.

"Not you too," Ruby says. "You're supposed to be here to support me."

"You're being irrational," I say.

"And luckily, you don't get to decide whether we bomb people," Ruby says.

"Why's that?" I ask. "Did you fire me when you dumped me?"

It's likely no one else notices, but I'm so used to watching her that it's obvious to me when Ruby flinches. I almost back down then—the last thing I want to do is hurt her more. But she hates aggression so much that she can't think straight when it comes to stuff like this.

"If you allow an attack like this to go unchecked, they'll assume that we either can't mount a proper defense, or that we're weak." I hate the idea of attacking—and the attendant collateral damage, but they started it. I never back down from a fight, especially one I know I'll win. "And in this instance, your bio father actually left us in a good position. Unless they've spent the last few years reverse engineering whatever weapons and tech they had, I doubt they can come close to matching us. Good old Solomon seized all the military stockpiles. I think we've got enough weapons to kill every human alive a few dozen times over."

"Brilliant." Ruby fumes. "Now that we've saved everyone from Tercera, finally, let's go ahead and finish off anyone still breathing."

"He's suggesting we protect ourselves," Rhonda says. "Prevent them from doing just that."

Adam stomps into the room. "The Port Heads have been informed of the attack." He glances from Ruby to Rhonda and then to me. "What's going on?"

Maybe her brother can talk some sense into her. "Ruby's insisting that we send Kimball a perfumed card apologizing that she didn't die yet."

Adam's face flushes. "You can't even consider *not* striking back. I never should have allowed Kimball such extensive access. That's entirely on me—he was disarmingly friendly, and I fell for it. He knows far, far too much. And if he knew about the phony schedule Sam disseminated, he left a few spies behind, too."

I can't even think about how close we came to Ruby being *gone*. Vaporized. Deceased. The rage that pulses through me at that thought is nearly incapacitating. The next time I see Kimball, I'm separating his head from his body.

Josephine jogs into the room, her sides heaving. "The Port Heads have all notified us that they're en route."

"No," I say. "They can't come here. If he has spies, he'll know and it'll make Galveston too attractive a target. It's already too attractive, but we really can't have every leader in one place."

"Once he finds out I'm here," Ruby says, "he'll—"

"Oh, no," I say. "That's why we should pretend you're dead."

She gasps. "You're kidding, right? Tell all of WPN and the Unmarked, and the Marked, for that matter, that their leader *died?* That will calm everyone down in the midst of this tragic crisis."

"We won't let them believe it for long," I say. "Only until we've wiped out CINOW."

She throws her hands up in the air. "Well. Then don't let me stop you. Go ahead and make plans to bomb a million and a half people, more than half the population of the earth as far as we know, out of existence. No big deal if they had no idea what the leaders may have ordered. No worries that it might be some kind of misunderstanding."

"What sort of misunderstanding results in leveling two cities?" I step toward her.

But she doesn't back down, not Ruby. "You said yourself that *we* have all the weapons. Why in the world would they attack us? If Kimball came and saw and knew, why would he pick a fight he can't possibly win? Have you thought of that?"

I hadn't, in fact. But if I acknowledge that she has a point, then anyone who might have been involved in this on our side—anyone who might have wanted to make it *look* like CINOW did this—will know that I suspect them. How is Ruby smarter than me at this stuff? She immediately suspects what I should already have been considering.

Who else wants her dead? And who else didn't know our real schedule?

We informed each Port Head we were coming only hours before our arrival. We hopscotched around, from Tampa to Jacksonville, to Mobile, to Miami, and only then to Savannah. Which means if any of the Port Heads are tired of everything changing . . . who had access to military support? As far as I can tell, all of them potentially could. There were an awful lot of jets and missiles and fighter planes taken by Solomon. Would they all have been accounted for? Or could his most trusted advisors have tucked a few away?

I can't let on that I know—especially when I'm not sure who's reporting to whom about our plans. "That's ridiculous," I say. "You think Kimball's smarter than I give him credit for, but I think he came here, took one look around, and decided to try and acquire you and everything else in front of him. When that didn't work, he wanted to eliminate the threat and come back and take whatever was left. You may not be greedy, but that doesn't mean everyone else is quite so altruistic."

Ruby's face falls. "Fine, then plan your attack." She spins around the room, eyeing everyone. "But no one launches a single jet. No one fires a single missile. No one so much as shoots a *gun* without my approval. Are we clear?" She storms out, Job and Adam on her heels.

Rhonda stays with me and the other military strategists.

I almost forget Lydia's there until she says, "What's the plan, then?"

It's hard to remember, once the planning is underway, that most of this is just an exercise—possibly helpful, but likely just a cover until we reveal the real threat. It's not like Ruby will sign off on us taking out the CINOW settlements. Or that we'll really be able to level the Capitol Building where Kimball and his dad live. But a guy can dream.

I watch everyone in the room carefully for any sign that they know more than they let on. So far, each person seems genuine. The only person here who's masking something is Lydia—and I know what that is. She's covering up how she feels about me. I ignore her redirection and accelerated heart rate as a matter of habit.

"You haven't eaten anything since breakfast," Lydia finally says.

The sun is starting to drop low in the sky. My belly rumbles as if on cue. "I'll eat later."

"I'll go get something for everyone," she offers.

"Fine," I say. "Thanks."

"But if you do that," Rhonda says, picking up on the flaw in the most recent suggestion, "then they'll be able to cut west. You said Kimball mentioned real time communications."

"We'd need to take those out first," I say. "But we have to locate them to do so. Any way we look at it, we can't even *plan* an effective strategy without a surveillance flight or two."

"Three would be better," General Coons says. "And as mentioned, we have the aircraft to spare."

It's hard to really take in the scope of resources that have been available to David Solomon all this time. "How much progress have we made on the communications upgrades that Ruby ordered?" I ask.

"It's only been three weeks," Lieutenant Parks says. "But the main lines have been run, and equipment has been installed or repaired in every port."

"What about Nashville? Memphis?" Rhonda asks.

"Or Baton Rouge?" I ask.

"Yes, the infrastructure is in place in each of the Phase One locations," Lieutenant Parks says. "But training the personnel to maintain it is more time consuming, as is manufacturing enough telecommunication devices to make it usable."

Logistics eat me alive, but we finally hammer out the basics we would need to accomplish to get the port-to-port and city-to-city communications up and running—beyond the phone lines and Internet for each Port Head, which Solomon always had. As the sun sets fully, I realize Lydia never came back with our food. I'll have to hunt her down later. I need to get Ruby to sign off on the surveillance flights at a baseline. Whether the attacks were made by CINOW or not, scoping out what they have and where they all live is just good sense. We should have done it before—the very second Kimball left. I'm ashamed I didn't.

"We'll reconvene here in one hour—get dinner, sit down and take a break, whatever you need. Tell no one outside of this room what we've been discussing."

Rhonda dogs my steps the entire way to Ruby's room. "I hate to be rude," I say. "But I need to talk to Ruby alone."

She lifts one eyebrow. "You used to get away with that nonsense, but you're not her boyfriend anymore. I think she'll want me there."

Ouch. "Not because I'm her boyfriend," I say. "I need to talk to her frankly as her Master of Strategic Defense, or whatever stupid title she made up and is likely regretting." I need to talk to her about what she *really* thinks is going on.

Rhonda's voice drops to a whisper. "Do you really think she won't want me in on the play? You and I both know she's positive that CINOW didn't do this."

If Rhonda knew I was setting up our strategy as a misdirect, how many others figured that out, too? I groan. "Fine. Come inside, but don't interrupt."

She shrugs. "No promises."

"No respect," I mutter. But I'm glad Rhonda's on my side. On our side. It always helps to be surrounded with people you know you can trust—and in this case, someone else who cares about Ruby almost as much as I do. I tap on the solid wood, and then I brace myself to be lambasted the second I shove through the doorway.

Only no one yells. No one shouts. In fact, Ruby isn't mad at all.

Because she's gone.

My heart skips a beat—and then another. The window's broken, glass scattered on the carpet, which means it was broken from the outside. I race across the room. There's a smear of blood on the pristine white of Ruby's bed, and drops that trail across the floor. She struggled with whoever took her. I can't force myself to rush to the window. My feet drag slowly, terrified at what I might find.

But the only other ominous sign is two drops of blood on the ground outside the window. No puddle or pool or ongoing trail.

Which means someone took her, but she's likely alive.

And I have no idea where they went.

❧ 19 ❧

RUBY

"Fine, then plan your attack." I make eye contact with every single person in the room, from the guards stationed near the doors to the haughty general who still can't stomach that I'm the queen. When I glare long enough, they all drop their eyes. "But no one launches a single jet. No one fires a single missile. No one so much as shoots a *gun* without my approval. Are we clear?" When I push my way past the press of soldiers and officers, Job and Adam tag along.

I'm actually glad that they do. I've barely seen Job in the three weeks since we left Baton Rouge. We left him behind when we went to the various Ports, counting on his expertise to spearhead the dosing of the local population with the hacker virus. It's not just to keep them safe from the much less terrifying Tercera—it's also because it'll keep them safe from *any* nasty virus they might encounter.

Some days I still pause and marvel that my dad invented it, and that we finally found it. Way too late, but still better than never.

I intend to race to my room and stuff my face against my pillows to scream. I'm sick of no one listening to me.

238

But then I realize that Sam paused a moment too long when I asked why Kimball would pick a fight he couldn't win. Sam's smart—but he's *wicked* smart about tactical and strategic things. He'd have already wondered why CINOW would attack when Kimball knew *just* how capable we were of returning the pain tenfold.

So Occam's Razor says . . . it's not CINOW who attacked us.

But then . . . who? Or rather, which disgruntled Port Head or displaced interim chancellor ordered me killed?

I turn on my heel and walk back the way we just came. Job grabs my arm. "What's going on?"

"I just realized that I need to read up on something I've specifically avoided until now."

"What's that?" Job asks.

"Just a little book of filth left me by my good old padre." Now who spent too much time in Mexico?

"I don't understand," Adam says. "What good will—"

"I'll explain in a bit." I duck into the office—full of miserable memories with David freaking Solomon—and force myself to sit in his chair. I pull the worn brown journal from the bottom of his drawer where I left it and pull out a sheet of clean, white paper. As if the purity of the paper can remove the stain of this terrible book.

"What are you reading?" Adam asks.

"Filthy, disgusting Solomon kept a little book, full of miserable secrets," I say.

Adam's eyebrows rise. "So you were telling the truth in Nashville."

I shrug. "Sort of. I hadn't read anything about Quinn specifically, but only because I never read most of this. Believe me, the first few pages are bad enough." But I plow my way through it, one terrible secret after another. Most of the people listed are political and social opponents David went on to squash, according to Adam. A few of them are still prominent business people and religious figures. The more notes I take, the more my fingers itch to toss this in the trash.

We're halfway through the book when Job notes the obvious. "None of these secrets are about Port Heads."

I drop my pen. "Either because he didn't write the secrets about them down—they were too close to his mind—or because he kept them around precisely because he didn't have dirt on them and trusted them."

Adam's laugh is bitter. "It wasn't that—he didn't trust anyone. People who are morally indefensible never do. They assume everyone is as bad as they are, and they won't put them in a position of power unless they can control them."

"So you think he just didn't write any of those things here?" I can't help my frown. "But then where does that leave us? Without more information on them, the kind of thing only David Solomon might have, how can I know which one of them attacked me?"

Job whistles. "You think the attack was from one of your own Port Heads?"

I drop my hands, palm down, on the face of the desk. "It had to be, Job. Think about it. Kimball spent weeks here, yes, and let's pretend I didn't believe him, which I did, or that he went home and was completely overruled, which is also possible. But he knew Solomon took over the United States' weaponry when he collapsed the government. Unless I'm missing something huge, that means that in spite of their more advanced tech, we can crush CINOW as easily as Solomon planned to annihilate the Marked. Why would he risk angering us like that? At least, without gutting our military forces first?"

Job blinks. "Which means this whole time, you've been trying to figure out *who* plans to kill you—not looking for something on someone working for or with CINOW."

We really should meld our brains somehow. It never occurred to me that it might have been an attack by CINOW . . . supported by someone here. "Actually." The cogs in my brain spin. "Kimball could have made friends here—he could be working *with* a greedy Port Head. They might be planning to take over WPN once I'm gone, and Kimball could get the single government he wanted." Even without marrying me.

"You're looking for anything at all," Adam says. "I think that about sums it up."

"Right," I say. "Remember when we work puzzles? And that one piece that fits nowhere finally drops into place? I feel like if the right information surfaces, we'll know it when we hear it. Or, at least, I hope that's true."

But we slog through the entire book and aren't one step closer to connecting Port Heads to wanting me dead, specifically, or to CINOW. In fact, there's nothing on them at all.

"What about his letters? Or didn't you say Solomon had email?" Adam asks. "No one else had the Internet, but he used it to communicate with them, didn't he?"

I'm an idiot. I've grown so accustomed to everything being paper or hard copy files that . . . of course he would have communicated with them in a faster way, one that didn't have too many prying eyes checking over it. Like delivery people. Too many ways for that to be infiltrated. "Here." I pull a rectangle out of a desk drawer. "It's his laptop."

It takes Job and I a minute to find the power cord and boot it up, but only three tries to crack his password. Ruby and my birthdate. My name was his password. I shudder.

"He did care about you in his twisted way," Adam says. "I know that's probably not very helpful, but it made me hate him just a tiny bit less that he kept promoting me on his security team."

I snort. "I couldn't care less whether he used the name of the daughter no one knew about for his password. It probably had more to do with being unlikely to be cracked . . . until I showed up, anyway." I toggle through icons until I find the email one. "Bingo."

And it pops up, just like that.

Unfortunately, there are a ridiculous amount of day-to-day affairs addressed in the various email correspondence. Everything from topics of Sunday sermons to the details of the Cleansing. If I didn't hate Solomon before . . .

"We don't have days and days to comb through this," Adam says. "Whoever failed to kill you will be planning their second attempt. We need to catch them."

I'm sure Sam's feeling the same pressure.

"Here, let me try some searches," Job says.

I stand up and surrender the office chair to him. He's better with things like this than I am anyway. And my typing skills are nonexistent. I'm sure it's painful for him to watch.

"I can't even see the screen right," Job complains. "How short *are* you?" He reaches under the seat to lower it down, presumably. But instead, he freezes.

"What's wrong?"

"There's something down here. Under the chair." He pulls his hand up slowly, and there's a folded parchment paper clutched in it. He flips it over, and the name Ruby is printed in almost perfect lettering.

My heart hammers inside my chest. Did David Solomon leave me a message? Did he know I'd kill him? I blink and my hands tremble. But I take it. I slide my finger under the flap and lift it up.

Dear Ruby,

You don't want to marry me. I suppose I should have expected that, but it hurts more than I expected it to. I know you love Sam, and I get that, actually. But I think it's a mistake. For you. For me. For the future. You and I are two sides of the same coin. We both want to heal—people, the world, everything. We want a better future, and I'm not sure your guy gets that about you.

Either way, I wanted to say thank you before I'm shoved out the door. I know I can't get back over to talk to you. Sam's seen to that. But I want you to be able to reach out to me at any time, for any thing. Since you won't have your communication system up and running until after I'm gone, I figured I'd at least give you the information you need to contact me. I told you that we hadn't expanded into Los Angeles yet, but that's not precisely true. My dad and I have had a residence there for quite some time—as well as a few thousand other people. It's been nice—like we're an advance team. It's small, and as you may be discovering, it's refreshing to have a place to go where you aren't constantly being evaluated and watched. I'll be studying there for my upcoming medical board exam when I finish my three-week rotation, and I'll be there for the next few months.

It would be easy for someone with a plane to fly into the airstrip less than a mile away. Unlike your government, we don't have the means to immediately shoot down anything that flies, so you'd land safely. I'm not sure we knew quite what we risked when we flew out near Houston on my trip over, but I'm glad of that. If Dad knew the military strength of WPN, he might not have sent me.

And we might never have met.

Whatever else you believe about me, believe this: I care about you and I'm impressed and I look forward with great excitement to stories of your success. You are doing the right thing—giving up the life you'd imagined for yourself for one that will right wrongs and restructure our world for a better place for generations to come. Don't ever doubt that.

Always yours,
Kimball Ryson

Another sheet of paper has the rudimentary basics of a

map, outlining where his Los Angeles residence is located, and where the airstrip is in proximity to the house.

"Still think it might have been CINOW, even working with one of the Port Heads?" Job asks.

I shake my head. "I think I might be safer there than I would be in any city here, honestly."

"Except that they aren't as strategically muscled," Adam says. "As he pointed out."

"So who in the world wants you dead here?" Job asks.

"The problem is that there are too many options," I moan. "Everyone has something to gain by offing me. Even you, Adam."

He shakes his head. "Wrong. You've offered me your place a million times. If I wanted that, I'd have taken it."

"Unless you thought I'd always be a threat." I smirk.

"You're always a nuisance." He shoves my shoulder playfully.

I bump into Job, whose hands bump the screen. "Watch it," he says. But then he leans closer to the screen. "Whoa."

"What?" I squint.

"This is a secret file." He blinks. Then he blinks more. "This is what we needed. Emails he sent to all the Port Heads, and then deleted, placing them in this weird file."

"*—those widows don't need their retirements now, but do you think God will really care? Do you think the people will? You were a grifter then, now, and you will be one forever. Don't forget it, Quentin. The difference is that now, you work for me, not yourself.*"

⚜

"*Many things have changed in the last decade, Rosa, but God has not become any more forgiving of women who lust after other women. Don't kid yourself there. They'd rip you to pieces if they knew, so you could kiss your comfortable life goodbye. You're where you are on my whim. Always. And if you ever try to deny*"

"And, Terry, how many of your children did we relocate into
your port? Adultery is as serious now as it ever was. I like
to think you've changed your ways, but Keri Johnson says you
haven't."

"She'll never forgive you, Sawyer. You married her sister, and
then you abandoned that sister to die. In what world will you
ever have a life together?"

"Loren Bray. Do I really need to say any more? I covered up
your murder at the time—but I will not hesitate to bury you
if you step out of line, Steve. One toe. One disloyal look and you're
gone."

"You serve a purpose, Dolores, while you do what I say and no
more. But if your worthless brother Quinn doesn't make his
move and oust Roth soon—as he promised—or if he becomes resis-
tant to our guidance, your position isn't irrevocable. Don't mistake
my patience for generosity. I'm not a generous man."

*"Y*our life has become quite blessed, thanks to me. But how long will those lovely girls look at you and Lilian with adoration once they know you shot their mother? I know what you'll say. But do you think they'll listen when you say she was attacking your home? Do you think they'll care that a hoodie hid her face, obscuring that she was a woman? No, they'll never forgive you from hiding the truth—that you killed the mother they loved. That you're the cause of their need for adoption. It's all very Les Miserable, but I doubt that will matter much."*

I need a bath after reading how Solomon twisted and threatened and belittled the people he chose to rule WPN for him.

"So let's recap," Job says. "Quentin was a con man."

I nod.

"Rosa's a gay woman . . . who also had an affair with dear old dad?" Adam shudders. "The world is a bizarre place, and it feels like every day I find out something worse about him."

"He used the secret of her sexual preference to force her to let him see their child?" I shake my head. "He was so disgusting."

"And who knows what he used to force her into a position where they got the child in the first place," Job says.

I don't even want to think about it.

"But in the most difficult to understand revelation, Sawyer loves Dolores Peabody?" Adam shakes his head. "I don't see how that could possibly—"

I blink. She told me about the man she loved. "She told me the man she loved married her sister." It's actually pretty tragic. "I think that might have been him. The email mentioned that Sawyer married someone's sister . . . and that he left the sister to die when she was Marked." I shake my head. "It's all so messed up."

Job's lip curls. "Now your freaky cousin wants to get with Dolores. Again, apparently. That's messed up."

Or it could be kind of sweet in a tragic way. Those two didn't have the feel of the other threats, really. Except for one. "Poor Jose. He defended his home from a break-in, shooting the assailant to protect his wife, presumably." I sigh. "And then they adopt the children of the woman he kills, possibly to try and set things right with the world, and Solomon uses that knowledge to make them do whatever he wants."

"Don't feel too bad for Jose," Adam says. "Solomon got him a job, and he could have found someone to adopt the kids. It's pretty strange he did it himself."

"We don't have enough information to decide whether it was twisted or an act of mercy," I say. "But we shouldn't assume all these people are as degraded and miserable as Solomon."

"Either way, Solomon's method of dealing with problems didn't give them faith that working things out was a good way to go." Job leans back in his chair. "But which things would impact who might want you dead?" He shakes his head. "I miss five hundred piece puzzles, honestly. At least those had a box with a photo you could use as a reference."

"Chancellor Quinn," I say.

"He's not even a Port Head." Job speaks slowly, as if I've gone nuts.

"Yes, thank you for that, but he's related to Dolores. So Dolores Peabody is in love with Sawyer Blevins . . . and—"

"Or at least, Sawyer loves her." Adam shrugs. "We don't know whether she still likes him."

"Fair," I say. "But her brother's the interim chancellor . . ."

"Or he was until you beat him without even trying." Job taps his lip with his index finger.

"Not sure how many of the particulars she knows," I
say. "Hopefully she has no idea that I attacked him and
threatened to out him."

"But we can assume they have a method of communication." Job frowns.

"It's weird that—" I freeze.

"What?"

"Lydia said that Quinn had some kind of multiple wife
situation, or something like that." I blink. "But Solomon
certainly had no evidence of that, at least, not in his book
or judging from the emails. I never saw his name, other
than as a byline in an email to Dolores."

"People might have hidden a few freaky things from
him," Job says. "It's shocking, I know, but possible."

"But what if Quinn realized I was bluffing," I say. "And
sent Lydia, knowing she had a connection to Sam that
would give her the inside track?"

"You're saying *Lydia* might be a spy?" Adam's jaw drops.
"I mean, I dislike her as much as you do, but that girl's feelings for Sam are legit."

"I'm not saying they aren't." Although I'm feeling decid-
edly stabby right now, after listening to him point that out.
"Look, I have no idea who she is or what her motives are,
but I'm just saying she *could* be not quite what she seems.
We have no idea who Quinn really is."

"It *is* bizarrely convenient that the person who has tried
to trash your and Sam's relationship since day one knows
Quinn—and that Quinn is secretly closely connected to
Peabody," Job says.

"And possibly Sawyer Blevins, the one person outside of
maybe Adam, who has a prominent leadership position and
a blood tie to David Solomon. It makes him uniquely
prepared to step in on my death," I say.

"Not quite the only person," Job says. "Rosa has a son,

too. With David Solomon, and everyone knows her name and face. She could claim the position on his behalf."

I swear under my breath. "Either way, I'm what's standing between them and taking over."

"But we have no proof that either of them were behind the bombings or want anything to do with the throne," Adam says.

"Not yet," I say. "But if someone kidnapped me, or if I *died* for real . . . "

"I'd prefer to avoid that," Job says. "Personally."

I laugh. "As would I. But if we can sell Sam on the lie that something has happened to me . . . I think the Port Heads would buy it too. One of them would step up, and if I had to guess—"

"Dolores Peabody or Rosa Alvarez," Adam says.

Yep. "One of those two—exactly."

"But if you're dead," Job says, "Sam really will burn CINOW to the ground. You must know that."

I slump in my chair. Every idea seems to dead end before we can make it work.

"Which is why we'll make it look like they *kidnapped* her instead of killing her," Adam says. "And then we watch to see who seizes the reins."

"I'm not hanging around here if she's gone," Job says. "Sam would figure it out, I know it. I've never been able to lie to him."

Which makes it unlikely that Lydia is anyone other than she says . . . He is really good at telling when people are lying. Something about being able to hear heartbeats, maybe. And if Lydia's legit, and Quinn really ran, then . . . all of this falls apart and we're back to square one. Unless it's Rosa.

But even if our ideas are all wrong, finding out who seizes control when I'm gone will be helpful.

"And they can't bomb CINOW if they have me—that

might kill me, either because they're angry, or inadvertently if they attack the wrong place."

"Which the person who wants you dead would be okay with," Adam says. "It's a risk—but with Sam here ostensibly in control until you're proven dead, that should be somewhat in check."

Everything is a gamble, any way I turn.

"Let's do it."

The blood is Job's idea. "Nothing will freak Sam out like that will," he says, looking at the splotches of red he artfully applied. "The thought of you injured, scared, and all alone." He shakes his head.

I won't lie and say I don't relish the thought of Sam worrying about me. I may have dumped him, but my heart's still tied to that big conflicted hunk. Even knowing this is the right play, I pause outside my own window, my heart in my throat.

"He'll be okay," Adam whispers. "Sam can handle himself. And then we can nail the jerks who want you dead and finally lay this ugliness to rest."

I think about all the people that these conspirators have killed, from the messengers weeks ago, to the residents of those settlements. "Nothing can make it right, but I'll feel better when we can punish the ones responsible."

"Me too." Adam frowns fiercely.

"And you're sure Kimball will welcome us?" Job asks.

"There aren't many things in life I'm positive about right now." I think about Kimball's eyes, and his words in the letter. "But that's one of them."

"Alright, well, let's go. The sun's setting. It's the perfect time to meet the pilot," Adam says. "And I want to get this show on the road—er, in the air."

Why does doing the right thing always feel like a mistake lately?

"Let's go," I say. "We have traitors to smoke out."

❦ 20 ❦

RUBY

Flying to a new place in the middle of the night might not have been the finest part of our plan.

"At least there's a full moon," Adam says.

Thadeus, our pilot, scowls. "Yes, that's very helpful. How'd you like to land a plane with a nightlight?"

Job clears his throat. "But you did say that the instrumentation still—"

"I'm so grateful that all of you are willing to be copilots," Thadeus says. "But I only really need one. Since Adam is the least irritating, maybe the two of you can go sit down and buckle in."

He's more polite than we deserve, probably. Job and I grumble, but we listen. My knuckles grip the armrests so tightly that they turn bright white, but a few moments later, we land. It's bumpy, but we don't die. I think that's about the best we could hope for with a last-minute flight to nowhere, based on a hand-drawn map.

"We have gas for a return trip, right?" I ask.

Job shrugs. "Might have been a question to ask *before* we took off."

"Probably," I say. "But seeing as I didn't even get to pack a toothbrush, details like gasoline didn't come up."

"I'm sure CINOW has jet fuel," Adam says. "And if they don't shoot us on sight, I bet they'll loan us some."

"I'll be crossing my fingers." I unbuckle and stand while Thadeus prepares to open the door.

"I'm even crossing my toes," Job says. "Just in case that helps."

"Gross. Your toes aren't that long," I say.

Job pins me with a stare. "You're sure of that?"

I think back to all the times we splashed in the lake at the cabin. "Pretty sure."

"You two going to reminisce all night? Or are you ready to wave the white flag and pray?" Adam points at the doorway. "As handsome as I am, I think Kimball's least likely to shoot at you, Rubes."

"The head of my royal guard is so brave," I say. "Shoving me out front, like an apple in the mouth of a pig."

"Ew," Job says. "That's not a peace offering. That's a shrively—"

"Let's just go." I walk past them both, my heart jammed somewhere between my lungs and my esophagus. "If we're going to get shot, we may as well get it over with."

But strangely, I'm less worried about getting shot, and more concerned about being shot down. Do I care what Kimball says? Whether he's angry at me for taking a month to find his letter? Was my relationship with Sam really holding me back? What's wrong with me?

My heart has plenty of time to descend from its place in my throat in the mile-long hike from the airstrip to the residence drawn on the map Kimball left. Which turns into two miles, thanks to a wrong turn.

"I'm sorry," Adam says. "I have a good sense of direction, but it's hard to orient in the dark."

"And I've got a blister now," Job says. "This sucks. I'd

almost have preferred that armed men met us on the runway, assuming they had a vehicle."

You'd never know we weren't blood related. He and I could definitely be real live siblings. "It's weird, you know," I say. Thadeus is back with the plane, in case we need to rush back for a quick departure. So I'm here with my two brothers. "A year ago, I thought I had no siblings."

Even in the moonlight, I can see Adam's affectionate glance.

"For a while, I hated Solomon even more because he stole my family from me." I bump Job with my hip. "But now I realize he didn't have that power. Instead of a cousin whom I saw as a brother, I guess now I feel like I have two brothers."

"Life is strange like that," Job says. "Perspective makes all the difference. A blood test could never make me love you more or less—and I couldn't love anyone more than you, not even Rhonda. If it took a sociopath and a pandemic to cement that bond, well, sometimes good things come from bad. Right?"

I hug him. "Yes, and I think that's God's message if he exists and has one. That the good can exist with or even sometimes alongside the bad, and it's our job to focus on that. To cultivate it."

"Guys," Adam says.

We turn toward his voice and our eyes fixate on the beach, where the ocean crashes against the sand. And an enormous white beach house, brightly lit against the night sky.

Why do rich people always paint their houses white?

I still my trembling hands and racing heart and walk purposely toward the edge of the light. I'm turning toward the front door when movement in the distance catches my eye.

Someone is walking out of the ocean and shoving their hair away from their eyes.

Kimball.

In swim trunks.

Perfect chest and six-pack abs, just like before.

Except this time he's all wet, and he's at home, and I've missed him.

I turn toward him without thinking, and my legs begin pumping as I jog his direction.

His eyes light up when they meet mine, and he starts to jog toward me, too. It's almost like something out of a movie from Before.

Until I stumble over something and fall forward, only the heels of my hands stopping me from face-planting in the sand. I reach backward for the object that tripped me. It's a towel—probably Kimball's—but it's wrapped around something else. I unwrap it carefully as Adam and Job catch up behind me and Kimball stumbles to a stop in front of me.

"Oh, that's nothing," he says. "I'll take it—"

Before he can snatch it out of my hands, I realize what I'm looking at. He's supposed to be studying for the medical boards. It should be a textbook. Or it could be notes. But it's neither of those things—it's a sketch. A pretty good one, actually. Stylized. Beautiful. Longing clear in every line, in every curve.

Of me.

It's my face, my hair tumbling around me, my lips curved into a knowing smile. Waves crash behind me, but that's not the thing that stands out. No, it's my eyes that he nailed. They're looking directly at him, and they're full of affection.

Affection isn't quite right.

In the sketch I'm looking at, I *adore* the person I'm staring at.

Is that how I look at Kimball?

I nearly choke.

Kimball takes the book and flips it against his wet chest. I'm worried the water will ruin it, but I can't bring myself to say that. "Kimball."

"You came." He's breathing heavily, his lips parted, his skin glistening.

"We all did." Adam waves. "Hey, there."

Kimball doesn't spare them a glance. "I'm so happy to see you."

"Why, thank you," Adam says. "It's been a while since anyone said that to me, and I won't lie. It's nice to hear."

I toss a handful of sand at him. "Shut up."

"Not likely," Adam says.

I stand up and brush sand from my pants and hands. "I'm guessing you didn't order an attack on Lake Charles and Beaumont."

Kimball drops the sketchpad and closes the space between us, his arms wrapping around me and drawing me against him. The water's cold against my skin and I shiver. "I would never hurt you."

"I know."

"Is that why you came?" His whisper blows warm air against my cheek. "To ask me that?"

I shake my head. "I was supposed to be there. Whoever attacked those places—"

"Was trying to kill you." He shudders. "You must stay here, then."

"If the attacks weren't from you guys, which I assumed they weren't," I say, "then my enemies are within WPN, and you can't keep me safe, as much as I appreciate the thought."

"I wasn't one hundred percent forthright on that," he says. "I hope you'll forgive me."

My arms stiffen and I press at his chest. "What?"

His expression is sheepish. "The thing is, all of the government was accelerated, as you know."

"Okay," I say.

"Except not up here. That's why we survived and have largely been fairly organized."

"I don't understand."

"What are you talking about?" Adam asks.

"I really did approach you in peace," he says. "Dad knew there had to be some kind of settlement down south—he knew what everyone else did. That David Solomon tricked the government and took over."

"But not up here?" I narrow my eyes at him. "What does that mean?"

"My mom was a senator," he says. "And so she was *supposed* to take the 'cure,' but there's a time delay, you know, and that caused some confusion. So they had reports out here that the cure wasn't a cure. And they didn't take it."

"So, wait." I swallow.

He tucks a stray curl behind my ear. "She didn't die, but my dad did take over for her a few years ago, and Dad is pretty sure we could level WPN if we had to."

I gasp.

"But we never would," he says. "Solomon was satisfied with the belief that the rest of the world had died, and he seized all the military assets in a reasonable perimeter. He dropped a handful of bombs on our hangars and supply warehouses, all of which had been emptied by that point."

Oh my goodness. "So you really came out to—"

"To get the cure," he says. "And to make sure you didn't pose a threat." He lowers his face until it's inches from mine. "Which you don't. We know that, but what I'm saying is that we're in a position to help. To protect you— or to help you eliminate anyone who *would* be a threat. To help ensure peace in our time, to facilitate the amazing things you're doing there."

But that means he *could* have attacked Beaumont and Lake Charles—to send me running out here.

He could have done it, but I don't believe he did.

He was too shocked when I showed up. And he was forthright about that lie immediately upon our arrival, not holding back. If he were guilty, he wouldn't have done that. Right?

Unless his dad did it and he doesn't know.

His hands come up on either side of my face, cupping my jaw. "Ruby, your brain is churning now, I can see it. Press pause. It's been a miserable twenty-four hours, I imagine. Come back with me. Eat something. Maybe take a nap, at least. Things will look better in the morning. I promise."

I nod, and he releases me, but it's reluctant, I can tell. He wants to hold my hand. He wants to wrap his arm around my shoulders. He wants to save me.

I'm sick of being saved.

But I'm also exhausted and tired of being attacked on all sides. That tiny town Sam wants has never looked more attractive than in this moment.

"You're right," I say. "I should rest. We can talk more later."

"You can meet my dad." Kimball's smile is absurdly hopeful. Eager, almost. Like a puppy, pawing at me for attention and maybe a scratch behind the ears.

"Alright," I say.

"But not right this second," he promises. "For now, food, shower, and rest. In that order."

"I'm liking you more every minute," Job says. "But for the record, I should say that I'm still Team Sam."

Kimball laughs. "Give me time, man. He's had years. You've known me five minutes."

By the time we're assigned rooms with running hot

water, Kimball has already had people bring us clothing and trays of food.

"You make a convincing argument," Job says, his mouth so full of a hamburger I can barely understand him. "I'll give you that."

"I'm ready to switch to Team Kimball," Adam says. "Sam's been way too moody and idiotic lately."

"Don't take this the wrong way," Kimball says with a half smile, "but the only person whose opinion matters looks a little uncomfortable by your jokes. So I'm going to ignore your comments for the time being." He squeezes my shoulder and then leaves us. He does pause by the door. "If you need me, I'm only a few rooms down. Shout and I'll come running."

The second the door closes, Adam asks, "How do you do it?"

I blink. "Do what?"

"You just draw guys to you like . . . I don't know. A back porch light draws bugs."

"What a flattering observation," Job says. "She's a bug zapper."

"And they're, what?" I smile. "June bugs?"

Adam shrugs. "Mosquitos?"

I shake my head. "I don't do anything."

"Wesley," Adam says. "Sam. And now Kimball."

"Look, can we not talk about this right now?" I ask. "I'm tired."

Adam and Job exchange a look I don't appreciate, but they respect my request. After we all three gorge ourselves, shower, and dress in clean clothing that Kimball procured from who knows where, we climb into bed. Or, I climb into bed. The other two refuse to go to their rooms. Job sleeps on the couch on the far wall, and Adam lies on the rug in the middle of the floor.

"How can you sleep there?" I ask.

But he's already asleep.

So much for being here to guard me. Asking him a direct question doesn't even wake him up. I suppose any would-be attackers might stumble over him and twist an ankle.

I toss.

I turn.

I cover my head with a pillow.

I flip around so my head is at the bottom of the bed.

My eyes are burning. My head feels stuffed with wool. I'm so annoyed that those two dropped off immediately that I consider kicking them in frustration. And yet I still can't sleep. Finally I slide out of bed and slip quietly through the sliding glass door. The ocean waves crash so reliably. The breeze blows my hair across my cheeks. This is exactly what I need.

Peace amid the chaos.

My life feels like nonstop upheaval lately. The people love me, but the leaders hate me. Like my dad, almost. He tried so hard to be good and to help people, but he lost his job and then his wife left him. His partner betrayed him. Maybe he took me at first to punish my mother, but when he tried to give me better life than the one I'd have with Solomon, it wrecked his future.

Sometimes I'm so angry at him.

And sometimes I miss him so badly it cuts like a knife.

Tears roll down my cheeks freely. No one can see me, not here. No one can judge me as weak. Or pathetic. Or wanting.

I've always been too small. Too skinny. Too young. Too naive. Too weak. Too empathetic. Too everything.

I hate it. I stand up, my pajama pants whipping against my legs in the ocean air, and I start to run toward the waves. The water's not warm like the gentle waves in the

Gulf when it slams against my legs. No, the Pacific Ocean is like an open palm slap against raw flesh.

The skin on my arms and legs pebbles.

And I welcome the onslaught.

Because it means I'm alive. I'm fighting. I don't stop moving forward until I'm up to my waist. The tears from my cheeks mix with the salty surf. A wave crashes over me, dunking me under the water momentarily. It's so dark, even with the full moon, that I almost can't find the shore again. But I do.

I'm paddling back in the right direction when another wave crashes over me, rolling me under.

This isn't the soft, calm water of the Gulf. I'm in the real ocean now, the angry ocean.

"Ruby!" Kimball's voice is urgent—distressed even. He's clearly a steady swimmer, reaching me quickly. "What are you doing?" His frantic eyes scan me for injury.

"I'm an idiot," I say. "I meant to walk out here and maybe swim for a bit."

Another wave crashes, but Kimball's arm keeps my head above it.

"And you didn't realize how much more powerful the surf is here."

I spit out ocean water and nod.

He helps drag me back to shore, slowly at first, but once we can walk, we both run. His hand never leaves mine. Once we're out of the water, we both drop to the sand— still a little warm from the long-gone sun. "You couldn't sleep."

"I broke up with him," I say.

Kimball was lying calmly next to me in the dark, and I'm not sure how I can tell, but I can. He freezes. He doesn't shift a hair, every muscle in his body tense. "Why?"

"I'm not entirely sure, but I think it's because he was hurting me."

Kimball exhales.

"But it still hurts," I whisper. "So much."

He flips over then, resting on his elbows, his face above mine, lit by the soft moonlight overhead. Shadows shift and tilt, making him look far more like Wesley than usual. "I'm sorry."

"I know."

"I wasn't lying," he says. "It's not the time to talk about it more, but I want you to know I was one hundred percent honest when I said I love you."

I believe him.

"I will protect you," he says. "I'll do anything you need."

"But you're not president," I say. "Your dad is."

"I'm all he has." Kimball's smile has the same cocky swagger Wesley's always did.

Is that why I like him? Do I regret losing Wesley? Or is it something else? For a brief moment, I wonder what it would feel like to kiss Kimball. Would it be hesitant and then eager, like kissing Wesley? Or steady, confident, and possessive, like Sam?

I shake my head.

"Are you alright?" he asks. "I can walk you back. Or get a blanket."

He'd love that, snuggling under a blanket.

"I shouldn't have come out here in my pajamas," I say. "I'm soaked now."

He laughs.

"How did you find me?" Was he just watching my room? That's a little creepy, honestly.

"We have motion sensors on the back of the house that alarm when we shut things down," he says. "Alerts went off, and someone let me know you were outside."

That's not skeevy, thankfully.

"Embarrassing," I say.

He shakes his head. "It's been a rough few months on you. I can't even imagine."

"It has been pretty crappy," I whisper. My eyes drop to his mouth. I shouldn't be looking at it. Like, I know that in my bones. The last thing I need right now is to kiss someone, but I can't stop thinking about it now. Do I only love Sam because he's the first guy I've ever really spent much time with? Was it only circumstances that forced us together?

Does he fit with the person I'm becoming?

Or does Kimball?

The corner of Kimball's mouth turns up. He has definitely noticed me staring. He leans toward me slowly, very, very slowly.

My heart lurches, and I can't tell whether it's in a good way.

A loud sound behind us—far beyond the beach house— yanks us both backward. "What was that?"

Kimball swears under his breath.

"Is everything okay?"

"That's a plane," he says.

"Is it your dad?"

He shakes his head. "He'd wait for morning. I sent him a message—he's *en route,* but he won't be here until ten or so."

I swallow.

"We need to get you away from here. Now." And before I realize what's happening, he's pulling me up to my feet.

"Who do you think it is?"

He grips my hand like he's worried it'll fly away. "It could be WPN—whatever Port Head failed before. Or it could be that Quinn guy you displaced. Who knows?" He pulls me close for a brief moment. "Whoever it is, they'll regret crossing me, I swear."

Adam and Job are shouting inside the house. "My brothers are freaking out."

"We need to go," Kimball says. "Right now."

I yell back at them. "Job! Adam!"

"Shh." Kimball presses his hand over my mouth. "We can't let anyone inside know where we're going or they'll lead whoever it is right to us."

"What do you mean?" I ask. "Where are we going?"

Job and Adam sprint down the beach toward us. "What's going on?" Adam asks. "Some noise woke me up and you were gone." He yanks me away from Kimball and hugs me so tightly that my bones creak. "I thought I'd lost you."

"I'm fine," I say. "The sound was a plane, probably landing not far from ours."

"Which means we need to go," Job says. "Before whoever it is comes looking for you."

"Right," Adam says. "All it takes is a single bullet." His voice catches and he clears his throat.

"We were already doing that," Kimball says. "I've got a bug out spot."

Now that we're all on the same page, Adam passes Kimball a gun, which is super odd. He can't really tuck it into his wet pajama pants. What a bizarre evening. He holds it in his hand as we jog down the sand. "There's a rocky outcropping a half mile or so from here," Kimball explains.

That's when we hear the first gunshot.

Then three more follow.

Our jog turns into a downright sprint.

"No one and nothing can get through the iron door once we reach it," Kimball says.

Another gunshot. Closer.

Shouting.

"It's right up here," Kimball says.

And then it's looming in front of us, a wall of rock riddled with holes, that extends nearly all the way out to the water. "Does it take water at high tide?" I ask.

Kimball shakes his head. "Only in storms."

Reassuring.

He presses some buttons, but his hand is shaking. After a series of beeps, a screen opens and he leans toward it. An eye scanner. Pretty impressive tech for a rocky outcropping in the middle of abandoned Los Angeles. He straightens and a door slides open.

And then a bullet hits the retinal scanner, shattering it.

I spin around.

Kimball grabs my hand, his gun pointed at the dark figure of the assailant.

But I throw my hands up in the air. "Wait. I'm the one you want."

When he grunts, I realize that the shooter . . . is Sam.

"They didn't kidnap me," I say.

"Kidnap you?" Kimball splutters. "Why would I ever—"

Sam's eyes widen. "What?"

"You don't need to save me." I start laughing, and then I can't stop. I know none of this is funny, but for some reason it all *seems* inexplicably hilarious. My attacker . . . is my savior. The one person I trust the most.

And the one who was supposed to be securing my throne in Galveston and sussing out the real threat. I did *such* a great job selling my kidnapping that I utterly failed in our purpose. But on a completely different front, I've been torn in two lately—between the future I wish I had, and the one I'm stuck inside of. I've been wondering whether I should kiss Kimball.

And I've been scared, so scared of all of it.

I broke up with Sam because he was scared of whether he was right for me, but it was me all along, again. Of course it was. And now, now I know. From the bottoms of my feet to the wisps of my topsy-turvy hair, including the snarls I'll barely be able to comb through, I'm *sure*.

Sam came for me.

Of course he did.

I don't even need rescuing, and he's still here. My heart expands a hundred times, and a frenzy of butterflies swarm eagerly.

And my insane, bizarre, confusing world narrows to one single point.

I race toward Sam, who holsters his guns in a flash and reaches for me. His arms wrap around me and pick me up, spinning me round and round. No matter what, no matter where, no matter when. Even when I'm lost. Stupid. Scared. He's always here. He always comes for me.

And deep down, I knew he would.

I kiss him then, and it's everything I ever needed. It's bold. It's apologetic. It's inviting. It's *mine*. *He* is mine. Always, and forever. "I love you," I say. "And if you'll forgive me for being an idiot, I will marry you."

Sam beams. "I'll always forgive you, and I'll punch anyone who calls you an idiot."

"Except not me," I say.

"Only Kimball has ever been dumb enough to punch you, and you wouldn't let me do anything about it."

Nothing has changed, not really. I'm still not sure who exactly tried to kill me. I'm not sure how Sam will manage while I'm transitioning things, but I'm not afraid anymore. Because if he comes for me now, after I dump and abandon him, then nothing between us can't be fixed. "Kimball's not the villain you thought," I say.

"No," he says. "I figured that much."

"You're not upset?" I can't stop looking at him—drinking him in. He's in all black, his typical tactical outfit. Even so, he fills the entire space, the whole world around him. He's got the gravitational pull of the sun. He sucks everything in and then destroys it. Except me. "Oh!"

"What?" he frowns.

"Did you kill anyone?"

Kimball swears.

"No," Sam says. "You hate when I do that, but Job, they might need your help. And a few first aid kits."

I laugh. Same old Sam. "Thank you."

"Always," he says.

I lean against his chest and close my tired eyes. "How did you find me?"

"I didn't find you," he says. "But I figured it was a safe bet that if he didn't take you, Kimball would know who did."

My neck complains, but I crane it to look up at him. "Huh?"

"If you think I let him traipse back home without tracking him, you don't know me very well."

I shake my head. "I don't even want to know."

"And I was right. Here you are." His smile is a little condescending, but it doesn't bother me. Not today.

"I am here, but only because I figured it was the only way to lure out the real culprit."

"And you knew I'd never sign off on using you as bait like this?" He lifts both eyebrows.

"I needed you there, panicking a bit, to sell it."

He sweeps me into his arms then, and starts to carry me back toward the house. "You're all wet, you brat."

"I went for a swim."

"With Kimball." He arches one eyebrow. "I noticed he's the only other person who's soaked."

"With Kimball," I say. "But only because I needed to—"

"Shh," he says. "I don't care. I don't own you."

"You kind of do," I say. "No matter how frustrated I

got, no matter how much time you spent with that Lydia, I never would've been happy without you."

"You could've been." He stops. "You could be. Life is a sequence of choices, always. And you're a wonderful person who could make any number of choices and still find joy." He whispers, "But I'm glad you decided to choose me."

"Me too," I say. "Deliriously happy, in fact."

"I hate to interrupt this little reunion," Adam says. "But did you come alone? And was it really wise to leave?"

"Wise or not, I wasn't going to sit around while Ruby was in trouble," Sam says. "And I should probably confess that I did have to shoot someone back in Texas."

"What?" I ask. "No, what, what I really want to know is . . . who?"

"Lydia," Sam says.

21

SAM

R uby wriggles so much that I nearly drop her.

I laugh.

She hits my chest. "Shooting someone isn't funny. What are you talking about?"

"Oh, calm down. I shot her with a tranq, and she's tied up in the plane. I thought I might drop her off here, once I'd found you, of course."

"I don't want her," Kimball says.

"Well, too bad," I say. "Because I'm not taking her back."

"I don't understand," Adam says.

"Me neither," Job says.

"When I told her I was coming for you, she told me I couldn't." I shake my head. "I'm ashamed to say that's the first time I realized it."

"That she's a ho?" Job asks. "Because we all noticed that way back."

"Please. No, I believed that she cared for me—"

"Oh, she did," Ruby says. "You were right there."

"I attributed anything she said or did that seemed *off* to

those feelings. That arrogance, that ego, it was my mistake." I clutch Ruby a little tighter. "You're shivering."

"I'll be dry soon enough," she says.

Even so, I rub my hands along her arms. "She lied about Quinn. He didn't have girlfriends galore. His secret, which I suppose he realized you didn't really know, was that he had been in contact with Peabody for years. Dolores Peabody, the Port Head in Mobile. He sold Unmarked secrets and favors to WPN as long as he was on the council."

"If we're talking about split loyalties, I was *queen* of WPN," Ruby says. "That didn't bother the council. Wouldn't they have liked that he had a connection to WPN?"

"But you were up front about your connections from the first day," Sam says. "They'd have hung him for treason if they found out Dolores was his sister and they had plans to bring the countries together, but with the Unmarked joining as second class citizens."

"Lydia told you all this?" Ruby asks.

I glance sideways at Adam. He winces. "Sure," I say. "She told me."

Ruby frowns.

"He tortured her," Kimball says.

I hate that guy. Like, really hate him. "Lydia had been working for him all along and sending messages to Dolores."

"But why would Dolores want me dead?" Ruby asks. "It's not like the people would want her as my replacement —" She chokes. "Oh."

"What?" Sometimes her brain moves so fast I can't keep up.

"She could have decided to forgive him." She looks at Job, her shoulders falling into the most pathetic, dejected pose ever.

"You think?" Job's brow furrows. "But he married her sister. That's so gross."

"People are complicated," I say. "Lydia insisted she loved me, right up until she came clean about all of it, and even then she said she'd betray Quinn for me if I'd give you up."

"She really is a ho." Job chuckles.

"So how did you leave things?" Ruby asks. "Can we just fly home?"

I shrug. "Not sure. Lydia left the room, ostensibly to grab food. Really she went to send a message to Quinn, but he told her that since their attack went awry, that Blevins would come up with something else. He was getting nervous and wanted her gone."

"You caught her talking to him?" Ruby asks.

Talking to him? She's so cute. "No, I wasn't thinking about her much. I discovered you were gone, and I might have freaked out a bit."

Ruby smiles then. "You did?"

I press a kiss to her forehead. "Just a little. And Lydia came in while I was . . . shouting at some people. She was shocked you were gone. I asked her if she'd seen anyone or heard anything since the kitchen was only a few doors down." I clench one fist. That's the first time I realized she was hiding something from me. Extracting the rest wasn't pleasant, but I don't regret it. "She . . . didn't want to share, but she did. After a little persuasion."

"Oh," Ruby says. "Well, I'm sorry."

I shake my head. "I just feel stupid." My ego got in the way of spotting a threat to Ruby, and Lydia widened the cracks in our relationship intentionally. I was so stupid that I let her.

Ruby presses a hand against my cheek. "Don't fault yourself. She really did care about you, and I think Quinn was brilliant to use that."

When we reach the beach house, Ruby wiggles until I reluctantly put her down. "I need a shower and we need to make a plan."

"How's this for a plan?" I ask. "You stay here with Kimball, who will lock Lydia up and throw away the key for conspiring to kill Ruby."

"Wait," Ruby says. "If Lydia was his inside man, then why didn't Quinn and Peabody know to attack the right place? They were *with* us."

"I don't think she looked at the documents I provided about our itinerary," I say. "But even if she did, everyone but Adam and me thought we *were* going to Lake Charles next."

"And we flew to Mexico instead," Ruby says.

"She had no way to call off the strike from Mexico, so by the time she could have . . . " I shake my head.

It was already done.

"But back to our next move," I say. "You stay with Kimball." I try not to scowl when I say his name. "And I fly back with Adam. We kill whoever is trying to step into your place, and then we come back for you."

Ruby sets her jaw.

I don't swear under my breath. I don't punch anyone or anything. But I want to, badly.

"I can't sit around while you deal with things," she says. "We go together."

My teeth grind against one another.

"Sam, I want you at my side. At boring meetings. At Sunday sermons. When we address people. As my husband."

My heart lurches at that word.

"But that means you have to take me with you. We have to vanquish the villains together."

I think about when we wound up in a holding cell. And again when Wesley and I were in iron shackles, chained to the wall. And again when I was bound and helpless while my dad almost killed her. "I've failed you too many times," I say. "I'm not sure I can risk you again, when you could be safe here." Even if it is with *him*.

"You don't have to do everything," she whispers. "And I can't risk you either. Luckily, we won't have to . . . because you won't be alone. We go as a team." She reaches for my hand and our fingers lace together.

We're on the other side of the continent, but the moment is the same. With her fingers threaded through mine, the sound of the surf behind us, I know we can do it. We can do anything. "Okay."

The beatific smile she turns on me makes the fear worth it.

"What if you didn't fly to Galveston?" Kimball asks.

"Um, that's a good idea," I say. "Far safer, anyway. Except that's the center of everything for WPN. She's going to have to go there eventually."

"But if you're virtually sure that it's, who did you say? Peabody? Is that who you think tried to have you killed? Maybe you fly into *her* home base. She won't expect that."

"It's actually either Sawyer or Rosa who's going to move to take my spot," Ruby says. "Peabody would be a facilitator either way. Sawyer is David Solomon's first cousin, and he always makes it clear to everyone that he's Solomon's only real blood relative, other than me." She looks at me apologetically. "And we recently discovered that Rosa and Solomon have a son—he would have a fair claim as well. Rosa could be planning to press that."

And it's pitifully clear that Ruby hopes, in spite of Sawyer's connection with Peabody, that her cousin didn't betray her and murder two settlements' worth of people simply to cover up murdering her.

"Okay, so Sawyer is where? New Orleans, isn't it?"

Kimball pays attention. I'll give him that. "And Rosa is in Miami?"

"That's right, yes," Ruby says. "But I'm not sure why I'd be better off flying to either of those places instead. Wouldn't Sawyer and Rosa have more supporters in their home ports than anywhere else?"

"First, whichever of them is guilty won't likely be staying at home," Kimball says. "I imagine the guilty party is headed for Galveston, if they're not already there."

"The people love her in all the Port Cities," Job says.

"Right," Adam says. "I think that's our best—"

"But to do things right, I need evidence." Ruby smiles. "Kimball's right about that."

I am so going to punch Kimball right in the nose the next time I have a reason. A broken nose would help blunt his stupid boy-next-door looks a bit. But in spite of my irritation with him, he's got a good point.

"I can't just go around shooting people," Ruby says. "Not if I want to be the kind of ruler that . . . Triptych . . . needs." She freezes, her eyes widening. "Triptych. That's what Dad called Tercera. Tri, for the three years it takes to fully run its course, but that word also fits for the three peoples. Marked. Unmarked. WPN."

"A triptych also means three pieces of art, meant to be displayed and appreciated together," Kimball says.

Ruby's eyes light up. "When this is past, I'm proposing that as our new name."

"It's good," I say. I hate that I sound like such a dope next to Mr. Eloquent, but Ruby doesn't seem to mind. She picked me, not him. That's enough to leave me beaming like an idiot, in spite of Kimball's irritatingly educated and insightful suggestions.

It takes us until well after sunup, only taking a break to make sure Lydia's still unconscious and hogtied, but we work up a plan. It's not nuanced, but it's as thorough as we can make it from here, and it hopefully gets Ruby the evidence she wants to use for a trial against Sawyer. Combined with Lydia's testimony, anyway.

Ruby rubs her eyes and shoves her messy, disheveled hair back. "When did you say your dad was going to be here?"

"I'm here now," a deep voice says.

Ruby springs to her feet and smooths her rumpled, salt-stained pajama pants as if that might make her look more presentable. I suppress a laugh. She never did get that shower or change of clothes. "Oh, sir. It's a pleasure to meet you."

A tall man with strawberry blonde hair and Kimball's insouciant smile strides across the room in an immaculate suit. "You must be Queen Ruby. I've heard a lot about you."

"I'm so sorry to greet you in pajamas." Her blushes are always so becoming.

"It's quite alright." He scans the people in his family room. "It appears you've had a very busy night. My son might have warned me, but I take it things have been intense."

Ruby nods and swallows. "My fiancé thought I had been kidnapped," she says. "And came to retrieve me."

"As any good fiancé would." If Kimball's father is disappointed to hear her refer to me as her fiancé, he doesn't show it. "I heard from the staff that he took out anyone who opposed him."

She bites her lip. "I'm very sorry about that. It really wasn't—"

"Suffice it to say that if he ever wants a spot on my security team, he's hired." Kimball's dad laughs. "But don't worry that we'll take offense. No permanent harm was done in any case. And it looks like you're already making plans to take care of whatever housekeeping is necessary on your end."

"Absolutely," I say.

"Well," he says, "don't let me interrupt. I've never seen my son look quite this earnest."

"I think we were all about to rest for a few hours." Ruby yawns. "And then perhaps eat dinner and talk to you about the future of CINOW and Triptych."

Mr. Ryson glances at Kimball.

"That's the new name Ruby's considering for the conglomeration of WPN, the Unmarked, and the Marked."

"I like it," Mr. Ryson says. "It's poetic."

"Thanks," Ruby says.

After we hammer out a few more details, Ruby stands up, yawning again. "I need a shower, and then I'm going to crash."

I stand up, too.

Mr. Ryson's eyebrows rise, but he doesn't object when I follow her back to her room, and neither does Ruby. I wait outside while she showers and changes. I'm tired, but nothing like her, I imagine. Once she's in clean clothes, with her wet but clean hair around her shoulders, she pads across the floor toward me. I pluck her up and swing her onto the bed next to me without a word, tucking her body against mine.

It fits as perfectly as it ever has, and some hidden tension in my heart I didn't realize was still there eases. She drops off to sleep, and then so do I. And for the first time in a very long time, all is right in the world. Because at last, I'm holding my tiny, perfect fiancée in my arms.

22

RUBY

The plan has come together. Part of me wants to prolong this moment in time—come up with a reason to delay. I'm sitting next to Sam at a long wooden table, eating scrambled eggs and toast. The waves crash outside, and seagulls swoop and call brightly. When I reach for Sam's hand, it's there.

His smile is open and genuine.

What is life, but a necklace full of moments, some perfect, some flawed, strung together in time—some behind us, some ahead. But this one bead in this single moment, it sparkles. I wish it could dangle suspended forever.

"You okay?" Sam's voice is deep, his eyes intent.

"I'm better than okay," I say.

"You don't have to do it, you know." His voice is gruff, almost as if he's forcing the words out when he doesn't want to.

"I know. I've thought about it from all angles, but I have to go. These are my people. What kind of leader sends some kind of advance guard to clean up all her mess-es?" I shake my head. "I may be small, and I may not be very intimidating, but I think that's the point. How many of Triptych's citizens are small like I am? I should show them that their size doesn't mean they can't move mountains."

Sam chuckles. "That's not what I meant."

My eyebrows draw together. "What?"

His hand brushes against mine gently. "You don't have to marry me." He sighs. "But you should know that I didn't propose because I was trying to pour glue into the cracks opening up between us."

So he did see them, too. "You were afraid. I get that."

He shakes his head. "It wasn't that either. I've never been afraid of anything other than losing you. That's the one constant in my life—my cross to bear. But that's not why I proposed either. A marriage isn't a guarantee. It's not a get out of jail certificate. I know that much, and I always have." His eyes go glassy for a second, and I figure he's thinking about his parents' miserable marriage. "No, I proposed because all we have are these perfect moments, and it was a perfect moment then, on that beach, with you. I felt like I wanted to string together as many as I could— like I wanted to express how perfect it felt to me, and that was the only way I could think to do it."

How much do his thoughts echo mine from a moment ago? We may not *seem* much alike, but in our hearts, we're almost the same. I shift my hand a bit, sliding my fingers against his. "I know just what you're saying." I lean against his shoulder. "And that's why I *want* to marry you, even though I'm young. Even though I don't have to. Even though it's no guarantee."

"The only guarantee in life is that I'll always come for you," he says. "Whether it's across the country, or through a boardroom. It may take me a week or two to figure out when I'm being a dope, but when I do, I'll come for you, guns blazing. Every single time."

I don't doubt that for a second. But if I ever do, he'll be there to reassure me, and that's why I want to marry him. "Once this is past, we'll pick a date."

"And we'll do it right," he says. "There will be a lot of people who want to celebrate with us, and I want them all to be there. You've missed out on a lot of things in life—from losing your dad, to hiding in a cabin, to being flung down a path you didn't choose. This wedding will be what you choose, every step of the way."

"Even if all you want is a small ceremony on the beach?"

His eyes flash greenish-gold. "Even if that's all I want, because more than I want that, I want what *you* want."

"You two ready?" Adam has been giving us space, but he's also itching to move. I get that, because I feel it too. Like a spider crawling between my shoulder blades that I can't quite reach.

I'm sick of waiting for it to bite me. I stand up. "I am."

The flight to Baton Rouge is long—longer because of all the logistics we can't seem to drop.

I keep coming back to asking one of the Marked kids to take my place. I don't like it, at all. It didn't work the last time we tried it. Solomon immediately realized it wasn't me. "Are you sure we should—"

"You won't make anyone do anything," Job says. "We'll just ask."

And then we're landing. And hiking through the muggy, hot underbrush. "How did it go from a little warm to an unbearable rainforest sauna in a month?" Kimball asks.

"Spoken like a California boy," I say. "It goes from one to the other in the blink of an eye down South."

The first person I recognize is Aunt Anne. She's talking to a kid with a mohawk that's clearly a copy of Rafe's at the edge of town. Her eyes widen and she sprints toward us. "You're alive."

"I am." I wonder how many times we've all had to worry

that a member of our family has died. So far, other than my dad, we haven't lost anyone.

Unless you count Wesley.

"What are you doing here?" Aunt Anne looks from me to Job, then to Sam, and then to Kimball and Adam. "Are you in trouble?"

"Aren't I always?" I ask.

But as we explain our plan, Aunt Anne falls into step next to us, making suggestions and clarifying a few details here and there.

"You need someone who's your size?" A girl who was following behind Aunt Anne asks softly.

My head whips toward her. She's my height and my weight. And she has high, pronounced cheekbones, blonde hair, and blue eyes. All she's lacking are the curls. "We are." I hate saying the words.

"I'd be honored to take your place," she says. "Unless you think I'm not regal enough."

Job snorts.

I open my mouth to tell her that we'd love it, but I can't get the words out. What kind of queen sends any of her people in her place? To take the risk that they might attack her instead? Rhonda stepped in on my behalf once, but I can't let anyone else do it, not now. I'm not sure what we'll do instead, but I just can't.

"Or if you'd like someone older," Rafe says from a few feet away, "I'm sure we won't have any lack of volunteers, *Your Majesty*. The people here practically worship you."

When did he get here? I hate the derision in his tone, because I feel the same way. It's ridiculous they should look up to me like they do, and that they're willing to sacrifice themselves to spare me.

"No." I shake my head.

The blonde girl's face falls.

"It's not that I don't appreciate your willingness to help,

truly," I say. "It's just that I know this was our plan, but I can't do it. I can't send someone to Galveston to be me, while I travel to New Orleans or Mobile or Miami instead. Even the thought makes me sick."

"We've been through this," Adam says. "The odds that—"

"I don't care," I say. "Any chance—"

"What if, instead," Kimball says, "*I* contact them, offering to sell you back . . . for a price?"

Interesting. "Keep going," I say.

Sam and Adam look like the same person in two bodies, scowling like they'd enjoy ending him slowly.

"We can do it from here. We tie you up, maybe add some makeup to sell it. I contact them—not sure how— and offer to ransom you. Whoever's in charge, well, they won't want you back, will they?"

"Or what if there are other people around and they feel they have no choice?" Sam asks. "Then they'll pay your ransom, and we'll know nothing for sure. We're safer sending a fake envoy to Galveston to distract them while the rest of us go to their home base and search for evidence of their duplicity."

"Except you know them, Ruby," Kimball says. "Will they be able to turn down the chance to eliminate you? Will they ransom you?"

I think about my interactions with the Port Heads. I hope Jose would do whatever it took to save me. I'm not sure about Terry or Rosa or Quentin. But I really believe that Sawyer Blevins cares about me. I shouldn't be hoping that it's Rosa. I shouldn't be looking for a way out, but he's the only family I have on David Solomon's side who hasn't let me down monstrously. Maybe that's why, more than any other reason, I need to know the truth about my enemies. "We'd need to really sell that I'm in peril for that to work."

"That won't be hard," Adam says. "Sam's gone, and no one's heard from you in days now."

Aunt Anne has a wonderful time applying makeup for this part.

"That's way too much fake blood," I say. "C'mon."

"Oh, fine." She wipes half of it off. "But mouth wounds do bleed pretty badly. It always looks much worse than it is."

I laugh.

"Watching you laughing with all those awful bruises and that bloody cut," Sam says, "is—" He shudders. "Let's get this over with already."

"Did we figure out the tech stuff?" I scrunch my nose. "I know nothing about that."

Job has been arguing with two of Rafe's guys and the representative from WPN for an hour now. "If we spoof the—"

"Hello?" Adam waves at Job. "Are we good to go?"

Job rolls his eyes. "I think so."

In the end, it takes them another forty-five minutes to agree.

"Oh come on," Kimball says. "Half that blood is on Sam's lower lip."

Sam's grinning, not at all worried. He shrugs. "Don't know what to tell you."

Aunt Anne's mostly faking being annoyed as she reapplies it. "Okay, now don't go glowing with joy on the video call and ruining this." But her eyes are twinkling, and I know she's happy.

I catch her hand. "Would you be willing to walk me down the aisle?"

Her breath catches in her throat. "Me?"

"I know I could ask Josephine, or Uncle Dan, but you're my real dad's twin. I think I'd rather have you do it than anyone else."

A tear slips down her cheek, and she nods soundlessly.

"Okay, thanks." The tears welling in my eyes will help sell this, I hope. "And I'd love to have Rose be our flower girl. By the time we have the wedding, I bet she'll be able to walk."

"Of course." She sniffles and then points at the camera. "Now. Focus."

I do. Kimball's hand hovers over the call button, but first he reaches up and runs his fingers through his hair, mussing the perfection just a bit. He glances back at me with a wild look in his eyes. "Ready?"

I nod.

He smiles, and then hits talk.

Frank answers, and I choke on a sob to really make sure he's worried. He looks ready to drop into a fetal ball and cry on the ground. Perfect. "I'll need to track down Mr. Blevins. Please don't disappear." He glances past Kimball at my bound form, his eyes wide and worried. "And please don't hurt her any more. We'll do whatever you want."

Kimball's laugh sounds legitimately unhinged. I love it.

It takes almost five minutes, but eventually, Sawyer's white hair and creased face shows up on the tiny screen in front of Kimball. "Ryson. It is you." He waves at the guards huddling behind him. "Out, all of you. Now."

My heart sinks. We need evidence. We need to catch them, but he's also my only blood relative, other than Adam and Josephine. Maybe he really wants to talk to me—to save me. Maybe he'll offer whatever it takes.

Once the last guard has gone—Frank practically has to be hauled out—Sawyer turns back to the screen, and he smiles.

But not a good smile. His smile is chilling in all the wrong ways.

He looks calculating, greedy, and possibly worst of all,

so very pleased with himself. "Your call is a stroke of luck, you know."

"It is?" Kimball asks. "Because we have need of quite a few things that I doubt you'll want to part with."

"Oh, I'm not going to pay you a dime for her return," Sawyer Blevins says, and my heart breaks right down the middle.

He told me about my father's limitations—about David Solomon's flaws. He told me about my grandfather, and how he was a good man. I hoped Sawyer was a good man too. He tried to step down. I don't understand how we could be here. I'd have let him marry Dolores, so what's the point?

I can't see Kimball's face, but I hear him spluttering from here. "You won't pay me for her? What does that mean?"

"What do you need?" Sawyer asks. "Because if you think I'll arm you so that you can attack us—"

"I don't care about that," Kimball says. "But the alleged cure she gave us didn't work. I think she double-crossed us. Our citizens are still Marked, and knowing a cure was coming, we have quite a few people who went to visit their lost family members and are now also Marked."

Sawyer chuckles. "Maybe she wasn't as unbearably noble as I thought. I'm actually a bit impressed."

"The point," Kimball says, "is that we need that cure. And we also need some of the manufacturing technology you've been hoarding. We aren't able to convert—"

My cousin waves his hand through the air. "Whatever. Yes, sure. We can send you the actual cure, and also manufacturing specs. I could even be convinced to part with some technicians to explain all of it. Is that all you need?"

"You said you won't pay for her," Kimball says. "But it appears that you will." He grunts. "It'll be my pleasure—"

"Not so fast," Sawyer says. "I won't pay you for her. That's true."

"Then what—"

"I don't ever want to see her insipid, cherubic little face again. I don't want to hear her whining voice. And most especially, I never, ever want that bobbing blonde halo of curls to float down the hall toward me."

"She's your cousin," Kimball says. "I don't get it."

"I've hated her father for so long that it's part of my DNA now," Sawyer says. "He's ruined everything in my life, and I've been forced to live off his crumbs, when I should have had it all."

"But she didn't have anything to do with that." Kimball tilts his head. "She's done nothing but good—"

"For which you kidnapped her." Sawyer laughs. "She's naive, and pretentious, and needy." He shakes his head. "And she'd never been strong enough to do what it takes. She'd have made a terrible ruler, but if we play this right, I'll come out of this tragedy with exactly what the world needs, finally in my rightful place."

A place he was willing to kill how many people to ascend? He's as bad as Solomon ever was. And I'm the fool who didn't see it.

"I don't want to kill her." Kimball's words are slow, practically pained. "You talk about her naiveté as though it's awful, but I feel pretty bad for kidnapping her, honestly."

"Don't kill her, then. Enjoy her. Dip her in bronze. Shoot her in the head." Sawyer shrugs. "I don't much care which you do, as long as we never hear from her again. Is that clear?"

"I don't understand," Kimball scratches his head. "She let you keep your job. She united the three nations."

"Oh, yes, she did that for me, and it makes things much easier. I'll be marrying Dolores Peabody soon, and her brother will be returned to the regent's seat for the Unmarked, but I'll rule them all."

"That's really what you want?" Kimball asks. "It was all about power? It's so cliché."

"I'm related to her, you know," Sawyer says. "And I'm old enough to be immune to whatever ingénue hormone she seems to exude that has all the morons with a Y chromosome stumbling all over themselves to save her."

"But—"

"I should have been Solomon's heir," Sawyer says. "I had the idea to create World Peace Now in the first place, you know. I was a pastor for a full five years before he uttered his first bumbly sermon. The second he told me what had happened, that his idiotic wife's ex had released an earth-destroying virus that only he knew about—I told him this was his chance. I told him to forget about duping wealthy widows out of their estates. Forget telethons begging morons to send us money for prayers. We'd prophesy the end of the world that we knew was coming—through insider trading as it were—and people would be so grateful for our prophecies for keeping them safe that they'd worship us. Tell me I was wrong."

Kimball doesn't say a word. I can only imagine how horrified he must be. *Sawyer* gave Solomon the idea—to create a cult that would worship him instead of trying to halt or mitigate the spread of the disease?

He's a monster. Worse even than my biological father.

"So let me be clear. If I keep her away from you, in exchange you'll send me—"

"Whatever you want, excepting military tech," Sawyer says. "And I'll even sign a peace treaty with you and your daddy, providing you pay an annual tribute to us. Ten percent, no wait, fifteen percent of your annual yield should be sufficient." His grin is positively disgusting. "I'm not a greedy man, as you can see. I only want what I'm due."

What more could he want than what he already had? I want, so badly, to stand up and shout at him. But he's in Galveston, and it's not the right time. Not yet, anyway. So I stay immobile on my side, but the fury I'm quaking with is real, right up until the very second that Kimball disconnects the call.

Sam steps into view and helps me stand. "And?"

"You know how I never want you to shoot anyone?"

He smiles.

"I think we probably need to hold a trial," I say. "But if things don't go smoothly with our return, don't aim for his extremities."

Sam beams at me. "It would be my pleasure, Your Majesty."

I punch his shoulder, and it freaking hurts as much as it always does. When will I remember never to punch Sam?

Sometimes, though, sometimes pain is just what you need. Sometimes you have to endure it so that you can come out the other side stronger.

23

RUBY

Two days later, I watch as I die.

On camera, no less.

Sawyer has huge screens erected in each city center. I'm standing on the edge of the crowd in Baton Rouge, my hair pulled back under a hat, baggy clothing concealing my tiny frame. When Sawyer starts the broadcast, he's impressively solemn. The Port Heads are all gathered. The ceremony is a nice one. They even pan around to show the crying and wailing from the audience.

It's a bizarre thing, watching people mourn you. It tears at me, like I'm complicit in the pain they're feeling.

But Sam's adamant that we can't stop the nonsense. "I let you manage the evidence gathering, but this next part?" He shakes his head. "This next part is tactical, and that's all me. It takes time to plan if you really want me to mitigate the death toll."

Which of course I do. So I wait like a good little girl, even when all I want to do is run down the street screaming, "I'm alive!"

But finally, a few days after the funeral, while the Port

Heads are still in conference, supposedly choosing my replacement, we finally reach the bridge to the island.

"I can't believe this is the only thing I get to do." I've been grumbling for hours, the whole way over in fact, but Sam just smiles and ignores me.

"You're lucky he's letting you do this," Job says. "And to be honest, you have the coolest job and you know it."

I do have high hopes. Our posse of SUVs rolls up to the guard gate at the base of bridge, the very place where I ran smack into Sam's chest when I turned around and sprinted back to the edge of the bridge so many, many weeks ago. That was the first time I realized something wasn't quite normal about him, when he didn't react the way he should have to my sleeping pills.

"No one's allowed across," the guard says gruffly, leveling a scary black gun at our vehicle.

Sam opens his mouth, probably to reverse his orders, but before he can, I snap my door open and hop out. I fling my hood back, clearly displaying my face and very recogniz-able hair. "Even me?"

The tip of the guard's gun dips and his mouth dangles open. "Your Majesty."

"That's right. It's me, Ruby Solomon, back from the presumed dead. Are you saying I can't cross the bridge?"

Sam's certainly prepared to shoot him dead if necessary. A quick glance confirms he's aiming in between the poor guy's eyes, his gun pointed across the top of the car.

I'm also prepared to present evidence of who I am. Identification, photographs. I'm prepared for him to yell, or to call me a liar.

I'm not prepared for him to break down sobbing. "You're alive! It's a miracle from God! Praise the Lord!" His gun clatters against the ground, and I cringe. We're lucky it didn't misfire. He's still bawling like a baby.

I walk toward him slowly. "It's alright," I say soothingly. "Truly. I'm alive, and everything is alright."

His arms wrap around me tightly, his tear-streaked face turned upward. "Thank you. Thank you, Your Majesty for coming back to us."

Uh. Like, from the beyond? "I actually—"

Adam's at my side then, gently removing the guard's arms and shooing the other approaching guards away. "As you can imagine, Her Majesty is very exhausted from her ordeal. She needs to get home quickly."

"Of course," they all mumble. "Yes, please, please go." But that first guy isn't the only one crying. The stocky lady behind him is hiccupping, tear tracks streaking her face.

Good heavens. I felt bad for the mourners, but . . .

"Let's go," Adam whispers. "Quick, before they find a lamb to slaughter or start a fire to roast it on."

"Now tell me that wasn't awesome," Job says. "For real."

He's kind of right. It was fun.

"I told you it was the best job," Sam says smugly.

"Oh, shut up."

But the second the wheels hit the pavement of the bridge, my Sam disappears. He's replaced with Terminator Sam. His eyes are devoid of life, his gaze constantly scanning. He barks commands through his earpiece. "Ready the feed."

"People might not even be out and about," I say.

"Oh, they'll be out," Adam says.

"We started the feed with a five minute loop. 'Announcement coming,' it's saying," Job says. "I'm sure Sawyer Blevins will be freaking out as the people gathering for the Sunday sermon and his coronation stop—wondering what announcement is coming."

Smart. I hadn't heard that. "Will it be playing inside the stadium as well?"

"It should be," Job says. "Since that's where he broadcast the montage of your time with them for the funeral. Remember?"

I think about the screens Sawyer installed, being used instead to out the truth about him. Making the video for Sawyer was actually kind of fun. I hope the citizens don't feel like I had anything to do with tricking them, but the important thing is that they're getting the truth now. Or, you know, five minutes from now.

We cross the edge of the bridge onto the island, stopping at the guard post again. This time we're on a timeline, so I'm much faster, but it's almost as fun. There's less crying, but more shouts of Hosanna. "I'm sorry," I say. "But we have to hurry. We have some demons to deal with."

The guard grips his gun tightly. "I'd be happy to come." His eyes are flinty. I almost wave him in, but our SUV is full. I shake my head. "I appreciate your willingness and your devoted service, but if you can keep holding the line here, that's the best thing you can do right now."

He salutes me and then smiles. "Welcome back, Your Majesty."

For the first time, I actually feel like I'm coming home to Galveston—the island I hated, the island I feared. Galveston feels like home to me now. Go figure.

I want to rush to our house—the house Josephine and David Solomon shared now feels like my house—because I'm worried about my mom and Rhonda, but I can't, not yet.

"It's time?"

Sam nods. "Now we wait. If things go right, half our job will be done by your people."

Like a mousetrap snapping shut, Sam said.

I imagine I'm there, watching the sermon—Sawyer's probably talking when it starts. "Announcement coming. Announcement coming." I imagine his people scurrying around, trying to get it to stop.

And then my face will pop up, huge. And very alive.

"My cousin held my funeral," I say, "and now you're all here to listen to him inspire you with the word of God before celebrating his coronation. But my death was just another falsehood in a long line of lies he has told."

Then a list will pop up, with every single lie we were able to document that people might know about. As we started digging, we found quite a few, starting at the beginning. "He was complicit in the foundational lie, the one that probably left many of your loved ones infected, Marked, sick, and then dead. He worked with David Solomon to ensure that their power increased, even as the people of the world died all around them. Deaths he could have stopped in several ways."

A few great shots of the world burning around them.

And then we roll forward, telling them about the accelerant, the retention of the virus in Solomon's death—we discovered Sawyer used it a few times too—and culminating with the footage of my darling cousin telling Kimball that he doesn't care what happens to me, as long as I never return. Finally it cuts back to me, only at the end, I'm addressing Sawyer himself. "Do you remember your welcome, the first time we met?" I bite my lip. "You told me you'd love to have me out for a visit." I smile. "Now it's my chance to tell you that I can't wait to see you again. In fact, I'm here on the island right now. I'll be waiting outside of the stadium to speak to you."

I've watched the video so many times that it practically plays in my mind as we wait outside for Sawyer Blevins to make his escape. Possibly for the first time in his life, he does exactly what I want, running out of the stage exit.

And right into the waiting embrace of Sam.

Who punches him in the nose. And in the stomach. And then kicks him.

I ought to stop him, but I can't quite bring myself to do it.

"He's unconscious," Adam says, sounding almost bored.

"So?" Sam asks.

Adam shrugs. "I'd rather inflict pain when he can feel it, but you do what makes you happy."

Sam sighs and steps away. "Take them all."

The men move forward to locate and apprehend the other Port Heads, but by the time they go inside, they're already caught—by my own citizens. They're not quite as vicious as Sam, but I think it's only for lack of training. They seem just as angry.

Until they see me. "Queen Ruby!"

They shout so loudly, and wail so fervently, that I walk up to the podium.

"Ruby!!" Job shouts.

I spin around. "Yes?"

"Do you want me to broadcast this?"

I blink. Do I want to speak to any one who is listening? Actually, I do. The girl who hated public speaking so much that she fumbled over her own words and puked down the front of her dress years ago now wants to address her people all over the world. "Yes, I actually do."

He taps his watch. He'll need a minute. As it turns out, that's alright. The audience is so worked up that they shout and scream and cry for quite some time. By the time they settle down, I glance back at Job and he nods.

I step up to the podium. "It's been a very long week," I say.

They laugh. Of course they do. Humor is the intersection of the taboo with the acceptable, and only I can make a joke about what we've been through—because I'm the one who died, and they're the ones who mourned me. We're joined, again, through our shared pain. "I want to start by saying that I love you all. I recognize that it sounds cheesy and almost unbelievable, but it's nevertheless true. You have become, well." I glance at Sam. "Not *everything* to me, but darn close. I want to make a world where all of my people can live, love, work, strive, and improve. I want the world to be like Before, only better. I want that for all of us, and for our children, too."

I gesture for Sam to join me. "And in light of that, I'd like to announce that I'm engaged. Samuel Roth, the love of my life and my very best friend, has asked me to marry him, and I've accepted with great joy."

To call the applause anything but thunderous would be a disservice.

Sam's even touched next to me. He wraps an arm around my shoulders. "And what have I learned from this?" I shake my head. "I want you all to listen. It's possibly the most profound thing I've ever uncovered, and it's simple, as most profound things are." I lick my lips. "Life is miserable, sometimes too short, and almost always ugly, but it's in the midst of that, it's *because of that ugliness* that we recognize its epic beauty. If I hadn't had such a terrible week, I might not have realized the joy Sam brings to my life. Those moments of perfection, they *are* the purpose in our lives. We appreciate them because of the difficult trials we endure. So as hard as it was to hear that I'd died not long ago, I hope you can now revel in the joy you feel at my survival. Appreciate the blessings we do have whenever we have them."

I gesture for Job to join me, and Adam too. "Life has been hard. I lost my best friend a few months ago. He died so that I could live." My eyes well with tears. "I'll never forget Wesley or his sacrifice. He wasn't perfect, but when he had the opportunity to do it, he always made the noble choice. He saved me, and together we saved the world. That's my goal, always. Survive the difficult, improve wherever I can, and then keep going to be better tomorrow than

I am today." I wipe a tear away. "And in light of that, I think it's a good time to tell you that I've come up with a name for our new nation. I hope it will reflect our past and my hope in our future."

"My father, Donald Carillon, developed a virus, a nasty, terrible, awful virus. He named it triptych. He wanted to use it so he could develop a vaccination that would be accessible to anyone, and keep us safe from a plethora of nasty things. It went wrong. It was released, and unknowingly, the world called it Tercera."

I wipe at my eyes again. "I've been amazed—no, astonished—that three very different communities are willing to follow me. After all, I'm a nobody. I had two fathers—and now none at all. I have an aunt I don't deserve and a mother I'm only now getting to know. I've never fit in anywhere. I tried every single path with the Unmarked, and none of them felt quite right."

Murmurs sound all around me. By now, I've learned that sound means they support me, and that they understand.

"And in spite of my shortcomings, the Unmarked—some of the bravest, kindest people I've known—chose me as their chancellor. Then the Marked, some of the fiercest, most tenacious people I've met, voted to join us, with me at the helm. And finally, I'm embarrassed to say that I've yet to ask my morally upright, loyal citizens of WPN to vote on me as their leader. That will be rectified within the month, I swear. But if you choose me too, then that will be three very distinct groups of people who have all agreed to come together as one in the wake of the devastation caused by Tercera—a virus my dad would never have agreed to release had he been given a choice. I'd like to call our new nation Triptych, in honor of the future my father *hoped for*, instead of the one that he got."

I have no idea how the citizens in other places react, but the ones in Galveston are wild for the idea. "I'll include a choice to ratify that, or to reject it. And if you reject it, that's alright. We'll go back to the drawing board and find a name that represents all of us, working together for a brighter future. And if you reject me, I'll help you find a replacement. But if you accept Triptych, and you accept me, I'll be delighted to serve you as I bring us all toward something we all want. Peace in our world, and peace in our hearts."

Because that's really the whole reason we're here at all.

For the first time, I think the citizens of WPN are starting to get that, but whatever they think, I can tell from Sam's goofy grin that he's finally fully on board.

And that's the only vote of confidence I really can't live without.

Nothing scares me, not anymore. Not now that Ruby's going to be my *wife*. The word rolls around in my brain like some kind of wood sprite, filling my mind with all kinds of flowers and butterflies and sunshine. I wish I could sit around and think about it all day. Ruby and wife. My wife, Ruby.

Except, I'm a little bit scared to stand up in front of nine-gazillion people and pledge my vows. I hate talking in front of a handful of people, much less every single person on Galveston Island.

"You didn't want to get married in California," Rhonda says.

I adjust the bow on my tux. "As if that was ever an option."

"But you told her it was fine if Kimball comes," Rhonda says. "I don't get it."

"She only suggested California because no one would travel that far," I say. "She never thought we'd really go there. But of course I want Kimball at our *wedding*. Wouldn't you want your archnemesis to watch you presented with the award you beat him to?"

"Are you really calling Ruby a trophy wife?" Adam shakes his head. "You're a braver man than I."

I clear my throat. "I would never call her that."

Adam smiles. "Good choice."

Rafe breezes through the door in a suit coat and black shorts, his hair still spiked into its signature mohawk. It looks a little less strange now that he's filling out and he has an Adam's apple. Not that you can see it with his leather-studded collar in the way.

Oh, well. Family is family.

"I'm here. That means the party can get started," Rafe says.

"Newsflash, rooster," Rhonda says. "This isn't *your* party. We're all waiting on the same person."

Rafe rolls his eyes. "I feel like my entire life has been spent waiting for her."

"Me too," I say. But Rafe's irritation only increases my joy. Maybe it's something about brothers, but getting under his skin makes me happy.

"It's time," Rhonda says.

"Time?" Adam looks out the window. "How do you know?"

Rhonda taps her ear. "Today, you boys aren't running things. I'm the one with the earpiece—the Maid of Honor earpiece."

"Wait," Adam says. "Why don't I get a radio? I'm the Head of her Guard."

Rhonda laughs. "Let's go, meatheads."

"Oh, don't call me that," Rafe says. "I'm definitely not a qualifying person."

"Fine, beefcakes?" Rhonda asks.

"Let's go," I say.

Rhonda takes my arm.

I pause, eyeing her purposefully. "Did I forget how to walk?"

"You don't know which direction to go." Her smug smile irritates me.

"Oh?" I glance at Adam, but he's not disagreeing. "You think I don't know how to get to the stadium?"

Rhonda shakes her head. "This is your gift from Ruby."

I blink. "My what?"

"She knew you wanted a small wedding, so that's what we're doing."

"I'm videotaping," Adam says. "And everyone else can watch it from those great screens good old cousin Sawyer installed before his execution." He shrugs. "But the wedding is just for the two of you."

My heart expands again. Ruby's always surprising me. And the more time I spend helping her make the decisions that keep cropping up, the more faith I have in her ability to do the right thing in the face of impossible problems. "Alright." If the people will forgive anyone for cutting them out, it's Ruby. "If that's what she wants."

We walk out the back door and start walking down the beach toward the surf. I expect hundreds of people, but I count barely more than a dozen. "Wait, who's going to be there?"

Rhonda points. "See for yourself."

Kimball and Sean and the brother-sister nerds from the Marked stand in the back. Kimball salutes me. Frank and a handful of other guards are on the next row. Dan's in front of them all, bouncing Rose on his knee, her little basket of rose petals on the ground next to them. Mr. Fairchild's standing next to him. Gemette and a few of Ruby's friends from Port Gibson are in front of them. And then on the front row, Job's standing there with a smile on his face, right next to Josephine. "Hey, Sam."

"This is it?"

It's the exact wedding I wanted. But I hope it's what Ruby wants, too.

Music pours out of a little black box on the ground next to Gemette.

"What's that?" I ask.

"That's my wedding gift," Kimball says. "State of the art sound system, so you don't even need a band out here."

I roll my eyes, but before I'm even done, I see her. Ruby steps down from the back porch of the house, her arm wrapped around Anne's. Her hair is down, curly tendrils framing her face, just like it was on the trip from Port Gibson to here—the trip that changed everything. The trip that set my life on the right path.

My eyes travel down, and I notice her dress for the first time. It's not big and full like a cupcake. It's not even white. It's an ivory silk that's much more flattering for her complexion, and it hugs her every curve. Most people see Ruby as childlike, almost, due to her size, but she's always been exactly perfect to me. Nothing ostentatious, nothing shoved in your face. She's like a meringue—light, airy, delicate, and not *too much* sugar. Nothing overwhelming.

Just right, in every way.

Clutched in her small hands is a huge bouquet of blood-red roses. They exactly match the tiny red tiara nestled in her hair. My Ruby. She couldn't look more perfect if she really were a princess in a fairy tale.

The only thing better than a helpless princess I can save is the strong capable queen walking toward me. Uncle Dan ushers Rose into the aisle and she walks toward me, chucking full handfuls of rose petals every two feet. It's a good thing she doesn't have far to go, or she'd need a bucket instead of a basket.

The music drops in volume just as Ruby reaches the back of the aisle, and every person she passes sighs or gasps or beams. Kimball winks at me as she passes, and surprisingly, I don't want to punch him.

I'm too happy to want to punch anyone at all. I'm not sure I've ever been this happy in my life.

"Sam," Ruby says as she reaches the front.

Just my name. And that's all I want to hear.

Until Job starts the ceremony, and then it's like he wrote the whole thing just for us. Maybe he did—I haven't ever been to a wedding.

"Did you have vows you wanted to share?" Job asks.

Ruby smiles. "Of course we do."

We do? Oh, no. I was sort of hoping we wouldn't have to do this publicly. It's not many people who are actually here, but they're all listening. And what's worse, stupid Adam's videotaping it so everyone can watch.

"I better go first," Ruby says. "Since we all know I'm the talker in this marriage."

This marriage. The words hit me then. She's my *wife*. It doesn't really matter what I say, or what she does. Our lives are profoundly different now. Better in every way.

"So, the question I keep getting is whether I'm going to change my name." Ruby's face is deadly serious. She looks from Rhonda to Job to Adam, and then to her aunt and uncle. "I can't believe anyone has even asked me that." Her laugh is bright and beautiful and it floods the entire area with joy, as though the sun is rising instead of setting. "Of *course* I am! The best thing about this wedding is that I won't have to stumble over who I am anymore." She giggles. "Am I Ruby Thomas? Ruby Carillon? Ruby Behl? Or Ruby Solomon? Who knows?!" She beams at me. "And now it doesn't matter, because I can be who I really am, who I was always meant to be."

She takes my hands in hers. "It's such a perfect example of what Sam is to me. Before I met him, I was lost, confused, unwanted, and just . . . unsure, about everything. I couldn't pick a future, a path, or a focus for my life. I had no idea what I wanted. I couldn't find my future because I had no idea who I really was. And what's so wonderful about Sam is that he lifts me up, he supports me, and he strengthens me to do what I never thought possible. With his help, I know who I am and what I want and how to get what I long for in life." She brings one hand up to my cheek. "And I'll never be lost again, because I'm Ruby Roth, wife to the most amazing man, best friend to the most incredible soldier, and confidante to the strongest warrior. I'll never be alone, and I'll never be lost, never again." This time her smile is just for me. "But if I ever am lost, I know he'll come and find me. Every time, no matter what."

She goes up on her tiptoes and kisses me then, softly but firmly.

And now it's my turn.

"I'm not someone who has much to say." I clear my throat. "Everyone knows that about me." I look around the crowd—every person I care about is here. "But that means that it'll be more impactful when I say this. I've never known anyone as good as Ruby. I've never known anyone as ferocious as Ruby. And I've never known someone who shines as brightly as she does. No matter how dark the night, no matter how deep the problems that lie ahead of us, with her at my side, there's nothing we can't do. There's no demon I won't face, there's no evil we can't vanquish." I look down at my beautiful bride. "You had a rough start and so did I, but the sins of our ancestors won't weigh us down anymore. We learned what matters: to fix the things we can and move ahead. To make every single day better than the one that came before."

I pick Ruby up in my arms and spin her around.

"My heart is full, Ruby. I didn't think that would ever happen. Before I met you, I had lost my mother. My father was a terrible person, even worse than I knew, and I only had three friends—your uncle, your cousin Job, and your cousin Rhonda. You were at the center of the only good things in my life. And now, you're still there, right in the middle. Since you stomped your way into my life, brandishing a honey pot in my face, I've found my brother Rafe, and defeated my father. I've grown from a jealous, sulky baby into someone who I hope is worthy of you. And when I'm not worthy, I know you'll kick me into shape."

"I will," she whispers. "But luckily, I kind of like the shape you're in right now."

Job races through the rest of the ceremony, and then . . . "With that, I'll pronounce you two husband and wife," he says.

Suddenly I'm kissing her, and it's the most perfect kiss we've ever had, which just means that it's the worst one we'll ever have.

Because every single day with her is better than the last.

When I kiss her this time, I don't care who's watching. Because I'm kissing my wife, the new President of the Republic of Triptych, and the future has never been brighter. Best of all, we're facing that future together. I can't wait to wake up for every single day of them, right next to the best person I've ever met, Ruby Ruth Roth.

When I hear it, I can't quite keep from laughing. "Are you positive you want to take my last name?"

"You finally thought my whole name out in your head, didn't you?" Her eyes sparkle with mirth. "With my middle name dropped in there."

"Ruby Ruth Roth." I shake my head. "I'm sorry."

"You never need to be sorry around me," she says. "At least this is a name I'm *choosing*." She presses a kiss to my lips, and this time she whispers. "Just like I'm choosing you —us—every single moment of every single day."

"Even so," I say.

"Let's do better for whatever children we have someday," she says.

"I couldn't agree more."

"We have a pretty good roadmap in place," she says. "We just have to get all the things right that our parents got wrong."

"It's a start." I pick her up and carry her down the beach. "And I can't think of anyone I'd rather be getting things right alongside."

"Neither can I." When she smiles at me, I don't care about the yellow house or the perfect job or the picturesque town. Whether we're in a huge city or in a tent in the wilderness, with her at my side, all is right in the world.

Bring it on. We're ready.

❧

I hope you enjoyed Renounced. It was a bear to write, but I think that even if it's not as "thrill a minute" as the first three books, it's nice to see what happens After, as it were. If you're looking for your next read, I hope you'll trust me with another series, also set on an Earth that's not quite like our Earth. Only, this next series has a bit more magic than the Sins of Our Ancestors did. . . Anchored is already out, as is the second book, Adrift.

Also, I've written an exclusive short story that I'll be releasing ONLY in my reader group on Facebook. It features Adam and Rhonda, in case you wanted *just a little bit more* of the post apocalyptic world from Sins of Our Ancestors. (And maybe one more happy ending.) You can join the group and grab your free copy of *Reclaimed* here: https://www.facebook.com/groups/750807222376182

SAMPLE CHAPTER OF ANCHORED

Prologue: Earth

The human brain interprets an image in thirteen milliseconds. At any given time, more than a hundred billion neurons are firing in the gray matter of an average kid. I learned that on my very last day of school.

The day before I escaped.

In spite of all those speedy, hard-working neurons, humans frequently make very poor split-second decisions. I'm kind of the expert on the consequences of bad calls.

If the semi-truck driver had serviced his brakes properly, my parents might still be alive. If I'd just lied about my bizarre dreams of Terra, Aunt Trina might not have surrendered us to the state. If I'd dealt with things better at the group home, well. There probably isn't any reality where that would have happened. But if I hadn't freaked out and screamed at my caseworker when he suggested separating me from my big brother Jesse, he might never have fixated on me.

If so many tiny details in my life had played out just a

smidge better, someone else could be stuck making this decision instead of me. Someone else could be responsible for saving the world, and that would probably be way better for, well, for everyone.

Because if I'm being honest, I'm not sure the world deserves to be saved.

❧

Chapter One: Terra

A few years ago, Abraham decided to add a chicken to the performing animals in the troupe's show. We all laughed. I mean, who's heard of a trained chicken?

Except the audiences went wild for her.

That chicken jumped up for treats. She pecked the poodle on the nose when he got too close. She fluffed up and strutted around on command.

A year later, Abraham's poodle caught a duck, and we ate it for dinner. We didn't find the honking little duckling until the next day.

It was all alone—doomed, really.

Or so we thought.

But our chicken adopted that duckling, ushering it around, feeding it, and grooming it. They were entirely different animals, but the chicken didn't care. Sometimes the duckling would hop into a puddle to splash around while the hen looked on with horror, but otherwise, they were inseparable.

I'm exactly like that duckling.

Although, at seventeen, I guess I'm technically a duck.

Either way, after Mom died, the troupe took care of me. Only, unlike the duck, I can't ever float or quack or honk. I have to pretend to be a chicken, and everyone outside of my troupe needs to believe my act.

When the first rays of the sun warm my face, I slide out of bed and dress. The first hour or two of every day are the very best—because there aren't any other ducks around to notice me.

I can be myself.

"Alora," Betty calls from outside. "Are you awake yet?"

"Mornings are the worst." My best friend Rosalinde pulls a blanket over her head. Her words are so muffled that if she didn't say the same thing every morning, I might not understand her. "And they just happen over and over."

"The alternative is probably worse."

"Too early for jokes." Rosalinde throws a pillow at me.

I duck and escape out the door of our wagon.

"Wait," Rosalinde mumbles. "Raisins!"

As if I'd forget.

I *love* our troupe's cook, Betty, but her porridge is disgusting. To be fair, it's not like anyone makes great porridge. It's essentially mush, after all. Sugar is too expensive for regular use, but raisins make the tasteless slop almost bearable. Unfortunately, they're usually gone by the time Rosalinde finally drags herself out of bed. Or, they would be, if I didn't fill my pockets for her.

"I need water from the stream for washing the pots and pans," Betty says. "And—"

"You need more firewood," I say.

"Exactly." Her mouth snaps shut, her hands drop to her belly, and her eyes look off into the distance. She's not paying attention to me anymore.

"Is the baby kicking?"

She nods. "He or she is a feisty little thing. Kicks like a mule."

"Do mules kick harder than horses?" I lift one eyebrow.

Betty rolls her eyes. "No idea, but that's the saying, Miss Sassy. Now get to Lifting."

I could physically reach down and stack the enormous

empty buckets and then lug them down to the stream with my capable bare hands, but it's so much easier to reach out with my duckling senses until I feel each bucket, and then Lift them into the air.

With the sun barely rising, it's dark enough that it's still enormously apparent when I do, because every time I Lift, light spills from my eyes—like a warning beacon that I'm a duckling to anyone close enough to see.

"At least you don't need a candle to keep from tripping." Betty laughs. "Now hurry along. I need water for the coffee right away—you've seen Martin without it. No one wants that."

The six large buckets float through the air next to me as I skip down the path to the stream. They're easy to Lift when they're empty, but even once I fill them up, it's not so bad to Lift them back to the wagon circle. I set them down carefully in their proper places around the makeshift kitchen—one on the table near the breakfast pots. One near the fire for coffee. The rest near the washrack. Betty can't lift anything heavy right now with her baby due any day, so I make her job as easy as possible.

By the time I come back with several dozen logs and stack them in a neat pile by the fire, Betty's porridge is almost ready and everyone else is turning out of their wagons, bleary eyed and stiff.

"I'm starving." I pick up a bowl and ladle it to the brim with porridge. Lifting works up an appetite, almost as much as if I had actually hauled everything myself.

"Don't be taking a double helping of raisins," Betty says. "If Rosalinde wants them, she can roll out of bed early enough to get them herself."

"Yes ma'am," I say.

But when Betty turns her back, I Lift a handful of raisins and tuck them into my pocket. We've been playing this game for years.

Betty looks at the raisins in my bowl and narrows her eyes at me.

I've never been caught, but she *knows* I'm doing it. She's mostly only pretending to be annoyed. Rosalinde isn't Betty's daughter, but we're all part of the same flock in this troupe. Which is why I can Lift here—safely. Without fear. At least until the citizens show up, the ones who would be appalled that a *woman* can do what only men can.

Everyone always says they want to be special, but in actuality they want fancy feathers or a shiny beak. They want to stand out. . .while fitting in perfectly.

If they really were different, they'd hate having to hide all the time. I scarf down the last few bites of my breakfast, carefully allocating one raisin to each bite, and head for the arena, dropping Rosalinde's raisins in her bowl with a wink.

"You better hurry, Alora. I hear the citizens of Spurlock wake up early," Martin says.

I can't allow any of them to see my eyes light up, or they'll know. I trot the rest of the way to the clearing where we'll be performing before too long.

The framework for the set is stacked against a thick copse of trees. I Lift each piece of wood quickly and, almost without thinking, assemble the risers and fix them in place. I'm careful to loop rope around each of my corners so they don't look anomalous, but I Bind it all nice and tight. Can't have anything falling apart mid-show. Once the risers are done, I move to the arena floor, the wooden support pieces flying through the air.

I've never talked to anyone else who can Lift, and I've certainly never been trained properly, but it comes as easily as breathing, as naturally as running or jumping or riding a horse. Maybe even more so.

Finally, I finish by setting up the tightrope across the top of the entire arena, with a rope ladder dangling from either side. Just after I Bind the last cords and cables in place, I notice little specks moving upward from far down-hill—from Spurlock castle. They're people, trekking up the hill toward us.

Martin wasn't wrong—they *do* wake up early here. Luck-ily, Dolores is already standing at the ticket booth, ready to take their money. Healers may not own any arable land, and they may rely on the patronage of citizens to support them-selves, but at least they're able to travel from place to place. Since they've taken me in, I can sleep under the stars and see all the sights Terra has to offer. Citizens may look down on Healers, but this life's not so bad. Not so bad at all.

By the time I walk back to the wagon ring to check in, Abraham has the animals ready in their pens. The horses stomp their hooves and toss their heads, their feather head-dresses shaking. Ironsides the elephant sprays the monkeys, and they shriek and throw clumps of what I really hope is dirt at Abraham. He should've moved her water bucket once the elephant finished drinking. I Lift it and shove it a few feet back. Abraham salutes by way of thanks.

Martin walks away from our circle and toward the arena, resplendent in his finest suit, the red lapels freshly pressed, his teeth gleaming when he smiles. Rosalinde's stretching to prepare for her contortionist act in the center of the circle, alarmingly close to Betty's banked fire. All around me the troupe's finalizing last-minute details for our performance, but there's still no sign of Thomas, my partner.

When a rock flies past my head, I whirl around, smiling. He's headed for the clearing, ready to warm up. I jog after him, excitement filling me along with big, heaving lungfuls of air.

We always warm up as the stands start filling to give people a little taste of what's to come. Citizens have been known to march all the way out here and balk at the ticket price without something to lure them into the show. Sometimes I Lift Thomas up to the wire for our warm up, but not today. The stands are already filling. My lovely fear-free morning is gone. Now it's time to follow my one cardinal rule.

No one outside of our troupe must ever discover that I can Lift.

Mom's been gone for a long time and my memories of her fade more every day, but I can still hear her voice in my head, repeating the same thing over and over. "Keep your ability hidden, Alora. It's the only way to stay safe."

Healers can't Lift like citizens—they can only Heal.

And among the Healers and citizens, only men have powers. Women can't Lift *or* Heal. They've never been able to do either. A woman's main purpose in life is to bring Mother Terra's new children into being.

Except for me.

Martin says if anyone finds out what I can do, the citizens will take me away, ripping me from the people and the life that I love. Or worse, they could decide that I'm dangerous. . .and destroy me.

I'd rather avoid both alternatives.

Thomas climbs up the ladder closest to us, one rung at a time, and I follow after him, a little impatient. Once we finally reach the top, I grab the rods sitting on the platform. Thomas snatches both of his staffs out of my right hand, clearly ready to begin, and maybe a bit annoyed that I've been following so close on his heels.

He lifts both sticks over his head immediately, but I land the first strike, our poles thwacking loudly, and we're off. Our routine has changed over the years as we've grown older and bolder. Last month I added the second wire, and that has been my favorite addition yet. We race up one side and down the other, striking and blocking slowly, and then a bit faster. We've just started when Martin waves at us, signaling that we're nearly ready to begin. Indeed, the stands below us are nearly full—which means we've accomplished our task.

Healers are allowed to camp near citizen settlements because of the service they provide—Healing for the injured. They pay for that, and it's enough to buy necessary provisions.

Most of the time.

But if citizens get lucky and avoid injury, or if there's a lean year, things get dicey.

More than fifty years ago, Martin's grandfather worked with several other wagon trains of Healers and came up with a plan. They needed another revenue stream, another way to earn money and purchase food and textiles from the citizens. Now pretty much every troupe of Healers performs as they travel. Our shows usually only draw a decent crowd for the first few days in a new place, but it's enough to cover what we need and set a bit aside. Plus, the performances alert the citizens in each area to our presence, and they bring anyone who's injured after the shows. It's a win all around.

When Martin stands up and begins talking to the crowd, the usual expectant buzzing begins in my arms and spreads through my body. It's always like this prior to a performance. Before my very first show, years ago now, I was terrified, worried that I would completely screw up. I thought the buzzing might make my hands shake, or worse, that I might fall.

Today, I watch, high on buzzy anticipation as Gibby the monkey rides Fuzz the donkey. Biff, Boff, and Buff, our three poodles, jump through hoops, and Ironsides stands on her hind feet, her massive trunk held straight up in the air. The buzzing amplifies when Martin announces Betty's singing and again when he brags about Rosalinde's incredible bending abilities. When Martin announces Roland's strength, the buzzing disappears, because I finally have something to do, some way to contribute. I hide behind the barricade while Roland starts off by lifting small objects. A heavy iron barbell. An enormous barrel with liquid in a chamber at the very top, so it sloshes out. That makes it look full when it really isn't, and then finally, it's my cue.

I help Roland by Lifting an empty wagon for his grand finale. The crowd gasps and cheers, absolutely stunned that he's a Healer, yet he's lifting an entire wagon. It's magical precisely because there's no way he could possibly do it other than using his own brute strength. His eyes aren't lit up, which is the first piece of evidence for the crowd that he's a Healer, not a citizen Lifting. But the second piece is that if he *could* Lift a wagon, he'd be powerful enough to join a Unit, the leaders of the citizen's standing army. No one strong enough to Lift a wagon would forego that kind of honor.

Unless they weren't supposed to Lift at all.

Martin announces Thomas and me next. We stroll out from opposite sides of the stage and climb the ladder up to the tightropes, our poles now tucked into the back of our waistbands. The key with any performance like this is to hold their attention while simultaneously building their anticipation. The beginning is actually the hardest part for me, although it's not at all tricky. It's the panache, the presentation aspect of it that stresses me out, because to prepare them for the second half, I have to make them believe I'm in danger, which means making intentional mistakes and fumbles.

I walk the wire slowly, inching forward, wiping my brow, glancing down at the ground below and wobbling. Thomas walks toward me slowly, steadily, holding out one hand to reassure me. When he finally reaches me, he feints at me threateningly, and we both whip out our sticks. That's when the fighting begins. He and I have practiced pole fighting on a tightrope since shortly after Mom and I joined the troupe. It comes easily to me, mostly because I sense the wire and have a natural understanding of rhythm. Moving fifty feet in the air feels almost as natural as it does on the ground.

After a moment of our sticks clacking as we turn, dodge, and duck, I leap across the three-foot gap to the cable that runs parallel to the one on which we began. No ladders connect it to the ground—it looks as though it hangs from two tall, thin poles. This crowd gasps, exactly as they always do. Thomas leaps across after me. While we jump back and forth, sticks still clacking, Rosalinde climbs up the ladder on my side. She's carrying a black sash in her hand. It's thick and dark and quite substantial. It has to be, or it won't work. Even with my eyes closed, light leaks through when I Lift.

Martin stops us with his booming voice. "This delightful audience is *bored*! We demand more." The audience leans forward in their seats, hooting and shouting, clearly agreeing with him wholeheartedly. They clutch snacks in their greedy hands, their mouths drop open, and their eyes widen.

Martin motions to Rosalinde, and I twirl my way down the wire until I'm standing in front of her. She makes a show of grabbing my wrist. I struggle, but she refuses to release me. Finally I relent, and she ties the sash around my eyes. Not once, not twice, but three times around, and then she knots the back. I can't see anything anymore, but I know that on the other end of the wire, Abraham's trading Thomas' sticks for two shiny, whip-thin long swords. They're blunt, but the crowd can't tell from so far away. They gasp and sigh and exclaim all around.

One woman, bless her, actually cries out. "Watch out! He has swords!"

Now that my eyes are covered, my other senses rush to fill the void. The wash of cool autumn air flows over my body, and the sun's rays lick the bare skin of my arms. People shift and murmur in the stands. Thomas dances across the wire to face me, but I stay still, fixed in place, while Rosalinde and Abraham climb back down the ladder. The smell of popcorn and apple pies wafts toward me from Betty's food stand. Based on the smacking of lips, the jangle of coins, and the crinkle of the pie's wrapping paper, she's doing brisk business for this early in the day.

The thin wire flexes beneath my feet, and I sense the parallel cord as well, Thomas moving toward me along it. Nearly three hundred people are watching down below. It's the perfect time to perform here, really. It's too early in the season for the fall harvest, and too late for watering to be necessary anymore. While the citizens wait for their crops to dry out enough to be cut, they have very little to do, so a troupe in the area is welcomed with giddy glee.

It's strange to think that I used to need my abilities to handle anything up here at all. After so many years, I'm completely comfortable standing blindfolded on a wire, high in the sky. I rush Thomas, leaning forward as I sprint along the cable. Just as I reach him, I leap into the air, grab a pivot point I've Bound with sand, and spin over his head. I smack him in the back and he stumbles forward. He spins around and comes after me with his swords. I block him easily with my sticks and leap to the parallel wire.

The crowd cheers as we hop back and forth again, much like we did at the beginning, except now I'm blindfolded and defending against Thomas' swords with my sticks. Eventually, we wind up near the platform on Thomas' side of the wire and I stumble backward and drop one stick. The same woman from before cries out again, and a young child sobs. Poor thing.

I hold up my remaining stick to block his sword strike and when he hits the stick with the dull blade, I release a

Binding and the top of the stick falls to the ground below as though he sliced it off.

I may never tire of the crowd's reaction.

The remaining piece of my stick falls from my hands, and I wobble in what I hope looks like fright, and fall, grabbing the wire with my bare hands, dangling pathetically from it. I swing back and forth a few times to get some momentum before I jump out and grab the parallel wire. I swing hand over hand the entire length of the cord until I reach the far end. Finally, I shimmy down the pole holding the wire up and land on the ground. I take a bow to pretty impressive applause for a morning show.

A startled yell from far above me and to the right can only be from Thomas. There's no time to try and sense what's happening that far away. I yank off my blindfold and spin toward the sound. Thomas's wire has broken and he's holding on to the end, swinging downward. I have a split second before he lands on the hard ground with a splat. I close my eyes as tightly as I can and slow his descent to the ground so that he lands more softly, probably only breaking his arm. I probably shouldn't have done anything, but I couldn't just watch and hope he wouldn't break his neck and die instantly.

You can't Heal dead.

Hopefully no one was watching me. I *was* facing away from the crowd, and my eyes were closed, so not much light would leak. I doubt anyone would notice the split second slowing of his fall.

But if they did. . .

The trouble is, very few people alive can Lift a person. Every single one of them has been born into or drafted for military service, and they're probably all ranked in a unit somewhere, commanding officers for either Isis or Amun. My eyes flaring to light while my friend's descent miraculously slowed could be a beacon for anyone who's looking.

I finally take a huge breath, let it out, and turn around.

Not a soul is looking at me—all eyes and attention are focused on Thomas. My heart rate gradually slows, and my breathing evens out.

"Alora," Martin says, his voice urgent and low.

"Yeah?" I brace myself for a monumental scolding.

"Betty's having her baby." Martin points. "That means—"

"I'll take care of her chores too," I say. "I know."

He winds his way back to the front of the ring and closes out the show. Even after the performance is over, he doesn't miss a beat. Not with Thomas falling—he heals his broken arm in front of the gathered audience as some kind of bonus—and not when Betty's baby decides to come early.

I race to complete all my tasks so that I can be there when the baby's born. I've never seen a Naming, and I'm desperate to be at my first. After all, if I'm ever blessed with a baby of my own, I'd like to know a little more about what's coming.

I race toward Betty's bright blue wagon, elbowing my way past my friends who are lined up outside. "She told me I could watch," I say.

"She told everyone that," Thomas says.

"You owe me," I hiss.

He rolls his eyes and shoves Roland back so that I can squeeze past and up the stairs. "Now we're even."

"Hardly," I say. I try to push past Sara, Betty's oldest daughter, who's standing on the top step.

"Um, family trumps friends." Sara crosses her arms. "I can barely see from here as it is."

I can't even argue with that, but I'm desperate to finally see a baby be born—and the magic that happens afterward, when Mother Terra names it. Then I notice the window off to the left. No one can see through the window, with it being almost ten feet off the ground. But. . .I Bind some dust in two places and leap across to it, dangling from my newly created handholds and peering through the window and into Abraham's wagon.

Betty's lying on her back on the bed, her head leaned back against the wagon wall, her hands braced on either side of her belly. Her face is bright red and her mouth is wide open. She's in obvious distress and possible pain. I blink. This is nothing like I was led to expect. I release my hold and drop to the ground.

Thomas throws his head back and laughs. "Serves you right."

"No one mentioned it would be so. . .disturbing." I frown.

"That's the birth." Sara smiles at me. "The birth is always hard. It's the Naming that people love to see. Give her a moment. The birth is nearly done."

"Will you tell me when it is?"

Sara nods with a half smile. "I will."

It doesn't feel like a moment. It feels like I'm pacing for an hour. Two. But finally, Sara points at the window. "The baby's born, and she's wrapped."

I Bind handholds again and leap upward, dragging my face up and into the window.

Sara's right. Betty no longer looks upset, or angry. She looks peaceful, and the tiny child wrapped in her arms looks pinker than I expected, but she looks healthy and strong, one arm waving back and forth next to her head.

And then a golden glow begins around Betty and the child. I rub my eyes, but everything looks the same. It really is otherworldly, just like I've heard, as if they're somehow lit from within. Then I notice that Abraham's glowing, too.

"Her name is Sheena," Betty whispers.

Abraham bows his head. "Her name is Sheena. Welcome to the world."

"Does he hear it too?" I hiss. "Or just the mother?"

Sara rolls her eyes. "Both mother and father hear the name when a child is born."

But sometimes there is no father—or no father who will claim a child, anyway. Like with me. I had only a mother, and when she Wasted. . .

I release my handholds and drop to the ground.

And not a moment too soon. Seconds later, a thundering of hooves sounds just past the ring—coming up the hill from the castle below. Most citizens who need Healing come by foot or in the back of a wagon.

A dozen mounted riders? That's nothing good.

I think back to the risk I took, Lifting Thomas to slow his fall. . .without the blindfold. No one did anything at the time, but what if someone noticed. . .and took the information back to Spurlock Castle? It would take them some time to determine what to do, and then to return here. My heart hammers, and my mouth goes dry. I consider hiding, but it's likely already too late for that.

The riders are already here. Eleven horses by my count, each of them ridden by a soldier in a bright red livery, halt just past our wagon ring.

That's far too many soldiers for me to do anything other than lift my chin and wait . . . and offer a silent prayer to Mother Terra that they aren't here for me.

***Did you like it? Grab Anchored now.

ACKNOWLEDGMENTS

Huge thanks to my husband, as always, for being the best supporter and the best spouse, and the very best friend a girl could ever imagine. No one can convince me the guys I write are unrealistically perfect, because I've got you to hold up as evidence these unicorns exist in the wild.

Big thanks to my kids for being my number two through six fans. (Number one is always the hubby, but they're sure close.) All FOUR of my older kids have read this entire series on their own, and most of them have reread them in anticipation of this release. Since Tessa's only eight—that's a big deal to me. Never think I take you babies for granted. You're the reason I write, and the reason I always think about quitting. Nothing matters to me more than you—the real life inhabitants of my little yellow house. (Even if it's not really yellow.)

Thanks to my mom, whose enthusiasm and support never wanes. Thanks to my editors, my mother among them. Without Carla and Carrie, this book would not have shined nearly as much.

Thanks to my ARC team and my fans for cheering me

on when I struggled. This book was hard—I won't lie. I wouldn't have gotten it done without you.

Bridget loves her husband (every day) and all five of her kids (most days). She's a lawyer, but does as little legal work as possible. She has three quarter horse geldings, a Holsteiner (jumping) horse, and she spends too much time riding and not enough time writing. (Or too much time writing and not enough time riding, depending on your perspective!)

She has more chickens than she'll admit to having, two lions head rabbits, a cat, two dogs (one bouncy and one yappy). She makes cookies waaaaay too often and believes they should be their own food group. In a (possibly misguided) attempt at balancing the scales, she kickboxes daily.

So if you don't like her books, her kids, her horses, her chickens, or her cookies, maybe don't tell her in person.

Bridget is active on social media, and has a facebook group she comments in often. Please feel free to join her there: https://www.facebook.com/groups/750807222376182

ALSO BY BRIDGET E. BAKER

The Birthright Series:

Displaced (1)

unForgiven (2)

Disillusioned (3)

misUnderstood (4)

Disavowed (5)

unRepentant (6)

Destroyed (7)

The Birthright Series Collection, Books 1-3

The Sins of Our Ancestors Series:

Marked (1)

Suppressed (2)

Redeemed (3)

Renounced (4)

The Anchored Series:

Anchored (1)

Adrift (2)

Awoken (3—releasing July 15, 2021)

Capsized (4—releasing September 15, 2021)

A stand alone YA romantic suspense:

Already Gone

Books by B.E. Baker

**(Same author—still me! But I use a penname for my
romance and women's fiction books to keep from
confusing Amazon's algorithms!)**

The Finding Home Series:

Finding Faith (1)

Finding Cupid (2)

Finding Spring (3)

Finding Liberty (4)

Finding Holly (5)

Finding Home (6)

Finding Balance (7)

Finding Peace (8)

The Finding Home Series Boxset Books 1-3

The Finding Home Series Boxset Books 4-6

Children's Picture Book

Yuck! What's for Dinner?

www.ingramcontent.com/pod-product-compliance
Lightning Source LLC
Chambersburg PA
CBHW010841190726
48286CB00012BA/2930